Ellipsis: A Love Story

This is a work of fiction. All of the characters, organizations, and events portrayed in this novel are either products of the author's imagination or are used fictitiously.

ISBN 978-65-00-56328-3 (Paperback)
ISBN 978-65-00-53050-6 (Ebook)

First U.S Edition: November 2022

For more information, contact the author at
www.ellieowen.com

CONTENT WARNING

This book contains explicit content, profanity, references to suicide ideation, discussion of domestic violence, discussion of murder, discussion of misogyny, and panic attacks.

To the talented artists who died dreamers.
To the artists who refuse to give up.

0

"I don't want to die," Thea whispers to the winds drying her tears as she rests her chin against the cold railing, gazing at the stars hidden under a veil of pollution.

The moon casts its silvery glow over the inky waters of East River, accentuating the one-hundred twenty-seven-foot drop between Thea and the water.

"I don't want to die," Thea repeats the mantra she'd been muttering as if trying to convince herself of something that's never been a lie. "It shouldn't be this hard. It shouldn't be this isolating. I shouldn't feel this hopeless."

Rejection shouldn't feel like a searing knife shredding Thea from the inside out, nor should it deprive her of air whenever she reads another automated and soulless rejection agents would send her way without a second to spare.

Thea shouldn't witness the success of others and see it as a verdict of worthlessness for her art, as a final judgment on her being obtuse. It shouldn't make her sob into her pillow and ponder whether she could live with a festered wound of failure.

But it's exhausting to cling to hope when each rejection pushes Thea into disillusion, withering a dream that sprouted between the pages of Thea's favorite novels, leading her to dream of writing her own stories.

Perhaps the world has enough stories, and people don't need me to tell mine, Thea muses with a sob raising through the lump in her throat.

Her nails bend as Thea grapples with the rusted railing, wanting so desperately to no longer feel the hollowness of a dreamer who was never meant to dream.

"I don't want to die," Thea repeats as she imagines her body hitting the wintry water.

Imagining how her bones would break, her organs bleeding from inside, and when she opened her mouth to scream in pain, it would be water that would fill her lungs, burning everything in its path as she yearned for the bliss of death.

But Thea didn't want to die. She was just tired of dreaming, of believing in herself when *no one* else cared enough to believe in her.

The bliss she so desperately seeks is the one she finds behind her computer screen, writing stories and imagining how people would react to them—wondering if strangers would cry where Thea cried or if they would laugh when she did.

Thea wanted her stories to invoke change or at least touch people in the same way writing had altered Thea's life. But publishing was an ungrateful lover, one who'd sell dreamers the stories about writers who'd been rejected many times before landing a book deal, becoming bestsellers as they grew a loyal fanbase.

Thea didn't want wealth or fame. All she wants is her stories to exist in the world, to be worthy of her dreams, but Thea often only feels worth in the form of an agonizing death, of throwing herself into the only thing she's less certain of than her future in publishing.

Only death would keep Thea from pleading with God, the Universe, or whatever entity who cares to listen, begging for a chance to make her dream come true as she doesn't want to die, but Thea doesn't want to live without achieving her dream.

"Five years," Thea answers her own prayer, weaving a promise between herself and Brooklyn Bridge. "I'll either die in five years or achieve my dreams and live."

The wind blows against her long brown hair, but Thea's met with nothing but soaring winds and the sound of the engines driving by as 1,826 days begin to countdown.

SIX MONTHS

1

A sliver of sunshine cuts through the dark studio apartment, illuminating dirty dishes Thea had left in her sink before stumbling into bed to cuddle the pile of clothes that acted as her closet.

Tears well in her brown eyes, remaining glassy on the moldy ceiling. Morbid amusement billows in some distant part of her at how the black mold reminds her of stars—that is, if stars were poisonous to her lungs.

Thank you for giving me the chance to take a look at your project. I'm afraid this isn't the best fit for me. Rest assured that this business is highly subjective.

I wish you the best on your writing journey.

Every rejection began and ended the same way, offering solace over a poor fit before including false optimism and a wish of good luck. Thea often wondered if the agents knew how their nonchalance kept pushing her further into the edge of a precipice.

Perhaps it's her fault that those tidal waves of rejection keep bringing tears to her eyes, that her body will tremble with sorrow despite her having more than five years of being a failure.

Thea knew that after five years of sending Marine, her best friend, a screenshot of the most recent rejection in her inbox, she'd receive the same meek support Marine had to offer before her friend would begin chatting about whatever TV show she'd been watching recently.

"Those fools don't know what they are missing out on," she'd reply with an angry emoji.

"One day soon, you'll be a bestseller! Just you wait."

Wait.

Isn't that what Thea had been doing? Slaving away as a waitress, putting up with the leering gaze of patrons throughout the night, so she could pay her bills while writing 365 days of the year without ever allowing herself a break as that would feel like a waste of those five years that have passed all too quickly.

Thea promised herself 1,826 days, but such a promise often seemed sacrilegious, bordering on torture to her creative soul that is often subjected to Thea's scrutiny as she'll spend hours lying awake in bed, wondering if she's at fault or if the industry is. Perhaps it's neither, and the one to blame is the consumer handing books to a cashier, dictating what is and isn't published with their Dollars and Euros.

Could the many stories Thea's written be worse than every single query that came up in an agent's email, or did they not like the sound of her name, didn't like the stories she had to tell, or maybe she was just another writer?

But even those have become bestsellers. After all, digestible mediocrity is an easy thing to sell.

182 days is all Thea has left for her dreams to begin taking form or for them to become the dirt tossed over her lacquered black coffin.

Purring coaxes Thea from dwelling on her ever-growing sorrow. The duvet with tiny red roses embroidered against a yellow background flies toward the

wall, pooling in the small gap between the worn-out mattress and a wall covered in sticky notes with motivational quotes.

"Good morning, Jolly," Thea murmurs to her cream-furred cat, whose eyes track as Thea replenishes the automatic feeder with the most expensive kibble the American dollar could buy—matching well with the automatic water dispenser settled beside it. "How is my morning, you ask? Well, I deeply regret the life decisions I made five years ago."

Meowing, Jolly rubs herself against Thea's legs, reminding the woman she wanted to shave before work as it's been too warm for pants lately, and showing her legs always granted better tips. A growing necessity when funerals are rather expensive, and Thea doesn't want her failures to become a responsibility for the people she loved.

"Behave, and I'll bring you some wet food when I get home from work. How does that sound?" Thea asks Jolly, whose tail sweeps the floor as Thea takes a seat on the wobbly table pushed against the window facing another building. "Now, be a good girl while I write."

Thea takes a deep breath as she presses the start button on her old laptop, swallowing the excited squeal as she's drawn back to the incredible feeling of writing. The one thing she would surely miss in paradise, hell, or the void of life.

Her nails click loudly on the side of the laptop, waiting for the machine to load the page her story had left off. A smile tugs on the edge of her lips as Thea reads her work—the grin cracking into a full smile as Thea is helpless against the love she has for writing, for creating stories of

made-up people, like she used to do with her childhood dolls.

It was in blank pages that Thea found comfort. Where she'd hide parts of her soul within characters she created, giving these stories all the secrets Thea would hide from people in real life, yet she hopes one day people will read those secrets despite not knowing them for what they are.

When writing, when filling those pages, Thea doesn't think about the shallow support from those around her. About how friends would read the first few chapters, offer feedback, and express their excitement before forgetting to read the rest of the story as they'd claim to be too busy with life to allocate time to the source of Thea's dwindling joy.

Yet, they've never been too busy to read books with a gold stamp branding them as bestsellers, nor were they too busy to rant about relationships fated to end in the course of a few weeks.

Have you ever stood on the edge of the world, only to find yourself alone? Thea writes, fingers gliding across the keyboard. The clicking sound fills the small apartment while horns and sirens echo down Brooklyn streets.

Thea sinks into the world that exists only in her mind, one that makes her heart thrum in tandem with her main character as the scenes unfold before her eyes.

Thea progresses in her scene, moving to the point where a dashing man asks if the heartbroken main character is quite alright—both oblivious to the love story that would unfold from the moment of human compassion.

Finishing the third chapter she's written since sitting down, Thea realizes the day has slipped between the

cracks of her fingers when Jolly purrs against her legs, compelling Thea to lift her gaze to find her apartment drenched in darkness.

The blue-colored sky is now dipped into the night, sprinkled with white stars that remain obscured by the pollution of the city. Thea curses at the green lights on her old microwave, showing it's six in the evening.

Scrambling out of her seat at the tiny desk, she pulls the oversized shirt she slept in over her head, throwing the item over the mountain of clothes she'd have to wash eventually.

Or were those the clothes she needed to fold and put away in her drawers? Thea wonders as she brushes her teeth while shimming into black jeans with her free hand.

Jolly meows as if judging her for not taking a shower that day or the day before. "We can't all lick ourselves clean, kitty kat. That's why Edna Murphey invented deodorant," Thea argues, spitting the white foam from her mouth while spraying deodorant and perfume, a dupe to some niche fragrance she saw online.

Although Thea doesn't know if it smells like the original, the notes of bitter peaches are quite pleasant even when drenching herself in perfume and deodorant until certain the fumes around her are more toxic than Chernobyl.

Pulling a tight-fitting black T-shirt over her head, Thea darts toward the small apartment's door, thrusting her feet into the same boots she wore when she stood over Brooklyn Bridge and decided to try for a little longer.

"Mommy loves you," Thea shouts as the door skids close and her boots slam against the sticky flooring in the narrow, poorly lit hallway. "Aaron is going to kill me."

Jumping two steps at a time, Thea runs on the sidewalk littered with black bags of trash, some pieces of furniture, and the everlasting scent of piss.

Home sweet home, Thea muses as she runs down the block without bothering to utter excuses when she pushes past people despite knowing her mother would abhor such behavior.

Pulling her phone from her small bag, Thea glances at the time entangled with the inspirational quote she used as a background.

I am an international best-seller, the quote declared while the clock informed Thea that she was thirteen minutes late, which in Aaron's mind meant she was an hour late—and judging by the line of patrons, he would be in a sour mood, stressed as he always is when it's a full night.

Which occurs more often than Aaron would like, preferring a steady flow of patrons instead of a line of people waiting outside, growing hungrier by the minute, and hunger brings a petty arrogance to demand food is served as soon as possible.

Thea saunters down the narrow alley lined with crates from deliveries made earlier that day. Another source of Aaron's poor mood as the man hates keeping inventory but doesn't trust anyone else to do the idle task.

Keeping her head low, Thea slips into the kitchen's backdoor, being welcomed by the heat and clamor of chefs and sous-chefs yelling for each other, by waitresses ably pilling dishes on the silver tray before they walk back into the parlor with a smile that didn't exist moments before.

"No sight of Aaron," Thea celebrates under her breath as she prances down the hallway immediately to the left side of the back entrance.

The small locker room is settled on the very corner of the building, squeezed between the restaurant portion of Ether and the next-door building.

"You are late."

Thea leaps backward, elbowing the doorframe as her boss leans against her locker. A tender smile on his kissable lips, a sight she loved and hated as it was a reminder of how good-looking the blonde man with emerald green eyes is.

But also a harbinger of his buried wrath.

"Sorry, Jolly puked on my boots."

"No, she didn't," Aaron drawls, seeming taller than he is when he's just tall enough to rest his chin on her head. "You can't be late three times a week."

"So far, I've been late only two days this week, but you don't praise me for it."

Aaron's smile becomes dangerous. Narrowing his eyes, he watches the sway of her hips a moment before his hand moves toward her waist, pulling her closer when Thea reaches for the apron behind him.

A moan raises over her throat at the squeeze Aaron gives on her waist, pulling her closer; Thea's chest flush against his until they practically share a heartbeat.

"You want to be praised, love?"

"Maybe." Thea plays his game, fighting against the shiver traveling down her spine as Aaron's teeth graze over the lobe of her ear. "I was quite productive today."

Writing and working took all of Thea's time. Leaving her too tired to join the rare outings her friends would plan from time to time as an excuse to announce a promotion or an engagement they'd learned about over social media first but still acted surprised upon inspecting the diamond-clad ring.

After one night a long time ago, when it'd been Thea's turn to stay back to help Aaron go through the inventory after service, run the books, and clean the parlor. Work ended with Aaron pouring Thea a drink, his green eyes focusing on her lips when Thea would ramble about whatever book she'd been working on at the time.

Somewhere between their chatty work routine, Thea found her back pressed against a brick wall as Aaron fucked her, their moans replacing the silence.

Since that night, Aaron had become the only person capable of consistently breaking her habit of overworking herself, replacing her squeals of excitement over a scene going well with Aaron's husky voice moaning her name.

A secret they only shared within the four walls of Aaron's apartment and an empty bar.

"Were you?"

"Three full chapters. I'm sure they need some editing."

"So you weren't late because you were thinking of me?"

Thea laughs, pulling away from Aaron as she wraps the apron around her waist, looping the long strand twice before spinning on her heels in a silent request.

"Why fantasize when I can have the real thing?"

A shiver runs down Thea's spine as his long fingers brush against hers. Taking the strands from her hand, Aaron drives Thea toward a wall, pressing his knee between her legs.

"A good girl who was bad," Aaron whispers into her ear as his hand moves toward her neck.

Pulling her toward him, so close their lips are a breath away from each other, her pupils widen with desire as Thea rolls her hips against his thigh.

"Tonight will be fun, won't it?"

"You tell me, Aaron."

A low chuckle echoes down the hallway as Aaron walks out of the small locker room without deigning to give her an answer, leaving Thea to press herself against the cool wall.

Despite teasing her with touches and words left unsaid, acting as if he's in control to play with her as he pleases, it was Aaron who broached the topic of a relationship after four years of fucking and six of working together, enough to know each other inside-out, to share conversations through glances.

Excuses rolled swiftly from her tongue as Thea explained why she didn't want to take that leap with Aaron. Offering meek excuses as to how their friendship was more important than labels, claiming to be afraid of how things could change between them.

Even though Aaron has always been the first person to read her manuscript from beginning to end, been the only one to offer feedback on her stories, Thea couldn't offer Aaron the happily-ever-after he deserves.

Not when there could be a day she might not be there to accept the hand Aaron faithfully proffers to her at the end of every night.

2

There's a pleasant thrum rippling across the parlor. A song of boisterous laughter and chatter entangled with the resonating sound of glass hitting each other in a cheer. All of it in juxtaposition to the soft music playing from the speakers built into the ceiling, where tiny LED lights turn the black-painted surface into the night sky with a constellation that follows Thea to a table tucked near a tinted window facing the street.

Tall glasses of beer nearly topple over when Thea swerves away from a drunk patron stumbling across the bar, expecting the world to carve a path for them as if they are Moses and the bar is the Red Sea.

A common occurrence that never failed to remind Thea how invisible she was to the world. Being merely a person one would glimpse at but never truly see.

"Gentlemen, your beers," Thea announces with a trained smile as she glances at the four men sharing a table —two of them wearing glasses and clothes they could've bought from a catalog, exuding as much personality as a gray wall.

One of the men, whose hair is nearly black, has gray eyes that seem to watch the world with keen interest, clears space at the table without taking the liberty to pick any of the four glasses of beer as if knowing he'd throw her balance off.

Thea distributes the glasses, ignoring how the oldest man in the group takes measure of her body. His indifference grows into a debauched interest that only middle-aged men are capable of when gawking at a woman closer to their daughter's age than their wife's.

"Anything else I can get you?"

"That would be al—"

The leering man with silver speckles in his brown hair speaks over the handsome stranger, "There is plenty I could order from a girl like you."

"You can order from the menu," Thea retorts, clutching the empty tray to her chest. "And no, sir. I'm not on it. As matter of fact, none of the waitresses are."

He laughs, glancing around the table to find his peers chuckling humorlessly except the handsome stranger, who instead beholds the man with something akin to scientific interest.

How very odd, Thea muses.

"I should talk to the manager about that. You are the most appetizing thing I've seen all night."

The handsome stranger raises a brow as he lifts the glass of foamy beer to his lips, his knuckles bleached as if irked by the words of his colleague. For a moment, Thea watches the column of his throat ebb as the cool, golden liquid washes away the poison of the older man's words.

He licks the foam clinging to his upper lip, keeping his laid gaze on Thea, almost as if coaxing her to speak. As if he's curious as to how she'll respond.

"Thank you, sir," Thea sustains her smile that only grows wider—proportional to her discomfort and anger. "It's been many years since I graduated high school. I've forgotten how horrific it is for creepy old fucks to hit on girls young enough to be their daughters and way too pretty to be in their line of sight. If being utterly disgusting is all you wanted, then have a good evening."

Spinning on her heels, Thea abandons the thick silence that'd fallen over the table, leaving the man to recompose himself before he can bawl like a child throwing a tantrum.

Threading around the patrons scattered throughout Ether—some of which weave their way to the bar in search of a refill—Thea's gaze flickers toward Aaron at the entrance of Ether, still finding herself surprised to find him greeting patrons there instead of playing host to the wealthy businessmen dining in the restaurant, some of which who could elevate Ether to new heights.

It'd taken Aaron eight years to make what had once been a dilapidated bar in a forgotten corner of Brooklyn into a not-so-secret hangout spot for people who deemed themselves too cool to drink at a bar with its name across social media.

At the two-year mark, Aaron bought the entire ground floor of the short five-story building, closing Ether for nine months as renovations expanded the bar into a restaurant.

The kitchen had relocated to the center of Ether, where it'd be the most efficient when serving both the bar and restaurant, allowing the kitchen staff to work in synchronicity, preparing exquisite dishes following the ingredients available throughout the seasons.

Orchestrating a fine balance, allowing each individual flavor to shine through each bite, and using spices from across the globe to ensure each dish would suit the palate of patrons from different cultures.

Gaining praise from Chinese businessmen after they closed a deal, to American housewives enjoying a night out with their girlfriends, giving every costumer an unique experience.

A theme that carried to the bar, where the dishes are less refined with burgers and onion rings, but also popular bar snacks from around the world, serving beer and the finest liquor, common in different countries.

With multiple entrances to the bar and the restaurant, the staff had placed bets on where Aaron would prefer to spend the nights working.

Thea had been certain Aaron would trade the dimly lit bar with music playing softly under the prattle of patrons for the restaurant bedecked with rounded tables adorned by fine linen and vintage silver cutlery, reflecting the pink art deco glass chandelier—an unique feast for one's eyes.

But Thea had been wrong as Aaron made Isabelle the restaurant's hostess. Slowly training her to be responsible for keeping the restaurant replenished and planning the new seasonal menu for Aaron to approve.

Through the years, it'd been rare for Aaron to mingle with those wealthy businessmen when he much preferred to welcome patrons into the bar or slip behind the bar and be the one serving drinks.

Aaron raises his eyes toward hers, inhaling a sharp breath before muttering excuses as he cuts through the throng of people caught between Thea and him.

"What happened?" Aaron asks, harboring the same worry in his eyes as he does when Thea weeps, and he cradles her face, peppering kisses down the bridge of her nose until her sorrow is too diluted for her to cry.

Thea jolts when his fingers brush against her hips. "Nothing?"

"Why were you just standing here?"

"I was enjoying the view. No need to be cutesy with me."

Rolling his green eyes, Aaron nudges her toward the bar, taking Thea across the busy kitchen with his hand sprawled on her back, so she has no option but to walk to the back exit of Ether.

The night is chilly against Thea's naked arms as the wind catches on the loose strands of her messy bun. Aaron watches as she yanks the elastic away, rolling it onto her wrist instead of tying the long strands back into another bun.

"I'm never cutesy," Aaron retorts, tugging on a strand of hair behind her ear. His hand lingers there, cupping her cheeks while restraining himself from pulling Thea closer.

"We are at work. We shouldn't be caught together, remember?"

That had been the one thing they agreed on about their relationship without quarreling. Aaron didn't want his employees to think he couldn't be fair when it came to Thea, who, in turn, didn't want to be the cliché girl known amongst her coworkers for sleeping with her boss. Losing their respect as they'd know why Thea was allowed to keep her job despite being late as often as she is.

Leisurely kicking a bag of trash a few steps from the backdoor, Aaron murmurs, cringing as a crate collapses onto the ground, "They know."

"You've told them?" Thea asks, hitting him with a tray.

"Of course they know! But not because I've told them or because we've been caught."

"Then how?"

Aaron rolls his eyes. Slipping an arm around her waist as he pulls Thea toward him, growing intoxicated by her scent as Aaron peppers a kiss from her jaw up to the shell of her ear.

"Do you not see how I look at you?" Aaron smiles as he feels Thea squirm with the shiver that runs down her spine a moment before she wraps her arms around his neck.

"Not really."

Thea savors the low grunt in his throat as his hands move to the small of her back, creeping dangerously close to the pockets of her jeans.

Aaron moves his lips from her ear down her throat, nibbling on the skin as she hums her words, getting lost in the kisses that make her blood sizzle. "I'm usually too busy looking at your lips or hands. You have nice hands."

"Tell me what happened, T."

Rolling her eyes, Thea pulls away from his embrace, beelining toward the metal door but Aaron is quicker, resting against the closed metal door to keep Thea from slipping back inside.

"Right now you're being an asshole."

"If someone is harassing my…staff, I don't want to serve them anything but the streets."

"Your staff, huh?"

Thea slowly takes a few steps away from Aaron, holding his searing gaze as he tries to carefully strip emotions from his voice, hiding the hurt within himself.

"You are the one who doesn't want to be my girlfriend even when neither of us has slept with anyone besides each other for four years. And you're my staff. I've kicked out countless patrons for harassing the members of my staff. You are not special when it comes to this, T."

"I can handle difficult clients. Plus, I need the tips."

"Why?"

One of the many annoying things about having a phenomenal boss is that every single member of Ether is paid well. No one needed the tips to make ends meet—nor to afford a weekend gateway from time to time.

"I won't ask again, T," Aaron warns, slipping entirely into that role she's always found so enticing to gaze at.

Adoring how Aaron was no longer the man who'd gone to university with her older brother, who hired her as a favor and kept their relationship a secret from Julien as the rising lawyer would find some juridical loophole to sue his best friend for sleeping with Thea.

Maybe Julien would find himself in jail for manslaughter as he'd be more furious over being lied to than about Thea and Aaron's odd relationship.

"Extra cash is always good," Thea lies, not daring to tell Aaron or anyone else about her funeral expenses in these upcoming six months.

Plans she desperately hopes won't come to fruition.

"If your rent increased, you can move in with me. You already spend a good chunk of the night with me."

"Did you suddenly heal from being allergic to cats? I'm fairly certain the last time you were in Jolly's vicinity, you sneezed for a few hours after."

"I'm fine with the risk of anaphylactic shock if it means you don't have to worry about rent. Waking up beside you is another decent benefit, a situation beneficial for the both of us."

"Sir, with all due respect," Thea mocks, swaying back and forth on the balls of her feet as Aaron steps closer, keeping his hands on his back while closing the distance between them. "You are painfully in love. It's cute."

"What if I am?"

"No denial?"

"You are the one who does the denying, love. Not me. There is nothing I would deny you. Nothing I wouldn't give you."

Thea gingerly lifts her shoulder in mocking innocence. Her eyes search his face, basking in the sharp angles that grow soft when Thea smacks their lips together in an all too fleeting kiss before pulling away, slipping back into Ether in hopes Aaron didn't catch sight of the blush spreading over her cheeks. "You have everything you could ever desire, Aaron. It's only fair you pant after something just out of your reach."

"You wicked woman," Aaron murmurs, planting a kiss on her shoulder before marching toward the entrance of the bar. Aaron smiles at patrons, embodying the charming and warm host he's always been.

Six months, Thea reminds herself. *Six months before I break his heart or sink into his embrace and claim Aaron for myself.*

That thought never failed to make Thea smile, the idea of getting to live the life she wanted, to share that joy with the man who'd been the person to reel her back from self-immolation when the weight of failure was a bit too heavy.

It'd been in Aaron's apartment where she finished her most recent draft and began writing a new one with Aaron working on the kitchen island in his apartment. He'd become a shadow in Thea's meager achievements, never too far from her memory when he'd also been the one to embrace her when she fell into the umbra of dejection.

"Burgers and fries for table forty-four, T," someone yells out, chuckling when Thea sighs, plastering a smile on her face as she places four plates and servings of fries atop the silver tray before slipping back into the parlor.

The boisterous laughter and excited voices thrum through Thea's veins, a painful reminder of how many still have a reason for happiness, being able to feel joy without much effort.

Perhaps others are merely better actors and actresses, able to sustain a character beyond their nine-to-five jobs, to hold themselves together until they are encased by the comfort of their home, finally allowing the mask of contentment to drop.

Welcoming the void that had been there the entire time was something Thea was far too proficient at even when she'd never been quite good at hiding her anger or joy, but fooling others into thinking something wasn't amiss is where she'd excel. Becoming a master at hiding her sorrow even from herself as she'd naively cling to hope, ignoring the grim reality of her life.

"You're back." The asshole greets her, taking the liberty to take two of the four plates off her tray. "What's your name, dear?"

"It's on the name tag, sir. But you would know that if you weren't so busy staring at my breast."

His leering brown eyes flit toward the silver plaque pinned to the left side of her chest—Thea would much rather put a sticker on her forehead than give patrons an excuse to glance at her cleavage.

"Thea," He savors her name despite pronouncing it as *tea*. "Would it change your mind if I said I fuck like a porn star?" He asks as the gray-eyed man sighs in what could pass as a grunt of annoyance.

A disingenuous smile spreads across her lips as Thea returns the favor of taking a measure of the man, from the thinning salt-and-pepper hairline, noticing the few wrinkles adorning his eyes, down to the thin lips and ragged shoes he wears.

The man rolls his shoulders, preening as his ego inflames like a spark igniting a wildfire with how Thea's gaze moves excruciatingly slow to meet his gaze.

"You do look like a man who fucks like a porn star. An A-list porn star, dare I say?"

He leans closer, breath smelling stale with alcohol, "What gave it away?"

"You are the kind of man who would be more preoccupied in trying to find the angles you look your best in as you stare at a mirror than in finding a woman's clitoris. I would say it would take maybe five long strokes before you stop to make sure the shoot is going well. You fuck like a man with an ego to stroke, like someone who would pay a woman extra cash for her to fake a loud moan and make her legs quiver with an orgasm you have never been able to give. So yeah, you fuck like a porn star. Only an imbecile would think that's a good thing."

Rouge creeps into his cheeks, spreading down to his neck as his thin lips contort into a dissatisfied snarl. "What a spiteful little mouth you have."

Placing the last of the small metal baskets holding french fries, mustard, and ketchup on the table, Thea blows him a kiss with a wink. "It looks even better around a cock, not that you'll ever see this mouth around yours."

"How charming."

"I do find it quite charming to not be desperate for male attention…If I can even call a drooling dog a man."

A bitter laugh rises from his chest as he brings a glass of dark beer to his lips, eyes moving down Thea's body once more before he says, "So what, you aren't like other girls? You wear boots instead of heels, refuse to wear makeup, and you find the male gaze abhorrent?"

"I could afford hundreds of shoes if I got a dollar for each dummy like yourself," Thea sighs under her breath. "I must remind you that I am a twenty-five-year-old woman, not the sixteen-year-old girls you'll prey upon because they are 'oh, so endearing' and 'so mature' for their age when in reality, it's their naivety that draws you to them. The gullibility in thinking lesser men like yourself see something in children they can't find in adult women. These girls don't know how much easier they are to manipulate. Don't worry about the tip. I'm sure you need to save up for your next blowjob. Anything else?"

The gray-eyed man speaks before the leering one can, "That will be all, Thea. Mr. Keane was just leaving." He offers Thea a gentle smile before his gaze grows cold as he faces the older man, "You should expect an email first thing in the morning. Now, please leave. We have seen enough of your...behavior."

Thea and Mr. Keane stare at the man.

Both notice the sharp line of his jaw and the tension between his shoulders as he pushes his glasses up with predatory grace that doesn't border on arrogance despite being aware of his prestige above those surrounding him. Demanding others to follow through with his orders as if they'd all been born in a world where he is the puppeteer.

Trading a protective asshole for an egocentric one, Thea muses as Mr. Keane chugs his beer before picking up his phone and wallet. Dragging the soles of his worn-out shoes, the older man slips between patrons with his head hung low.

"If he had a tail, it would be between his legs," Thea murmurs, lifting her gaze back to the handsome stranger. "I can handle myself, sir."

"I can tell. But I merely did not want Mr. Keane's company nor to work with him. Thank you for showing me his vile nature. There is a reason I bring people I might work with to a bar."

"Being a guinea pig to you isn't on the menu, sir. I expect a bountiful tip," Thea jokes, ignoring the sketch of a smile adorning the stranger's handsome face as she whirls away.

The rest of the night is easy, serving a variety of cocktails and snacks to patrons who imbibe further as the night deepens and music flutters louder through the speakers once the restaurant portion of Ether is closed; allowing half the kitchen staff to drink at the bar while the other half goes home.

Somewhere along the night, patrons gather around the bar, growing bewitched as Aaron rolls his sleeves with a smirk. They watch him pour vodka into a shaker with sugar and lime juice—a slight variation of the Brazilian cocktail called Caipirinha.

A recipe he learned during the gap year he took after dropping out of law school, traveling the world, and discovering his passion for mixology as he learned to enjoy the required artistry.

In a blur of repetitive actions and conversations, Thea doesn't stop herself from ogling Aaron, savoring the sight of the veins on his hand as he cradles the shaker with that smile that draws people in.

Leaving most of the tables vacant, people move closer, seeking space to lean against the quartz bar, oblivious that once the bar is closed down and there is no one other than Thea and Aaron tidying up, she'll be the one he takes home.

"You aren't very helpful," Thea complains, resting her head against Aaron's shoulders. "Your arms would be better used cleaning tables instead of around my waist."

Cuddling closer, Aaron hums in agreement. The tip of his nose trails a path over the length of her neck as he breathes her in, holding Thea close enough for his expensive perfume with notes of leather, tonka bean, cashmere, white woods, and amber to entangle with the scent of her skin.

"I missed you."

"We've been in each other's presence for approximately five hours."

"Still, I miss you," Aaron argues, reaching for the bottle of disinfectant in Thea's hands and a rag she'd placed in the back pocket of her jeans.

With a kiss on the back of her neck, Aaron drags himself toward the bar, throwing the remaining liquor from glasses littering the bar into the sink before he carefully places cups varying in size in a white bin.

Stealing glances over her shoulder, Thea wipes down a table, putting the stools upside down on top before moving to the next one in an absent-minded routine.

A process she repeats a few more times before reaching table forty-four to find a phone left behind. Thea taps the screen to find it's one in the morning and that the phone's owner never bothered to change the lock screen background.

"Someone forgot their phone?" Thea speaks in a question, sauntering toward the bar her gilded boss wiped clean. "Who forgets a phone in this day and age?"

Aaron chuckles, pouring two fingers of vodka before pushing a rounded glass across the counter as Thea slithers toward him. "Perhaps people who aren't glued to their phones?"

"Who? Grandparents? Even they are addicted to their puzzle games. My nana says it's the new sudoku, whatever that means. Besides, in the height of technology and amazing digital art, who is lazy enough not to change their background?"

"A psychopath?" Aaron speaks in mocking horror. "Does it have a password on?"

Thea sips on the vodka as she tries 0000 as a password, the phone vibrates, and she tries 0011. After a few attempts, the phone won't let her try again for another minute.

"I'm locked out," Thea pouts, leaning into the counter with her lips puckered. "What's your phone password?" Aaron blushes, clearing his throat as he pivots toward the shelves holding a plethora of liquor bottles. "Is it my birthday?"

"No."

"Your sister's birthday?"

"What is your password?"

"I am a bestseller," Thea shares nonchalantly, fingers reaching for the back of his dress shirt. "You answer me, little Aaron."

"August 21st."

"Why?"

Sighing, Aaron walks around the bar before spinning Thea's stool. He stations himself between her legs as Thea's small fingers slip over the unbuttoned sliver of his shirt, a smile spreading as she feels his heart beating quicker at their proximity.

Aaron brushes her hair over her shoulder, hand lingering on the back of her head as he trails kisses from her jaw to the shell of her ears. "It's the day we first kissed. August is also the month we met, although that happened years before you cared to learn my name."

"I knew your name. You were the rascal who introduced my innocent Julien to being hungover on school nights."

"There is nothing innocent about your brother. One time I walked into our dorm to find a girl straddling his face while another slobbered over his—"

"Don't tell me! I formally and eternally request to never hear about my brother's sex life. I'll keep pretending he is a respectable not-so-young man. Better yet, I'll think of him as someone who made a vow of celibacy while you remain the depraved bestie."

"One condition," Aaron pleads, planting a kiss on the tip of Thea's nose. "You take the blame when Jules finds out about us. In a way, you are at fault. You did seduce the depraved best friend."

"Did I? How?"

Thea tips her head back, holding Aaron's gaze as she leans forward, catching his lips between her teeth when someone clears their throat behind her near the pub's entrance.

"Am I interrupting?"

Thea glances over Aaron's shoulders to find the gray-eyed stranger looking at them with an arched brow as he slips his hands into the pockets of his well-fitted jeans.

"Did you forget your phone?" Thea asks, planting a kiss on Aaron's cheek before she slips out of his embrace. "If so, I may or may not have locked myself out of it for a minute?"

The man moves his middle finger to push his glasses up on the bridge of his nose, blushing when he seems to remember the black frame is currently resting against the neckline of his shirt. Thea smiles as he swerves his hand to the nape of his neck and takes a ginger step forward.

"I came back for your tip," He says, patting down his pockets. "I guess I also forgot my phone."

"How convenient," Aaron murmurs as he slithers past Thea, standing between her and the handsome stranger. "She doesn't need your tip, sir."

Thea peaks over Aaron's shoulder, resting her chin as she says, "I was joking about the tip. I'm still not on the menu, bu—"

"Is this the asshole you told me about?"

The soles of his expensive shoes drag against the dark flooring as Aaron adjusts the cuffs of his shirt, cracking his neck and knuckles as if he's about to punch one of his patrons.

"Who are you?" The man probes, crooking his head as if it's a novelty that someone could want to punch him—or he's just confident Aaron's punch wouldn't hit his face as the handsome stranger is quite a bit taller than Ether's owner.

"Her boy—friend. Her boss," Aaron stammers as Thea prods his waist, earning a delightful grumpy groan from him. "And you are leaving."

"Actually, I'm Adrian."

Thea holds Aaron back, wrapping her arms around his waist when he tries to take another step between them and the stranger, who offers Aaron a lop-sided grin, looking far too amused for a man about to be punched.

"You keep cleaning, I'll go get my tip, and then we can go home."

Thea doesn't wait for an answer before retrieving the phone from the counter and marching toward Adrian, steering him back to the door he came from.

The city has fallen silent, at least as silent as a city like New York could ever be, with the echo of sirens zooming through nearly empty streets. The distant bellow of drunkards and the even more faint sound of moans echoing from open windows.

"You need a background," Thea blabs, proffering the phone to the man.

"You snooped?"

"I don't need a password to see you never bothered to change from the default background."

"And why would I?"

"Because it shows you have a personality?"

"A background holds that much power?" Adrian probes, seeming genuinely curious. "Does that mean I am a brainless vampire?"

Thea crosses her arms over her chest. The corner of her lips curls into something akin to disgust as she glares at him—nearly wishing someone would drop a vase from their apartment building right onto his head that insists on twisting her words.

"I said it shows personality, not that it grants you one. Now, if you excuse me—"

"Don't forget your tip," Adrian calls out, bouncing between the heels of his feet and tips of his toes as he unlocks the phone, opening an app before extending the mobile back to Thea. "Your number?"

Thea snorts a laugh, rubbing her arms against the cold wind laced with a subtle whiff of puke. Adrian moves to block the air current from brushing against her skin, looming over Thea so close his body heat spreads over her.

"That's the cheapest way I've been asked for my number."

"You demanded a tip, and I don't carry cash with me. So, your number?"

"It's not like you are sending me a thousand dollars. Five bucks will do."

"Just type your freaking name and number. I would like to get some sleep before work."

"Jesus, aren't you a grouchy little boy," Thea complains, snatching the sleek black phone from the tips of his long fingers.

Under Adrian's attentive gaze, Thea quickly types the required information before thrusting the phone into Adrian's chest.

"Happy? Or does the grumpy young man require a forehead kiss and a lullaby?"

"A kiss would be nice."

"Then I hope you remember your dreams," Thea carols, pushing Ether's door open. "Goodnight, Adrian."

3

"It's utterly adorable when you are jealous," Thea sing songs as she follows after Aaron, watching him flick the switch in his dark living room.

The spacious living room becomes drenched in warm, golden light, softening the cold gray walls and black steel strewn around in different elements—the lightning, the window frames that grant them a corner view of Brooklyn, and the stairs leading to a mezzanine.

Without a word, Aaron throws his blazer over the back of an armchair before he plops down on the black leather couch inhabiting the space in front of the gas fireplace.

Aaron rests his head against the slope of the backrest. Sustaining the scowl contorting his face as his lids flutter close, he runs a hand through those gilded strands as Thea gingerly removes her boots, carefully placing them near the entrance where she hangs her bag on a little hook Aaron put up just for her.

It wasn't necessarily rare for Aaron to have moments of jealousy, becoming miffed when patrons were a bit libertine with their gaze and words, but usually, it would last as long as the patron's beverage or as long as it took for Aaron to cruise to where Thea had been, glowering at those patrons with some sort of male understanding.

Thea lights the fireplace before her socks propel her toward Aaron, gliding across the floor before climbing on top of him.

"Are you mad at me?"

"No."

"Are you sure?"

Aaron doesn't answer with anything other than a low grunt as Thea runs her fingers through his hair, smirking when his lids remain closed, but fingers uncurl from a fist to rake over Thea's thighs.

"You don't have to be jealous over someone we'll never see again," Thea reasons with Aaron, lips brushing against his jaw.

"Is he the asshole you told me about?"

"No, pinky promise. He was at the same table, but he wasn't the asshole."

"I don't like him."

"And I don't like when you are grumpy. I like when you smile. When you kiss me and make me laugh."

A soft smile curls on the edge of his lips, green eyes landing on Thea's gaze as she pulls back, gliding a finger from his chin down the column of his throat before slipping her hand under the soft fabric of his shirt.

Aaron groans as her nails leave vermillion lines against his pale skin, savoring how her hips undulate against his groin as her fingers nab the buttons—nearly ripping them off in her need to explore Aaron's defined stomach.

"Will you touch me?" Thea speaks with her mouth above his thundering heart.

"Where should I touch you, T?"

"Everywhere."

"With my fingers or my mouth?"

"Both."

"Gluttony is a deadly sin," Aaron drawls, allowing her to pull his shirt off his body before he does the same to

Thea, deftly undoing her bra with his lips sucking on her neck. "Are you a sinner?"

Thea stands up, shimming out of her tight jeans under Aaron's hungry gaze. He savors each inch of skin that becomes exposed, beholding Thea with the same intensity Aaron had studied the delicate marble sculptures he'd seen a long time ago when visiting the Cappella Sansevero when Aaron believed he could never lay eyes on anything as breathtaking.

Yet, the man has to remind himself how to inhale and exhale before pulling Thea back toward him. His lips ravish her neck, sucking on the skin until certain there will be a trail of purple marks marring the silk of her flesh.

"Tell me, are you a sinner, or are you sin herself?"

"I'm the song of oblivion, and we'll dance together."

"Good. There is no hell I'd rather burn in than yours," Aaron hisses, throwing her on the couch. Looming over her while goosebumps spread over her naked skin. "No devil I'd rather worship than you."

Aaron kneels between her legs, branding her skin with searing kisses across Thea's collarbone, moving down her shoulders as his tongue leaves a path between her breasts while holding her gaze. Pride swells in his chest as Thea writhes under the warm breath Aaron blows over her rosy buds.

Pinching her other nipple, Thea purrs with desire, her short nails sinking into his flesh in a silent prayer for more —a command and a plea for Aaron to go further south.

A hand on her hip, Aaron lingers there. Savoring the taste of her skin as he kisses her stomach, planting kisses on Thea's hip while imbibing on the breathy moans that arouse him, leaving those black trousers all too tight, his very skin too taut around him.

"Please," Thea begs as his digits sink around her hips, tight enough to mar her skin.

"Please, what?"

Thea rolls her hips, trying to find any friction between the two, but Aaron pushes her legs apart, toying with her as the tip of his tongue brushes against the wet patch in her underwear without allowing any release.

"I want you to fuck me."

"Do you?"

Aaron leisurely kisses her ankles, moving up her thighs, grinning when Thea tugs on his hair, pushing him down between her legs. Obliging only partially to her request, Aaron kisses her inner thighs while his fingers are a ghost of touch against her long legs.

Eliciting goosebumps, Aaron caresses her, his hands moving further down as his tongue and lips explore her legs, sure not to neglect either of them until his breath hits her warm core.

“Not yet, T."

There is power in plucking every nerve that thrums for him. Power in making the blood in her veins pool near his lips as her underwear becomes evidence of her pleasure.

“Please?”

“You were late for work today, were you not, T?" Aaron asks, moving so he can pull her white panty down her legs, repeating the kisses he'd laid there a moment before. "No reward for you yet.”

“I hate you.”

"Maybe you do, but you love tasting yourself on my tongue, tasting your sweetness around my cock. Don't you?" Thea mewls in response, fingers digging into the leather couch. "How should I fuck you, T?"

Her hands cup her breasts, squeezing them as she refuses to answer, craving for release, for pleasure but being too proud to cave so easily.

Aaron topples on top of her, propping himself with a hand on the backrest of the couch as he stares into her dark eyes, silently demanding an answer.

"Do you want me to fuck you?"

"Yes, please."

His fingers trace the shape of her lips, gliding them down her chin, stopping a few inches shy of the wetness between her legs. "Wait for me in bed."

Aaron marches toward the sink within his kitchen island. Through his blonde lashes, Aaron watches Thea tiptoe from the couch, stepping over their discarded clothes littering the dark flooring as she practically runs to the bed nestled in a nook facing the kitchen, caught between the large windows that run along the entirety of the apartment, and the luxurious bathroom he plans on washing her body in when she's too tired to even stand.

The loft wasn't necessarily big, but it was spacious. Each room shares a common area while still allowing a king-size bed to be out of sight despite the lack of walls.

Thea once asked him why he used that space as a bedroom when the loft in the mezzanine following the steel staircase allowed for far more privacy.

Aaron claimed his clothes needed more space than he did, but truthfully, he liked how the sun warmed her skin in the morning, the way Thea would grunt at the luminosity before tucking her head in the crook of his neck.

Aaron washes his hands as if preparing to walk into surgery, brushing underneath his fingernails as he should've before ever touching her, yet the movements are mechanical as his attention remains on Thea rolling on the black silk sheets.

A satisfied smile graces her face as Thea basks in the small luxury, oblivious to Aaron rinsing his hands and patting them dry before he walking toward the bed.

"It's unfair that I'm naked and you aren't," She complains as the man stands on the foot of the bed, etching the image to his memory as she writhes under his gaze.

"The only unfair thing is that my sheets get a taste of you before I do," Aaron drawls, nestling between her knees, fingers trailing over Thea's legs once more, "Where were we?"

"Don't tease me, Mariani."

"Break eye contact, and I'll stop," he warns. "Ah, yes. Do you want me this badly? You're so wet, love."

Thea mewls a breathy *yes* as her hips roll against the tips of his fingers, the tender sound morphing into a startled yelp when Aaron thrusts three fingers inside of her, stretching her entirely.

"So very tight," Aaron hisses, pulling his fingers back out before pushing them inside once more. "Do you like that?"

"Yes," She moans, wrapping her legs around his waist, trying to pull Aaron down toward her, but the man refuses to cave.

He strokes her in a rhythm Aaron mastered a long time ago, learning to evoke a different reaction from her with nothing but his fingers, where to touch her to make her come within moments, where to stimulate her ever so slightly to build her pleasure until it became overwhelming to her senses.

And right now, he's pushing her to the edge until she nearly falls into an abyss that makes her entire body quiver, but Aaron pulls his fingers out just before she reaches that ecstasy.

Sucking his wet fingers, Aaron slithers to the floor, pulling Thea to the edge of the bed in a single swift movement. Without warning, Aaron flickers his tongue against her wet cunt, drawing that breathy moan that makes time run too fast yet too slow.

Aaron's tongue moves slowly, teeth grazing over the bundle of nerves just as Thea instructed him the first time Aaron had her in his bed—the first time her taste coated his tongue, and he knew he'd rather die than go a day without tasting her.

So far, he'd succeeded in that.

"That feels so fucking good," Thea purrs, running her fingers through his hair as Aaron takes note of every emotion flitting across her face. "But I need more."

With a smirk on his lips, Aaron sprawls a hand on Thea's stomach. Pushing her down into the mattress, he thrusts his tongue inside her, grunting and humming while his body craves more.

Aching to be closer, to thrust into her as their tongues brush against each other, to feel her chest against his as he licks the sweat on her neck as pleasure reaches a culmination.

But tonight, like all the other nights, is about Thea. About following her lead, allowing her to dictate how far they go and for how long.

Thea sinks her nails in the blankets as Aaron holds her down, inserting a finger and then another, pushing his hand on her stomach to intensify the pleasure that quickly overflows her body.

Wetting Aaron's face as he keeps sucking her, thrusting his tongue in tandem with his fingers, making Thea scream against a pillow as she rolls her hips against his face.

Pulling back, Aaron watches as her body trembles, eyes rolling into the back of her head, taken to a realm of her own. One where she doesn't see as he strips down to nothing, where she doesn't feel his fingers curl around her ankles.

Aaron flips her in bed, so her stomach touches the silk. A resounding slap on her ass fills the apartment as Aaron teases her entrance with his cock leaking pre-cum.

Aaron wouldn't dare to thrust into Thea until she descends from her climax. Until she takes notes of her surroundings and moves down his cock with another loud moan.

The sun assaults Thea's closed lids.

Coaxing her out of a peaceful slumber, Thea rolls on silk rather than scratchy cotton sheets, frowning at how the air is laced with the bitter scent of coffee and Aaron's shampoo—a combination of citrus and floral.

Thea rolls onto her stomach, eyes raking over the luxurious apartment while stretching like a cat under the sun as she listens to the sound of the shower running in the adjacent bathroom.

Slumping out of bed, Thea tiptoes toward the living room in search of her underwear and clothes that she finds neatly folded on the couch, exuding the smell of the expensive detergent Aaron buys, spending forty dollars on a single bottle.

Thea stealthily slips her panties on, ignoring the inviting smell of coffee, the rumble of hunger, and the certainty that Aaron would gladly make her breakfast if she stays a few moments too long. But breakfast often ended in sex, and as pleasurable as it was, Thea still has a book to write.

"Good morning, T," Aaron's voice strikes her like the tip of a whip. Making her leap at the raspy sound, a telltale Aaron didn't sleep much. "Running away without goodbyes?"

"I'm guilty, your honor."

With nothing but a white towel wrapped around his slim waist, Aaron's gentle footsteps lead him to his giant steel fridge; it doesn't take long for the clatter of mugs to fill the silent loft as he cracks an egg into a white ceramic bowl.

Damp skin glistens under the auric sunlight, accentuating the ridges of his stomach as Aaron asks, "Why?"

"I want to write, and you are too good at distracting me into spending the day cuddling or fucking you."

"Would make a difference if I said I went to your apartment an hour ago to feed Jolly and bring your laptop here?" Aaron asks, flashing her that toe-curling smile. "And your battery died last night, so I charged your phone for you."

Thea prances toward him, pressing her naked chest to his back as she wears only her panty when wrapping her arms around his waist, hands wandering over the ridges of his stomach as she bemoans, "My valiant hero."

"Bacon?"

Humming, Thea slips around Aaron. Gazing at his slightly red nose and irritated green eyes before rolling onto the tip of her toes to kiss him. Aaron's hands wander from her waist down south to her ass as Thea tastes the coffee on his tongue.

"Did you sleep well?"

"I always sleep well when I'm with you." Thea's lips travel across his chest, savoring the warmth radiating from Aaron's skin to the tip of her tongue. "Did you?"

"No," Aaron hums. "I dread the mornings when you are here. It always means you'll leave me to spend the day without you."

"Not today, boss-friend. I'll hog your couch and coffee machine. The payment for my company will come in the form of kisses from my fearsome employer."

"Fearsome?"

Thea slips away, sauntering toward the meek laundry pile beside Aaron's bed, where the white dress shirt he wore yesterday remains, waiting for his cleaning lady to come over tomorrow to clean his apartment and take his clothes to be dry-cleaned.

A moment after slipping her clothes on, Thea unplugs her phone from the borrowed charger, holding the power button until her home screen comes to life with a photo of the Brooklyn Bridge—a reminder of her self-imposed ultimatum.

Color slowly bleaches from Aaron's face as Thea takes languid steps into the kitchen, dragging her barefoot over the cool flooring as she turns her gaze to bask in how the morning sun pours into the loft, painting his pale skin gold.

"Oh, you have no idea the viperine whispers we, your employees, will share behind your back."

Green eyes widen in horror, and his grip on the frying pan handle tightens until the knuckles of his fingers are white as Aaron's chest raises rapidly.

"How bad of a boss have I been?" He asks in a strained whisper. "I know I've been a bit less patie—"

"We don't talk about you as a boss. You are a great boss, and we know you are busy. Stressed. We are curious as to what has kept you so busy, but what we'll talk about for most of our shift is good your butt looks in those tailored trousers you wear. It's heaven sent."

"Should I wear jeans instead?" Aaron ponders. A gleam of worry laces his gaze as he watches Thea scroll through her notifications.

"Do that, and I'll quit. I'll move to Seattle and hog Julien's couch instead," She threatens meekly. Brow arching when she sees the two notifications she received hours apart from her wiring app. "Oh."

"What '*oh*'?"

For a moment, Thea doesn't say anything, grinning and shaking her head at the blue logo preceding the first notification that came in maybe fifteen minutes after the gray-eyed stranger left Ether.

Adrian Friedman sent you $1000.
"For the tip."

The second notification was similar, although it came two hours later with a longer attachment.

Adrian Friedman sent you $1000.
"I plan to see you again. Consider this as credit."

Ignoring Aaron, Thea sends the money back with a simple message.

You sent Adrian Friedman $2000
"My time is not for sale."

"What is it, T? Did something happen with Jules?"

"Oh, no. Sorry. That guy from yesterday sent me two-thousand dollars as a tip, don't worry, I sent—" A ring interrupts her pulling Thea's gaze to see the money sent back.

Adrian Friedman sent you $2000.
"Take the money. It's yours."

"No fucking way," Thea murmurs, typing the same thing before sending the money back.

Adrian Friedman sent you $2001.
"Don't devalue your time."

You sent Adrian Friedman $2001

"Stop sending me money. I get paid enough to tolerate customers!!!!"

"Thea?"

"Sorry, he keeps sending the money back."

"Take his money and ignore him," Aaron murmurs, pushing a plate with bacon and scrambled eggs toward Thea. "I don't like him. He seems...arrogant."

"I don't know, he just seems wealthy to me. Who gives two-thousand dollars as a tip? Maybe he's just one of those out-of-touch rich guys who think a couple thousand is pocket money?" Thea murmurs, glancing at her phone, waiting for Adrian to send the money back.

Grunting, Aaron walks around the island to take the seat beside Thea, weaving their fingers together as he brings a warm mug of coffee to his lips.

Thea had always wondered how the man could take his coffee without a drop of milk or sugar. She's convinced it's some threshold one passes once they become legitimate adults—the kind of adult who lives the life they planned instead of being a twenty-five-year-old struggling to chase their dreams.

"What?" Aaron asks, noticing the weight of her gaze. "Do I look extra handsome this morning?"

"You always do, but I was thinking about how much more of a grown-up you are compared to me. You own an apartment, and you run Ether, which is a dream come true. There is nothing you have dreamt that you haven't achieved."

"And that makes me the superior adult?"

Thea nods while Aaron remains silent as he eats his breakfast. Thumb running over Thea's knuckles, Aaron allows the silence to prolong itself for long enough for Thea to think he won't say anything else.

Thea eats her food with a soft smile on the edge of her lips as she squeezes his hand.

Scraping his plate clean, Aaron turns his gaze toward the buildings framing the view out of his apartment, staring down at the avenue painted in the blue and gold of a fresh spring day.

"Do you know why I dropped out of law school? Has Jules told you why?"

"Jules only told me you were traveling the world in your rich boy suit, getting drunk and laid every other night," Thea replies, leaning into her stool as she watches him. Trying to catch his gaze, Aaron doesn't look her way. "You can talk to me, you know?"

Aaron chuckles, planting a kiss on her cheek, pulling her close enough for his arms to envelop Thea as he speaks, "I had maybe a year left before graduating when I dropped out during summer break. I went to Italy with my parents and my sister, a dream vacation to many, only my mother would drink from dawn to dusk. It'd been years since she accepted her loveless marriage. My parents agreed they could fuck whoever they pleased as long as their friends didn't hear about it, a dirty little secret meant to maintain my father's status as a loving husband and present father."

Thea watches as his chest puffs with a deep breath, steadying himself as if the memory brings out all the emotions he'd felt at the time, painting Aaron in a way she'd never seen before.

"My mother hated these vacations. It forced her to see how fucked up her life had become, how her grand love story ended with my dad fucking girls who'd just turned legal. A disgusting fact we all pretended to ignore, pretending it didn't leave us nauseated with the certainty he'd go younger if the law allowed. My mom hates that my sister grew up with their fucked up version of love, that my father taught me everything I know about business, shaping me into a shadow of himself."

"Is that why I've never met your parents?"

"Because my family is a stereotypical old money mess? Yes, it is. I don't want you tainted by that. You're too good for them."

Aaron lets go of Thea's hand, marching toward the few bottles of liquor he keeps at home. But instead of pouring himself a drink, Aaron spins the bottles until their labels are all facing the same direction, fidgeting with them as he continues.

"One day, while my mom and sister were gods knows where, my father held my face between his hands to proclaim 'Son, I'm so proud of you.' Not once before had my father ever said he was proud of me. Not with my straight A's in high school, not when I got accepted into the best universities in the country. It felt so good, T. That was when I realized how much I craved my father's approval. It nearly brought tears to my eyes until he continued, 'You are becoming the man I always wanted you to be.'"

Julien used to tell Thea stories of what he and Aaron used to get up to, going to classes straight from a frat party, the never-ending liquor, and how Aaron would use those parties to collect blackmail material on their classmates, building an archive capable of ruining lives.

Knowing one day, Aaron and most of his classmates would be powerful like their parents, and those dirty little secrets would be beneficial down the road.

For many years, those stories convinced Thea stay away from her brother's best friend, not trusting Jules's sermons about how Aaron has changed since their college days. That is until Thea needed a job in New York, and Aaron was willing to hire her despite her lack of experience.

"My father wasn't proud of me. He was proud of himself. Becoming the man my father wanted me to be meant becoming the man my mother hated, the man who my sister has been dating for so many years despite treating her like trash."

Aaron keeps his back to Thea, muscles flexing as his fingers grip the edge of his cabinets, exerting too much force to keep himself from crying, unleashing the anger he's harbored for years.

"That morning I dropped out, my father cut me from the family wealth the same day. My sister fell out of his grace when he arranged a marriage that would benefit the company, and she refused not to marry for anything other than love, but I was the one he taught about business. So, when that sabbatical year of drinking and fucking came to an end, I came back to New York and began making money with the only valuable thing my father gave me."

Thea leaps from her stool, sauntering toward Aaron, whose body becomes taut when her fingers brush against his back, her lips planting a kiss above his heart.

"The man is a fucking bastard, but he knows how to make a thousand dollars become millions. Every day since that vacation, I've done everything I could to shed the skin my father made me wear. The skin I enjoyed wearing until that day. I wonder if I've ever truly escaped from his shadows. If I've managed to become the kind of man my father would loathe."

"Of course you have," Thea murmurs, slipping around him, as she raises a hand to his cheek, coercing Aaron to look at her. "I don't know your dad, but I know the kind of man you are, Aaron. You are good. You woke up early to go feed my cat and get my laptop just so we could spend the day together. You're unlike any man I've ever met."

Green eyes darken with sorrow as Aaron leans down, resting his forehead against hers, arms wrapping Thea in a loose embrace, almost as if telling her she can run away, turn her back on him, and he'll let her go.

Aaron would never become a jailer, preferring to sacrifice his happiness than to asphyxiate Thea's happiness.

"Before Jules asked me to give you a job, I promised myself I wouldn't drag a woman into my life as my dad did, that I wouldn't allow myself to fall in love and be happy. I'm not deserving of it when my mother never had that joy, but you ruined that plan as soon as you walked into Ether with a goddamn book, nearly knocking the waitresses out as you couldn't peel your eyes from whatever you'd been reading. You dismantled that promise as soon as you looked me up and down, scowling as if I'd been a giant rat."

Rolling onto the tips of her toes, Thea wraps her arms around his neck, closing any distance between their bodies. They stay with the sun warming their skin, bodies swaying to a melody that exists only in their embrace.

"Give me a reason, T."

Not this again, Thea broods, tightening her embrace when a part of her wants to take a step back, to put distance between herself and Aaron, to not give him hope when there might not be any.

"I just don't want to ruin what we have with a label," Thea lies, unable to tell Aaron that it would feel cruel for her to become his girlfriend when, in six months, she could no longer be waking up next to him.

Moving on from a fling seems easier than from a partner who chooses the precipice of death.

"Aaron, I love you. I just don't think I—"

Thea's phone interrupts her, vibrating on top of the quartz countertop. An unknown number flashes on the screen before she picks up—almost thankful for the disturbance as Aaron rolls his eyes before slipping away.

Thea watches as he walks from the kitchen toward the mezzanine, seeking a change of clothes from the towel around his waist or seeking the reclusion of his office settled between his expensive clothes.

"Hello?"

"Will you stop sending your tip back?"

"Adrian?"

"Are you that popular?" The man's voice is husky, as if he'd just woken up. "Who else is sending you tips?"

"There is only one moron who'd send thousand dollar tips. Which I decline, so you should stop sending me money."

"'*Being a guinea pig to you isn't on the menu, sir. I expect a bountiful tip.*' That's what you said, isn't it?" Adrian quotes her, oblivious to Thea rolling her eyes as she misses Aaron's comforting presence. "You got your tip. Please keep it."

Silence prolongs between them, the only sound being their breathing as Thea finishes her breakfast while listening to condiments settle on a fridge clattering as Adrian swings his fridge open. A few moments later, a ceramic mug sets on top of a counter.

The soft thud of a tea bag precedes the sizzling sound of warm water pouring when Thea finally breaks the silence. "And the other thousand?"

"Well, later this week, I have another meeting," Adrian explains. "I'll take them to Ether. Consider it an advancement for you to be a guinea pig."

"Good luck getting in, sir."

"Why?"

"My boss-friend has a policy of not serving morons."

Adrian laughs, muffling the plummeting sound of sugar cubes sinking into his tea, yet Thea muses how his chuckle doesn't quite match his persona—then again, Thea doesn't know the man enough to know his personality.

"Is that why he made you a waitress?"

"Aren't you funny?"

"Hilarious even."

"You can tell by how much I'm laughing," Thea's voice is clipped, her words unamused. "If you excuse me, I have a book to write."

"Oh, you are a—"

Thea hangs up on Adrian before he can finish his question, drinking the rest of her coffee before she puts her phone on *Do Not Disturb.*

Tiptoeing up the metal staircase, Thea follows the sound of Aaron furiously typing on his laptop. The blue light doesn't do justice to how handsome the man is, bleaching his sharp features of any sharpness, contrasting how the low light in Ether accentuates every line and curve of his face, often adorned by the easy smile he's mastered.

A smile one would expect to find on the face of a villain, but on Aaron, it lacked all venom and sadism, granting him nothing but a beauty that draws people in, making gay men flirt while straight girls blush and swoon when Aaron glances at them.

Fingernails brush against the clothes perfectly lined up, reminding Thea of a department store with a vast collection of dress shirts varying from black and white, while his trousers collection varies in shades of black and navy.

It's quicker to get dressed, Aaron argues when Thea teases him about it, keeping it secret how he wants to be at Ether in case Thea needs him, how he enjoys the sight of the wind pulling on Thea's golden brown hair as her cheeks would be rosy from running to avoid being late—or rather, avoid being too late.

Aaron's back becomes taut when her fingers brush against his naked skin. Thea waits for him to pull her into his lap, assaulting her neck with bites and her lips with kisses, yet he doesn't move, doesn't recoil nor stop Thea as she glides into his lap.

Her brown eyes search the planes of his face, noting the tightness on his lips as Aaron avoids her gaze, focusing on the spreadsheet open on the screen.

"I do love you," Thea murmurs, resting her head against his shoulder as her writer's brain seeks the right words to offer a half-truth. "Even when I didn't like you, I loved you. You turned my introverted brother into a slut by pulling Julien from his shell. Every adventure he went on was with you by his side."

The edge of his lips loosens into a meek smile—*a small victory*, Thea thinks, knowing too well Aaron's moods are a lot like diffusing a bomb.

Not particularly difficult once one knows their way around it, but one wrong move and the man cuts people out of his life in a way only death can emulate.

"I don't think he'd be the big shot lawyer he is without you, and not because of connections. You are like the horse-shit that allowed my brother to blossom into who he is, into the man he was meant to be."

"Are you making amends or offending me by calling me a fertilizer?"

"Both?" Thea asks, snaking an arm around his neck, her fingers playing with his auric hair. "I do hate how much trouble Jules got into because of you, but you never allowed him to take the fall alone. You protected him long before you protected me. How could I not love you?"

"So why won't you make us become *us*?"

"I've made myself a promise, Aaron. I gave myself five years to do nothing except chase my dream, to make it a reality, or die trying. You just got unlucky that I'm close to the end and nowhere near fulfilling my dreams."

"And if they'd come true long ago?"

"We would have moved to Idaho. You'd plow the land while I'd write novels with your rascal children pestering me. They would have these green eyes that sparkle when they looked at me, you know how children seem utterly infatuated when looking at their mom."

"Idaho?" Aaron jests, hand abandoning the keyboard to rest on Thea's thighs. "How many rascals would we have?"

"Five? God, you'd ruin my body."

"That's impossible. How long until your promise comes to an end?"

"181 days."

"Six months of single-hood?" Aaron asks mischievously, pepping kisses down her collarbone. "I should download a dating app and enjoy this time."

"Eh, you can just go to work and not reject every single one of your customers. Although Ether would become a sex dungeon if you accepted the advances of our loyal patrons."

"We could turn my apartment into a sex dungeon?"

Thea laughs, slipping out of his lap as she reaches for his computer, slamming the screen shut before walking back the path she'd taken to the mezzanine.

"We will, but first I write. And I demand your handsome company downstairs."

4

Words fly from the tips of Thea's fingers, sentences growing into paragraphs until pages upon pages are written, flowing easily and wildly with the story unfurling before her eyes.

Each comma and period steal a smile from her face. A sight Aaron marvels in. Resting his head against the leather couch as he takes frequent breaks from filling orders and looking at drafts architects have sent him for the possible expansion of Ether.

"Okay!" Thea announces for a third time, marking the end of another chapter—the third she's written, as being in Aaron's apartment meant she could pout and be spoiled with snacks. "Read this?"

Aaron smiles, scooting closer. An arm draped around her shoulder, he watches as she scrolls a few pages before the chapter header comes into view.

The bartender sheds all emotions from his face, adoring how frustrated Thea becomes when trying to depict his emotions, always so nervous about what he might think when there's never been a writer Aaron liked better.

When Julien told Aaron about his little sister's dream of becoming a romance bestseller, Aaron scolded the idea as his sister is an avid romance reader. Rambling endlessly about those allegedly grand love stories that in real life would end in a funeral home or a courtroom as far too many of those novels romanticize abuse, making a possessive man appear as someone merely too protective.

But Thea's work is different.

Maybe it's because she never had the patience for jerks.

Offering them saccharine smiles before drizzling poison over their ever-so-fragile egos as she rejects them with a cruel efficiency—something Aaron experienced a few too many times.

Or maybe Thea just has a natural talent for seeing people.

Understanding them and identifying their flaws in a way many won't realize their flawed nature is being scrutinized, managing to make the mundane seem like the deepest declarations of love, turning ordinary events into something ethereal without it being outrageously fanciful.

Heart pounding against her ribs, her stomach twisting in fear, Thea bites on her nails. Clinging to every chuckle and curl on Aaron's mouth, she nearly mounts him to assess the glisten in his eyes as he reads her work.

There's something daunting in sharing her stories, evoking a vulnerability that surpasses the fragility Thea experienced when standing on Brooklyn Bridge as she pondered on whether she should jump or give herself more time.

Death looming ahead of her had been less nerve-wracking than witnessing someone reading her work.

"Well?"

"I'm not done, T," Aaron murmurs, stealing a kiss as he reads the last page. "Honest opinion?"

"Always. Even if you break my heart."

There isn't much left to be broken, Thea mulls as Aaron nods, slowly closing the laptop that sounds like the engine of an airplane, settling the device on the coffee table in front of the couch—where he'd taken Thea more than once, perching her on the edge of it as he knelt before her, thrusting slowly and drawing each purr of pleasure.

"I love when you add bits of our sex life into your work. It inflates my ego."

"Is it good? Don't you think the—"

"It's good, T. People have a terrible tendency of being moronic. The quality of your work has nothing to do with how far you've come in your career."

Aaron plants a kiss on the tip of Thea's nose before pulling her into his lap as she nods, cuddling against his chest and burying her face against the crook of his neck. Thea purrs as Aaron runs the tips of his fingers up and down her spine.

Undoing the knots of anxiety that blossom every time Thea finishes a writing session and begins to overthink, to hate the words that had her smiling not even a second ago as she wonders if this time around, the story will be good enough for someone to see value in her and the stories she has to tell.

Content to be in Aaron's embrace, Thea watches as the buildings shrouded in shadows slowly come to life, with lights sprouting between the closed curtains.

"Are you hungry?" Aaron murmurs when Thea's stomach warbles. "Are we ordering pizza, or do you want some home-cooked food?"

"Both?"

"A home-cooked pizza? In a gas stove? My ancestors would call you a barbarian while cursing your bloodline."

"At least I don't put pineapple on my pizza. That counts for something," Thea retorts, prodding his chest before lazily gliding down from Aaron's lap.

Aaron lingers behind for a few moments, watching her tiptoe toward the steel staircase leading to the mezzanine as the floors are cold against the soles of her feet.

With long steps, Aaron catches up to Thea in a heartbeat, becoming a second shadow as she gingerly approaches the black dresser he bought for her. Filling the drawers with a range of extra small up to extra large clothes after Thea continuously refused to bring a few pieces of clothing to his apartment, claiming it would make them too much of a couple.

Cheeks growing rosy, Thea lets the dress shirt she'd been wearing pool around her feet as Aaron moves toward a drawer dedicated to plain t-shirts. Green eyes rake down Thea's body, mesmerized by her curves as he regrets wearing sweatpants after his shower earlier in the day.

Aaron's gaze lingers on the pair of black leggings accentuating the contour of her legs and butt—a sight that would plunge even the holiest of men into hell with the wickedness of their fantasies.

Fantasies that would grant Aaron a few broken bones if Julien ever knew Aaron broke the one rule Julien stipulated when asking to hire Thea.

Do not fool around with my sister. She deserves better than your no-relationship antics, Julien said over the phone on a random night years ago.

And if we fall terribly in love? Shall we hide our love from the fearsome older brother? Aaron had jested, having no intention to even befriend Thea as he'd been certain the younger woman despised him, and Aaron wasn't one to grovel for respect or affection. *What if she can't resist me? I'm quite handsome, according to my mom, as well as yours.*

To that, Julien laughed before threatening to end their friendship if he ever broke Thea's heart, yet Aaron would've preferred Julien threatening to kill him in a few different ways as death would be less difficult than life without his best friend.

"What are you staring at, sir?" Thea asks, tucking the front of the T-shirt she stole from Aaron into her leggings, leaving out part of it to cover her butt.

Pouting as Aaron slides a T-shirt on, she waits for him to reply, "Your brother would push me in front of a train if he knew the answer to that. If he knew the extent that I explored your body with my tongue."

Thea laughs as she prances toward Aaron, arms wrapping around his waist as she rests her chin above his beating heart, giggling when the man sweeps her off her feet, tramping down the stairs that thrum loudly with each heavy step Aaron takes.

Carrying Thea, Aaron walks across his living room, not bothering to turn off the large TV hung on the wall as the entrance hall is his destination.

"Won't you be cold?" Thea asks when her feet touch the floor.

Aaron shrugs, pocketing his wallet and phone before procuring a coat for Thea—one that practically swallows her as he retorts, "I have you to warm me."

She laughs, pushing socks over her cold feet before slipping into the combat boots she has loved for many years—a gift Thea bought upon finishing the first book she ever wrote, one that remained her favorite even after querying so many agents and receiving so many rejections that forced her to shelve the book.

There is still a part of Thea that hopes, one day, her favorite book will be displayed on the shelves of her favorite bookstore.

"This will cost you over time, you know?" She teases, pulling up the zipper of her boots.

"As you can see, money isn't a problem."

"How snotty. I require my payment in massages and a good bottle of wine."

The electronic lock of the door dings when Aaron pulls the handle down. Wrapping an arm around Thea's waist, he gently nudges her into the poorly lit hallway—which is the most *New Yorker* thing about his apartment building, when each unit costs close to a few million.

"You don't even like wine. You claim it tastes like vinegar," Aaron says as the lock dings once more, bidding them farewell as they walk toward the elevator.

"But you like it. It's cute seeing you sniff it like it's supposed to do something."

"It is suppose to do something!" Aaron yelps. Prodding her waist as they walk into the bright elevator, they are greeted by nothing except their reflection in the mirror taking up the whole back wall.

Aaron presses the *G* button that lights up before closing the elevator door as he props his chin on the crown of Thea's head, hands slipping into the pockets of her coat.

"I've bought you a five dollar wine that you loved. We should buy you a sippy cup since you are such a connoisseur of grape juice."

"I have so many distributors that would consider hiring a hitman on you if they heard that," Aaron grumbles, rolling his eyes in a rare display of emotions as his father taught him how a single emotion can be weaponized in negotiation.

"Lucky me, you love your Persian rugs too much to have them stained with my blood," Thea jests, tipping her head back against his chest. "Besides, I know you would just throw your sippy cup at their head to deter them."

"I'll use that tactic if Jules surprises me with a visit and finds us like this," Aaron chuckles, dropping his head to the crook of her neck as the blue light above informs them of the floors they are quickly going down. "I've had nightmares about that. They'll start as sex dreams and end up with your brother throwing me off a balcony my apartment doesn't have."

Laughter echoes against the steel walls, reverberating endlessly like the ripples in a lake that's been placid for far too long—a sound Aaron always wished he could preserve beyond the videos he'd take of her, beyond the voice notes she'd text him.

All things he held dear but inevitably paled in comparison to the richness her joy brought into his life.

Sometimes Aaron wonders if his sole purpose in life is to make Thea laugh, to pull her out as she pulls him into the fleeting blues whose call she'd often heed to, asphyxiating in doubt while smothered by insecurity.

The elevator stops on the ground floor, its doors sliding open to show them a resident that'd been waiting for the elevator with groceries bags piled on their arm.

"Good evening," Aaron says politely, following Thea, who is too busy giggling to be courteous. "What is so funny about my nightmares?"

Thea slips her hand into the pocket of her coat, weaving her fingers through his as she takes the lead, her boots slamming against the marble flooring that integrates into the concrete of the sidewalk.

They remain enmeshed as they saunter toward the expensive supermarket at the end of the block, dodging people who are too focused on their conversations shared through text and the people who seem to demand others carve a path for them.

"You are so in love with my family. It's just cute," Thea explains between her giggles, squeezing his hand as Aaron drops a kiss on her cheek, his lips moving down to her neck.

She squirms as his teeth sink into the sensitive flesh, but Aaron doesn't say anything, clinging to her against the nippy spring breeze.

It was always odd to Aaron how the whole of New York, the world even, fades into a blurry background whenever Thea is in his arms, choosing to stay there instead of walking ahead as she often did.

Almost as if life is a race and she's always one too many laps behind, like she can't relax for a moment, or everything will crumble into nothing.

Thea slips away from his grasp when they reach the supermarket, skipping toward the shopping carts as she marches into the warm light of the store. She takes the lead once more, guiding Aaron to the aisles divided by black matte steel shelves with signs marking the different products in each corridor.

"What do we need to make pizza dough? Will you look up?" Thea asks as she beelines to the flour section of the supermarket, replenished with more brands and types of flour than she judged necessary.

"Didn't you bring your phone?" Aaron asks, laying his hands over hers on the handle of the cart.

"Battery died. It's been acting up for a while. Regardless, Italian boy, tell me los secretos."

"That's Spanish, not Italian, but you'll need flour, yeast, sugar, salt, olive oil, water," Aaron lists things, not arguing when Thea puts three packets of flour on their cart. "All things I have at home," he murmurs, but Thea doesn't bother listening to him.

Pushing the cart through different aisles, Thea gets distracted with imported products that they have no use for in pizza, stealthily adding random items in their cart—from Japanese candy and Swiss chocolate bars to dehydrated sheets of tomato sauce.

Aaron doesn't say anything about the copious amount of cheese Thea adds to the cart, a range of mozzarella, Emmental, gouda, and parmesan—a combination more likely to be used to make fondue than a pizza.

"Black olives or green olives?" Thea asks.

"Black," They say in unison, both reaching for the closest green item around them.

Thea spins on her heels, triumphantly holding a plastic package of green olives as she asks, "Will I have luck today or tomorrow?"

"Tomorrow," Aaron murmurs, stealing a kiss from her as he plays into the little game that originated in the Scriven family, something Aaron first witnessed with Jules.

Leaving him puzzled for a few moments before bursting into laughter at the oddness of it all, yet with time he began to cave to the lure of the game, and by the time he met Thea, he was a near professional at finding something green to touch when he and someone else spoke at the same time.

"Does that mean I get tomorrow off from work?"

Aaron's hand moves from her hips to her neck, giving it a quick squeeze that makes Thea gasp as she nervously cranes her neck to glance around, granting Aaron enough space to lean down, his teeth nibbling on her ear lobe.

"That means, T," Aaron whispers so that she's the only one to hear as a woman hurries down the corridor with a toddler beside her. "That I get to taste you before and after work."

"Uhum," She hums, nails exploring his abdomen as her hands slip under the white tee. "I think that just means you are getting lucky, not me."

"And why is that?"

"Well, you get to have me sitting on your face, you get to taste me, you get to make me cum, and you spend the day with me on your tongue before getting a second taste. All things you get out of this arrangement. If I considered myself lucky to cum then I wouldn't have a vibrator at home, nor my fingers and a pillow."

Aaron grunts, pulling her so close that Thea can feel the effect those words have on him, the effect of imagining her lying naked in bed, rocking her hips back and forth as her neighbors get to hear the breathy moans she lets out.

"Fuck. When you put it like that," Aaron concedes, grabbing her ass. "How about if I promise to make it extra good?"

"I'll think about it, sir. But, we should get some eggs, too, don't you think?"

"God, you are cute," Aaron says, not wanting to argue even when he dreads what kind of pizza Thea will put together by the items in their cart. "Get whatever you want, T."

Flour falls on the disinfected countertop, reminding Thea of when her mother would have her and Julien as helpers when baking. Turning an evening after school into some of Thea's most cherished memories as their mother would teach them skills everyone should have.

Or maybe it just reminds Thea of fresh snow sprinkling over the city, giving her an idea for a retelling of *Charlie and the Chocolate Factory* in a world with towers built of chocolate.

"Okay, I'm done," Aaron announces, setting his phone down before walking toward the pink, heart-shaped ceramic bowl Thea insisted on buying for his otherwise monochromatic apartment.

Claiming it was the perfect feminine touch for an apartment that reminded her so much of New York's polluted sky—something Thea makes a point to comment on often.

"What were you doing on your phone?"

"A surprise."

"For who? Me? Jules?"

"There are more people in my life that I care about."

"Ah, so it's a gift to my mom?" Thea teases, propping her chin between her floured hands as she watches Aaron pour the elastic dough over the counter.

The veins in Aaron's hands slowly pop out as he kneads the floured dough, repeating the movements three times before turning the dough over or flipping it.

"Some Sicilian grandma is very proud of you in Italian paradise," Thea murmurs, mesmerized by how the muscles in his arms flex over the minute movement of spreading the dough in a perfect circle.

"My family is originally from Ghedi, and both my grandmas are alive."

"I know, but you look like you should be on a Mediterranean island. Kneading dough under the sizzling sun with sweat dripping down the tip of your nose, gliding between the grooves of your muscles. You'd be rich if you moved to Sicily and became a pizza guy."

"Well, I'm a rich guy on an island, an overly populated island that becomes a swamp in the summer, but an island nonetheless."

"I'm fairly certain I wouldn't need a cat to eat roaches the size of my fist, nor would rent be absurd when you share a cubicle with rats."

Aaron flashes her a smirk as he shakes his head. "The bubonic plague spread through Europe after reaching Sicily with rats. I don't think you'd be very safe from rodents there, but you can always move in with me."

"And live in your non-existing guest bedroom?"

"I have a perfectly good bed, one you've slept in many, many, many times."

Thea chortles, walking toward the stove, pulling a few eggs from the boiling water, and dropping them into cold water. "You know, I'll move in with you if you call Jules and tell him I'm moving into a loft with you."

"Smart woman, you'd have the loft to yourself after my funeral."

"Sauce?"

"Sauce," Aaron says, grinning as she places the pot beside him. Edging between the counter and Aaron, Thea slips a hand under his shirt, holding him flush against her chest. "How much sauce, T?"

"Do it the Sicilian way."

A sigh tangled with a chuckle slips past his lips as Aaron scoops the chunky tomato sauce—a personal preference more than tradition.

Peppering kisses on his chest, Thea doesn't watch as Aaron uses the back of the spoon to spread the sauce, nor when he sprinkles a generous amount of mozzarella before prodding her waist in a silent request.

Thea turns toward the pizza as Aaron slips his hand under her T-shirt, watching the concoction she comes up with as Thea adds shreds of ham, peas, and corn before taking a break to remove the egg shells and cutting a hard-boiled egg into small pieces that she adds to the pizza as well.

Black olives and a handful of sliced onions for the final touches before Aaron places the pizza in the preheated oven.

Pouring a glass of the five-thousand-dollar wine she'd demanded Aaron buy himself, Thea leads the man by the hand to the couch, giving him the glass of red wine as she searches for a movie to watch.

"Are we crying, laughing, or watching a superhero movie?"

"Crying," He says, planting a kiss on Thea's temple before pulling a cashmere throw blanket over them.

Knees to her chest and head nestled against Aaron's chest, Thea sighs contently, savoring the fingers running through her hair and the kisses planted on her head every so often.

Enveloped in a cocoon that allows Thea to forget how life often feels as if she's walking on a sisal rope. Trying to find a balance between her dreams and not breaking the hearts of those who wouldn't understand why she doesn't want to live in a world where her writing isn't valued.

A paradox between not wanting to die and where being a writer isn't enough. Thea needs her work to touch others, for her books to exist in the collective mind, and to touch and heal others as writing has done to her.

Thea could have a good life, being taken care of by Aaron, loved and cherished by him. A life that she craves. Wanting to see the world and write until she's old, but anything short of being a writer is hollow and lifeless, preferring the death of a dreamer over life as a failure.

5

Fire has always been enthralling.

Perhaps it's the beauty in deadly things that captivate Thea. Bewitching her as the bright orange melding into a lively blue is something capable of ending a life just as much as it can nourish it.

Something controllable but can just as quickly get out of control, Thea muses as she watches the chef and sous-chef prepare for the night ahead with sweat sodding the bandanas around their heads.

"Enjoying the view?"

"It's fascinating, isn't it?" Thea retorts, glancing to find Isabelle standing beside her, dressed in tailored trousers and a vest, allowing her arms to be kissed by the heat of the kitchen. "Shouldn't you be upfront?"

The woman chuckles, her long box-braids swaying gently as she shifts her weight from one foot to the other. "Aaron wants to have his eyes on the entrance. There's a patron he doesn't want in Ether, but he hadn't had the opportunity to inform the man he isn't welcomed."

"Ah," Thea mutters, biting down on a smile while holding back the urge to march toward Aaron since her legs are still a bit weak from the morning they had as the man refused to not keep his word. "I don't know anything about that if that's what you're curious about."

"I'm sure you don't. Regardless, good luck tonight. Aaron has that predatory gleam in his eyes."

"The one that makes our patrons test the limits of our lovely state indecent exposure laws?"

"That's the one," Isabelle concedes with a knowing smile on her face. "Some people might consider you to be very lucky."

Thea peels her gaze toward the salt and pepper shakers she was designated to refill while the other waitresses handle the custom-made napkin dispensers.

"I am. Jolly is quite adorable," Thea feigns ignorance. "Although, she could be a bit better at hunting down roaches."

"Mine is scared of them. He'll run in the opposite direction." Isabelle saunters away, clapping to silence the loud prattle amongst the staff, the chefs halting what they are doing as they listen to her. "Okay people, we have sixty seconds to go. Good luck."

There is a collective sigh as Isa dawdles back to Aaron, who smiles as she mutters something to him before disappearing into the restaurant, preferring the atmosphere there as she'd been the one to help Aaron make final decisions about decor and the liquor served exclusively for those wealthy businessmen.

It'd been Isa who arranged for food critics from around the world to make visits to Ether in the restaurant's first few months of existence, granting her more responsibilities over the restaurant until only major decisions needed to pass through Aaron—more often than not, he'd leave those for her too.

Thea walks toward the polished silver trays, picking one up as she takes a deep breath, rolling her shoulders back as the music playing on the speakers is overpowered by the steady flow of patrons streaming into the pub.

As the sound of stools being drawn out, bags settling on empty seats, and conversations melding into laughter fills the space, Thea armors herself in her customer service voice and smile.

Thea often pretended walking into Ether's parlor was akin to becoming a character in an epic fantasy book, that dealing with hungry patrons who are cranky after a day at work is more daunting than marching into battle.

Sometimes she's convinced a magical villain would be easier to defeat than a patron who requests something that isn't on the menu—wanting apple pie when apples aren't in season or a salad without half the ingredients.

"Good evening. How may I help you?" Thea's voice carries that trained cheeriness as she approaches a table of college-aged women.

Thea waits those few seconds it takes for them to take her measure, not out of judgment but rather to memorize the face of someone they can trust, someone they can pull aside in case another patron pesters them.

"What do you recommend, Thea?" A red-haired girl with beautiful blue eyes asks, leaning closer to offer Thea her undivided attention.

"That depends on what are you in the mood for. Is the goal tonight to end up leaning over the toilet retching your life away, to get buzzed but not drunk to the point a trashcan of a man becomes attractive, or do you want to drink something yummy yet slightly alcoholic?"

"I want the first option. Ginger here will have the last option and those two," A girl with platinum blonde hair and captivating brown eyes chimes in, jerking her chin toward a girl with long brown hair styled in a slight curl and a Southeast Asian girl who also has platinum hair—reminding Thea of a K-pop idol she's seen on social media.

"We'll have the middle option. Can we also get some fries?" The idol-looking girl interrupts in a clipped tone. "Oh, and that guy's number?"

Thea follows the manicured finger, pointing at Aaron, who sustains a smile as a patron runs her hands down his arms, leaning into the narrow front desk, where some restaurant patrons mix the entrances, needing Aaron to guide them to the right place.

The man pulls back the further the woman leans toward him, nearly laying on top of the desk before Aaron walks around, leading her to the restaurant.

"Ah, you're out of luck," Thea says, leaning as if to share a secret. "He's not currently interested in...women. You should try in six months."

"He's figuring himself out? Awn, that's so cute."

Thea laughs as she ambles away, jotting down the concoction of drinks for the bartenders to prepare while the kitchen works on the fries.

An hour or two passes of tending tables, collecting orders, and waltzing between the kitchen, bar, and the section of Ether designated to her—each waitress and waiter having a few tables they remain responsible for throughout night, not overwhelming anyone nor allowing fights for tips.

Gaze drifting to the ceiling dotted with lights that flicker like stars, Thea's steps become languid between her rounds of checking in on customers. She watches as the soft golden lights sparkle to the thrum of a pop song, wondering if perhaps the stars dance to the melody of human life.

A star for each life. Flickering in tandem with the joy they feel, dimming with heartbreaks and hopelessness, Thea muses, wishing she could pull her phone out of her pocket to write down her thoughts.

"Hi there."

Thea peels her gaze from the ceiling toward the stranger wearing a grin and a different pair of glasses than she'd last seen him. Glancing over Adrian's shoulder, she finds the entrance of Ether mysteriously empty.

"How did you get in?"

"You do know there is a front door, don't you?"

"Wow, in the two days you left me alone, I managed to forget how irritating you are. Thank you for the reminder. Now, if you could please—"

"Do you know her?" A woman standing a few steps behind Adrian asks, glancing at him and a man beside her —one of the three guys who'd been with Adrian the previous night.

"No," Thea says.

"Yes, we do know each other," Adrian retorts, patting the top of Thea's head. "I spent $2000 just to spend time with her, a very expensive lady."

"Okay," the other man says with a slight quiver in his voice as he gestures for the woman to keep walking. "We've heard too much."

Thea crosses her arms over her tray, brow eyes meeting his gray ones. "Why are you here? And why do you make it sound like I'm a sex worker?"

"We are all whoring ourselves under capitalism, and I told you, I want to use your skills."

"What skills? Transferring money that isn't mine?"

Mimicking Thea, Adrian rolls his eyes as he crosses his arms over his broad chest. "It is your money, and you have this unique aptitude to be blunt? Well, I suppose it's bravery rather than a skill."

"Don't be mistaken, being a bitch is a skill. I've been working on it for most of my life."

Adrian smirks at that, eyes flitting over the planes of her face—seeking the slight fullness of her lips, the curve of her lashes, and the way her dark brows furrow together as Thea glares at him.

Hissing when Adrian takes the liberty to smooth down her hair, fingers lingering there. Gliding down to her neck, ever so slowly, until the tips of Adrian's fingers brush against her jaw, and Thea pulls away.

"Talented indeed," He mutters, pretending not to see the flush in Thea's cheeks. "Where is your boyfriend?"

"Not that you are entitled to this information, but he's my boss, a friend, and my brother's best friend. Not my boyfriend."

"Regardless, come on, I'm certain my friends over there want to order something."

Adrian spins on his heel, sauntering toward table forty-four, where his companions had been sitting in silence with menus covering their eyes, pretending they weren't craning their necks to eavesdrop on Thea and Adrian's conversation.

The menus are held in place even after Adrian has taken a seat. He glances over to where Thea lingers, watching his lips moving as she can't hear him through the boisterous laughter and chatting in the pub.

Come here, Adrian mouths, watching as Thea rolls her eyes with a sigh before pivoting toward the kitchen, where she's greeted by the clank of pots and steam of boiling water.

"Logan," She calls for the youngest member of Ether, an eighteen-year-old responsible for frying everything. "Can I have some french fries?"

"You can have anything you want from me."

"Lo, you're practically a toddler. I'll take the fries, and you can keep the flirting to yourself."

"I'm eighteen," He argues, pouring a fresh portion of fries into the bubbling oil. "Seven years isn't a lot, gorgeous."

"If you are willing to date a thirteen-year-old, that's your own criminal agenda. Personally, there isn't anything that could make me opt to become a child predator."

"I'm eighteen," Logan repeats himself, scooping a batch of fries. "I've been legal for a few months already.

"Legality and morality aren't the same things. Anyone who says otherwise is preying on you, but thanks for the fries. I'm sure you'll find an age-appropriate girl for you."

Thea plants a kiss on his cheek as she takes the little metal basket from Logan's hands before marching toward the kitchen's exit door, where the mishmash of the kitchen fades into the distant echo of sirens and the engine of cars.

The concoction of sounds nearly caves into silence when one has grown used to ignoring New York's growing pains. Thea remembers how intimidating the city had been when she first moved there with a small bag and dreams.

But New York has a way of crushing dreams, turning them into the sand made to build the pillars of high-rise buildings far too expensive for one to live.

"The city of dreams," Thea murmurs bitterly, perching on an empty crate as the tips of her fingers burn when touching a fry sprinkled with salt. "Fucking bullshit."

Head tipped back, Thea surveys the starless night, ignoring that painful pang in her chest as she yearns for her home, where the sky is always clear for her to decipher the stories written in silvery stars.

Thea wonders if her story is teeming with ellipses. Perhaps her dreams and ambitions were meant to be suppressed, and she was supposed to omit herself from life —plummeting into the torrential water beneath Brooklyn Bridge as her life isn't one needed in the story of others.

With greasy fingers, Thea pulls her phone from her pocket with tears lining her eyes as she scrolls through a bottomless list of rejections—there should be more of them, but not every agent deigns to email someone they rejected.

"Books are subjective," Thea scorns as she reads a prevalent line from those automated forms that never give a pithy reason for their lack of interest. "I hope you'll consider me again for your next work."

Thea hated the false sense of camaraderie agents try to weave into their rejections as if they weren't in a position of privilege—as if they couldn't nudge authors toward fixing the things that weren't working for them.

Yet, there's nothing Thea hated more than the writers who'd speak about how easy their publishing experience has been while hiding how they have friends in the industry or share a surname with a founder of a well-established agency.

Publishing reeks of misogyny and racism just as much as it reeks of nepotism. If Aaron had been a YA bestseller, she would have signed with an agent and gotten a book deal long ago, clad in compliments she likely wouldn't deserve.

"Sometimes it's easier to prefer the death of a dreamer than the dream itself," Thea sighs as her soul aches for the one thing she loves with every fiber of her body.

Yet, there are nights she'll find herself on Brooklyn Bridge once more, gazing at the murky waters and lamenting she didn't leap five years ago.

Nights when she'd regret clinging to hope that those five years wouldn't be trivial torture, wishing she hadn't thought about how her death would affect Julien, Aaron, and so many other people.

At the same time, Thea knows they wouldn't mourn her but rather the role she'd taken in their life. Mourning the friend, sister, and daughter, not the writer who pours everything she has to offer into the one thing she's truly ever had, and if her writing didn't have meaning, then neither did she.

If the stories she carefully curated were all a waste of time, what did that say about her? Was she any better than a Victorian ghost haunting homes? Was she any more tangible if she couldn't touch people in the way it mattered to her?

"Six months, and I can be forgettable like everything I have created," Thea murmurs, wishing time would go by quicker as leaping from the bridge would be easier now that the sketch of her insignificance is taking its final form.

Rubbing the tears out of her eyes with salt on her fingers, Thea hopes her eyes aren't red with sorrow as she rubs her greasy fingers on the sides of the black dress she wears on top of a white T-shirt—something Aaron laid out for Thea to wear.

The kitchen's fire door squeals like a strangled cat when Thea forces it open, welcoming her into the pandemonium that quickly erases her thoughts as the sweltering air licks her skin when she walks further into Ether.

"Thea, table forty-four," Someone shouts, voices mingling into one akin to the echoing villain voice in the video games Julien used to play.

"Fucking fuck," She cusses under her breath, marching toward the little baskets holding french fries, a Brazilian snack called Coxinha, and three plates of hamburgers.

Positioning the items on her silver tray, Thea salivates at the smell of bacon and melted cheese as she balances the tray on the palm of her hand, stomping toward the parlor without bothering to plaster a smile on her face.

Her trudging becomes heavier with each of the sixteen steps it takes from the kitchen to table forty-four. On step eight, she feels Adrian's gaze on her, and on step thirteen, his grin is wide as he pushes aside the pitcher of beer on the table.

"Thea, how are you?"

"Adrian," She carols as if happy to greet him once more. "Stop, will you?"

"All I ever did to you was bring that guy here, and at the time, I didn't know he was disgusting. You have no real reason not to like me."

Thea gapes at him, head crooked to the left as her hand lingers in the air, holding onto the tiny metal basket lined with a waxy black paper.

She watches as the man raises a brow at her, gaze flickering over her face as a surgeon might do when faced with a complex diagnosis.

"Nor do I have reasons to like you," Thea mutters, placing the remaining items from her tray on the table. "It's not my fault you have an annoying aura around you."

"You can read auras?" The woman asks, halting her search for something in her tote bag. "Will you read mine?

"I only read annoying auras. His is the only aura I can see."

Adrian chuckles, raising a single french fry to his mouth under Thea's glare, amused by how she claims to loathe him while the edge of her lips has the faintest of smiles before she glances away, and that smile grows nervous.

Those at the table follow Thea's gaze, both women sigh at the sight of Aaron striding toward them with a phone to his ear, but his gaze is attentively on Adrian.

"Let me put you on mute for a bit," Aaron speaks to the person on the other side of the line. "Thea, who do we have here?"

"I'm Theresa," The woman says, proffering a hand to Aaron. She smiles at the brush of his fingers and the tender smile on his lips.

Hiding the low rumble of jealousy clouding his eyes, Aaron drops a hand on Thea's lower back, tugging her closer until his arms are around her waist.

"I hope Thea has been treating you well."

"Oh, she's delightful," Adrian chimes in, gawking at the two with curiosity in his eyes as he ignores the stack of paper Theresa lays in front of the plate of his burger. "There's a reason I keep coming back."

"It's definitely not because you are welcome here. As I've made abundantly clear before."

"It must have slipped my mind."

Aaron smiles.

The full display of teeth reminds Thea of when Jolly will hiss at her when she doesn't let the cat chase after a particularly large rat.

"I hope you won't forget this," Aaron drawls, fingers caressing Thea's hips. "Finish your food and get out, sir. My office, T?"

Adrian watches the column of Thea's throat as she swallows hard, placing her weight on one foot, then the other before lifting her gaze toward the table—arching a brow at the stack of paper for a fleeting moment.

"Just your boss, huh?"

"In more ways than one. Now, if you excuse me, I'd hate to keep Aaron waiting. Enjoy your meal," Thea carols, trailing the same path Aaron took to his office.

Pushing past the throng of patrons, Thea slips into the kitchen, discarding her silver tray on a pile of clean treys as she runs down the stairs leading to the basement that serves as Ether's storage area, where crates of liquor are stored in a dark and cold corner while produce is in the walk-in refrigerator built with steel walls.

The cramped space allows for a long yet narrow office devoid of windows, the only light coming from an extra fixture of the same pink chandeliers adorning the restaurant's ceilings.

"Jules, I'll call you later for you to gush about your new crush. Yes, your sister is in trouble," Aaron says, discarding his phone on his desk when Thea peeks her head inside his office. "Your brother said hi."

Slipping into the room, Thea locks the door as Aaron strides toward the small steel sink settled in the corner of the room—a small luxury to Aaron as there are few things he hates more than feeling his hands dirty.

"Have I not been a good girl?" Thea ridicules with a mischievous wiggle of her brows.

Ignoring the questioning arch in Aaron's brow, she prowls toward him, behaving as if she was the one with the upper hand in the situation.

Something that's not too far from the truth.

"Care to tell me why you were serving that douchebag?"

Thea doesn't answer him as her hands wander toward the lace tied around her waist, tugging on it before throwing the piece of cloth toward Aaron, who catches it long before the item can touch his face.

Patting his hand dry, Aaron tracks every movement of hers as he stalks back toward his desk, watching as Thea reaches for the zipper in the back of her dress.

The silent room fills with the faint chirr of the zipper moving down, of her black dress shuffling down her legs. "What are you doing?" Aaron asks as he reaches for her, hand moving to the nape of her neck while his fingers hook around her underwear. "Trying to distract me?"

"Depends. Is it working?"

"No."

"I'll have to try harder," Thea whispers, planting a kiss on the base of his throat as her hand travels down his chest. The heel of her hand presses against his groin, stealing a groan from Aaron, "Much like you are."

"You are wicked evil."

Aaron pulls on her hair, taking her lips between his teeth, savoring the whimper that slips past her throat as he slaps her ass and pulls her closer.

A moan raises in Thea's throat, bubbling past her lips when Aaron slips his fingers between her legs, stroking her through the thin fabric of her cotton panty.

"Care to explain your sudden libido?"

"You just look so good when you are protective of your staff, very hot," Thea mutters, rolling onto the tips of her toes as she wraps her arms around his neck, stealing a kiss and sighing at the brush of his tongue. "If I'm not mistaken, these walls are soundproof, no?"

"They are. But we are still at work, love."

"That we are, but today is my lucky day, isn't it? I can't think of a luckier way to spend my shift than with you inside of me. You fill me up so well...unless you want me to find someone who fills me up even better."

"You wouldn't dare."

"You said people know about us. Why not take advantage of it?"

Thea's giggle morphs into a yelp when Aaron whirls with her in his arms, hoisting her onto the table littered with receipts and contracts from distributors.

"You plan on screaming, T?" Aaron spreads Thea's legs open, nestling himself against her as he undoes the buckle of his Italian leather belt—throwing it against a wall as if it didn't cost hundreds of dollars.

Thea teases Aaron through his pants, eliciting a grunt from him as she rubs his length over the layers of clothing between them. Her skin prickles with the excitement of danger, knowing anyone could come knocking at his door when she's half-naked.

"I listened to your brother blab about this new girl he met for an hour," Aaron grunts against the crook of her neck. "Yet, all I could think about is how Jules would kill me if I complimented you like he was complementing this girl."

"Is there a point to this, or are you trying to turn me off?"

"You'll be the death of me, Thea Scriven. You walk into my office, and all warnings go out the fucking window, but first tell me—"

"I didn't let Adrian in," Thea states, not deigning to offer more of an explanation when she doesn't owe him one. "But it's a five-hour flight from Seattle to New York. You could spend those final hours of your life in a much delightful way."

"Shirt," Aaron demands in a rumble.

With that simple request, Thea's hands move to her white T-shirt, pulling it over her head, removing her bra before sprawling herself on his desk—barely missing the monitor of his computer as she pushes her black panty down.

Thea has always felt utterly perfect in how Aaron relishes the sight of her body, exploring every curve, every mole adorning her skin while his hands remain placid against the side of his body, beholding her like an artist would appraise a masterpiece, eyes filled with pride and a sense of longing, things that don't quite seem to belong.

"What are you waiting for?"

"You are beautiful, T," Aaron mutters, the tips of his fingers brushing against her ankle, raking up ever so lightly. "A feast of all my favorite things."

Aaron glides a finger over her sternum, moving it down her stomach as Thea arches toward his touch, whimpering at the languid touch, with how teasing it is.

A low hum of approval rises in his throat as his thumb brushes against the curve of Thea's breast. Aaron's hand rakes over her legs, moving to the apex of her thighs.

Thea gasps at the brush of his finger with the way his thumb circles around her clit, the way he squeezes her breast. Turning her gasp into a moan, Aaron bends toward her, licking a path from her stomach to her breast.

His teeth nibble over the pink bud. His eyes focused on Thea's face—how her lips part and her lids flutter, on her nails sinking into his back.

"What should I eat first?" He asks before sucking on her nipple, tongue swirling, and teeth grazing as he pulls back.

Peppering kisses on her chest, he strokes her, spreading the wetness between her legs, allowing his fingers to glide easily.

“On your knees, Mariani,” Thea says, and Aaron chuckles, knees hitting the floor with a thud as his hand moves to her inner thighs.

Nibbling on her thigh, Aaron pushes two fingers inside Thea as his thumb tends to her clit. His teeth nip her flesh as she writhes, whimpering, and jerking ever so slightly.

Aaron trails a path from her knees up to her apex, his warm breath steals a moan from Thea, making her slide further to the edge of his desk, but Aaron continues teasing her. Kissing her opposite leg, he places it over his shoulder, allowing him ample access to her core.

"Oh, God."

"Seeing him already?" Aaron preens, curling the tips of his fingers as he nibbles and sucks on her inner thighs. "This won't do, love. I barely started."

"For fuck's sake, just fuck me."

"But a feast is meant to be relished, savoring a bite at a time. Each kiss and flick of my tongue is a moment of degustation, T."

"God, I hate you."

"God has nothing with this, little lamb."

"He sent the devil instead," Thea hisses, running her fingers through Aaron's hair, disheveling the perfectly styled golden locks. "You should amend for your sins."

"I plan to, but you make things so hard for me. I can barely think when I see you glistening for me. It's beautiful, Thea. You are beautiful."

Aaron snakes a hand around Thea's waist, pinning her to the desk as he licks her in a long stroke. Tongue splayed over her mound, humming against her, eliciting moans of pleasure.

Her fingers keep running through his hair, tugging it when Aaron uses the tip of his tongue to draw circles over her clit, drawing the humming into moans.

"That feels good," She cries, rolling her hips against his face, against the fingers that remain teasing inside her.

Coercing her climax into building at an agonizing pace, so slowly there are moments Thea feels the pleasure ebbing before Aaron goes a little deeper and faster.

Aaron teases her with light pressure and speed. From languid strokes that are feather light to flicking his tongue almost too fast, too strongly, all before ebbing back into that feathery touch, changing things to gradually bring Thea to the edge of her climax only to negate her of it.

"You taste so good." The vibration of his husky voice steals a moan from Thea. "What a sweet little pussy you have. Do you want to cum before I fuck you?"

Thea doesn't answer, tugging at his hair as Aaron's hand slithers over her chest. Pinching her nipple and twisting the bud as Aaron thrusts a third finger inside her, torturing Thea with all the little things he learned throughout the years of pleasuring her—knowing how to get her off quickly or deny her orgasm for hours.

Her voice echoes against the walls, amplifying itself as Aaron falls into the rhythm he knows too well, thrusting his finger as he sucks on her clit.

Pushing gently on her lower stomach, Aaron smiles when Thea wraps her quivering legs around his head. Holding him there, he nearly drowns in her overflowing bliss that gushes over his face.

Forcing him to suck on her, to stretch her as her body shakes, and her eyes roll to the back of her head while the computer monitor sways back and forth, threatening to fall when Aaron pushes Thea beyond cloud nine.

Thea's legs fall limp, yet her body still trembles as Aaron stands up, looming over her while working on the buttons of his damp white shirt.

His eyes lavish the sight of her nudity, the faint gleam of sweat making her shimmer like a sculpture carved from the finest of marbles.

Thea's lids flutter open at the ruffle of clothes falling on the ground. Head lolling to the side, she watches Aaron undoing the button of his black tailored pants.

She licks her lips as the zipper on his pants chirr, and he allows the expensive fabric to glide down his legs. Thea's fingers wrap around the edge of the desk as she gazes at the sight of his bulge—the little wet spot darkening his equally black briefs.

"Spin around," Thea's voice is a low whisper, yet Aaron complies with her request, barking a laugh when her toes glide down his back, all the way to his butt. "With a cute butt like that, you should wear a thong instead of a brief."

"Really?"

"I could bite into your butt, Aaron Mariani. It is quite yummy," Thea rambles in her sex-drunk state as she pushes herself from the top of the desk. "You should offer that to VIP clients. Oh, the wealth you'd accumulate!"

Aaron whirls back around, snaking an arm around her waist as he doesn't trust her legs won't buckle.

"Shut up, Thea Scriven."

Thea rolls onto the tips of her toes, stretching herself until her mouth is on top of Aaron's as her hands slip inside his briefs. Squeezing him, Thea whispers in a drawl, "Make me."

A rapacious smile spreads over Aaron's lips, his eyes gleaming with mischief as he raises a hand to Thea's neck, squeezing the sides of it for a few moments before releasing his hold.

"You want to suck me off?" Aaron asks, bringing his wet fingers toward her mouth. He smiles as Thea sucks on his fingers, letting him push them down her throat. "You are so ready for me, aren't you, little lamb?"

Thea smiles, bobbing her head as she presses her tongue to his digits. If Aaron knows how to prolong her pleasure, then Thea knows how to make Aaron beg and moan loudly, knowing that if she'd been on her knees, the man would soon be thrusting into her throat, driven by lust.

"Want me to fuck your throat, love?"

Instead of nodding, Thea moves her hand up and down his shaft before Aaron closes his fingers around her wrist, spinning her around and pushing her body down onto the desk.

A slap resounds against the walls, followed by a yelp that slips past Thea's lips. "Fuck," She hisses, raising her hands to the edge of the desk, savoring how the cold wood feels pressed against her warm nipples, how his body feels pressed against the warmth of her body.

"Uhm, I really want to fall back on my knees."

"Don't you dare, Mariani," Thea threatens a moment before she hears Aaron spitting in his hand.

Thea pushes her butt up, spreading her legs in a blatant invitation Aaron takes without a second thought, sinking into her with a growl in the back of his throat.

"How do you want it, little lamb?" Aaron drawls, pulling back almost to the tip.

"Hard."

"Always so good to me."

6

Cum drips into Thea's knickers as she saunters back into the parlor of Ether, an easy smile on her lips and a ruddy glow to her cheeks as she remembers the way she'd left Aaron in his office; sprawled in his chair with his lids closed and too exhausted to put his clothes back on.

Thea ignores the knowing smirk adorning her coworkers' faces; and the curious glances filled with envy —far too many of Ether's staff have daydreamed about getting bonuses by spending an hour alone with Aaron in his office.

The busy kitchen falls into clean-up duty, leaving only a small area dedicated to serving the customers on the bar, although, this deep into the night, the bartenders will be busier than the cooks.

Humming, Thea prances toward the few silver trays stacked on one another. She reaches for one, ignoring how Aaron asked her to go home early, wanting Thea to get the rest he couldn't.

"You can go home early," A strident voice raises behind Thea.

"How so, Ana?"

Thea glances over her shoulder to the brunette with big brown eyes that rarely match the kind smile she plasters on her lips from the beginning of each shift, long before there are any customers in sight, down to when she's bidding goodbyes to the staff, making sure to plant a kiss on Aaron's cheek by the end of each shift.

"I've been serving your section since you...left for Aaron's office. I think table forty-four will leave a rather hefty tip."

"Thank you for covering for me. Enjoy your tip, Ana."

Thea whirls toward Ether's backdoor, taking a few steps before curiosity creeps over from the deepest recess of her mind, prompting Thea to spin on her heels back toward the parlor.

Greeted by soft music and loud patrons, Thea rolls onto the tips of her boots to peek at table forty-four, where plates of food surround Adrian while his companions are nowhere to be seen.

"For fucks sake," Thea curses softly. Ducking between a group of patrons with a prayer on her lips, she trails behind the group walking at a snail's pace toward Ether's front door.

When the night air brushes against her skin, Thea realized just how warm Aaron left her—too used to the warmth of his skin and sweat clamming their skin; to the brush of his lips exploring the curves of her body as she'd catch her breath when coming down from cloud nine.

Thea lingers there, watching the group of friends venturing in the opposite direction of where she'd be walking home. Their voices mingled into the song of Brooklyn, with the echoes of distant brawls and music playing a few streets down.

With that song playing in her ears, Thea closes her eyes, allowing the chilly wind to erase Aaron's fingerprints from her skin and the kisses he'd planted on the divots of her spine.

A dangerous game we've been playing for far too long, Thea muses as she drags her boots against the concrete sidewalk, wishing she'd taken up on Aaron's offer to spend the night with him.

But a day away from Jolly was cruel enough on the kitty, and Thea also knows that if she allowed a day, it would bleed into a week, then she'd soon be living under Aaron's roof, and she'd have more to lose than a dream that never became anything beyond that.

Thea keeps her gaze high, seeking the stars that seem to be perpetually hidden by a veil of pollution from cars and the bright lights from the growing high-rise buildings spread across Brooklyn.

If fate was truly written in the stars, if they were the thing dictating the lives of those on earth as the moon dictates the tides, then it seems the cosmo doesn't want Thea to read her fate.

Not wanting Thea to have hope nor for her to fall into despair and find herself sinking into the bottom of a river —a cruel mystery, it seems.

Thea reaches the end of the street, standing on the side of a faded crosswalk as she waits for an opportunity to cross as she's never quite acquired the brazen New York style of demanding cars to stop for pedestrians.

"Thea Tea," Adrian's annoying voice rises in the distance.

He smiles when she glances over her shoulder before deciding to force herself into that brazen New Yorker disposition—forcing the drivers to step on the brake or be hit with a lawsuit.

Honking mingles with drivers cussing at Thea as an arm drapes around her shoulder. "Let me walk you home. It's late."

"No, thank you."

"In case you didn't notice, Thea Tea, I wasn't asking."

"Are you too stupid to know what 'no' means?"

Adrian chuckles. Leaning down until his warm breath tickles the slope of her neck, eliciting a shiver down her spine.

"Glance over your shoulder. You'll see a guy staring at you and trailing after us," He whispers before pivoting and taking Thea with him, voice raising as if he'd been too drunk to be aware of his surroundings. "Come on, let's go back for another drink."

Thea smacks the back of her hand against Adrian's chest, making him laugh as her eyes land on a guy wearing a beanie a few steps behind them. He quickly stops walking, turning to the street as if he'd suddenly realized he needs to cruise it, yet he steals glances at them.

"Okay, you can walk me home."

"I was going to regardless. I'd rather not wake up and see in the news that a woman in Brooklyn was brutally murdered or raped, or both."

"The wonders of being a woman on planet Earth. Joining the seven-hundred thirty-six million women who are victims of physical or sexual violence, if not both."

Adrian steals a glance at her, thinking she doesn't notice the slight tilt of his head or the smile adorning his lips. "Not tonight. That much I can promise you."

"Very heroic of you," Thea jests, rolling her eyes as they stroll down the street. "You could always send him a tip since you have such a gross disposable income."

Adrian laughs, pulling Thea from the outside of the sidewalk to the inside before draping his arms over her shoulder again, keeping her body close to his, as if afraid the guy trailing after them could just grab Thea and run away with her.

“You are in New York, Thea Tea. You either meet someone really broke or someone extremely wealthy. This is a city of extremes and exploitation. There is a reason so many are miserable here.”

Thea rolls her eyes, but she doesn't rebut when Adrian is right. She has first-hand experience with both realities, living in Aaron's wealth during their stolen nights while sharing her apartment with rats and roaches.

Head lolling to the side, Thea notices how the city seems to fade away, the rattle of trash bags becoming nothing as her attention falls on how soundless Adrian's steps are.

Contrasting to how Thea drags her boots against the coarse sidewalk, reminding herself of the many times she'd see drunk patrons tumbling over, skinning their knees and the palms of their hands before being dragged down by their friends.

Sometimes Ether's staff bets on which patrons will retch outside Ether and which unlucky patron will fall into it—their only secret from Aaron as the man would most definitely repudiate betting against customers.

"What are you smiling about, Thea Tea? Does my company delight you?"

She snorts a laugh, dramatically rolling her eyes before saying, "How optimistic of you. The only thing I enjoy is that your company is keeping me somewhat safe. You are like a wildly uncomfortable injection, the ones where your butt hurts for a full week? Reminding you of how miserable it was, but you know it's for the better even if you do not enjoy the process."

"Not even one bit? Although, let's keep this PG when I say that, I too could leave your...muscles hurting for a week."

Laughter billows into the air as Thea throws her head back, laughing freely as Adrian's eyes flit over her face. Noticing how her nose scrunches with her laughter as Thea's eyes nearly disappear with how high her cheekbones are, her perfect teeth that aren't pearly white but make her seem more humane and less like a goddess.

Adrian wonders how someone of divine beauty could be working in a pub of all places, wondering how he'd been lucky enough to stumble on someone so beautiful, but Adrian wasn't one to question his blessings.

He wonders how someone can be beautiful even under the limelight of stores that have been closed for hours, their windows displaying goods any drunk person would forget about in the morning.

"Why do you care?" She asks with a giggle slipping into her words as they walk past her apartment building, ambling without a destination.

"My parents instilled in me this ravaging need to be liked, and you, Thea Tea, don't seem to like me very much. It's been years since someone didn't instantly like me. It's harrowing."

"What? They are usually charmed until you send them $2000, and they suddenly get the ick?"

"Why would anyone get mad over free money?" Adrian asks, steering Thea toward a twenty-four-hour bakery with a pale yellow awning and a pink neon light hung in its interior, informing customers that after five in the afternoon, all coffee is decaf. "But no, they get this so-called ick when I say their work is subpar, at least in parts.

If they sucked all around, I wouldn't work with them, but I did have someone using strikethroughs. Can you imagine?"

Thea doesn't stop Adrian when he drops a hand to her lower back while pushing open the bakery's matching yellow door, encasing them in the smell of warm carrot cake.

Large paintings bring color to the lime-washed brick walls, where posters and photographs scatter above the oak benches, and its pink cushion runs perpendicular to the wall.

The mellow colors blend well with the art using contrasting colors, nearly electrifying the canvas as they practically jump out, visually fighting each other in a way that works beautifully.

Thea meanders further into the bakery while Adrian disappears to order them something. She stops in front of a framed poster with the entirety of The Great Gatsby written in tiny letters.

Stealing a smile from the edge of her lips as Thea hopes to one day steal the idea, bedecking her walls with her books instead of their covers as some designer might have a vendetta against her.

"I didn't know what you wanted, so I went for a classic," Adrian says, startling Thea as she'd almost forgotten he was with her. "Red velvet cake, also known as the only cake that matters."

"That's something we can agree on."

Adrian takes a seat, smiling as he watches Thea sprawl herself on the bench before pulling a fluffy pillow into her lap like another layer of defense between her and Adrian.

"A woman of taste."

"Yeah yeah, whatever you say."

They stare at each other as silence prolongs itself, disrupted only by the cutlery of other customers and the chiming of the coffee machine.

The air's laced with a caramelized and almost nutty scent of beans, sugar, and chocolate used in many of the cakes on display, some with beautiful frosting resembling dainty flowers.

It seems wrong for Thea to have never been to a bakery so close to her apartment, yet there are only three places she's had the energy to visit in nearly five years.

"So..."

"So..." Thea echoes, gaze darting across the bakery in search of something to talk about with him; there is nothing quite as dreadful as a meal shared in silence.

"So, you are a writer?"

Perhaps that is more dreadful, Thea broods.

"Depends on what you consider a writer." Adrian arches a brow at her reply, almost as if asking her to elaborate. "My relatives don't think of me as a writer because I have yet to traditionally publish a book. They claim any seven-year-old can write, but unless it's a career, my craft has no value. Other people will differentiate between a writer and an author, which to me is merely semantics."

"There are many published books with no value. What do you consider yourself to be, Thea Tea?"

"A writer that's been fucked over by a nepotic industry? Do you know how many people only sign with an agent because they are friends or went to school with the right people? This industry is built on connections, and I'm particularly unskillful when it comes to pleasantries."

"If you write good novels, then you are a writer. Publishing simply means quite a few people will profit from something that only exists because you exist. There are plenty of people involved in polishing a manuscript and making it look good to consumers, but they'd all be jobless if there was no one to write it."

"Or anyone to read it," Thea points out, knowing there is no reason for her to write if no one is interested in reading her work. Something that makes her heart tight with despair, needing someone beyond Aaron to see the value in her stories.

Maybe that's why Aaron was so important in her life, as Thea knew he meant every word when saying he was excited to read a new chapter, knowing even when there'd been something demanding his attention, and he had to postpone reading her work, Aaron would inevitably ask for the promised chapter.

Aaron was the one constant in her life.

Thea would slip through the cracks of her brother's mind, pushed under the things that mattered most to him as Jules would forget to read her books, yet her brother never forgot to watch Formula 1 races despite their erratic timezones or which LEGO sets would be released throughout the year.

"What do you work with, Adrian? Or are you simply a trust fund baby?"

"I am indeed a trust fund baby, but I'm also an editor."

There is triumph sparkling in gray eyes, in the way the edge of Adrian's lips curl into an arrogant smile as if he's gloating for keeping that knowledge a secret.

Oblivious to how Thea wonders if those medieval executioners felt the same way as Adrian does; if they too had a cavalier attitude in coming to have power over the lives of others, a power that stands between whether someone lives or dies.

"What?"

"Fantasy editor. If you want, I can take a look at your manuscript unless there is a strikethrough. In that case, I refuse to even look at you anymore."

"What?" Thea repeats.

"I said I'm a—"

"I heard what you said," Thea hisses. Fingers curling into a fist as she tries to rein in her wrath over how Adrian allowed her to expose a side of publishing those within the industry prefer to turn a blind eye to, letting her dig her own grave and throw five years down Brooklyn Bridge by ruining all of her chances of ever getting a book deal when she'd been nothing but unpleasant to an editor. The publishing world is far too small for any editor to want to work with her—for any agent to sign her when she committed career suicide.

"Don't do that. Don't change your nasty little self to be all smiles, " Adrian says, tipping his head to the waitress that comes to their table as he leans into the back of his chair. "I wouldn't offer to read your book if I didn't enjoy your nasty little self. I have a terrible inclination that there could be several strikethroughs, and I would continue liking you. You are quite something, Thea Tea. Unless your boyfriend forbids that too."

"Aaron isn't my boyfriend." Thea clings to the one thing that makes sense to her. "And I don't have money to pay for an editor, especially a trust fund editor."

Adrian nods.

Pushing a heart-shaped plate toward Thea as he brings a cup of coffee to his lips, hiding the smile on his lips when he notices Thea biting the side of her lips and the blush in her cheeks deepened by the neon light not too distant advertising fresh-out-of-the-oven cookies.

Fidgeting with the cake rather than eating it, Thea wonders how her night ended in such a way; it went from being in Aaron's office for hours to feeling as if she'd been exposed.

Thea tastes blood as she bites into her tongue to keep herself from unraveling, anchoring herself to that coppery taste reminding her of when she'd been a child fascinated with licking batteries.

The phone in her back pocket pings, steering her attention away from her gnarling worry. Thea glances at Adrian, finding his lips still contorted with a little grin, before taking a bite of the red velvet cake.

Adrian Friedman sent you $8000.
"Ur cute."

"Adrian," Thea sighs before sending the money back.

Seconds later, his phone vibrates with a notification. Adrian's grin blossoms into a full smile as he says, "Oh, look, you paid for my editing fee, which doesn't exist, but you just paid for it. So, what is your book about?"

"I was just giving your money back."

"The moment it left my account, it became yours. So, the book?"

"It's a fucking romance, and you don't edit romance. What's the point?"

Adrian takes another bite of the cake, moaning obnoxiously loud as he savors the taste, rolling his eyes heavenwards in exaggerated satisfaction.

Thea's eyes flit over his face.

Noticing the sharp angles that make him conventionally handsome, there is a glimmer in his eyes, a child-like curiosity that intrigues her.

"Fantasy is what I prefer to work in. I'm good at my job, Thea Tea. I'm pretty sure I could make the bible a more engaging story."

She laughs once more, rolling her eyes at him. "You are ridiculous, and your ego is bountiful."

"I've been told my ego is expanding faster than the universe. You are the one breaking my inertia."

"Are you sure you are an editor? You sound more like an astrophysicist," Thea jests, cutting a piece of cake before she moans at the slightly tart edge of cocoa. "Which one should I send you? The first book I wrote or the tenth and last book I've written?"

"The one you are the proudest of."

Thea's smile falters.

At one point or another, she'd been proud of all the books she'd written, loving each and everyone, but then rejections dimmed the love and pride, making her think of those books as worthless, a waste of time—much like how she sees herself.

Believing that with each vague rejection, each no she'd get in the form of *'no reply means no'* or the *'a no from one agent is a no from the agency as a whole,'* in the rejection she'd face when friends claimed to be so very excited yet a month would go, they wouldn't read past the first chapter.

"They are all failures," She mutters, hating the sadness that sinks to her core and corrodes every positive thing Thea ever saw in herself.

"Are they failures, or have others failed you? I can't tell you which one it is, but I assure you, not every person is born to be a writer, not every bestseller should reach that place, nor every fan-favorite author should be anyone's but their mom favorite author, yet when those people succeed it means countless of deserving writers failed, and they aren't the ones to blame."

"Strikethrough writer?"

"Strikethrough writer."

Thea smiles, biting back on another laugh as she isn't used to laughing as often as she did with Adrian, nor with anyone other than the characters she'd created as a mirror of herself—from the things she loves to all the things she hates.

"Very well, Adrian Friedman. Can I have your e-mail?"

"I thought you'd never ask."

7

Keys jiggle in her hand as Thea tries to find the keyhole of her door in the dark hallway, struggling to find it as if she hasn't lived in that apartment for years.

"You know you don't need to physically see me walking into my apartment."

"I know. I just like your company," Adrian says, placing his hands on the door frame as Thea glances at him from over her shoulder, noticing just how close he'd gotten. "And now, I must see your cat."

"Jolly doesn't want to see you."

As if the cream-shaded British shorthair cat has a personal vendetta against Thea, Jolly meows adorably, hitting the door with those deadly claws that have left one too many scars on her wrist, ones curving into the palms of her hands.

Finding the keyhole, Thea carefully pushes the door open, trying not to hurt Jolly, who slips into the hallway. Purring as she rubs herself against Adrian's legs.

Thea ignores the little giggle that escapes Adrian's lips as the man picks up Jolly while she slips into her apartment, leaving the door open for Adrian, who peppers kisses on Jolly's rounded head while the cat gently paws his face.

"Oh God, she's the cutest thing in the whole world."

"She eats roaches and rats for me," Thea points out.

Collecting dirty clothes scattered in her studio apartment that could pass as a prison cell, Thea hides them under the blanket pooled between the gap of the walls covered in sticky notes with motivational quotes and her bed.

"Disgusting, but she's like you," Adrian jokes, running his hands over Jolly's fur while glancing around, almost as if he'd never seen a shabby apartment. "A beauty with a filthy mouth, isn't that right, Jolly Bean?"

"I have a filthy mouth?"

"Yes, you do." Adrian presses his nose against Jolly's pink snout, getting a gentle nibble on it before the man sets the cat on top of her small dining table that functions as an office desk. "And you know it."

"Whatever you say."

Thea expects Adrian to walk toward her and take a seat beside her on the bed, for his hands to glide to the side of her neck, thumb caressing her jaw before pulling her into a kiss.

Yet, he takes a keen interest in her microwave with a green light. Thea hopes he doesn't open the door and find it will break apart in his hand and possibly fall from the broken hinges—something her landlord refuses to fix.

Adrian leans over her table, peeking out of her small window as he ignores the few cups she'd left in the sink for far too long, but that will have to wait until morning for her to wash them.

"Nice view," He teases as she has a sliver of street view, most of it blocked by the building built beside hers. "Bet you get a lot of sunlight."

"I do, actually."

A lie, but not something he needs to know the truth about as she only gets sunlight in the mornings when she's sleeping the day away after writing all night.

Adrian raises a brow at the pile hidden under her blankets before he finally takes the seat next to her, laying down on his elbows without saying anything.

The silence becomes thick as they stare into each other's eyes, neither knowing what to say but feeling as if there is something to say, something they wish the other to know but don't know what it is yet.

As if there is something between them that the silence threatens to sever.

"Adrian?"

"Huh?"

"Promise you'll actually read it."

"Of course, I'll read it. I wouldn't have charged you $8000 if I didn't plan on reading it," He quips, gloating silently as a smile blooms on her lips. "How disappointed have you been with people saying they'd read your book and never doing so?"

Thea sprawls herself beside him, smiling as Jolly meows once more without leaping down from the table—the cat did always enjoy the view she'd get from there.

"Three years ago, when I was writing a novel, my very best friend read the first five chapters, claiming she loved it and was utterly excited to read more. The next day she texted me saying she just wanted to go home and read the chapter six and seven, but she never sent me any opinions on it."

"Ouch."

"Yeah. A few days later, I stopped sharing the document with her. Whenever I brought it up, she'd say how she was excited about it, and couldn't wait. A month passed, and she didn't realize the document sharing was turned off, but she'd text me about the books she'd been reading. To this day, she hasn't realized the document sharing has been turned off, even when I finished. I offered to send her a printed copy of it, but she said she'd just read from the document sharing."

"Ouch again."

"Yeah. A part of me still wants people to care, but I'm getting to a point where it's harder and harder to pretend they ever will. Why should I care when they don't?"

"And Aaron is different?"

Thea turns her head to look at Adrian, only to find him looking at her, his gray eyes laced with something too similar to sadness.

"He is. Aaron will always text me to ask how the writing is going. I can change the topic, and he'll always go back to '*you didn't tell me how writing is going,*' it means the world. Doesn't it?"

"It does. People always bring back the things they are truly curious and interested in."

Thea pokes his ribs, earning a squeal from Adrian as she continues her assault. "Oh my, did it hurt? Are you okay after not insulting Aaron?"

"He's your boyfriend, that's not your boyfriend. He can't be that awful."

"I told you, he's not my boyfriend."

Adrian rolls onto his side so he's facing Thea.

His hand glides the side of her neck, thumb caressing her jaw but instead of pulling her into a kiss, he leans down. Warm breath becomes the air she breathes, yet it's easy for Thea to ignore the little voice telling her to slip away.

"So if I kissed you, he wouldn't be mad?"

"He would, but I wouldn't be a cheater."

"Do you want *me* to kiss you, Thea?"

"Do *you* want to kiss me, Adrian?"

The man smiles. Pupils consume the gray of his eyes as his gaze flits over her face before dropping to the length of her body.

"You know I do. I've wanted to kiss you since the moment I laid eyes on you."

"Why haven't you?" Thea asks, dropping her hand to his wrist, keeping him there when Adrian threatens to pull away.

"Because, Thea Tea, I'll only kiss you when you ask me to. When you are breathless with how much you need me to kiss you. Then and only then will I kiss you."

"Why?"

"Because I know what I want," Adrian says, planting a kiss on her cheek, almost kissing her lips. "And I want you. With time, we'll learn if we want each other for the rest of our lives."

Thea snorts a laugh, rolling her eyes as Adrian pulls away, taking two steps toward Jolly under her gaze. "You are very arrogant. Has anyone ever told you that?"

Planting a kiss on Jolly's head, Adrian drags his boots toward the door. Moving all too slowly, giving Thea a display of his body as he walks into the hallway, reaching for the doorframe and leaning on it.

"People usually won't state the obvious. Goodnight, Thea, don't forget to lock your door before you go to bed."

Fuck, she thinks as Adrian closes the door for her, steps echoing faintly as Jolly meows longingly. *I really did want him to kiss me.*

The world rumbles, quivering and bending into itself as colors bleed into one another, becoming murky like the walls in her apartment. Even the mellow sounds become thunderous, clapping against something hard, melding into a meow.

Jolly smacks Thea's cheeks with her paw, her coarse tongue dragging against her soft skin. Stirring Thea awake to realize the claps of thunder is actually someone knocking on her door, the sound reverberating against the thin walls of the apartment building.

"Coming!" She mutters, wrapping the comforter around herself before meandering toward the front door with her eyes barely open.

Thea works on the door chain that dingles against the wall, adding a new scratch to the white paint marred black long before she moved into the shoebox of an apartment.

Unlocking the door, Thea rests her temple against it, eyes drifting close before seeing who is standing before her.

"Good morning, love," Aaron greets her, planting a kiss on her cheek as he slips into the apartment, taking a moment to lock the door before venturing deeper into her apartment. "You forgot your laptop at my place."

"My hero."

Aaron chuckles at the raspiness of her voice. He glances over his shoulder while settling the device on her table, smiling when Thea wraps her arms around his waist, laying her head over his back, his heart beating a little faster as she listens to it.

They stay like that for a few moments in silence, disrupted only by Jolly's purring as the cat rubs herself against Aaron's legs, demanding attention from him, but Aaron busies himself by running the tips of his fingers over the back of Thea's hands.

"You are so warm."

"Don't you mean hot?"

"Hum, that too," Thea concedes.

Snaking around his taut body so her head is laid on his chest instead of on his back, she purrs in tandem with Jolly, approving of the caress as Aaron dips his fingers underneath Thea's oversized T-shirt.

"Want me to tuck you back in bed?" The man whispers, biting his tongue against the sneeze, threatening to ruin the moment as he explores the divots of her spine.

"What time is it?"

Turning his head toward the microwave displaying 11:11 in its hideous green light, Aaron lies as he squeezes Thea against his chest, "Seven, too early for you, isn't it?"

"Uhm."

"Do you want to sleep for a few more hours?"

"Uh-huh."

Aaron smiles against her temple, planting a kiss there before leading her back to bed in three short steps—one of the odd perks of living in a small apartment is how quick it makes for them to stumble into bed.

With arms wrapped around his waist, Aaron contorts himself to remove his shoes under Jolly's attentive gaze, almost as if the cat is waiting for the succession of sneezes that torment Aaron practically when he's in the hallway.

"Not today, Jolly," He whispers, scratching behind her pointed ears before leaning against the wrought metal headboard. "I took two allergy pills today. You are harmless to me...at least for a few hours."

The cat meows before elegantly leaping into the twin-sized bed. Jolly threads carefully around Aaron and Thea before settling on the curve of Thea's legs as she cuddles against Aaron.

Sighing contently with the circles his hand draws on her spine, Aaron's free hand finds its way to the nape of her neck, playing with her hair as she drifts back asleep to the sound of his beating heart.

A small part of him feels guilty for lying to her, knowing she'd prefer to have him grab breakfast loaded with coffee so she could work on writing, but far too often, Thea pursues her dreams to the detriment of herself.

Spending days on little sleep and even less food, as cooking is too laborious of a task, too time-consuming when she's in the middle of a scene, especially when scenes tend to morph into pages, growing into chapters as the day slips between the pages in front of her.

So, he lied about the time.

Forcing Thea into catching up on lost sleep before he takes her out for a late lunch or gets food delivered to her apartment so she can eat and he can bask in the way her cheeks grow ruddy with joy.

The way Thea will practically glow when immersed in the one thing that brings her nearly as much joy as it sucks out of her.

It's exhausting to care when no one else does, Thea once told him, long before he'd grown to care about her and her writing, but even in that moment, with Thea asleep in his arms, he knew it wasn't enough.

Every day since, Aaron has worried about what that exhaustion and loneliness could morph into, worrying it could steal Thea from the one thing she truly loves.

Now he's thankful for every day with her, preferring to stare at the walls of her apartment filled with motivational quotes, for his arms to go numb, and his back to ache as she sleeps on him more than anything else.

Aaron would trade decades of his life for her dreams to come true, for her to have one year where everything goes just as she wants.

If only New York had a genie in a bottle rather than rats in the walls.

8

Thea glances at her phone, noticing how quickly the battery has drained in the short commute from her apartment to Ether.

"Are you waiting for a call?" Aaron asks, peeking at her phone just as Thea presses the side button before sliding the phone back into her pocket.

"A text from an editor."

"That's...new. Why didn't you tell me about it?"

"It just happened yesterday."

A yelp bubbles past Thea's lips when Aaron stops walking and pulls her close. Ignoring the loud sighs of passersby, Aaron leans toward her.

Fingers find their way to the nape of her neck, his thumb caressing the soft arch of her jaw as green eyes flit over her face—noting the meek smile on her lips, the way the city lights seem to dim as Thea comes into focus.

"Are we celebrating tonight, love? Because if so, I'll need to call Isa and tell her she's responsible for Ether for a few days, maybe two weeks."

"Oh really? And where would we be? Locked in your apartment, becoming nudists for two weeks?"

Thea laughs as Aaron peppers kisses on her face, moving from her cheeks to her forehead before his lips land a final kiss on the tip of her nose.

"I know you always wanted to go to Svalbard," Aaron says, resting his forehead on hers, fighting the urge to flip off the next passerby, who sighs loudly, rolling their eyes at the inconvenience of walking around them. "Although, I think that'd be rather dull. It seems like something that requires a long stay to fully enjoy. So, how about I take you to Monaco, or maybe we can take a road trip through the Swiss Alps?"

"One condition, I demand we rent a little cabin and eat all the fondue we can stomach."

"Anything you want, T. So, should I buy us flights and book hotels?"

"I wish," Thea says, rolling onto the tips of her toes as she wraps her arms around his neck. "It's not that kind of editor, not one that would acquire my book. Just one that wanted to help me with some feedback. Hopefully, you can take me on that trip soon."

"I'm sorry, love."

"For what?"

"That people are fucking morons."

Thea raises her shoulders in a nonchalant shrug, not deigning to show Aaron just how quickly she's running out of time as she lies to him, "Well, it's never too late. Besides, people can't all be like you."

"One day, there will be more people like me. Your wrists will cramp with how many books you'll have to sign for more people like me, the ones who appreciate you, value your work, and whose lives are better for it."

Thea pulls Aaron down toward her.

Smiling against his lips as his hand dips toward the small of her back, inching closer to her ass. A moan lingers between them as Aaron deepens the kiss, whirling Thea around and pressing her against the window of a coffee shop.

Grabbing her ass, Aaron settles Thea between his knees, trapping her there as he slips his tongue into her mouth, savoring the taste of her lips as their bodies meld together.

Creating a chasm between them and the nugatory world that fades. Demolishing the brick-and-mortar buildings, emptying the streets littered with cars stuck in traffic, and stilling the soft spring breeze that runs its fingers through Thea's hair.

"Get a fucking room!" Someone shouts from across the street, eliciting a laugh from Thea as she entangles her fingers in Aaron's hair, smiling against his lips.

"We should obey that request."

Thea nudges Aaron away as her laugh comes in tandem with the coffee shop customers knocking on the window she'd been leaning on.

"We should, but we can't," Thea says between fits of laughter, resting her chin against his chest. "Time to stop whoring yourself to me and get to work, boss-friend. You are late."

"So are you," Aaron argues as Thea drops her arms from around his neck, sprinting ahead of him to sustain the fallacy of their relationship being strictly professional as if there is a single employee that hasn't figured out why Thea is the one employee always held back to help Aaron close Ether.

Thea can feel those green eyes on her, watching as she skips, walking with a bounce on her heel, giddy over a quick kiss that has her heart hammering against her chest long after she slips inside Ether.

She halts at the door, confused as they are late enough for the bar and restaurant to be brimming with patrons, yet the parlor is empty except for staff.

There's a clear divide between the bar and the restaurant waiters, each lingering on opposite ends of the room while the cooks gather in the center of the bar, where they share a bottle of bourbon.

How odd, she thinks, venturing into the room that's more raucous than when there are customers but isn't nearly as rowdy as when it's just Thea and Aaron cleaning up before closing for the day.

"Thea, come here," Ana calls from the same table Adrian hogged for the nights he'd been there.

A vulpine gleam adorns Ana's big brown eyes as Thea drags her boots toward table forty-four, where Isabelle and Logan are seated beside Ana.

"If you are looking for Aaron, he isn't here yet," Ana says with enough poison dripping in her words for both Isa and Logan to raise their brows. Shoulders inching toward their ears, acting as if Ana had broken a glass in an abandoned theater, the sound echoing against the cushioned walls that once amplified the thrum of loud speaks while not allowing the battle in a superhero movie to bleed into the mellowness of a romance-comedy.

Thea mirrors the tender smile on Ana's face as air flows into Ether when Aaron pushes the front door open, not bothering to wait outside to give enough time between the two to appease gossip.

"It seems you knew that already." There is somewhat of a challenge in the girl's eyes, despite her voice slightly quivering.

"I did, Ana. I was tearing his clothes off in my apartment before I came...Well, we both came before we made our way here. And no, we aren't dating, so drop the petty attitude before it even starts, okay? *I don't care* if you give him kisses and flirt with him."

Blood rushes to Ana's rounded cheeks, giving her a youthful appearance, almost as if she was a blushing bride in some Archaic English novel that has inspired many to view and write women as objects to be sold.

The portrait of a coy virgin, Thea muses, wondering how the woman was raised for those doe eyes to foment a newfound hatred as if Thea had stolen her betrothal—as if Aaron was a prize Thea was competing for.

Without a word, Ana rises from her seat as Thea takes hers, watching the petite woman march toward Aaron in a display of her age, reminding Thea that she just turned twenty-one.

"Is that why you keep rejecting me?" Logan asks, raising a glass of apple juice to his lips.

"No. If my options were celibacy and having sex with an eighteen-year-old, I'd sign my life away to God as a nun."

"Ouch, why?"

"Because if I were attracted to minors, I would sign up to become a priest?"

Isabelle's boisterous laugh echoes against Ether, ricocheting against its walls until Aaron glances at them from over Ana's head.

"My grandma would wash your mouth with a bar of soap for saying that," Isa quips, arching a brow as she raises a glass of Schwarzbier beer—a beverage so dark it nearly blends with the color of her skin.

Thea remembers the night the staff had pestered her to allocate each a cocktail or beverage that matched them, except she needed to justify it with the flowery poetry of a writer.

There'd been skeptical glances when she said Isa was Schwarzbier, some had even been offended and didn't want to hear what Thea had to say, but Isa waited until the end of their shift to ask her why.

This might sound weird, Thea preambled before explaining how Isa managed to be strong and delicate—her face carved in sharp lines and angles, but with a softness to them in how her face was heart-shaped.

How the bridge of her nose down to her deep cupid bow added depth and her lips, added fullness to her face, as well as her deep brown eyes, striking balance between being doe-eyed and like a doll while remaining strong and powerful.

Traits reminding Thea of the lightly roasted flavor of Schwarzbier beer, its clean yet nuanced hints of caramel, and airy wafts of coffee, striking an equal balance between the intensity and sweetness Isa had, being kind without being someone others could walk over and powerful without harshness.

"Regardless, why are we closed today?"

"Aaron sent an e-mail earlier today informing everyone Ether would be closed for the night, but he wanted to buy everyone drinks and pizza."

"A confraternization," Logan chimes in. "He also said it wasn't mandatory, but I guess everyone wanted a free meal and drinks."

"You know what that means, don't you?"

Isabelle nods while Logan's eyes dart between the two, oblivious that the last time Aaron closed Ether for a gathering with the staff, he announced the expansion of the bar into a restaurant.

"He's been planning this for a while," Isa says, running her fingers around the rim of her glass. "Didn't he tell you anything?"

"We usually don't talk about work outside of work."

Logan still holds traces of confusion on his face, arching a brow at Isa in a silent request for her to explain when Thea's phone vibrates in her pocket.

Adrian Friedman sent you $1000.
"Today has been a busy day, I only got to read the first chapter so far. Color me intrigued and pissed off."

You sent Adrian Friedman $0.10
"Why are you pissed?"

A smile tugs on the edge of her lips as she rolls her eyes at the ridiculous amount of money, yet she refuses to play his game, refusing to chide him for it, letting Adrian send her as much money as he wants. Soon enough, she'll send it all back.

Searching her bag for her charger, Thea doesn't pay attention to Isa explaining how the few times Aaron has called for these "confraternization nights," they'd all been used to announce renovations that would close Ether for a few months, but he always made sure everyone would receive their usual paycheck unless they wanted to secure work elsewhere.

Adrian Friedman sent you $100.

"This is too good to not have agents and editors fighting for it. Your girl Cecilia has a corrosiveness to her that's usually found in the male characters. I'm curious as to where the story will go."

Thea's smile widens, yet she hates how it makes her giddy, hates the excitement that comes when people praise her work before forgetting it exists.

That's always been the problem.

Not writing or developing characters and their plot but captivating a stranger into moving from a blurb to the first few pages of a book. Trying to break the herd mentality imbued in people, where they'll be dismissive of anything that has yet to captivate the collective.

Thea reins in her excitement, not allowing that joy to take root when there is nothing to be joyous about. Not yet, at least.

It doesn't take long before fifteen pizza boxes are delivered to Ether, demanding Isa's attention as Aaron doesn't carry cash in his wallet, being resolute in handling things with a black credit card.

Thea watches as the man seems confused as to why Isabelle is scolding him for ordering pizza from a place that costs $50 a box—painfully oblivious that most people wouldn't pay that much for a pizza, much less when ordering fifteen.

With a promise of paying Isa back by the end of the night, Aaron saunters away with five boxes cradled in his arms. He practically dances in the parlor, moving from one end to the other as he offers slices of pizza to the staff.

Aaron jumbles with the boxes as some people want a pepperoni slice, others mushroom and broccoli, while most stick to the classic Margherita pizza.

Knowing Aaron is extra charming for her delight, he captures her attention. Thea peels her gaze away from him as she opens the document with the first book she'd ever written—a story inspired by Jules's phase where he only cared about Formula 1, blabbing about the sport until Thea took the liberty of writing a romance between a team principal and the world champion pilot.

"Don't tell me you're writing?" Aaron asks, settling the last pizza box on the table. "Logan, I think Isa was calling for you."

"I didn't hear...oh yeah, I'll go find her," The boy amends upon noticing the way Aaron widens his eyes, pleading for him to leave without being asked. "Bye, Thea. Enjoy your pizza."

"So," Aaron preambles, taking the seat next to her while fidgeting with the pizza box as Thea raises her gaze to meet his. "Ana told me you told her that we've been...sleeping together."

"I did."

Nodding and humming in understanding, Aaron pulls a slice of cheesy pizza, offering it to Thea before taking one himself.

"Does that mean I get to kiss you at work whenever I want?"

"What do you think?"

Aaron bites his lips, his green eyes focusing on Thea as she licks the tomato sauce on the corner of her mouth. Whimpering in delight over the pizza in the same tone she whimpered hours ago when his tongue lapped between her legs.

"I think I should take you to my office and eat something far better than pizza."

"Aaron!" Thea yelps with heat rushing to her cheeks as she smacks his shoulder, ignoring the delicious tingle in her lower abdomen.

"Should we?"

"You are wicked cruel."

"And you love every single second of it. Am I wrong?"

"I said you are wicked, not that you are a liar. But no, you shouldn't take me to your office, but maybe if I'm in a good mood, I might let you take me to your bed."

"I did suck up my allergies to spend the day with you."

"Free will is a beautiful thing, isn't it?"

"It is," Aaron agrees before his hand finds its way to the nape of her neck, pulling her into a kiss that makes Thea drop her slice of pizza on her phone as she moves toward him.

Stumbling from her seat as she closes the distance between them, Thea presses her body against his, careful not to allow her digits covered in cheese grease to touch his expensive suit.

"You taste like oregano," Aaron mutters against her lips, shivering at the laugh bubbling from her chest as Thea buries her head against the crook of his neck, breathing him in as if her life depended on it.

"You taste like tomato sauce. We taste quite good together. Now, tell me what are your plans for Ether?"

Aaron snakes his arm around Thea, keeping her there as he peppers kisses from her jaw down the slope of her neck, nibbling on the sensitive skin before licking the slight ache.

His teeth sink a little stronger as Thea whimpers against his neck, planting kisses along Aaron's jaw. Thea arches toward him when his fingers slip under her T-shirt, caressing the divots of her spine, moving from her jeans to her bra.

"You know, I really want to eat that pizza," Thea says as his slender fingers move toward her breast. "I am starving."

Humming in agreement, Aaron gingerly spins Thea around before settling her in his lap. "You have to forgive me, love. I'm using you to hide the fact I have a boner right now."

"Oh, I can feel it. You are nasty, Aaron Mariani."

"Yet, you are the one who stripped down in my office, and practically begged me to fuck you."

"And you loved every single second of it," Thea mimics the pretentious tone of his voice as she lifts the slice of pizza from her phone, throwing a napkin over it without bothering to clean the device. "Quite the mess you made, fucking me until my pussy couldn't take any more of you."

"We enjoy messy."

Adrian Friedman sent you $100.
"Should I stop by Ether tonight?"

Thea rolls her eyes at the text, ignoring Adrian for a few moments as the vodka martini burns down her throat, making her regret not sticking to the peach liquor she prefers over everything else in Ether.

Her stomach flutters as she reads the wiring notification once more, enjoying how ridiculous Adrian is to keep sending her $1000 without any real reason.

You sent Adrian Friedman $0.10
"No, the bar and restaurant are closed for the day."

Thea props her chin against the palm of her hand, watching as the cooks bellow to some 2012 summer song, leaving the younger members of the staff confused.

Adrian Friedman sent you $1000.
"Then where can I see you tonight?"

Adrian Friedman sent you $1000.
"If you say your apartment, should I buy something?"

You sent Adrian Friedman $1
"Who says I want to see you tonight? Especially when you are thinking about buying condoms."

Adrian Friedman sent you $100.
"Take your mind out of the gutter, Thea Tea. I'll wait for you in our bakery. Cake is on me."

Thea chuckles at the bold assumption she'd want to see him badly enough to walk past her apartment to share some cake with him when she could just cuddle with Jolly and write a little before sleep sunk its claws into her.

The music blasting through the speakers dims to a low hum as Aaron ventures from the closed kitchen with a black matte cart they often use to unload delivered produce into the large fridge.

Instead of being loaded with heads of lettuce and sacks of potatoes, the cart has more or less seventy gift-wrapped square boxes.

Reading the names on a little tag, Aaron hands out each box to its corresponding staff. Working through half of them before Isa chimes in, "As many of us know, whenever Mr. Mariani shuts Ether down for a day, it means he's finally ready to share something he'd been planning in secrecy for a while."

"I wanted to show my gratitude to each and every one of you," Aaron says, ambling toward Thea, to whom he hands the last box, holding her gaze as he continues. "To show how much I care and appreciate having you in my life."

Heat spreads over her cheeks, a grin tugging on the edge of her lips as Aaron weaves their hands together. Thumb running over her knuckles for a few moments before his attention drifts back to the staff.

"For the next four months, the bar will be closed down for renovations. Isa and I have been discussing how to optimize Ether's space. The restaurant will be open during lunch hours once the renovations are over, and the bar will serve as a bakery mixed with bunch kind of place during the day, closing a few hours earlier than our competitors for us to prep for the night. Tomorrow Isa can tell you more about the changes. Enjoy the rest of the night."

When the attention on Aaron dissipates, he turns his gaze back toward Thea, eyes gleaming with a request, wanting Thea to unwrap her gift as he wraps an arm around her waist.

"How much did you spend on this little gift for everyone?" Thea chides as Aaron smiles against her shoulder, watching her crumble the wrapping paper before pulling the smartphone from its white packaging.

"Almost $100k, but it came from a few investments I've made, so no real money was spent."

"Aaron, that's a lot of money."

"Well, it's your fault." Thea raises a brow at him, holding his gaze as he leans down to whisper in her ears. "If I bought you a new phone, you wouldn't accept it, but if I bought a new phone for everyone in Ether, then you'd have to accept. I could have spent a $1000 on it, but I'm happy to spend a hundred thousand on you."

"You are disgustingly rich."

"And infatuated, but you tend to ignore that. You know I'd take you to Las Vegas to get married by Elvis Presley in a costume that reeks of whiskey and tequila. The hangover would be the only thing I'd regret."

"I'm pretty sure New York has city halls to officiate weddings, and if you are proposing to me, you'd be skipping quite a few steps, don't you think?"

Aaron shrugs as he bends his knees to rest his chin against Thea's shoulder, watching as she turns her new phone on, greeted by the 'Hello' transitioning into different languages.

"Jules would be the only one bothered by us. Your mom would love to have me join the family."

"My mom would divorce my dad to marry you. That's how she'd want you to join the family. She has a puppy love infatuation toward you. Your rich boy vacations were a real reason of torment to her."

"It's Jules' fault. You know I'd much rather go to your hometown during school breaks than to Europe," Aaron whispers against the shell of her ears, lips raising a shiver on Thea's spine as his breath tickles her. "Your mom is hot, but I must admit that I quite like the idea of you calling me daddy."

Thea rolls her eyes at him, pretending to be too focused on typing her passwords before the apps transfer.

"What, no *'you're disgusting, Aaron'* comments to throw at me?"

"You're filthy, Aaron Mariani," Thea concedes, bumping her head against his forehead. "Be nice to me, and I'll go back to your apartment with a surprise...*daddy*."

A dry chuckle bubbles past his lips, echoing into the pit of Thea's stomach as Aaron nibbles on her collarbone. "Fuck. I like how that sounds, and I feel wrong for it."

"Oh, so now you don't like being called 'daddy', daddy?" Thea asks with a malicious gleam in her eyes as she prods at his waist. "You go talk to the rest of the staff. I've been monopolizing you too much tonight."

"What will you do?"

"I'll prepare your surprise, *daddy*."

9

The kitten eats her kibble without as much as a glance at Thea, who washes Jolly's water bowl before finally rinsing the few cups she'd abandoned in the sink a few too many days ago.

"You are a good girl, Jolly. I'd hate to take care of your seven lives from paradise," Thea tells the cat as her robe falls before she slips into the scarlet lingerie—one of the few things she'll allow Aaron to buy since it's something she'd only use for him.

Jolly's tail sweeps the faded flooring of Thea's apartment before abandoning her food to leap into the pile of clothes Thea has yet to be bothered enough to take to the laundromat.

A meow echoes against the thin walls as Thea pulls a beige coat over her scandalous outfit, but Jolly hisses when the woman pulls the only pair of high heels she owns.

"I love you. I'll be back by the morning, and I promise tomorrow will be just you and I."

Thea drops her phone into her pocket, holding her coat flush against her body, fearing the tie around her waist will come undone, and expose that she's wearing nothing but lingerie beneath it.

No pretty Aaron or bratty Adrian to disturb our peace, Thea muses as she locks her door, breathing in the smell of cheap cigarettes that permeates the dark hallway. Yellowing the walls scribbled with markers marred by the furniture of long-gone tenants.

Walking down the stairwell built in the center of the building, Thea listens to snippets of her neighbors' life—a pop song filtering past the gap underneath the front door, entangling itself with the cry of a baby and the pacing of a nervous parent.

A few floors down, she can hear a couple yelling at each other and the thrum of glass shattering against the wall. A shiver runs through her body as she walks faster down the steps, trying to outrun the urge to call the police when she knows how that can often make things worse.

High heels clank against the soiled flooring as Thea's fingers cling to the wood railing that'd ben smoothed down by years of people running up and down and college kids sliding down floors by sitting on it.

Thoughts flickering between the couple arguing and her own memories, Thea slips into the streets of Brooklyn, ambling to her destination as guilt gnaws at her, blinding her to the headlights of cars and items displayed near shop windows.

Thea stops when a pale yellow awning comes into view, her eyes flitting toward a pink neon light hung in the bakery interior, where Adrian is sitting at the same table they picked the night before.

Before she even realizes what she's doing, Thea slips into the bakery, marching toward Adrian as her voice raises into a whisper, "You really came here?"

Adrian glances up.

The faint pout adorning his face melts into a grin. Pointing to the bench in front of him, Adrian watches as Thea plops down on the pink cushion.

"I was just thinking of leaving," He says, gray eyes gliding down the length of Thea's body as she raises a hand to catch the waitresses' attention while clinging to the front of her coat. "You look beautiful, Thea Tea."

"Thank you, but I have a mirror at home."

"Funny, I didn't see one last night."

"Maybe next time."

Adrian smiles, leaning into the table to whisper, "Is that an invitation? Because I'll gladly come knocking at your door, Thea Tea."

"I might let you in if you crawl," Thea mumbles, peeling her gaze from Adrian as the waitress approaches. "Hi, can I get a cake to go? Whatever you have is fine. He's paying."

"Not tired of ripping me off? I've sent you thousands today."

"You are a trust fund baby," Is the only explanation Thea gives him. "Besides, you have my number. No need to keep wiring me money."

"I know, but money is often the only thing people want from me. As soon as I stop giving them money, they stop caring about me."

"Poor trust fund baby."

Thea pouts for a moment as she pulls the small plate of chocolate cake toward her. Reaching for the fork in Adrian's hand when he asks, "What's with the coat? A surprise for boss-friend?"

Adrian chuckles dryly at the blush tinting Thea's cheeks and the tips of her ears, yet it's the way she rolls her shoulders back and tips her chin forward that Adrian finds too endearing.

Making him wish he'd been born with the artistic inclination cover designers had; perhaps he'd be able to fill a sketchbook with drawings of the woman in front of him, allowing him not to dwell on the way Thea scrunches her nose before coating her words with poison.

Or the way she fights against smiles as if her honor depended on it, the way her tongue pokes at her cheek whenever she rolls her eyes toward the heavens.

Yet, the one thing he's tormented most about Thea is the intrusive thoughts that have made work so difficult, as he wonders if the poison of her words is sweet when tasting her lips and if her kisses are as intoxicating as her cruelty is akin to a bath of ice water.

"Is it that obvious?" Thea asks in a whisper—hair nearly falling into the cake's frosting as she leans over the table, blush deepening once more as Adrian raises a hand toward her locks, brushing them away.

"You are clinging to your coat rather vehemently, Tea. You are either cold during spring or naked underneath it. What color lingerie?"

"Red."

"He should buy you green or purple."

"I don't like purple nor green."

"They'd accentuate the color of your eyes, making your complexion seem doll-like. I suppose it's a good thing you don't like those colors, or the world would be in disarray, drivers crashing into each other as they crane their necks to look at you, doctors cutting chests open to gift their patient's hearts."

"And you?"

"I'd crawl toward you, getting on my knees at the snap of your fingers."

"Like a dog? I say, 'come here, boy,' and you wag your tail in excitement?"

"Something does move when I'm excited."

Thea's laugh billows against the bakery walls; the few customers there glance at Thea before their eyes land on Adrian, who watches as she leans back into the bench, painfully unaware of how much he enjoys making her laugh.

"You are terrible."

"I just like to make you laugh."

"Why?" Thea asks with a giggle lingering on her lips. "My laugh isn't very *doll-like*. The kids I went to school with made sure I knew that."

"You know how fingerprints are unique? How no one else in the world has the exact same ridges, curves, and lines on the very tips of their fingers? How not even identical twins share fingerprints when they share everything else? Or how handwriting is also unique to oneself? Even if what you write always looks different, the difference in that is still unique to you?"

"Yes, what's your point, trust fund baby?"

"I believe laughs are the same way, I believe no one else among the seven billion people in the world will have the same laugh as you, no one will sound like you do, and I quite like the imprint of your happiness."

Thea laughs at that, except Adrian now knows her laughs and this one isn't joyous nor scornful, but rather a nervous giggle as if Thea isn't used to being seen.

And she isn't.

"You sound like Aaron."

"The boss-friend who you totally aren't wearing lingerie for?" Adrian asks, stealing the fork in her hand to take a bite of the cake he'd left untouched until she'd arrived.

"Yes. Why don't you like him?"

Adrian doesn't answer her.

Instead, tipping his head to the ceiling painted in a deep shade of green, the exact color he knows would look beautiful on Thea.

"I was the ugly duck of high society until college, but my best friend, Liam, was the complete opposite. Liam had been modeling since he was six months old, and all the mothers wished to marry their daughters to him. A golden child in every aspect, but Liam never made me feel less than him."

"Yet, it doesn't sound like he's still your best friend?"

Adrian keeps his gaze on the ceiling, gathering his thoughts over memories that'd faded from his mind as he grew older, preferring to look ahead than back at the people who'd betrayed him, clinging to the idea of someone new rather than an ex who'd broken his heart.

"No, he isn't. We went to University together, where he set me up on a date and by a miracle, I started dating my first girlfriend, Lauren. In retrospect, she was never the kind of woman I found beautiful, nor did we share the same...morals. But she was nice, and I thought she loved me."

Thea drags the fork against the ceramic plate, bothered by the way his brows knit together as if he has yet to understand what happened to him and his best friend.

"I dreaded the idea of summer break as I knew we'd both go back home, and for the first time ever, Liam didn't spend the summer with me. He claimed he wanted to travel alone for a bit, which was fine, until I got bored and lonely without Lauren. So, I decided to catch a flight from New York to Santa Barbara."

"Oh no," Thea mutters, knowing where the story is going before he finishes it.

"I found Lauren slobbering on Liam's cock with cum dripping down her thighs. The worst thing is that it made sense, you know? She was beautiful, Liam was beautiful and charming, and I was neither. I don't remember much of what he said, but they'd been fucking around before I began dating Lauren, and Liam kindly asked if she'd be willing to fuck me."

Adrian peels his gaze from the ceiling, expecting to find the shadows of pity adorning Thea's face, but there is nothing but a simmering anger.

"Problem is, I'm no longer shy once I'm comfortable with someone. I can be quite charming, so Lauren took fucking into dating, and Liam didn't quite care."

"You are not shy."

"Oh, I am. Why do you think I didn't speak a word while you went on to that poor guy about how fucking like a porn star isn't good? You are so incredibly authentic that I feel comfortable with you, Thea Tea, and your boss-friend reminds me of Liam."

"Well, you aren't an ugly duck anymore," Thea concedes, another blush tinting her cheeks. "And I'd tackle Liam if I saw him, what a jerk...my brother was cheated on by his high school sweetheart. It broke his heart, then Aaron came along claiming men fix broken hearts with pussy while girls fix theirs with cum."

"A poet," Adrian jests. "Is that what you've been doing?"

Thea shrugs, pushing the plate of a half-eaten cake toward Adrian before crossing her arms over her chest.

"In a way. Maybe that's why or maybe I just like sex, and finding strangers to have sex with is quite difficult in this economy. Condoms are very expensive after all."

"Good thing I'm a trust fund baby with phenomenal health insurance. I can give you my blood test results in a few days if you'd like?"

"What? You aren't worried about a baby? Just STDs?"

"Is Aaron infertile? If not, I take it you are on the pill, or maybe you are infertile. Regardless, I can afford to raise a baby."

"Yes, trust fund money, I remember it now," Thea jests, smacking a hand against her forehead in mockery as she rolls to her feet. A moment after, Adrian stands up, taking the plate with him as he trails after Thea, shadowing her every step toward the curvaceous marble counter where cookies are on display alongside flyers with all the baked goods offered by the store.

Adrian reaches for the yellow bag where the name of the bakery, *Ina,* is written in an elegant font. "Thank you," he says to the cashier, who takes his plate before accepting his card.

"That's my cake," Thea prods his waist, trying to reach for the bag as Adrian raises it over his head. "Give me my cake, Adrian Friedman. If you want cake, you can buy the entire bakery."

Thea pokes his waist, standing on his feet as she tries to steal the bag from him, but Adrian wraps his arm around her, pulling Thea flush against his chest as the cashier chuckles while ripping the receipt from the machine.

Closing his teeth around his credit card and receipt, Adrian mutters his farewell before hurling Thea with him, ambling toward the bakery's front door.

"Let go of me," Thea says as Adrian unravels his arm from around her. Pulling his card from his mouth before settling it in the pocket of his jeans instead of his wallet. "My cake?"

"It's late, and I'll walk you to your boss-friend."

"Why?"

Thea tips her head back, finding gray eyes a little darker as Adrian leans toward her, his lips brushing against the shell of her ear, a hand moving to the nape of her neck.

For a moment, Adrian doesn't say anything, nor does Thea, hesitating to pull back, waiting for him to decide their next move as if strung to each other, their limbs meant to move in tandem.

"Because, Thea Tea, you're naked under that coat, and I'd hate to miss out if you just so happen to let it slip off your body."

"I won't."

"And I won't take the risk with you."

"I can carry my cake though."

"And I can throw you over my shoulder and carry you," Adrian says, planting a kiss on her cheek before standing up straight. "Lead the way."

Thea takes three steps back, nearly hitting the back of a street sign as she crosses her arms over her chest, glowering at Adrian, who keeps holding the cake over his head.

"What's next? You want to hold my hand?"

"I do, actually. You look like you have soft hands," Adrian blabs as he proffers his hand out. Nearly expecting Thea to huff and walk away, she instead grabs his fingers before whirling in the direction of her apartment.

Thea takes the lead, stomping her feet against the sidewalk while Adrian ambles behind her, long legs allowing him to leisurely keep up.

Without Thea even noticing, Adrian slowly digs his heels into the concrete, slowing her down until her stomping march comes down to a gentle stride with Adrian behind her, feeling the warmth radiating from her body.

Thea can feel the weight of his gaze, much like how she's noticed his fingers gingerly weaving with hers, thumb caressing her knuckles in a way that tells her the caress is one Adrian isn't aware of.

"Thea Tea?" Adrian calls, tugging at her hand.

"Yeah?"

"Why didn't you stand your ground?"

"How so?" She asks, glancing at him from over her shoulder, enjoying how a traffic light paints him in a soft hue of red.

"You asked for your cake twice and gave up on walking to boss-friend's alone. If you had asked me to go home, I would've."

Some unconscious part of her knew that. Thea knows Adrian can read her, and if she truly wanted him gone, he would've seen that on the planes of her face. But she enjoyed the banter, enjoyed the way his presence allowed her to lower her guards and take a deep breath.

"Bold of you to assume I don't enjoy your company. After all, you keep me from getting into headlines."

Adrian gasps loudly, dropping his arm over her shoulder, trapping her between his chest and the yellow bag swelled with the cake box.

"You are just using my body? What am I? A whore?"

"*We are all whores under capitalism*. Isn't that what you told me?"

"You do pay attention to me," Adrian preens, resting his chin against her head. "Don't tell me you are growing fond of me?"

"You're like a period. I hate when you're here, but I worry if you are late."

Adrian's laugh billows past his lips, making Thea smile as she feels it reverberate against her body. She rests her head against his chest, allowing him to be closer than she probably should, but for some odd reason, Thea has felt safe in his company since they met.

When she thought she'd never see him again, fate clouded by New York's pollution had a different idea.

They walk by Ether, where some of the staff are still inside, sweeping clean the liquor stock as they dance, not bothered by the windows facing the streets.

Adrian's thumb caresses the length of her collarbone as Adrian slips his hand over the flap of her coat, keeping her close enough for Thea to feel the frantic beat of his heart.

Her fingers itch to touch him. Curiosity surges in her mind as Thea wonders how Adrian would react if she raised her hand to caress his wrist or if she tipped her head to plant a kiss on his forearm.

The curiosity lingers as Aaron's building comes into view, bringing a sense of doom that Thea juts off as being related to an awkward farewell.

"That's me," She says, spinning on her heels as Adrian drops his arm from her shoulder, locking their fingers together instead. "Can I ask you something?"

Adrian proffers the bag toward her, smiling as she rolls her eyes before taking an almost unnoticeable step toward him.

"Anything, Thea Tea."

"Are you only reading my book because you want to fuck me?"

"Do you know why I send you money?"

"Why?"

"Because I'd rather win someone's affection with meaningless dollars than with praise they don't deserve," Adrian says, brushing a stray bit of hair behind her ear.

His hand lingers there, running over the highest point of her cheekbone as Thea's lids flutter slightly, head tipping toward the warmth of his hand.

"I do want you. It's very strange how drawn I am to you, but don't think I'll spare your feeling if your book turns out to be shit. Books are far more important than someone else's feelings."

"Ice cold."

Thea smiles as her thumb caresses the back of his hand, stomach fluttering at how his gray eyes flit toward her lips —not bothering to hide how desperately he wants to kiss her.

"I've been dumped because a girlfriend of mine wanted to be a writer, and I wouldn't recommend her to a single agent or editor."

"Strikethrough writer?"

Adrian leans down until his forehead is nearly touching hers. Their breath tangles together, lips all too close for Thea's liking.

"God no, I avoid stupidity at all costs. But Thea, when I say you are, so far, a very good writer, don't think I'm saying it just to fuck you. You'll decide if that happens."

"Don't hold your breath."

"Ah, but you already leave me breathless," Adrian teases, smiling as she chuckles. His hand on her neck pulls her an inch closer. "Can I kiss you?"

"Not tonight. Not when I'm wearing lingerie for someone else. Good night, Adrian. Dream of me."

Thea pulls away, taking long steps toward the luxurious building, where the lobby is empty, yet the bright LED lights illuminate the entire ground floor.

Fighting the urge to glance over her shoulder, Thea enters the password allowing her into the building. Her steps echo through the ample lobby before reaching the tall ceiling and glass doors.

Waiting for the elevator, Thea fishes her phone from the deep pockets of her coat before gingerly tugging on the belt, pulling on it only when the doors slide open to reveal a blissfully empty elevator.

Thea settles the yellow bag on the floor as she presses the button for the penthouse, her coat slipping open, allowing her to see her reflection in the mirror glued to the back of the elevator.

The scarlet lingerie leaves her a bit paler, yet the bra makes her breasts look perkier. With a hand sprawled over her chest, Thea takes a few photos of herself before sending them to Adrian, along with all the money he sent her that day.

Adrian Friedman sent you $150000.
"I'm saving these for later."

10

A week locked in her apartment, not leaving for anything other than to take the trash out, and buy snacks, has usually been synonymous with paradise.

Yet, a week without hearing anything from Adrian, and Aaron being a tad too busy, has left Thea awfully restless. Something Jolly has noticed, leaving her prone to accept cuddles.

"You are a lucky lady, Jolly."

The cat meows, paw pressing down on her chest as Thea slams her computer closed for the fifteenth time today, caught between trying to write, pacing her apartment, and typing messages to both the men plaguing her thoughts.

"You have never had sex. You don't know how stupid it makes you when you haven't had it in a while," Thea complains, planting a kiss on Jolly's fluffy head. "Or when you haven't heard feedback on your book. You have never even written a book. Next life, I want to be a pretty kitten like you."

Thea's phone vibrates on the table, erasing her sour mood as a laugh slips past her lips at the notification overlaying the photo of the Brooklyn Bridge.

Adrian Friedman sent you a request for $15000.
"You made me cry, Thea Tea. This goddamn book is supposed to be a romance. Romance is supposed to be cheesy. Your cardiologist needs to scowl you."

Ignoring the request for money, Thea calls Adrian with Jolly climbing onto the table, prowling toward the post in front of the window, oblivious to how Thea's heart beats faster with each second the man doesn't pick up his phone.

She hangs up when it goes to voicemail, but Thea calls him again as she stands up, marching up and down the narrow hallways between the kitchen and her bed.

"Pick up," Thea whispers, clinging to the smartphone. "Please pick up."

The seconds stretch eternally, nearly going to voicemail again when the metallic sound of Adrian's voice graces her ears. "You are cruel."

"Me? You are cruel. You haven't sent me an update all week. It's been pure agony."

"Between work, being a handsome trust fund baby, reading your book, and staring at those elevator pictures, two of those things have been neglected."

"Which ones?"

"Are you flirting with me?" Adrian asks.

Thea doesn't say anything as she listens to his soft breaths, the sound of sheets rustling as if he'd kicked his blankets away.

The faint echo of his steps reaches her ears, too muffled of a sound for him not to be barefoot.

"If I am?"

"Then I'd tell you I haven't gone to work for a few days. My boss isn't happy about that. If you aren't flirting, then I haven't read a word you've written, and I deleted those photos."

"Oh, you poor thing."

"You should send new ones if you feel so bad."

Thea's breath catches at that, feeling as if Adrian had been watching her all week. Something that would be impossible as none of the buildings surrounding hers has a view into her apartment.

Yet she'd been taking quite a few photos of herself, renewing her archive of nudes with the excuse of having a better camera.

Most of which she'd send to Aaron, but a few of those, she'd been thinking of someone else after taking a shower and laying in bed naked, too warm to think of putting on clothes but too bothered not to find relief.

Those photos are the evidence of what she'd been doing early in the morning or late at night when she'd buck her hips and bite down on her pillow with a name lodged in her throat.

"Thea Tea?"

"You are so annoying."

Thea drags her feet on the floor, ambling toward her bed while shimming out of her black knickers.

"What have I done now?"

"You keep teasing me. It's frustrating."

Adrian laughs through the phone, a sound that muffles the breathy moan as her fingers rake over her naked thighs.

"You are the one who sends me photos in lingerie, and I'm the one teasing you?"

"Indeed."

Silence falls between them, neither saying anything as they listen to each other's silence—Thea doesn't dare to touch herself, not when she can hear more fabric rustling and his footsteps echoing.

"What are you doing?" She asks.

"Thinking about you."

"Why?"

"If I had a reason for it, I would have a way not to think about you, and I really don't want to be thinking about you when I'm talking to you."

"Are you fucking looking at those photos right now?"

"And if I am? They have phenomenal lighting."

"And the model? Do you like her?"

"Thea." There is a warning in his voice, her name coming almost clipped. "Don't torture me."

"But she's thinking about you too," Thea says, fingers finally reaching her wet mound. She explores her slit, gliding back and forth without too much care. "She's wondering if you've found your way back to bed, or maybe you're sitting on your couch butt-naked."

"Are we doing this right now?"

"Doing what?"

Adrian laughs at her innocent voice before a moan slips past her lips, and Thea hears him walking once more. She hears the springs in his mattress bounding under his body.

"Why are we doing this?" He asks. "I can be there in an hour."

"I don't want to wait an hour, nor am I doing anything."

Thea lets go of her phone as she pulls her T-shirt over her head before waddling toward her kitchen, wherein one of its drawers, she keeps a few of her toys.

Unsure of which one to use, she takes the vibrator and the transparent dildo back to her bed, where she plots her back against her pillows.

"Have you...done anything to those photos?"

"What haven't I done to those photos is a better question, Thea Tea."

"Have you wrapped your fingers around yourself? Moving up and down along your shaft? Have you used lube or do you spit on your hands?"

"Both, depending on where I am in the house."

"Oh," Thea says, falling silent as she takes the dildo to her mouth, sucking on it as she knows Adrian can hear her.

"I jacked off to you in the shower, in bed, in the living room, in the kitchen. The elevator has been my favorite place."

"That's risky."

"Being a trust fund baby means my building has an elevator just to my apartment. No one but myself can use it. Don't worry, I've cleaned up after myself."

"That's good," Thea says as she drags the toy between her breasts, going down her stomach before brushing against her clit. "Adrian?"

"Huh?"

"It's been so long since I've had sex."

The man's laugh is nearly a grunt, "A week is a long time for you?"

"It is, isn't it? Why you haven't sent me an update?"

"I wanted to have an excuse to see you again. An hour is a short time, Thea," Adrian's voice is needy, coercing

Thea to slip the toy inside her. "An hour is a really fucking short time, Thea."

"No. Tell me, do you move fast or slow?"

"I'd rather show you."

"I can't wait that long. I want you now," Thea says, pulling the toy out before thrusting it back into her with a moan. "I want you to fuck me so good. I want you to pull on my hair as you pound into me, want you so fucking deep in my pussy. Do you want me like that? Do you want to taste me? To suck on my breast as you fuck me nice and slow? Or would you fuck me like you need me? Maybe you'd fuck me like you hate me. Tell me, Adrian, do you hate me? Because I hate how much I want you, I really do. God, Adrian, I need you so bad. Will you come for me?"

"Fuck Thea, I'm going to fucking—" Thea sits up in her bed, heart beating fast as sweat clings to her skin.

Glancing around her empty apartment, Thea's eyes land on the green light of the microwave, telling her it's three in the morning and she'd been dreaming.

A too realistic dream that makes her reach for her phone, seeking evidence it was just a dream, that she didn't fall asleep after having phone sex with Adrian.

"Fuck," She curses, both content and disappointed as the last communication they had was a week ago, with him sending her $150,000 for no good reason.

Thea sends the money back with an attachment too similar to what she wondered about in her dream, "Why you haven't sent me an update all week?"

Not waiting for a response, she falls back asleep with that same breathy moan on her lips.

Before moving to New York, Thea would fantasize about starting her days with a jog in Central Park, having picnics during the spring and summer, and ice-skating in the winter.

While the reality of rent had forced Thea to live in Brooklyn, it was the myriad of birds pooping everywhere and trying to steal her food with those tiny beady eyes intently staring at her that made Thea loathe the park despite its beauty.

It certainly didn't help to learn Central Park is a migratory route for birds from South America to Greenland, granting the park not only a flock of tourists but a few hundred species of birds to torment her throughout the year too.

"A perfect place for a picnic," Thea grunts as she keeps her head low, boots sinking into the fluffy grass as she marches toward Cherry Hill Fountain, the spot she and Marine have always met up before picking a place to settle down.

Clad in a blood orange milkmaid dress, Marine stands out from the crowd of tourists and New Yorkers that happen to have time to stroll through the park.

The wind pulls on her long hair that's been curled to perfection, making Marine look like she belongs in the Filipino dramas she watches to keep her from losing her fluency in Tagalog.

An easy smile adorns her tanned face, growing a little bit wider with each step the petite woman takes around the fountain. Her cheeks tinted with a coral blush accentuating the rich brown of her eyes.

"Riri!" Thea calls out, watching Marine come to a halt before spinning and running toward her. Throwing her arms around her in a hug, Marine nearly crushes Thea's ribs as she steals the air out of her lungs.

"Guess what?" Marine says as a way of greeting, squeezing Thea once more before letting Thea go.

Sometimes Thea wishes she could hate Marine for how little she cares about Thea's writing, and it would be a lie if Marine denied her slight disinterest in what Thea has written, but it would also be a lie to say Marine wouldn't do anything for Thea to achieve her dreams.

There is little they wouldn't do for each other despite their tastes and preference rarely aligning—a constant reminder that it would be far too easy for them to drift apart as finding a middle ground had always been difficult between them.

Yet, the universe has a way of striking balance instead of cleaving them apart.

"You've decided to be kind and not have a picnic in Central Park? You're taking me to brunch in some nice french bakery instead?"

"You can't hate Central Park when we met here." Marine pokes her waist before looping her arms through Thea's. "Greyson loves telling his friends the story of how we met."

"You were topless! I'd been in New York for two days, and I didn't think people actually went nude despite it not being illegal. You do have great boobs. Consider me envious of you."

"Thank you," Marine bows with a giggle on her lips. "You wouldn't be envious if it was your back that hurt at the end of the day."

Resting her head against Thea's shoulder, Marine falls silent as they aimlessly walk, their steps marked by the clanking of glass bottles and ceramic plates disrupting the silence between them.

A notification echoes faintly, making both of them reach for their phones, but Marine puts her phone back into her pocket, turning to see the ghost of a smile on Thea's lips as she reads the notification.

Adrian Friedman has sent you $1000.
"Are you free today?"

Thea doesn't answer, wanting Adrian to suffer as she suffered in the week that went by without him sending her updates as he read her book.

"Is that a smile I see on your cute little face?"

"No," Thea denies too quickly, flicking the tip of Marine's nose. "Now, tell me your news."

"In a bit. Just know one is about my boobs."

Thea's blood curdles at that, but she doesn't press for more, allowing Marine to speak when she wants and lead them to the lake where they usually settle down for their picnics.

Worry gnaws on her as Marine flicks a blanket over a sunny patch of grass. Anxiety swells in Thea's chest as she helps set the plates, pulling a bottle of orange juice and a bottle of mini champagne while Marine picks up the little bento boxes she prepared that morning.

"Unfortunately, my boobs won't be mine for much longer," Marine breaks the silence, and Thea straightens her spine, biting down on her tongue as she fights against the prick of tears in her eyes.

A fissure spreads over her heart at the idea of fulfilling a promise she made five years ago, adding to the hardships those closest to her would face as life is built on suffering, and not everyone is ready to give up on it.

Thea didn't consider how cruel it would be of her to leave them, to venture into the greatest unknown without being certain her friends and family would be well, certain they wouldn't carry any of the blame she tries so hard not to pin on them.

"In a way, I suppose my whole body won't be mine. I think that's usually what happens with pregnancy."

"Marine!" Thea cries out, throwing her arms around her friend as her heart beats faster, ears ringing with the blood coursing through her veins. "When did you find out?"

"Two days ago. I wanted you to know before telling anyone else. You, me, and Greyson are the only ones who know."

Thea tips her head back, refusing to shed tears over something so joyous, refusing to cry when that might break her in a different way.

"I'm so happy for you and Greyson."

"I know, but I need to ask you something else," Marine holds Thea's face between the palms of her dainty hands. "Will you be my maid of honor?"

"You mean godmother?"

"No, Greyson proposed."

A scream of joy bubbles past Thea's lips, making birds fly with a croon in their beaks. Yet she doesn't hug Marine once more; instead, she topples back, staring into the blue sky through the canopy of trees.

"A baby and a wedding?"

"A wedding in seven months before the baby is here."

Thea's smile falters at that.

Hating how close to her deadline they are planning their wedding to be, knowing it would break Marine's heart for her to choose between postponing it or proceeding with it so soon after whatever fate has in store for Thea.

"I always find it adorable when weddings have the baby."

"You just love babies."

"Exactly, don't deprive me of that joy," Thea points out, concealing how she likely won't get to feel the joy of either event. "You know, one way or another, I'll be there for it all, don't you?"

"Even if I have to move across the county because raising a baby in New York sounds like hell?"

"Always Riri, I'll come to you as a pretty sunset, as a breeze on an impossibly warm day, or as the first snow of the year. I'll always be with you."

"I'll hire you as my full-time nanny."

"I'll gladly be your baby's guardian angel."

Marine proffers a ham sandwich to Thea before popping the champagne open and forcing it into Thea's hand.

"Now, tell me, who made you smile with a single text?"

"It wasn't a text. Someone sent me a thousand dollars. Why don't you have a ring? Do I need to go sell Greyson's car so he can buy you the largest diamond?"

"We were in a grocery store when he proposed. I asked if he wanted oat milk or rice milk, and he said that he wanted to marry me. I nearly threw both cartons of milk at him."

"What a jerk," Thea jests, rolling her eyes while Marine laughs. "It's kinda romantic if you think about it. He must have been thinking about how you are the greatest thing that ever happened to him."

"It only took him three years."

"I only ask you one thing, Riri," Thea says as she takes a bite of her sandwich, munching on it while Marine raises a brow. "Don't let Greyson name your baby. After he named his boat, Bertrude, I don't trust him to name things."

Marine's laugh nearly obscures the sound of another notification that steals Thea's attention as she glances down at another transference from Adrian.

Adrian Friedman sent you $1000.
"I'll send you a million dollars tomorrow if I don't see you today. Your place or mine?"

You sent Adrian Friedman $2
"I don't know where you live, and I'm in Central Park today."

Adrian Friedman sent you $100.
"I'll meet you at the information kiosk on the South end in an hour."

One hour, Thea thinks, taking another bite of her sandwich, swallowing the sorrow lodged in her throat.

One hour where I get to be happy without thinking about the future.

"What color are we thinking for the wedding?" Thea asks, the bottle of champagne inches away from her lips. "I quite like green."

"You hate green!"

"Someone told me I'd look good in green."

Marine laughs, throwing a grape at Thea as she argues, "It's my wedding. Although it would be a good day for you to find a husband if you are tired of fucking Aaron."

"One doesn't get tired of a dick like his."

"State-of-the-art dick with a man that has the craftsmanship of an artist in how he uses his schlong."

Thea laughs at the memory of how Marine slept with Aaron before she did—one of the few customers Aaron ever allowed to take him into Ether's bathroom before a smiley Marine walked out minutes after Aaron did.

The food trickles into nothing as they chat about flowers and cake flavors, about how to convince Greyson not to get the eyebrow piercing he's been talking about for months—although that's an idea Marine wants to postpone forever, not just until after the wedding.

Eventually, they pack up and throw away their trash before heading back to Cherry Hill Fountain, where Thea lingers for a few moments, watching as Marine skips while walking away, unable to contain her happiness and excitement for her future.

Boots dragging against the pavement, Thea heads toward the south end of Central Park. Each step abrades the joy Thea harbored for an hour, overcasting her happiness for Marine with tears and worry as she faces how much she'd miss out if life continued refusing to be kind.

Happiness melts into guilt over the sorrow she'd cause her friends, knowing Marine would never be the same without her—never be able to forgive or understand Thea's choices.

Thea stops a few meters shy of the phthalo green kiosk, where tourists stop to buy maps of the park while New Yorkers don't bother.

"Thea Tea!" Adrian calls out, waving at her before bringing his hand to his back.

He smiles at her, his face glowing in the soft afternoon light, painting Adrian in a swat of light, nearly stealing the air out of her lungs as he closes the distance between them.

"I was expecting your book to be something that if I twisted the manuscript it would drip cum."

"What?" Thea asks, brows knitting in confusion. Tipping her head back to look into his gray eyes, wondering if he too has been plagued by dreams.

"Some books do that."

"Do they?"

Adrian brushes a lock of hair behind her ear. His smile fading as he searches her eyes while snaking a hand around her waist, pulling Thea closer to his chest.

"Your eyes are reddened."

"I was crying."

"Why?"

"My best friend is engaged and pregnant. I'm going to be an auntie."

"Why do you look sad then?"

Thea wraps her fingers around his wrist, holding his hand against her face as she tries to find the words to tell Adrian how she'd been late to meet Marine after missing the subway three times when her legs refused to move.

Her body petrified over the idea running in her mind, the thoughts pleading Thea to just step in front of a train—a quick but agonizing death, one that would traumatize those on the platform, but then Thea would at least be remembered.

Thea's free hand travels over the length of Adrian's chest, stopping inches shy of his heart as if the reminder of life, the reminder of what she'd be giving up on if her thoughts had won that battle, was still too painful for her to allow herself the sensation of his beating heart under the tips of her fingers.

"Has your life ever felt like you are standing on a beach, and a wave crashes gently over the shore, pulling at the sand as it ebbs away? And you know you are standing, but it feels like the world is crumbling beneath your feet? Your heart begs you to run toward the safety of land, begging you to find the shore, but you never left it?"

His gray eyes capture the sadness in her smile. Leaning down, Adrian rests his forehead against hers, laying a hand over hers as a single tear rolls down her cheek.

"Where are you standing, Thea Tea?"

"Sometimes, I think the Earth has swallowed me whole. Other times, I wonder if it has propelled me into space, leaving me adrift to watch life on Earth without truly touching it, without experiencing the joy and excitement others feel, but I'm so happy for her. She deserves the world, and she's getting everything she deserves."

"You deserve the world too."

"Then why am I stuck? Why isn't there anything tethering me to life?"

"You have me, and I have you. For now, that'll have to be enough. A team of two," Adrian says, planting a kiss against her forehead.

With a hand on the back of her head, Adrian holds Thea close, wishing he could meld their bodies together so he could protect her from the deepest recess of her mind.

11

There is a perpetual blush adorning Thea's cheeks as she glances around the coffee shop Adrian took her to, where people are bedecked in designer items, belonging more to a flagship store in Dubai than a coffee shop in New York. Leaving Thea to feel out of place in her vintage black jeans and an old T-shirt from a band Jules was a part of during high school—being a member for a few weeks until he suggested the name *Death Grip*[1] and his bandmates kicked him out from the band when they learned what it meant.

"You know," Adrian severs the silence that fell between them since they met up in Central Park.

Thea watches as he brings a cup of coffee to his lips, savoring the warm beverage in a loud slurp that makes people turn their heads at him.

Their scowls only deepen when eyes flit toward Thea, scowling at her through the lenses of their privilege.

"I'll admit, I expected Cecilia to wear figurative blinkers that blinded her to red flags, or for this book to be another misogynistic, men-loving novel negating any resemblance between the female main character and other women who enjoy makeup or dressing up."

"You have a lovely view of romance books."

---

[1] Death-grip and death-grip syndrome are slang terms for suffering adverse effects from one's aggressive and recurrent male masturbation technique, which result in an unsatisfactory experience when engaging in regular sexual intercourse with a partner.

"Can you blame me?" Adrian asks, gingerly pushing a small plate with a triple-chocolate chip cookie toward Thea. “Romance is often made out to be a genre where a woman’s goals and ambitions are secondary to whichever male character she’s fucking, or am I wrong?”

Thea remains silent, fidgeting with her cookie as she doesn't dare negate his opinion when it's so similar to her own, hating how the genre has morphed into another form of oppression.

Yet, she yearns to hear his opinions on the genre she loves so much.

"Male writers demonize and demoralize women in their work. I don't see what difference it makes when a woman is the one perpetuating this narrative that subjugates women to the whims of men, treating them as an object to be possessed, as something no better than breeding cattle."

Arching a brow at his strong words, Thea notices the way his cheeks flush, how Adrian's hands quiver ever so slightly, making her adore him a little bit more for his passion, wishing more people in publishing would think as he does.

"Sorry," He apologizes, pushing his glasses back on the bridge of his nose. "I just can't understand why women would write stories that reinforce the power men are told they possess over women, nor why women would read such things and strive for such relationships. I didn't mean to offend you."

"You didn't. I see tremendous potential in how this genre can advocate for women, but no part of me seeks community among peers with views like that, or has any interest in writing such uncanny betrayal, in making fictional women, but women nonetheless, be treated like accessories or sexualized for wearing jeans and a T-shirt."

Adrian smiles as Thea breaks her cookie in half, offering him the other piece with the sketch of a blush adorning her cheeks as she slides to the edge of her chair when Adrian gestures for her to lean in as if he's about to share a secret.

"You did fail to escape the cliche of an athlete love story," Adrian whispers, eyes flitting over her face. "Although, it was still surprising how you did it."

"I once read an article about this retired MMA fighter who murdered his wife and son before killing himself. In the autopsy, they saw his brain had the same kind of damage expected in a late-stage dementia patient. It prompted studies about what kind of brain damage athletes are facing down the line when partaking in MMA fighters, hockey, football, really any sport where concussions are frequent, and these men can often have fits of rage that end in violence."

"Isn't brain damage somewhat common amongst serial killers?"

Thea reaches for her mug of hot chocolate and nods before continuing, "After reading that article, I no longer found it enticing to read or write stories that could end in a funeral if they were to take place in the real world. Romance requires beating hearts long after the epilogue is over."

"God, you are smart. I am curious as to why you write romance?"

Thea smiles as she nibbles on her half of the cookie, feeling that giddy joy swelling in her chest whenever she's given the space to speak about something she's passionate about.

"Because I'm tired of the harm this narrative has perpetuated. You said it yourself, women are made to be side characters in their own stories, lovable only when they are doormats to possessive men. It's tiring to read book after book where the man holds all the power, where he walks all over her, but it's all forgiven if he sings to her or promises to go to therapy."

Thea eats the last bit of her cookie, her hands move as if she's weaving a tapestry of all the things she loves while oblivious to the cookie crumbles adorning the corner of her mouth.

"I'll never write a book that erodes the FMC's personality and voice until she's nothing but the object of his desire, depriving her of goals and ambitions to make her a ploy to his development. A way for him to become successful, to receive his inheritance, or whatever other trope is used in the story. Women can have a career, and be in love, we...am I talking too much?"

Thea waits for an answer, fingers tracing the rim of her mug as Adrian bites down on his lips, eyes gliding over her face in a near caress.

"I like hearing you talk. It's cute. I think I'll always be curious about what romance means to you."

"This," Thea states simply, everting her eyes to the window behind Adrian as heat spreads over her cheeks.

"Sitting in a coffee shop?"

"It often feels like the more I write, the fewer people care. So when you asked to read my book, asked to see me today so we could talk about it, that makes me feel seen. There is romance in that, isn't it? In taking genuine interest in what I like, paying attention to what I say without thinking of it as silly. People don't fall in love because of grand gestures. They fall in love because of a memorized coffee order, because of a tiny gift that reminded their significant other of them, because of a good morning text, little love letters, and acts of service."

"You are a very simple woman to understand, Thea Tea," Adrian concedes with a grin. His fingers tighten around his mug, fighting the urge to take Thea's hand in his. "Tell me, what is the worst thing a man can say to the woman they are falling for?"

Thea leans back into her seat, knowing he's asking her anything that crosses his mind just to keep her talking, but her eyes still move across the coffee shop as she ponders his question.

"You make me want to be a better man," Thea says as if she could read the minds of the women gathered inside. "A wise woman will hear that as *gugu-dada*."

"And an unwise woman? What will she hear?"

"She'll believe she found the perfect man because he's willing to *try* to be better for her, instead of just *being* better. They'll hear things like, *'you are the one person in the world who makes me want to live,'* and take it as anything but codependency. Someone wise wouldn't settle for being a lifeline, but people still fall for a tale as old as time."

"I could marry you right now."

"Why?"

"Because you scare me."

Thea offers him a vulpine smile, marking Adrian as her prey when that's what he's been since the moment he laid eyes on her.

She holds his gaze, biting down on her tongue as a silly grin blooms on his face, eyes sparking with something that makes her nervous.

Like a fire, she's drawn to but knows is too dangerous to get near. Something, or in this case, someone she should run away from, but she's been cold for far too long.

"Why did you want to see me?"

"Mainly, because I missed your laugh," Adrian says, and she laughs, oblivious to how the man sinks into the sound, allowing her to pull on the strings of his heart like the moon commands the tides. "But I have a gala coming up soon, and I'd like for you to go with me."

"Convince me."

"I will...over dinner."

"Is that a request or an order?"

"It's whatever it takes to convince you to join me for dinner. I promise you my chef is phenomenal."

"You have a chef?"

"I don't have a chef." Adrian stands, weaving his fingers through hers, pulling Thea to her feet, taking the lead out of the coffee shop as he paid for their meek break. "She meal preps on Sunday, and I eat that."

"Today isn't Sunday."

"I'm well aware. I just asked her to make dinner for two because I wanted to see you. So now you truly need to join me for dinner, or all of her hard work will be useless."

Thea lets Adrian pull her closer as she wraps her arms around his waist, stealing a single nervous giggle from the man before he clears his throat.

"Did you just giggle because of me?"

"No."

"Oh, you did! Do you like when I wrap my arms around you?" Thea jests, slithering around Adrian, her arms letting go of his waist as she coils them once more around his neck. "How about this?"

The bell hung by the coffee shop entrance sings as Adrian pulls the matte black door open, slipping onto the street facing Central Park.

Thea doesn't let go of him, rolling to the tips of her toes as Adrian presses his legs over hers, forcing her to keep walking even with her back to the world.

"Do *you* like when I hold you close?"

"I'm not answering th—Oh."

Adrian stifles a laugh as bird poop falls onto Thea's head, making her stumble away from him with her mouth agape, arms raised as if she'd been yielding to an invisible force.

"I fucking hate this park," Thea shrieks, cheeks reddened with anger as the poop drizzles down her T-shirt.

"Come on, let me take you home."

"But—"

"No buts, I'll take you home. You'll wash your hair, and we'll have dinner," Adrian says, pulling a handkerchief from the back pocket of his jeans.

Thea doesn't argue as he wipes away most of the white mess out of her hair, nor does she when he plants a kiss on her cheek before weaving their fingers together.

Rolling his shoulder back with pride, Adrian leads Thea down the street with a light bounce to his step, humming contently as he beelines toward a limestone-clad building facing Central Park.

Men wearing preppy uniforms push open the large double doors, greeting Adrian by his surname as they make no fuss about the precarious condition Thea finds herself in.

Thea stares at the marble flooring, focusing on the thumb caressing her knuckles, the warmth radiating from Adrian's body as she follows him closely, matching him step by step.

The concierge also greets Adrian, who raises a hand toward the young-looking man as he guides Thea down to the elevator, stealing a wow from her lips as the golden doors open without Adrian needing to press any buttons.

"You are so rude," Adrian's voice is cold, compelling Thea to raise her head to look at him as the doors swing close and the elevator moves up.

Thea takes a step back as he takes one forward. They do that three more times until her back presses against the golden wall of the elevator.

Her hands move to his waist, fingers snaking around the hooks of his jeans where his belt is settled. Adrian glances down between them, taking another step until their bodies press together.

"Why?" She asks in a near purr.

"You have literal shit in your head, and I still want to kiss you."

"Why?" She repeats, but Adrian hears the words she doesn't say.

Why don't you?

"If I kiss you right now, I'll carry you to my bedroom instead of to my bathroom, and I want you to be comfortable when I kiss you. Even more comfortable when

I remove every piece of clothing on your body as I explore every inch of naked skin."

Thea's breath catches in her throat, her lips parting as she breathes him in, wanting to kiss him.

Fuck, she thinks, rolling to the tips of her toes, hand moving to the nape of his neck, pulling him down toward her.

"Thea Tea," Adrian mutters against her lips, shuddering at the brief touch. "Don't play with me."

"Why?"

"Because the things you can overcome don't remain as scars, and if you kiss me right now to never kiss me again...I'll be scarred for life."

"And if...what if I want to mar you?"

"You already left a mark on me. Just don't ruin me for everyone else," Adrian pleads, resting his forehead against hers. "Not until I have the chance to be your man."

The mechanical and metallic sound of the elevator halting and the door opening doesn't tear them apart or stop Thea and Adrian from tasting the air between them as one would lose themselves in a kiss.

His fingers dig into her waist, pulling Thea close while keeping her distant enough for Adrian to resist the swelling temptation as her fingers caress the nape of his neck.

"Adrian, if you aren't going to kiss me, then I really want to wash my hair," Thea whispers, planting a kiss on his cheek before uncoiling herself from around him, slipping out of the elevator to find herself in a long hallway disemboguing in a living room.

Despite taking a few moments to remove her boots, Thea's footsteps echo faintly against the pale walls that aren't quite white but remain neutral enough to accentuate the paintings.

"Is that a replica of a Van Gogh painting?"

"The replica is in the museum," Adrian says, trailing close to Thea as if he wants to see his home through her eyes. "That is an original Van Gogh. Don't ask me the name of it. My mother is a fan of the arts. She's the one you'd want to talk about the art here."

Thea nods as she walks past the yellow painting, eyes flitting through the hallway with ancient vases protected by cases. Everything in it seems to belong to a museum rather than someone's house.

“Adrian, just how expensive is this place?”

“A few million”

“A few million as in five million, or a few million where you have three digits before the ‘million’ is spelled out?”

“A few as in $333 million,” He says, and Thea shrinks into herself, holding her hands close to her chest, afraid the faintest brush of her fingers will break something.

Somehow impair the entire building, fracturing the floor-to-ceiling window framing Central Park in the center of the living room where cognac Italian leather couches bedeck the room.

Matching well with the brightly colored designer throw blankets adorning the seats and the Persian rug bringing more warmth to the cold flooring.

Thea walks toward the giant window, mesmerized by how she could count the trees if she wanted, seeing the lake in the center of the park, yet the people ambling there are too small, seeming almost fake—as if they too were part of a painting.

The city stretches out in front of her, granting Thea a view of the water surrounding the island and impossibly tall buildings that seem small when she looks down on them.

"Do you truly own this place?" She asks, whirling around to face Adrian.

"My dad owns it, I just live here rent-free. Don't worry, he plans on signing the apartment to my wife’s name once I'm married, until then most properties remain under my parents name.”

"Is your dad some super-rich mobster?"

"No, just the founder and CEO of one of the biggest publishing houses in the country."

"So, you aren't just some random editor? You are really important to the world of publishing, and I'm rude to you all the time. Great."

"I like when you are rude to me. It's endearing."

Thea laughs, dropping her head against his chest, arms wrapping around him, anchoring herself to the one thing she knows she won't break by touching, the one thing Thea feels drawn to.

"Can I wash your hair?"

"If you want to touch bird shit, I won't stop you," Thea jests, resting her chin against his beating heart. "Adrian?"

"Thea Tea?"

"What did you do to me for me to like you in such a short time? This is dangerous."

"I know."

Adrian slides his hand in hers, tugging Thea after him as he leads her down through the maze of corridors, each bedecked with what she presumes is an original Monet painting that consumes most of the long hallway before tapestries, and vases take up the rest of the space—some of which once belonged to ancient Chinese Dynasties.

Heat spreads over Thea's cheeks as Adrian leads her to a bedroom where books are piled close to the bed on one side while the other overflows with stacks of loose paper.

Following Adrian into a bathroom, her gaze lingers on the duvet thrown to the side, the pillows wrinkled from a night of tossing and turning in bed, unable to fall asleep.

"One moment," Adrian says before dipping out of the room, his footsteps growing distant.

The light marble flooring of the entire apartment is halted abruptly in the threshold between the bedroom and bathroom, where a matte black stone replaces the sleek marble.

Thea traces the light veins with the tip of her toe, fuzzy sock smoothly gliding as she walks toward one of the counters, where she spies on the aftershave and fragrances Adrian owns, all of the labels written in foreign languages, from brands she's never heard about.

"Weird," She mutters, confused as to how he owns so many perfumes when Adrian just smells clean and warm.

A scent that reminds Thea of books and old libraries, some cottage in a forgotten corner of Earth where the only neighbors to see are squirrels, and a path of aster flowers, painting the world in soft lilac.

Something entirely too comfortable and homey.

"Aren't you a curious little thing," Adrian's voice echoes against the walls, making Thea leap away from his vanity. "Judging my perfume choices?"

"I don't recognize any of these brands, but I'm certain they cost more than my rent."

Thea watches as Adrian settles a beige pillow near an impossibly big bathtub that would take up her entire apartment.

Sitting on the pillow, Thea tips her head into the bathtub, listening to the water spraying against the white walls while Adrian adjusts the temperature.

They remain silent as he soddens her hair before cursing under his breath, running toward the large shower in the most distant corner of the room.

"I only have ginger-scented shampoo and rinse," Adrian sounds almost apologetic as he settles back down beside Thea. "You'll have to forgive me if you hate ginger."

"More brands I don't know?"

"Yeah, my hairdresser said she'd stab my neck with her scissors if I used a different brand."

"She sounds fun," Thea mutters, hand fluttering toward his thigh as Adrian lathers the shampoo against her scalp.

Massaging it until Thea is practically moaning, yet the whole thing is over too soon as Adrian rinses her hair, and Thea stands up, turning off the faucet for him as water drips down her clothes.

Adrian opens his mouth to ask if he did something wrong, but Thea lifts her T-shirt over her head, fingers working the button of her jeans.

"Thea?"

"I still feel dirty. I think I need a shower."

Silver rakes over Thea's body, watching as she shimmies her jeans down, kicking the piece away with her socks. A smile graces Adrian's lips at the green bra that doesn't match the purple panty she wears.

Thea takes Adrian's hand, hurling him after her as she marches toward the opposing shower. Turning on the faucet, she gasps as freezing cold water hits her spine.

"Let me just," Adrian mutters, stepping into the water to adjust the temperature, yet his eyes refuse to leave her glistening body. "And I'm wet now."

"So am I."

Thea arches a brow at him, hands undoing her bra, discarding the item on the floor as Adrian takes a step toward her, but she doesn't take one way from him.

"I can see that."

"Can you?" She asks, taking his hand and placing it on her waist, inching his digits down. "Maybe you should feel it?"

"Thea..."

"Have you been dreaming of me too?"

That very last word undoes something in Adrian, granting him permission to dip his fingers underneath her panty, stroking her slit.

"I have. You deprive me of sleep, Thea," Adrian says, burying a hand on the nape of her neck, pulling her toward him, but he doesn't kiss her. "I'm not going to make you cum."

"I don't want you to. I want you to touch me."

Adrian thrusts two fingers inside her, not bothering to ease into her, not wanting to take it slow when her nails sink into his arms, teeth biting down on his shoulder.

"I want you so bad," Thea says, wrapping an arm around his neck, rolling her hips against the stroke of his fingers, moaning with the pressure of his thumb.

"You have me, Thea. I think you had me long before I saw you, but I'm not fucking you today."

"Will you taste me?"

Adrian grunts at that, forcing himself to reach for a sponge, soddening the item with soap before bringing it down to her body.

"I want to."

"You can."

"First things first," Adrian says, sinking his fingers deeper into her, going faster as she mewls against his chest.

Shaky hands pull on his wet clothes, removing his T-shirt before Thea peppers kisses across his chest, nibbling on his skin as he takes her further into cloud nine.

"What have you done to me?" She whimpers, legs weakened as Adrian pulls his fingers out of her before she can climax.

Damp hair clings to her skin as Thea sits uncomfortably still in Adrian's kitchen, watching his chef garnish their dinner while Adrian is busy putting their wet clothes in the washer.

Thea wonders if there is something wrong with her, for the in-unit washer to be the only thing she's envious of instead of the Italian marble. Well, the Italian everything, or even the view of Central Park. She is merely envious of the ability to wash her clothes in her humble abode.

"You are the first girl Adrian has asked me to make dinner for," The chef slices through the silence. "And I've worked for him since he was a freshman in college."

"How was he back then?"

"A total nerd? Shakespeare was ten-out-of-five words he'd speak, then a girl broke his heart, and he became a normal person."

"No longer a pretentious brat?"

"Exactly."

The chef watches Thea glide a finger against the ridges on the stainless steel countertop as she takes a measure of the chef, whose luscious dark brown hair is in a tight braid, ensuring not a single strand of hair finds its way into the food.

"What is your name?"

"Devyani," The woman says, brown eyes peeling from Thea as she glances at a pot with something slowly simmering.

"You're beautiful."

"Are you wondering if Adrian and I ever had a relationship beyond a professional one? I've slept with his sister before, but white girls aren't quite my type. My parents accepted me being a lesbian very well, but they refuse to let me date someone who isn't Indian."

"I didn't know he had a sister."

Devyani smiles at the scowl between Thea's brows, reading the lines of hurt in not knowing something so important.

"He has two. One moved to London a few years ago."

"Are you talking about Ollie?"

"Ollie?" Thea asks, glancing over her shoulder to find Adrian wearing gray sweatpants and a white T-shirt. Nothing she hadn't seen countless men wearing, something even she's worn before, yet her eyes cling to the contort of his body.

"Olivie Friedman. A psychic told my parents they were going to only have boys, so they'd been set on Adrian and Oliver. When she was born, they decided to drop the R. To this day, she thinks her name is the Czech variant of Olivia. We let her believe it because no parent wants to say they were disappointed with their child the day they were born."

"You're the eldest?"

"He is," Devyani chimes in, settling a plate in front of Thea before walking to the end of the small dining table in the kitchen, where the staff will have their meals during the weekdays. "Adrian, Olivie, and Cove."

"Same mom and dad?"

"Yup." Adrian's hands brush against her shoulder as he ambles toward his seat, planting a kiss on Devyani's cheek. "Thank you, Dev. You're free to spend the night here—"

"No, thank you. I'd rather not stay up because my neighbors are moaning all night."

Thea pulls her hands to her lap, tugging on the hem of the t-shirt Adrian gave her as a blush raises in her cheeks, making Devyani's laugh echo against the stainless steel walls and appliances, morphing the boisterous and warm sound into something metallic, reverberating endlessly until the chef is out of the kitchen.

A snicker flutters toward them as she ambles down the hallway, somehow knowing her way through the maze of the apartment across all four floors.

"I can keep quiet," Adrian mumbles. "Can you?"

Thea shrugs with a poisonous smile on her lips, emancipating the initial discomfort she'd been feeling since the shower she shared with Adrian.

"I often like to keep my mouth busy."

"As do I," Adrian replies, raising his fork and knife to the juicy steak on his plate, where he keeps his gaze. "But that's not what I wanted to talk to you about. Well, there are a few things I want to talk about."

"About me or my book?"

"Both."

"Will you look at me?"

"No," He says matter-of-factly. "You look awfully beautiful in my T-shirt. It makes my mind a puddle of debauchery. I need a moment to not think of you in that shirt."

Thea laughs, turning her attention to her plate. Slicing the steak and taking a bite of the caramelized carrot, she tries not to moan at the explosion of flavor that unfolds from spicy to sweet.

Every bite is unique, whether she eats only the steak, the carrots, the mashed potatoes, or combinations of them in varying proportions. Regardless of what she does, they are all unique.

All a feast for her senses in a way that nothing she's eaten at Ether could compare, and the thought alone feels like a betrayal.

Thea scrapes her plate before she stands up and leaves Adrian alone at the dining table, ambling down the hallway that leads her to the first floor, where she faintly remembers seeing a sitting area.

Or maybe it was a small cinema with velvet couches and dark ruby walls, Thea wonders as she stumbles into a second living room, a mirror to the one she'd seen before, except there, the large couch had a shearling upholstery instead of an elegant Italian leather.

Thea plops down on one of them, running her hand over the fuzzy cushions as her gaze lands on a more distant view of Central Park.

"You left me?" Adrian's voice sounds off from the hallway, his footsteps growing nearer. "Why did you leave me?"

Thea pats the empty spot beside her, inviting him closer as she says, "I don't sit around at a dining table after I've eaten."

Silver rakes over her naked legs, yet Adrian doesn't walk toward Thea as his fingers curl into a fist, knuckles bleached with a restrain his dark pupils don't allow, consuming the silver of his eyes how he'd like to consume her.

"You could put on a movie to distract yourself since my presence is all-consuming."

Nodding, Adrian walks toward a side table, picking up a sleek black remote. With a press of a button, a projector screen unravels from within the ceiling.

"What movie?"

Thea hums while thinking, waiting until Adrian is sat beside her before saying with a giggle, "I'd suggest porn, but that might not end well for you."

"You enjoy this, don't you?" His head lolls against the back of the couch, moving closer to Thea to catch sight of her mischievous smile. "You enjoy torturing me."

With a dignified huff, Thea stands up, taking two steps away from the couch before asking, "Should I go home? I'll leave if my presence is bothersome."

Adrian glides to the edge of the couch, hands reaching for her, the tips of his fingers curling around the back of her thighs, pulling her closer one step at a time.

His large hands glide over her legs as he moves back to the couch, sinking into it, his touch never leaving her skin, coercing her to straddle him rather than sit beside him.

"I don't ever want you to leave, Thea, and that's the problem, isn't it?"

Thea tangles her fingers in his hair, smiling at the dampness of it. "It is, but it doesn't have to be one. Not today, at least."

"Then stay."

"Then tell me what you wanted to talk about," She demands, resting her forehead against his, ignoring the little voice in the back of her mind reminding her that she barely knows the man.

Yet, she yearns to.

A shiver rakes over her spine at the phantom touch of his fingers, an idle and soft caress on her legs gingerly moving to her waist, passing the bottom of the shirt he'd given Thea after he nearly made her climax in the shower. A favor she repaid by nearly making him cum with the sight of her glistening body as she used his lotion on her silky skin, etching his smell on her as if they'd been one.

"You are positively wicked."

"And you are positively...stiff."

"Shut up," Adrian murmurs, grunting as Thea rolls her hips against his groin while moving to rest her chin against his shoulder.

"Come on, trust fund baby, tell me what you want."

"First thing," Adrian begins, resting his head against hers, fingers raking over her spine. Savoring the warmth of her skin in an all too naive touch. "Three weeks from now, I have this gala my father is forcing me to attend. It's something he would attend with my mom, but Cove got herself in trouble, and my mom is demanding they go on a father-daughter getaway."

"Why?"

"Because my father has this tendency to ramble about the great minds of human history, using their philosophy for battle or great times of recession as motivation to high school drama."

Slouching against his embrace, Thea laughs, burying her face against the crook of his neck to muffle the billowing sound.

"I mean, why take me to the gala? I'm not asking about your family dynamic."

"Because if you think this place is a gross display of money, then wait to see the gala and its attendants all trying to out-rich and outsmart each other. And you, Thea Tea, you are smarter than the lot of us."

"Prettier too."

"The most beautiful of them all."

"Really?" Thea asks, pulling back to see the truth in his eyes, but she finds so much more.

There is far more adoration than there is lust. Adrian looks at her with more respect and care than she has ever held for herself, with something so pure it makes her heart tight in a way that only writing has ever made her feel.

"You can see it, can't you?" Thea nods at that simple question that makes her throat tighten. "I don't know who raised you, but they did one hell of a job, or maybe I should thank whatever God made you."

"Adrian, I'm going to kiss you in three seconds. Stop me if you don't want—"

His mouth is on hers before Thea can finish talking, but the kiss isn't the passionate, fiery kiss she expected.

No.

Adrian explores her mouth, savoring the softness of her lips while she tries not to giggle at the scratchy feeling of his stubble.

Thea opens her mouth to him, welcoming his tongue as she rolls her hips against his groin—not to make them move faster, but as an invitation, wanting him to know that, in that moment, she belongs to him.

A mewl slips past her throat with the soft touch of his tongue, the hand he lays on the back of her head, keeping her close as they blindly explore each other.

Behaving in the same way Thea would fantasize when she was a little girl who had yet to have her first kiss. Dreaming it would be softly passionate, that they'd move in sync, neither going faster or slower than the other.

Adrian pulls away, gasping for air as his lids flutter open, once more etching to memory the faint blush of her cheeks and the way she bites down on her lips with a tiny satisfied grin tugging on them.

"Great kiss, Thea...what is your last name?"

"Scriven," She whispers. Brows knit in confusion as her fingers move over the nape of his neck, fairly certain he'd know her surname from the wiring app. "Are you sufficiently scarred, or can I kiss you again?"

"Ah yes, but one thing before we do. I want to send your book to editors, but I won't do anything without your permission."

12

Very few things have stolen the air from Thea's lungs.

Her first kiss had been bad enough for her not to want to breathe, and so was losing her virginity.

Getting accepted into her dream college was the first time she'd ever been unable to breathe through tears of joy, and so was the first time an agent requested a partial of her book before they forgot to send a rejection.

The hundreds of rejections she's received also stole the air from her lungs as she'd cry alone in her shitty apartment, holding onto Jolly as a landline.

Until the moment Adrian spoke of sending her book to editors, the last time Thea had been deprived of air was when she stood on Brooklyn Bridge, staring down at the blue water that grew pink under the red sunset painting the sky.

She'd been on that bridge the entire day, taking photos so the passersby wouldn't bother her as Thea pondered on whether she should end it all.

The night before she received her three hundredth rejection, something broke in a way even the death of her grandparents didn't.

Like the ideas that chose her to bring them to life, were all regretting it as she'd failed them, much how she failed herself.

Or maybe, just maybe, how every single agent she queried had failed her, failing to see anything worthy in her stories, to see how she'd been eager to learn and improve, willing to do anything to have her books in a bookstore.

There'd been countless nights where Thea wondered if her blood would have been on those agents' hands if she had jumped in the water, if any of them would've felt guilty had she not decided to give herself five years.

Five years that are so close to ending, and now, she has a real line to the safety of the shore, a possibility to no longer be adrift in the unknown.

"Are you serious?"

"Yes."

"Please don't play with me, not with this. If you wish to break me, do not break me with this."

"Thea, I'm serious."

Thea pushes herself away from him. Tears well in her eyes, hands trembling as if the world began to split itself in half.

“For five years, I have not mattered, Adrian. I’ve mattered to others, been someone’s sister, someone’s daughter, someone’s friends-with-benefits, but I, Thea, have not mattered."

Nails bend as Thea curls her fingers into a fist, cutting through her palms as she tries not to break into a million little pieces, trying to rein in the deluge of sorrow that pours out from her.

"Writing has always been what mattered the most to me, and if my writing hasn’t mattered to anyone, then neither have I. Do you know how soul-crushing that is? To be adrift in an ocean of dreams? To see so many disgusting humans achieving the things that are so distant to me? To see misogyny in books sold as feminism, to see racism treated as world-building, and yet…yet they are praised.

They are cherished, uplifted, adored, and I'm forgotten. I'm left to be adrift, to starve for the life I've dreamt."

Adrian stands up, walking toward Thea, but she pulls away from him, meandering toward the large windows showing the night as it swallows the city whole.

"Do not joke with this. I know I need an agent to be published, but I'm so fucking tired. Tired of not mattering, of being the only person who believes in me. No one cares, Adrian! No one can understand just how broken this dream has made me. No one understands that if I could be happy doing anything else, I wouldn't still be trying to be a writer, but I was cursed to only be happy over the thing that has broken me the most."

Tears well in Adrian's eyes, feeling as if his soul is shredded by the sheer pain in her voice, by her despair that is tangible, carving deep into himself as he's helpless against it, seeking a way to make her pain disappear but there is nothing he can do.

"This is the only thing I care about. When I think about fucking killing myself, putting an end to the travesty my life has been, it's not the fear of death that kept me from jumping down Brooklyn Bridge, it's knowing that if I'm gone, then no one will fight for the books I've written. I'm so tired. So, so tired."

Thea can't breathe through the tears ripping through her, succumbing to the exhaustion, feelings, and thoughts she's never shared with anyone but Adrian, weighing him down to the bottom of East River with her, stringing him into a promise she made and shared with no one else—she didn't even intend on sharing it with Adrian, but he needed to understand that she can't handle more rejections.

"Who will care for my books when I'm gone if no one other than myself cares for them now? I just want one person to care, one single person who truly cares about the things I've written. Why is that too much to ask for? Why? Am I so fucking worthless?" Her voice drops into a whisper as her knees hit the marble flooring. Her hands that'd been waving in tandem with her despair; now wrap around her. "I don't even fucking know why I'm so terrible because not a single agent will tell me why they don't care, won't tell me what is so terrible that they just wish me luck and go on their merry way. I'm fucking tired, so fucking tired. Why am I not good enough, Adrian?"

Adrian takes a single step toward her, afraid if he touches her, she'll crumble away like shattered tempered glass, exploding into a million little pieces that neither one of them will be able to piece back together.

But Adrian knows something needs to happen, knows there needs to be a change in how things work, in the way everyone handed out their rejections because seeing Thea that broken, that close to oblivion, made him realize she wouldn't be the first nor the last writer to feel that way. He dreaded thinking about the manuscripts abandoned on someone's computer, the manuscripts the world will never see because so many failed that dreamer.

The world needs dreamers. It needs the artists that elicit the beauty in life. And he needed her to smile, to see Thea achieving all of her dreams.

Adrian proffers his hand to Thea, hoping she'll take it, even if she leaves his apartment to sleep in Aaron's bed, wanting her to accept his help because one way or another, from that day onward, he'll be dreaming with her.

From that day to the day he dies, Adrian will dream for Thea even if she never dreams of him.

"Writing books is easy, Adrian," She says, gazing at the distant park. "Being rejected without even being given a chance, surviving long enough to see them in the world… that's hard. That might be too much to ask for, and I don't want—"

"You don't want to achieve your dreams because of me, because people would publish anything I ask them to publish?"

Thea nods, glancing at the hand he still offers her.

Instead of laying her hand in his, she crawls toward him, wrapping her arms around him, allowing him to hold her just as she always wished someone would be there to hold her through the worst of it all.

"I promise I won't tell anyone of our connection. I'll act like your manuscript ended up in my mailbox, and I'll redirect it to some of my colleagues. How does that sound?"

"The world is a fucked up place. Don't you think?" Thea mutters against his chest with a faint nod, not wanting to voice that she's okay with that plan, not wanting to have hope for what that might bring her.

"It is. We'll have to break the world and put it back together, Thea Tea."

13

Hands move up and down Thea's back, Adrian's lips planting a kiss on her temple every so often, enjoying the intimacy while believing she's still asleep when she, too, is enjoying the warmth of his arms.

She keeps her face slack and lids closed as he brushes a few brown strands of her hair away from her face, his finger tracing the shape of her jaw down to her chin before he trails the contour of her pouty lips.

Thea cuddles closer to him, rolling on top of Adrian as she buries her face against the crook of his neck, enjoying the way his fingers reach the nape of her neck before dipping down her spine, caressing her down to the back of her thighs before moving back up.

"Are you comfy?"

Thea nibbles on his neck, too tired to speak, but her hands move toward his chest, marking the ridges of his stomach before her hand slips under his body, hiding her hand between him and the shearling couch.

"Do you always enjoy cuddling this much, or am I just special?"

"Shut up so I can sleep."

"But I'm hungry, Thea Tea," Adrian whispers, wrapping his arms around her. "Hold tight, will you?"

Before she answers, Adrian sits up with a grunt, hand moving to the back of her head, holding her against him as one would a baby.

Thea giggles against his neck, raising a shiver that reaches his soul. She tightens her embrace, wrapping her legs around him as he stands, taking painfully careful steps not to disturb her.

"You could have left me on the couch," She points out the obvious.

"I won't let go of you until you ask me to."

"Good."

They fall silent once more, Adrian's thumb caressing her butt and the back of her head as he walks to the kitchen with a foolish grin on his lips.

Thea doesn't pay attention to the art on the walls when her mind revolves around the way Adrian smells, his unshaven face tickling the slope of her shoulder; focusing on how his heart beats steadily against her chest until Thea plants a kiss on his jaw, lips moving down to his pulse that quickens.

"Do I make you nervous?" She asks in a sultry voice, teeth grazing against the rim of his ear. "Your pulse is pounding, Adrian."

"You do. You make me feel things I don't think a man should feel."

Brows knit together as Thea leans back, forcing him to flex his arms and stomach to balance her weight. Thea fights the urge to mirror the smile that sprouts on his face when he sees her face still swollen from crying and sleep.

"In a good or bad way?"

"And why do you care?"

"Who says I do?" Thea locks her fingers behind the nape of his neck as he stops walking halfway into the kitchen. "Perhaps, I am perversely indifferent."

"There is this artist who cuts all of her finished paintings, selling these two-by-two pieces to people all around the world. She says it's because it feels wrong to have her art existing in a single place, that she'd much rather have its ashes spread around the globe."

"Why are you telling me this, Adrian?"

"Because publishing a book is a lot like that, it allows something so deeply personal to exist in the minds and hearts of countless others. That's why art without meaning is vacant. It's a vessel without a soul."

The frown between her brows deepens, confused as to what that story has to do with how she made him feel, but Thea doesn't prod him for an explanation, allowing him to resume his path to the kitchen, trusting he'll elaborate eventually.

Thea cuddles against him once more, knowing they are in the kitchen when a chill spreads over her skin, a drop in the temperature almost unnoticeable if it wasn't for how warm half of her body is.

Through the hazy reflection on the stainless steel appliances, Thea sees Adrian adding water to a kettle before throwing a tea bag in a mug.

"You can set me down if you want to," She suggests again as he walks into a pantry the size of her apartment.

"Nope, just need you to open this jar of honey."

She rolls her eyes but doesn't say anything as he pivots so she can reach for the honey before doing what he asked. The five minutes it would take for one to make tea becomes ten as Adrian slouches through the steps, muttering to himself about having to eventually learn how to navigate his kitchen beyond knowing how to use the kettle—that even Dev had to take a few weeks to teach him how to use the item as she would put it back where it belonged in the pantry before giving up and leaving the kettle on the counter.

Adrian settles Thea on the stainless countertop as he pours honey and water into his mug before marching back to where they spent the night in each other's arms.

Thea holds the mug for him as Adrian sits back down on the shearling couch, a triumphant smile and a glimmer in his eyes that search her face.

"Remember how I said art without meaning is a vessel without a soul?"

Thea nods, running her fingers through his hair.

"You seem to give meaning to my life, because for a very long time, I've felt vacant, devoid of a reason that made life something meaningful. You reminded me things can be beautiful without having meaning, and you have given me something I longed for."

"That's a big claim to make."

"It is, but you've made me excited in a way I haven't been in a long time, Thea Tea."

"Don't fall for me, Adrian Friedman. I don't need another heart to break."

"Why? Because of what you said yesterday?" Thea nods, hands moving over his chest. "I've never understood why one would take their own life."

"Consider yourself lucky." Thea smiles at him as she cradles his hand over the warm tea, settling the mug between them like a bulwark protecting both sides. "For a long time, I didn't understand either. There was a time when the future was filled with more hope than uncertainties. But rejections began to weigh down on me, wearing down my sense of worth until I was no longer puzzled by why someone would see life as a burden. It can often feel so heavy, like an anchor hurling you to the bottom of a river."

"Meaning?"

"Meaning that I don't want to die, but I'm desperate for a gulp of air. All I want is to live, for my books to not wither with me, but I can't keep going if this is all life has to offer."

"You don't want to live if you don't get to be a published author?" He asks, pulling his hand away to settle the mug on the ground. "Why?"

Thea wishes she knew the answer to that question.

It's something she pondered about during many sleepless nights, unable to calm her mind when she sought to understand why writing meant so much to her.

It just did.

There wasn't a nice little story to encompass everything writing made Thea feel, no words capable of explaining the sense of belonging that only existed when she sat in front of a computer and allowed the stories in her mind to take place in the physical world.

Thea wishes there was an easy way to explain how something she loves so deeply can be the very same thing that makes her contemplate self-immolation over the mere idea of her work not existing in the world.

Something far too devastating that Thea prefers to cling to a false sense of hope, ignoring impending doom as her destiny isn't in her hands.

"Some nights I wonder if there aren't as many stars in the galaxies as there are dreams that remained as such, never meant or capable of coming true. If maybe every supernova isn't a physical representation of a world ending when a life-altering dream doesn't come true due to the incompetence of others. I just pray I'm not a supernova. I want to be part of a constellation that shines brightly."

"I'm sorry, Thea Tea. I wish I could dismantle every step of the system that has failed you so far."

"It is what it is. I probably should go home. I need to feed Jolly and work on my book."

Yet, she doesn't move away, instead leans closer, resting her forehead against his. Their lips are a breath away when Adrian whispers, "I'll take you home."

Closing the distance between them, Thea kisses him, not caring that neither brushed their teeth the night before, not caring for anything other than the hand she pulls toward her waist.

Wanting Adrian to explore her body, but he doesn't move a single inch toward her breast or the apex of her thighs as he kisses her with the same sweet innocence of the first kiss they shared.

"I was hoping you'd say that," Thea whispers against his mouth. "But I'm not going to cum with my cat staring at us, so you better kiss me a little deeper and palm my body properly."

"My pleasure," Adrian's voice is husky to her ears, making her core tingle.

A giggle bubbles past her lips as Adrian throws her onto the couch, kicking the mug that shatters against the floor, spilling tea over the marble, but Adrian's attention focuses on pulling Thea's t-shirt over her head.

Each inch of skin that becomes exposed is accompanied by a kiss, the first on her neck, then her collarbone. Adrian moves a few inches down, planting a kiss on her breast before kissing her sternum as he settles between her legs.

Thea arches toward him as she brings her arms over her head, wanting him to explore her body however he wishes, wanting to see where his instincts lead him rather than her guiding him with the feather-light touch she'd touch herself with.

Adrian's lips mar her skin, igniting a fire as the soft palm of his hand glides from her thighs to her chest, palming her breast while taking the other in his mouth—his tongue lapping around her nipples, stealing a breathy moan.

Thea rolls her hips against the knee Adrian keeps between her legs as he focuses on her chest. "Look at me, Thea," He says, hot breath making her nipples harden into pink peaks. "Peel your eyes from me, and I'll stop what I'm doing. I want you to see as I worship your body."

"Worship?"

"You are either a gift from God or a Goddess. Either way, I'll show you how much I...how much I care for you. I want you to see how much I enjoy pleasuring you."

"And you?"

Adrian flicks his tongue, teeth grazing against her nipple. He doesn't answer for a moment as his attention moves to her other breast, sucking on it until Thea purrs.

"There will be opportunities for you to pleasure me if that's what you mean. Fuck, Thea, there have been times already," He says, dipping his hand to her unclothed mound, thumb drawing circles as he kisses just above her belly button.

Adrian makes a mental note to thank whatever God allowed his fate to cross Thea's life, granting him a night of sleep with only the thin cotton of the t-shirt she borrowed between their bodies, thin enough for him to feel every curve of her body, for his sweatpants to have dampened when she'd grind against him with his name on her lips in her sleep, begging for the Adrian to go faster in her dream.

A secret he'd never tell her, fearing she'd be too embarrassed by it.

"Meaning?" Thea asks, a wicked smile on her lips. "Elevator pics?"

"Do you have any idea how hard it was for me not to jerk off in the metro? For me to ride the elevator to my apartment and walk into my room before I could have my cock in one hand and my phone in another? I've cummed to you many times already. Let me make you come for me."

"What if we are even?"

Adrian practically growls at the idea, forgetting his fingers as he dips his head between her thighs, tongue pressed against her wet pussy, tasting her with a grunt of satisfaction.

His tongue works her much like how they'd kissed before. Being all too tender for Thea, making her squirm with each kiss he gives her lips, for each lap his tongue takes against her.

"Fuck, I need your fingers too," Thea says, and Adrian obliges without a second of delay, slipping two fingers inside of her. Curling the tips, Adrian thrusts his digits into her as his mouth focuses on her clit. "Just like that."

"Fucking delicious."

The vibration of his voice makes Thea grab his hair with a moan on her lips, forcing him closer as she moves her hips in tandem with his fingers.

"I want you to ride my face, Thea," Adrian says, savoring how she bites the back of her hand to muffle her moan. "You taste so fucking good."

Rolling onto the small couch, Adrian pulls Thea with him, careful around the shards of ceramic spread across the floor as Adrian slaps her ass before pulling her down toward his lips.

"Fuck Adrian."

With a leg on the couch and the other stepping on the spilled tea that's grown cold, Thea rolls her hips against him, a hand still in his hair, pulling him closer as she sinks deeper onto his tongue.

Thea mewls with the second slap in her ass, making her move faster, taking his free hand that isn't thrusting inside of her, to her breast—Adrian pinches her nipples, tugging on it as Thea sinks her nails into his forearm.

His tongue and his fingers against her pussy, the way gray eyes stay focused on her while Adrian's face grows red with his need for air, the way he tugs on her nipples is too much.

It's all too much, sending Thea into a sweet abyss of pleasure, where she loses herself in a chase for bliss, moving her hips against his face, allowing her moans to meld into a scream that reverberates against their bones.

Adrian doesn't stop fingering her, doesn't stop sucking her, slapping her ass, and grabbing it, stringing one orgasm into another and another.

"It's too much," Thea says with closes lids, but she doesn't stop fucking his face, doesn't stop until his grunts of pleasure sound a little too much like pain. "Oh god—I'm so sorry."

Thea sits on his chest, wiping the blood that dribbles down his cheeks. "It's not broken," He consoles her, a slight grin tugging at his lips before wiping his hand on his chest. "Even if it was, it would have been worth it."

"Nearly having your nose broken from a girl riding your face would be worth it?"

"That too," Adrian concedes, raising his hand toward her breast. "But I fucking came just from the way you look when cumming."

Thea lays down beside Adrian, peppering kisses on his shoulder as he wipes the blood from his face, yet for some reason, the sight of his satisfied grin and the arm he snakes around her makes her giddy.

It seems wrong for someone to be so content in holding her naked body, so at ease in having his face wet with her release and his pants sodden with cum while still seeming so completely content.

"Shower and then Brooklyn?"

"Yeah, just let me catch my breath."

"Jolly, I think I met the biggest idiot," Thea says as a greeting. "I nearly broke his nose, and he dropped me off before going down the block to buy us lunch. That's idiotic, isn't it?"

Jolly meows as if saying, *Then why are you smiling so much?*

"Don't judge me. You like him too."

Thea doesn't lock her door as she walks toward the unmade bed with a pile of clothes pressed against the corner. Falling on it with a toothy grin, Thea kicks her blankets away, burying her face in her pillow as she squeals against it.

Jolly leaps into the bed, pawing at Thea's back in a request for the woman to cuddle her before squeezing between the gaps of her arms.

"Turns out you aren't a lucky lady, Jolly," Thea whispers conspiratorially. "The things he can do with his tongue? Yeah, that's something only deities should experience. Even he might be able to change things. It's scary, Jolly. I haven't felt hope like this in a long time."

Five years is a long time for one to try to achieve their dreams. It's plenty of time for someone to finish a degree and watch their newborn child grow past most of their most significant milestones, getting a car and a computer, long enough to grow old enough to trade in.

Yet, it's been more than 1826 days since Thea had felt hope that her dream could come true, and now she has a chance, a very small chance. One that might be the push she needs to leap into the water of the unknown, but one way or another, Thea's life will change as those five years she promised herself are coming to an end.

"I'm scared, Jolly. Hope is a cruel thing at times. Having trust in something I can't quite see...that's terrifying."

Jolly meows, coarse tongue licking under Thea's chin, pink paws pressing against her chest as the cat slithers in her embrace, pulling away to lick Thea's cheeks.

A knock on the door pulls Thea from her reverie. "It's open," she says, leaping with a smile on her face that falls when Aaron walks in. "Oh."

"Oh?"

"I wasn't expecting you," She explains, setting Jolly back on the bed as Aaron cruises toward her, wrapping his arms around her. "How are you?"

"I missed you. I always forget how stressful renovations are, but I mainly miss you."

Aaron buries his hand in her damp hair, pulling Thea into a kiss as he presses her against the small dining table where she left her computer.

His tongue explores hers before he pulls back to sneeze, much to Jolly's delight, who meows in tandem with Aaron.

The cat watches as he takes a few steps back, pinching his pinkie to fight against more sneezes. "You were holding her, weren't you?"

"Jolly is a cuddly girl."

"She takes after you," Aaron jests with a sniff. "I can't stay long, but I wanted to stop by to say your brother set me up on a date."

"With who?"

"Someone he worked with in Seattle. She moved to New York a while back, and Jules thinks I'm the perfect candidate to help her get used to the city."

"Is this a '*let's see if we can date*' or is this a '*let's pretend it's a date before you take me home and my neighbors hate me by how loud you make me moan*' kind of date?"

"It's whatever you want it to be," Aaron holds her gaze. "If you want me to get through appetizers before I fake an emergency and go back home to fuck you, then I will."

"I want you to be happy, Aaron."

"And I want to be happy with yo—"

"Thea Tea," Adrian's carol cuts through Aaron's voice.

The blonde man whirls to find Adrian frozen on the threshold of her apartment with a nondescript parchment bag and a yellow one with *Ina* written on it.

"What are you doing here?" They ask in astonishing synchrony, leaving Thea in awe for all but seconds as she remembers just how much each man dislikes the other.

"Adrian is the editor I told you about." Thea slips past Aaron, wrapping her fingers around Adrian's wrist as she hurls him into her apartment, forcing him down on her bed just as quickly as Jolly pounces onto him, sinking her claws into the cotton T-shirt as she climbs to his shoulder.

"Can you work tonight?" Aaron asks Thea, but his green eyes are focused on Adrian.

"Sure, I'm not used to the restaurant, but I can fill in if you need me."

"I'll always need you, love."

"I know," Thea says, escorting Aaron down the few steps between her kitchen and the front door. "Now, go work and then fresh up for your date. It's only—"

Aaron pulls Thea into another kiss, a crash of lips and tongue. His hand moves to her ass, pulling Thea into him as his fingers dip between her legs.

Only when a moan bubbles past her lips does Aaron pull back, cheeks ruddy as he plants a quick kiss on her lips before closing the door behind himself.

"Sorry about that," She whispers, wiping her mouth as she walks toward Adrian without looking at him.

"Don't be. He's the one acting like a dog pissing somewhere to mark his domain. It's childish and shows insecurity."

"We have history, and he is my brother's best friend. Aaron's a good guy."

"Do you love him?"

"I do."

"Are you in love with him?" Adrian asks as he stands up with Jolly on his shoulder.

Thea doesn't answer him as she has never asked herself that question before. Often feeling as if loving someone and being in love are too synonymous of a feeling, but now she wonders if she'd been wrong.

Wonders if she could be falling for someone she shouldn't. Thea knows there's a difference in how Aaron and Adrian make her feel, but none of it will matter if she doesn't survive the next few months.

"What did you get us, and what's the plan?"

"I got lasagna, and the plan is you work on the book you are writing while I revise your other book. I don't think there is anything major you need to change. I just want to be sure I give you your best fighting chance."

"You already did," Thea mutters, ambling toward Adrian, wanting to wrap her arms around him but feeling as if she shouldn't touch him when she can taste Aaron in her mouth. "You, Adrian, are my best fighting chance."

"Soon."

Adrian rakes his hands down her arms, weaving their fingers together before sprawling himself on her bed, taking Thea with him as she laughs, hitting his chest when he wraps an arm around her waist, resting his chin on her shoulder as Thea pulls the lid off the lasagna.

She tries to stand to pick up cutlery other than the plastic ones from the bag, but Adrian doesn't let her go.

"Really? You want to eat with a plastic fork?"

"Yup, as long as you stay right here."

"Sitting on your boner?"

"I don't have a boner."

"Not yet."

Thea offers him a wicked smile before turning back to the lasagna, rolling her hips in tandem with a plastic knife more likely to break than cut through the first layer.

"I'm not going to stop you," Adrian says, laying a hand on her hips. "Although, if you almost break my dick instead of almost breaking my nose, that would be very bad."

"If your dick is half as good as your tongue, I'll stop."

"It's better," Adrian whispers against the shell of her ear, delighting himself in the soundless moan as Thea opens her mouth in a gasp.

Thea untangles from his embrace, crossing to the kitchen to fetch them a pair of steel forks before taking a seat in the only chair around her dining table as Adrian remains on her bed.

Gray eyes twinkle at the blush staining her cheeks, how she bites her lips, caught between the desire for him and, well, for food and the prospect of writing.

"If it's better, how come you are single?

Adrian laughs, stealing one of the two forks Thea cradles against her chest. He cuts a piece of the lasagna with the side of the utensil, offering it to her first.

"Because I hadn't met you yet," He says matter-of-factly, without jest to his voice or a smirk on his lips. "I've met plenty of people, but no one like you."

"I'm warning you not to fall for me."

"Why?"

"Because a window is just another door for the brave," She mocks.

"Tell me about it. Explain it to me."

"Isn't that enough?"

"I know how you feel, but why does it seem you are on a countdown?"

Thea doesn't say anything, turning her attention to the lasagna, cutting a piece for Adrian as he did for her, and with silly grins on their lips, they feed each other, wanting to spoil the other instead of merely eating at their own will.

Jolly watches the interaction, waiting for them to finish the lasagna before leaping from Adrian's shoulder to the table, where she licks the tomato sauce from the parchment box it came in.

Stalling before giving Adrian an explanation, Thea washes the cutlery, cleaning the countertop under his watchful gaze.

She hears as he moves on her bed, resting his back against the mountain of pillows she has while patiently waiting, not daring to speak, giving her a getaway from explaining the promise she'd made.

Eventually, Jolly has licked all the sauce from the box, finding a patch of sunlight to lie under as she watches Thea cruise toward the bed.

Adrian pulls her into him, hands moving over her thighs as she straddles him. Thea sprawls her hands on his chest, feeling his heart hammering against his ribs.

"I don't want to die. Let's start there."

"You told me that already, and I'm glad."

"Five years ago, I was ready to give up on...myself, on my dream. I'd gotten enough vague rejections, not enough partial requests. I didn't and still don't see the value in what I've written because no one else has."

"What changed your mind?" Adrian squeezes her thighs, sitting straighter to close the distance between them. "Was it Aaron? Because if so, I'll get on my knees and thank him for it."

"Fate did. I spent the entire day standing on Brooklyn Bridge, trying to get the courage to jump while also talking myself out of it. I decided if my battery died after 1:15 AM, the time I was born, I would jump. If it died before, I would give myself five years. My battery died at 11:47 PM."

"That's the time I was born."

"Really?"

Adrian smiles as he nods, silver lining his eyes.

"And the five years?"

"Months from running down, so don't fall for me, Adrian. I don't want to break your heart."

"You won't," He lies to Thea with his lips against hers. "But the day your book is released, you'll go on a date with me. Deal?"

Thea nods, unable to speak through the lump in her throat, to voice just how much she has grown to cherish the most infuriating man.

14

There is something fundamentally different about working in the restaurant compared to the bar. People are usually very polite and talkative or exceptionally rude and flirty.

But in the restaurant, the waiters and waitresses are virtually invisible to the wealthy and balding men trying so hard to impress women while spewing their orders without as much as a thank you.

Thea hated it.

And the tips were terrible. Only the most anti-social members of Ether's staff enjoyed working there, getting to speak as little as possible with better salaries to compensate for the rudeness.

"You've been smiling since the last customer left the restaurant," Isa says as she takes note of inventory while Thea keeps her company. "You hate working for the restaurant. Why are you here tonight?"

"Aaron has a date."

Thea rests her cheek against the cold marble in the restaurant's reception area. Her eyes study Isa's face, noticing how the woman seems tired as Aaron is certainly running all decisions through her too.

Seeming to forget Isa has enough responsibilities to handle for him without her running around with him to meet with his architect friend and local bakeries to negotiate having their bestsellers sold at Ether.

"Didn't you just make it public you've been fucking?" Isa peels her gaze from the clipboard, watching Thea's nails tap against the counter. "Are you jealous?"

"No, just want to know if it went well," Thea says, nails continuing to tap against the tabletop. "He deserves to be happy, and I don't know if I'm the one to give him that. But God, I love fucking Aaron?"

"I love fucking you too," Aaron says, a sharp smile adorning his lips as he saunters into Ether, glancing at the empty restaurant that's already cleaned. "How was the night, Isa?"

"The same as they've always been under my watch."

Aaron beholds the woman with a mix of utmost respect and adoration as she rolls her shoulders over, sustaining Aaron's gaze until a smirk curls on the edge of his lips, baring the arrogant trust he has in her.

"Once the renovation is done, we can officially start thinking about the second unit," Aaron doesn't peel his gaze from Isa as Thea glances between the two with a frown.

"What second unit?"

"Your brother wants to invest in Ether, but he wants a unit on Upper East Side because that's where lawyers prefer to meet. Jules was also smart enough to demand Isa is the one to administrate the new unit."

Thea's frown deepens as she knows her brother is the last person to demand something from the people he loves while managing to be the most pretentious lawyer she's ever seen.

Albeit, she hasn't seen many lawyers—especially lawyers who have yet to lose a case in whatever kind of law Jules practices.

"Does that mean he's visiting soon?" Thea asks, allowing Aaron to wrap his arms around her, pulling her toward him while Isa rolls her eyes.

"Not until we find a location for the second unit."

"You two can talk about how much you miss your brother and best friend on your merry way," Isa chides, waving them off without deigning to hide how much she enjoys working in silence, something neither Thea nor Aaron are good company for. "Thank you for helping tonight, Thea."

Aaron leads her out of Ether as she blows Isa one kiss after another until the restaurant door closes behind her and Aaron. His lips find her neck, planting kisses in tandem with every step she takes down the streets shrouded in darkness.

Strolling toward his building, Thea enjoys the kisses Aaron plants on her flesh. Savoring the hand trailing her body, warming her down to her core.

It should feel wrong, Thea muses, wondering how her body can crave Aaron between her legs just as much as it desires Adrian, leaving her entangled in the tenuous line of wanting them to contend for her pleasure, to explore her body but not for them to fall in love with her.

Yet, Thea is helpless as her thoughts wander to one of them, curious if he's gotten home safely, if he's taking notes on her book, or if he's in bed thinking of her.

Thea doesn't know which one she'd rather have Adrian do, which one would ignite a fire within her soul.

"You are awfully silent," Aaron says, pulling Thea from her reverie as she finds herself in the elevator of his building.

"I'm a little tired. Sorry."

"That's okay. We can just sleep."

Thea smiles at him, glancing at the numbers increasing floor by floor as the elevator rises. The smile becomes dangerous as she lays a hand on his chest, nails tracing patterns on his skin.

"A week is too long without sex."

"I know you haven't gone that long without playing with yourself," Aaron drawls, watching her eyes as he brings his hand around her neck, pushing her against the elevator wall as his thumb caresses her throat. "Have you?"

"Allow me to rectify myself, Aaron Mariani," Thea teases him in a pompous tone while her hand drifts toward the buckle of his belt. "A week is too long to go by without a dick inside of me, but we can just sleep if you want?"

Before Aaron can answer, the elevator comes to a halt on the top floor. Hand still wrapped around her neck, Aaron pulls Thea with him, kissing her as they stumble into the hallway.

The digital lock on his door illuminates the dark hallway as Thea slips her hand down his pants, enjoying how Aaron opens his mouth to grunt against her lips.

His jacket hits the floor when the door swings open, closing behind Thea as he presses her against it, ripping her dress to shreds, his thumb pressing on her windpipe.

"Rough."

"I'm starved for you, love."

"Good," She moans, returning the favor by pulling at his shirt until buttons trickle to the floor.

Lips find warm skin as Aaron slips out of his trousers before he hoists her up, wrapping her legs around his waist. He moves her body against the bulge in his briefs, stealing a moan from Thea, driving her kisses into bites.

Trudging deeper into the apartment, Aaron fidgets with the band of her thong, pulling on it, causing the band to snap against her flesh.

"I want you in my mouth," Aaron says as he sprawls on the couch.

"You don't tell me what to do, Mariani."

Thea glides from his lap, kissing his thighs as she undoes the hook of her bra, throwing the item at his face before allowing her nails to dig into his skin.

She teases him with kisses that grow nearer to his cock, hands moving from his inner thighs to the shaft pulsating against the palm of her hand.

"How did your date go?"

"Fuck, Thea. I don't want to think about that."

"Why?" She asks, tugging on his underwear, smiling as his cock springs free, nearly hitting her face. "Was she pretty? Did you want to fuck her?"

"I did fuck her."

With her fingers around his cock, Thea halts for a moment, arching a brow, but Aaron's lids are closed, jaw tight, fingers grabbing the cushion beneath him.

"You fucked her?" Thea moves her hand against his shaft as she waits for some envy or irritation to spark somewhere within herself.

"I did, in the restaurant's bathroom," Aaron confesses, and Thea plants a kiss on his cock, lips moving down without taking him in her mouth. "Then, she sucked me off while I drove her car and fingered her."

"Did you really? Then what?"

At first, Aaron is silent, brows contorted with guilt and pleasure as Thea spits on his cock, spreading her saliva around as she strokes him too slowly and lightly for his pleasure to build up but enough stimulation not to get soft.

In fact, Aaron gets harder as he tells her about his date.

"Then we got to her condo. I bent her over her couch as she pulled her skirt up to her waist, waiting for me to put a condom on before pounding her wet pussy."

Thea dips her hand between her legs, touching herself over the image Aaron paints in her mind, imagining Aaron's hand wrapped around his date's hair, a hand on her breast as he thrusts into her.

"I told her I was about to cum, and she pushed me back, dropping to her knees as she took off the condom, stroking me until I painted the back of her throat."

"That's it?"

"She took me to her bedroom, pushing me onto the bed before she climbed on top of me with my cock in her mouth and her pussy in mine."

Thea licks his shaft, tongue wrapping around him before she settles for licking the little bit of skin on the back of his cock, enjoying the way Aaron moans, fingers curling around the edge of his couch.

"Did she taste good?"

Grunting, Aaron takes a fistful of Thea's hair in a silent answer that tells her how much he liked his date's taste—a taste that lingers on his tongue.

"Then you left?"

"Then she fucked me. Can you taste her on my cock, Thea?" Aaron asks, opening his eyes to see as Thea takes him into her mouth, humming as she can taste the stranger. "Do you like how she tastes?"

"It tastes like she stole something from me."

"Did she?"

Thea doesn't answer, taking him deep in her throat and holding him there until she needs air. Saliva dribbles down her chin as Thea bobs her head, using her hand to stroke him as she pulls back.

Aaron thrusts into her mouth, going deeper and faster until he's standing up. A hand wrapped around Thea's wrist as he fucks her mouth, moaning and grunting as her teeth graze against his length.

Thea pushes away from him, spit and cum dripping down her chin as Aaron strokes himself, cumming on her face and chest.

Aaron plots down on the couch, growing soft as Thea walks to the kitchen, wiping her face and chest while her wetness glides down her tights.

"Sorry to ruin your plans, but I don't think I can cum again tonight," He says, voice weak and tired.

"Go to bed, Aaron Mariani. I want you inside of me."

"Fuck," he curses, pushing himself to his feet. Green eyes on Thea as she licks her lips, smiling as he strokes himself to get hard once more. "I love when you get bossy."

Guilt is a funny thing.

Something capable of being tyrannical to the point of squeezing the life out of a person, choking them with its burden. Yet, there are times when guilt is unjustified, making it easy to push it aside with the reminder that guilt and guilty aren't synonymous.

Thea's mind catches between guilt and lust as she grabs onto Aaron's hair, moaning with each flick of his tongue while the sun warms their skin, painting the white sheets an auric color that matches the hair tangled between her fingers as her body trembles with pleasure.

"Good morning, love," Aaron mutters with his lips raking up her stomach.

His fingers slide inside her, allowing Thea to nurture her climax as she rolls her hips against his fingers. Teeth graze over her breast as Aaron savors the way Thea clings to the blankets kicked aside, body taut and quivering with the last wave of pleasure.

Aaron nibbles on her neck, smiling against her feverish skin as Thea's moan reverberates against the brick walls in his apartment. "Please let me wake you up like that more often."

"I will." Thea hums, nails lazily digging into his back as she wraps her legs around him, holding Aaron against her body as if she'd crackle into oblivion within him to tether her to reality.

With a hand around his neck, Thea blindly palms the bedside table in search of her phone, smiling as the bright screen shows a notification from Adrian.

Adrian Friedman sent you $1000.
"Good morning, Thea Tea. I've been making progress in your manuscript."

"Will you tell me about Adrian?" Aaron murmurs against her neck, sitting up between her legs to study her face as Thea smiles at her phone before rolling on the bed and pushing her ass toward Aaron.

"He's editing my manuscript. He wants to send it to a few of his colleagues."

"Really? That's good."

You sent Adrian Friedman $5

"Morning, Friedman. Should I stop by so we can go through the edits together?"

Aaron brushes her hair to one side as he kisses a trail from the top of her spine, moving down the divots as he grabs her ass, holding it up until his lips are over it, biting into her flesh, savoring the moan he steals from Thea.

"Has his feedback been valuable?"

"I'm just asking him if we should meet up for lunch to go over edits."

"He's probably working, no?"

"Probably," Thea moans as Aaron licks from the front to the back. "Uhm, I like that. Did you learn that from your date?"

"Are you jealous?"

"You are a free man, Mariani. Did you eat her ass?"

"And if I did?"

"Then I'd ask if you are trying to eat mine."

"And if I am?" He asks, spreading her cheeks, but his thumb only caresses her entrance. "Should I?"

Thea doesn't answer as her phone vibrates in her hand.

Adrian Friedman sent you $1000.
"I have work, but I can stop by tonight?"

You sent Adrian Friedman $5
"I'll see you then."

Throwing her phone to the side, Thea ignores the guilt and excitement bubbling in her chest at the idea of seeing Adrian.

Glancing over her shoulder to look at Aaron, she asks, "Do you plan on going on more dates with her?"

"Jules demanded I take her on five dates, claiming I'm too hard to please because I don't give girls a chance."

"Poor Jules...oblivious that his best friend daydreams about eating ass."

"I don't daydream about eating ass, Thea."

"Good, because I want your cock in my pussy."

"So bossy."

"Well, you are the one who got soft before I could cum," Thea jests, gasping as Aaron adjusts himself behind Thea. Teasing her with the tip of his cock. "Fuck, Mariani."

Aaron laughs, fingers sinking into her hips, leaving red marks as he inches forward, grunting as he sinks to the hilt before pulling back slowly, but there is nothing gentle in how he thrusts into Thea in deep and fast strokes, quickly taking Thea to a summit as she's all too sensitive.

Thea bites down on a pillow, muffling her moan as Aaron's cock twitches inside her.

He gets harder before cumming inside her, grunting against the crook of her neck, moaning close to her ear as

Aaron knows how horny it makes her, amplifying her own pleasure.

With Aaron on top of her, Thea feels as he grows soft, his lips lavishing her shoulder and neck with kisses before he grunts, "I'm sorry, love, I have work to do. Will I see you tonight?"

Thea rolls in bed, bathing in the sunlight as she watches Aaron trudge toward the kitchen island with a hand on his cock—seeming to remember the buildings facing his allow them a view of his dick. Meanwhile, Thea's eyes never leave his ass.

"No, Adrian is coming over for us to edit," Thea murmurs as Aaron tosses her a box of tissues before he disappears into the bathroom, leaving the door open in an invitation.

Thea's phone vibrates on the nightstand. Reaching for it, she giggles at the notification.

Adrian Friedman sent you $1000.
"I miss you, and I might steal your cat from you."

"Nooo, Jolly bean is mine," She writes, sending a text rather than wiring him money as she attaches a photo of herself pouting—a photo that may or may not include her breast.

Adrian Friedman sent you $1000.
"You torture me."

Adrian Friedman sent you $1000.

"And my coworkers nearly saw you naked. A shared torture."

Adrian Friedman sent you $1000.
"I am, however, saving those for later."

You sent Adrian Friedman $1
"I'll let you see them in real life."

Thea bites down on her lips, kicking away the blankets as she can't quite contain the fit of joy that surges in her chest when it comes to teasing Adrian, enjoying how much he enjoys her. Throwing her phone on Aaron's bed, she slouches out of it, prancing toward his large shower.

"You torture me, T," Aaron draws a heart over the fogged glass pane on his shower.

"I keep hearing that for some reason. You scrub my back, and I'll scrub yours?"

"Come on in."

15

Jolly meows, pawing at Thea's hand as if prodding the woman on why she'd been smiling—or maybe to remind Thea she should be writing instead of daydreaming about Adrian's good morning texts, something that's been a new norm for a week, or at least it had been a norm, with Adrian sending Thea a text as soon as he woke up instead of waiting for a time he knew Thea would be awake.

"Don't look at me like that. It's hard to write a sex scene when I keep thinking about a dork who wakes up at six am every morning. You know the one who sends good morning texts with their plans for the day?"

Thea asks, expecting a meow that doesn't come as Jolly paws her hand once more, complaining when Thea lifts Jolly from the table before bringing the cat to her chest.

"A man in love, Jolly. That's who."

Picking up her phone, warm from being used as Jolly's pillow, a grin unravels on Thea's lips as she rereads the notification.

Adrian Friedman sent you $1000.

"Good morning, Thea Tea. I am pleased to inform you I had a dream about you. So, while I miss you, I can still remember the way your hair felt against the tips of my fingers. It was a lovely dream. It will give me plenty to think about during this morning's pilates session."

"He does pilates, Jolly. That's what wealthy people do, isn't it? Marine does it, but I doubt Adrian goes to a studio. He probably has a pilates room in his apartment, don't you think, Jolly?"

Jolly tips her head back, baring her sharp teeth in a harmless hiss that Thea always takes as an agreement. Peppering kisses on Jolly's head, Thea settles the cat in her lap, only for Jolly to sink her claws into Thea's sleep shirt as she climbs back toward Thea's chest.

Hands hover back to the keyboard as Thea stares at the red brick wall in front of her window, noticing how the sliver of sunlight accentuates its texture, leaving Thea to wonder if the wall would feel as scratchy to the tips of her fingers as Adrian's stubble, stealing startled laughs from her whenever he managed to creep up behind her, dragging his chin against the nape of her neck or the slope of her shoulder.

Fingers brushing against the keyboard, Thea thinks of how Adrian would wrap his arms around her waist, pulling her against his chest, clinging to her as he smiled against her skin.

Thea smiles at the memory, wishing he didn't have to work. Wishing Adrian could just spend every day with her, making her blood warm and fuzzy as her skin tickled; much how she'd wish to touch him but felt as if they weren't close enough for such liberty.

Words slip from Thea's mind as Adrian conquers every single one of her thoughts, leaving Thea to wonder if he's already at work or if maybe Adrian is running late after pilates and showering.

Planting a foolish grin on her lips, Thea wishes she could see Adrian at work, wondering if he's more gentle with other manuscripts or if he's far more incisive, sparing no kindness to comment on things he finds moronic.

Thea smiles as she opens the shared document she has with Adrian. Reading a few of his notes on lines that he deemed to be below Thea's talent, leaving suggestions on how to rework a paragraph and somehow maintain Thea's voice, having the line exude the exact meaning she'd been aiming for but lacked the right words.

"Focus, Thea. You have a chapter to write today," Thea chides herself as strands of hair whip against her face when she shakes her head.

Reading over where she'd left off, Thea cracks her fingers, forcing her mind back into that odd space where she becomes a spectator in whatever scene unfolds before her eyes.

Only, the scene remains stagnant as Thea drums her fingers on the side of her computer, trying to think of what to write next, but words are failing her.

Evading from her mind as she tries to think of how to write a sex scene without feeling repetitive, removing the awkward interactions and forced lines that were meant to be erotic but instead had the opposite effect. Those scenes lacked the warmth and intimacy she'd feel with Aaron or Adrian, even when they hadn't slept together but had spent nights fondling.

When Adrian would patiently wait for Thea to settle her computer down, spreading his arms open as she clambered toward him, watching a smile unravel on his lips the closer she got.

Letting Thea straddle him as they held each other's gaze, trying to see who'd be the first to cave and lean in for a kiss—oddly enough, the score is tied between the two.

Thea lets the sex scene unfold akin to her memories with Adrian, lids fluttering as she writes the love interest's hand moving against the main character's waist, fingers dipping under her blouse to tease and toy with her without realizing she's the one in control.

Adrian always made Thea feel in control, knowing he'd drop his hands from her body before she needed to voice her discomfort, knowing he'd watch her through the bliss Adrian felt in seeing her body writhe for him.

So Thea allows the MMC to prowl toward the FMC until the back of her knees bumps against the edge of his bed, and she moves out of the way to let him fall on the bed while she slowly removes her clothing, savoring the way the MMC writhes in bed.

Pretending it's Adrian who curls his fingers around the luxurious duvet as his eyes move over her body, the scene moves quickly while Thea shifts in her seat. Sinking into a fantasy, Thea eternalizes within the pages of her book, hoping Adrian will never know she craves for him to touch her as the love interest touches the main character.

Wanting Adrian's fingers to brush against her inner thigh as if asking for permission, inching closer and closer to her core while maintaining eye contact. Watching how she gasps in need, the way her body clamors for him.

"Fuck," Thea mumbles as she realizes how her hands tremble and sweat clings to her skin while Jolly judges her for it. "Who writes a sex scene with a person in mind, Jolly?"

A woman in love, Jolly purrs as Thea closes her laptop, not daring to write more of the sex scene when the characters had climaxed, as she now wanted to.

"Don't be blasphemous, Jolly. I'm not in love. I may be crazy because of how often I'll talk with you, but I'm not in love. What?" Thea asks as Jolly prances toward the window, perching herself on the only spot that grants her a view of the street. "Don't act offended."

Jolly meows, ignoring Thea as her tail sweeps the dust mites accumulated on the table while Thea tiptoes toward the kitchen drawer where she keeps her toys.

Picking her only vibrator, Thea jumps in bed before shimming out of the sweatpants she'd stolen from Adrian a few nights ago when they agreed to meet at his place to work together.

Hand dropping between her legs, Thea brushes her fingers over her damp underwear as she scrolls through her phone, trying to find a single photo or video she'd taken of Adrian that she could use to lust after him.

But Adrian seems incapable of being anything less than adorable and dorky, keeping his little smirks and suggestive glances or touches for Thea's eyes only—never even daring to send her a single nude of himself when she'd send him countless of her.

Thea dips her hand under her panty, moaning as her digits touch the wetness pooling between her legs, spreading her labia before sliding a finger inside, trying to match the way Adrian touches her.

Gliding and exploring.

Reaching deeper than Thea's fingers, leaving her craving for him like Thea's never craved for anyone else to touch her.

Thea opens her phone camera, filming herself as she thinks of Adrian's lips on her shoulder, sternum, belly, and thighs—all places Adrian would kiss her as his free hand roamed her body.

Touching Thea all over, never giving her a second without feeling his touch as Adrian would curl his fingers inside of her.

"I need you in me," She moans, stroking herself as she imagines what Adrian would do beyond fingering and eating her out, wondering if he'd pull her hair, slap her ass, or what. "Need you to pull my hair as you fuck me. I'm so wet for your cock. God, Adrian, I want you so bad."

Jolly's fluffy tail tickles Thea as the cat serpentines between her ankles, softly purring until Thea picks her up, settling Jolly against her chest as she adds water to Jolly's wet food.

"You're lucky to be so cute," Thea says when Jolly meows, showing those sharp white teeth. "It grants you spoiled brat privileges, like getting me to make a soup out of your wet food."

Jolly meows once more, almost chiding Thea for criticizing her preferences in liking her kibble wet and her wet food to be more water than food.

Thea hums contently, settling the wide bowl on the table, clinging to Jolly for a few more moments as she glides toward the petite fridge in search of a can of Pepsi—the last she had in there.

Placing Jolly on the table, the cat gingerly approaches her elevated bowl, sniffing the mix as Thea taps on her phone screen.

Adrian Friedman sent you $100,000.
"One of these days, you'll get me fired for indecent exposure because of your videos."

Adrian Friedman sent you $1000.
"At least let me watch live :("

Thea doesn't answer him. Enjoying the idea of Adrian suffering for a bit, leaving him to believe she's orgasming over and over while fantasizing about him, craving for the one thing spacetime deprived her of.

Not entirely wrong, but Thea had given him two hours of her day.

"Okay, Jolly, should I edit or write?" Thea asks as Jolly shimmies closer to her bowl, tail sweeping from right to left. "Thank you, Jolly. Writing it is."

Enveloped by the soft scuffle of her neighbors walking around their apartments, of unoiled hinges moaning louder than she'd been moaning not even thirty minutes ago, Thea falls into the story.

Heart beating faster as the paragraphs duplicate quickly, Thea squeals with excitement when a line is good enough, knowing if she had the privilege to read her story through the lenses of a reader instead of its writer, she would have highlighted those lines and added a tab to the side of her book.

Thea couldn't remember the exact moment she began to look at those twenty-six letters and see vast possibilities, seeing all the words she could wield as a weapon. She couldn't remember when she fell in love with writing or creating stories or when one melded into the other and gave her something she'd cherish until her dying breath.

But Thea remembers when she'd been a little girl who'd devour books and would spend hours writing stories with her dolls—stories that'd been erased from her memory and forgotten by time.

Perhaps that's when Thea saw literature as a way to eternalize her mind. Regardless of when or how there's never been anything else Thea could give herself to wholeheartedly.

Trusting the weft of her books to catch her, envelop her, and shield her from the real world. Giving Thea a place for her to exist without fear of judgment, where she could simply state her thoughts and opinions without cushioning for the comfort of others.

An art that has given Thea so much while taking just as much from her. Yet Thea couldn't let the stories in her mind go untold or be erased from her memory and forgotten by time.

Through writing, Thea found the comfort children sought when building blanket forts, bulwarking themselves from the world.

"Thea Tea," Adrian carols through the closed door of her apartment, giving three quick raps that are a bit stronger than they usually are.

Lifting her eyes from the bright screen in front of herself, Thea finds her apartment shrouded in darkness; the heinous green light of her microwave acting as a lighthouse, guiding her to the light switch beside the door leading into the minuscule bathroom.

Adrian is leaning against her door frame, mustering his best Don Juan impression with a brow arched and a smirk adorning his lips. All of it melts into confusion as his gaze travels down her body.

"Why aren't you naked?"

"What is that?" Thea asks at the same time.

Raising a cake box and a plastic bag toward Thea's face, Adrian mutters, "Cake? Oh, and lube, I thought you weren't responding to me because you were too busy flicking the bean."

"Flicking the bean?" Thea arches a brow, fighting against the laugh lodged in her chest as she juts her chin toward his other hand. "Why are you carrying a skateboard?"

"Because I was skating?"

"Don't lie to me, Friedman."

Adrian gasps loudly, stumbling into Thea's arms, hiding his face against the crook of her neck, smiling into her warm skin when Thea wraps an arm around his waist.

"I'm wounded that you don't believe I'm a skater boy."

"Okay then, Avril Lavigne, show me."

Thea pokes his waist before Adrian rolls his shoulders as he hands her the cake box and plastic bag, standing a little taller with each step he takes back.

"Do the flip thingy, you know, when they do a little jump, and the skateboard flips over?"

"If I fail, do know it's performance anxiety, but this is the only time I'll have performance anxiety," Adrian says as he wiggles his brows suggestively, basking in the faint blush spreading over Thea's cheeks.

The board's front wheels hit the wood flooring of the hallways with a resounding thud, making Adrian cringe, glancing left and right as if waiting for a neighbor to complain about the noise.

Jolly meows, nudging herself between Thea's hands as they watch Adrian skate back and forth in the hallway—waving and blowing kisses before doing the flip thingy.

In a medley of meowing and clapping, Adrian does the trick once more, disappearing down the hallway before he skates into her apartment.

Adrian stands in front of Thea, swaying back and forth as he waits for compliments. Dark brows knit as Thea turns her back to him, placing their cake and lube on her small table.

"Well?" Adrian probes, stepping down from his board as he wraps an arm around Thea and pets a purring Jolly. "Are you proud of your skater boy?"

"I'm thinking, if I can fit ballet into my schedule, maybe we can buy Jolly a tutu skirt."

"Because she secretly wants me? Luckily, there is plenty of me to go around the Scriven girls."

"Lucky me to be stuck with you." Thea turns around in his arms, smiling as Adrian leans down to rest his forehead against hers.

"Pretty damn lucky. My mom would say you won something better than the lotto."

I'm inclined to agree, Thea thinks without daring to voice it, without daring to acknowledge the fleeting thought that makes her heart beat as quickly and contently as when immersed in a story.

"Close the door, Friedman," Thea whispers, rolling onto the tips of her toes to brush her lips against his. "We have a cake to eat."

"It's red velvet. Our favorite."

16

When Adrian asked Thea to attend some gala with him, she didn't expect Adrian would have a team of stylists and makeup artists waiting for her at his apartment on the night of the gala.

Nor did she expect to be so uncomfortable with every aspect of being dolled up—from the several hands working on her hair, adding extensions for volume and length, to how they practically fry her hair to add a slight curl to it.

Even the products layered on her skin, beginning with an esthetician pampering her skin with luxurious yet delicate procedures before handing Thea over to the makeup artist with all the talent Thea always wished she'd inherited from her mother or managed to learn from Marine.

Instead, she'd been puzzled by the entire thing. Studying herself in the mirror as the young woman added primer, foundation, concealer, powder, blush contour, bronzer, eyeshadows, eyeliner, fake lashes, mascara, and a mist making it hard to breathe.

"You seem uncomfortable," the makeup artist says. "Is there something you don't like?"

"No, no, I love it! Truly! I'm just not used to seeing myself with makeup. I wish I did, but I'm not good at it, and it's not for lack of trying."

Thea cringes at the memory of the dreadful picture she'd took of herself when she was a teenager and thought she could blend eyeshadows; years before contenting herself with mastering eyeliner.

"It's not like you need makeup. Well, no one does."

Thea arches a brow, somewhat confused as to why a makeup artist is saying something akin to writers saying people don't need books—however, people do need better books.

"Makeup is a form of art. A really good artist will use light and shadow to completely alter one's face. SFX makeup is even more of a masterful art form, and while it's something that *can* give people confidence, I don't believe people *need* makeup for them to be beautiful."

"Beauty is both objective and subjective," Thea mutters. This time, it's Aria who raises a brow at her. "What we consider beautiful is a concoction of genetic, cultural, and objective factors. In ancient days, someone being tan was a sign of poverty; now, it's a sign of luxury, making a tan something beautiful. On the other hand, symmetry is something our brains seek, therefore its something people will always find to be beautiful."

"Kinda how I find cockroaches disgusting, but my youngest sister has one as a pet?" She asks, holding a brush a few inches away from Thea's face, who tries not to laugh at the idea while nodding in agreement. "I hope this doesn't mean my work is making you feel like a roach."

"Don't twist my words," Thea argues, crossing her arms over her chest while the hair stylist finishes her hair.

Sweeping all of it to one side, allowing the big diamond earring the stylist chose for Thea to stand out—another thing that leaves her uncomfortable, although not as uncomfortable as the gigantic choker sitting in its jewelry box makes her feel.

A tiny note beside the box informs Thea of the three thousand diamonds surrounding a 21-carat green diamond, emphasizing on the rarity of green diamonds when Thea didn't even know diamonds could be anything but clear.

"Dress before the necklace and jewelry," Aria says as she notices where Thea's gaze is locked.

"I don't think I should wear that."

"Why?"

"It looks expensive. I don't like expensive things."

"It is expensive, but if you are dating someone in the Friedman clan, you should get used to it. They love spoiling the people near them."

"Stop, Aria. You'll scare her off," Giulia says, gesturing for Thea to follow her to the large mirror on the opposite side of the room, where a clothing rack holds several gowns, each longer and more elaborate than the next. Yet the one thing they have in common is they are all a variant of green or purple.

Thea smiles at that, clinging to the silk robe she's been clad in since she stepped out of the shower despite already showering in the morning.

"Does he have a preference?" Thea asks, hands touching the expensive fabric, some of which are beaded, while others maneuver the fabric to create texture.

"He does, but Adrian told us not to give suggestions or hints about what he likes. You are to pick whatever dress you feel most comfortable with."

The velvet hangers are soft beneath Thea's fingers, gliding against the steel clothing rack as her eyes imbibe in the beauty bared for her to luxuriate in.

Eyes land on a forest green dress so deep and rich in color it nearly passes for black. Picking it off the rack, Thea places the dress in front of her as she assesses the plunging slit on the right side, where the fabric gathers near where her hipbone would be.

The fabric appears almost wet in the moonlight spilling through the floor-to-ceiling windows in Adrian's bedroom, stealing Thea's breath over how such a simple design can be so elegant yet sensual.

"This one." Thea glances over her shoulder to find grins adorning the girls' lips, almost like they also yearn to see Adrian's face when his eyes fall on her.

The stylist steps forward, gesturing for the robe to come off as she unzips the dress before Thea slips inside, holding her breath and breasts as Giulia pulls the zipper up.

It's tight enough for it to slightly hurt when Thea takes a deep breath, but that ensures, no matter what, the dress won't slip down to expose her chest.

"No underwear with this one, huh," Thea murmurs as Aria approaches her with a little powder puff in hand, patting highlighter on Thea's legs as if the moisturizer she used with diamond dust didn't make her skin seem like silk already.

"I'll tell you a secret," Aria says, adding shimmer to Thea's shoulders and collarbone. "It's moments like this when I thank God for making me bisexual. Imagine looking at a beautiful woman and thinking, *'I want to be her'* instead of wishing you'd be the one fucking her at the end of the night."

"Aria!"

"What? You are too straight to understand, Giulia."

Giulia and Aria push and poke at each as they saunter back to the vanity teeming with makeup and hair products —where the hairdresser remains stone-faced while watching the girls.

"You'd be surprised by how creative these Friedman heirs can get," Giulia speaks wistfully. "Isn't that right, Aria? You have been taken to bed by one of them."

Thea raises her brow, staring at the petite woman— well, a girl, much younger than Thea herself, far too young for her not to be grossed out with Adrian if that's the Friedman she slept with.

A faint blush rises in her cheeks, speckled with soft freckles, as she says, "I love helping people, and Cove was exploring her sexuality. She didn't take me to her bed."

Keeping her gaze on the gown adorning her body, Thea doesn't notice as Giulia takes the diamond choker to her. Stealing a gasp from Thea as the cold jewelry kisses the sensitive skin of her neck, raising goosebumps down her body.

Thea gasps once more as she lifts her gaze toward her reflection, peeling back at the details of how the boning in the corset makes her waist look slim like an hourglass, how her skin shimmers elegantly, not with chunky glitter, but almost as if she'd been bathing in moonlight.

The simplicity of her gown with the breathtaking beauty of the necklace strikes a perfect balance between displaying the Friedman's wealth without making Thea look like she raided their treasury.

It all blends perfectly, but her face is the thing Thea's eyes keep going back to, wondering if she'd always been this beautiful or if it was all thanks to Aria's work.

"Put on your black heels, and you'll find Adrian in the room next door. He should be ready by now," Aria says, and Thea doesn't linger, tiptoeing to where Giulia had lined up at least twenty pairs of high heels from different designers.

Hobbling down the hallway, Thea reaches the guest room door with one shoe in hand, wearing the other as she rolls her shoulders and tips her head back before knocking on the door.

Gingerly pressing her ear to the door, Thea listens to the ruffling of clothes a moment before Adrian's muffled voice flutters toward her. "Come in," he says, and Thea doesn't wait a second longer before slipping inside.

"What are you wearing?"

Brows knitting close together, Thea's eyes glide down Adrian's body, taking in the form-fitting suit made of black and gold jacquard woven in an intricate pattern, more fitting for a grandmother's couch than a suit.

"What? You don't like it?"

"You look like a couch from the eighties. Why would you wear that?" Thea asks, biting down a laugh at the gold shirt he wears underneath the well-fitting jacket.

"Perhaps I just want you to take a seat on me, preferably on my face."

"What an enticing offer, but I'll pass. I'd hate to ruin the family heirloom."

Adrian's chuckle drifts into nothing as he raises his gaze from his suit to look at Thea, his smile falling as silver rakes over the length of her body, lingering on her exposed leg, the swell of her breast before a smile returns to his face when his eyes meet hers.

Adrian sketches a step toward Thea before halting as he takes a sharp breath. His eyes flit down her body once more, seeking the details of her beauty as if she were a mirage, wanting to be certain Thea isn't a figment of his imagination.

"What?" Thea asks, glancing down at herself. "Should I change into a different dress? I can put something else on. Maybe Giulia has a different set of jewelry."

"Don't ruin perfection."

"I think I'd need a few plastic surgeries before I'm considered perfect."

"Bullshit," Adrian says, closing the distance between himself and Thea, wanting to snake an arm an around her waist but not daring to touch her for fear of ruining perfection. "You smell good."

"Thank you. It's a dupe I bought for twenty bucks."

"Want me to buy you the original?"

"No, I want you to change suits."

"Don't I look dashing?"

Thea laughs, rolling onto the tips of her toes as she plants a kiss on his lips. Slipping past him, Thea struts toward the clothes rack beside his bed, where suits of varying shades of darkness hang.

"Should we wear matching colors?" Adrian asks, trailing behind Thea like a shadow.

Fingers glide up her spine as Adrian savors the shiver he elicits as his thumb reaches the nape of her neck. Brushing against the sensitive skin he has kissed countless times already, but it never seems to be enough.

"I like my men in black."

Adrian giggles, meeting her eyes when Thea's head lolls back against his chest. "Am I your man?"

Ignoring him, Thea picks a simple black suit and tailored pants from the clothing rack. Thrusting the items into his chest as she arches a brow as if saying, *Get naked.*

So he does.

Holding her gaze as his heinous jacket falls to the floor, Adrian works on the buttons of his gold shirt in an agonizing rhythm, each taking three beats of Thea's heart.

Her pupils grow wide.

Blood rushes to her already blushed cheeks, painting her like a porcelain doll, with bright red cheeks and lips that Adrian knows the taste of.

“Like what you see?” Adrian teases as the shirt glides down his broad shoulders, pooling around his feet as he savors the way Thea licks her lips before biting them.

Small hands brush against Adrian's defined stomach, savoring the soft ridges beneath her fingers. A stark contrast to how Aaron has sculpted his muscles after hours spent with his personal trainer in his condo's gym.

"You are beautiful," Thea murmurs, taking a step closer to kiss his chest, lips moving up to his throat as she'd been dying to do for nearly three weeks.

Days spent getting to know each other's bodies after working on her book, but Thea had been the only one getting naked—the only one to receive pleasure with Adrian's lips between her legs, riding his face as he didn't want her to ride anything else.

Thea drops her gaze, shivering as Adrian undoes the zipper of his atrocious gold pants, standing before her in nothing but white briefs. "Can I touch you?" She whispers, dipping her hand underneath the band of Adrian's underwear when he nods, sucking in a breath as her fingers curl around his shaft. "Girthy."

Adrian doesn't stop her as Thea pushes his briefs down, stroking him with a breath caught in her throat—not because it's the biggest dick she'd ever seen, nor something she'd never be able to fit inside of her without crying in pain, although Adrian would stretch her.

“Like what you see?” Adrian repeats the question, a slight quiver in his voice as Thea runs her thumb around his circumcision scar.

"Did you not hear me before?" She asks, and Adrian grunts as she squeezes him lightly before letting go. "Promise, I'll feel it when we get back from the gala?"

Adrian arches a brow at her, curious as to whether or not she's joking. He doesn't question her, watching as the pout on her lips grows with each piece of clothing he puts back on, except this time, he looks dashing.

Beautiful in the simplicity of a black suit, but beautiful, nonetheless. Thea watches as he walks to the vanity in the room, cladding his fingers in silver rings that make her smile.

"What?"

"I like your hands. They look good with rings."

"Keep the compliments up, and I'll start to think you like me, Thea Tea."

"And if I do?"

"Then I know you'll choose me," Adrian prowls toward her, weaving their hands together. "Sooner or later, you'll choose to stay with me, choose to build a life woven with mine, and you'll choose to say *I do*, for as long as you do."

"Whatever you say, Friedman."

With a parting glance at the perfectly made bed with sheets more expensive and luxurious than the presidential suite in a hotel, Thea lets Adrian lead her down the hallway with a shared sense of grief, both sighing as he guides Thea through the maze of hallways she truly despises.

Always needing Adrian beside her whenever she visited, or else she'd get lost, taking Adrian an ungodly amount of time before finding her—something that's happened a few too many times.

Aria is waiting for them in the living room, a clutch bag in hand, "You forgot your bag with your phone and ID."

"Thank you," Thea tips her head slightly, sinking her heels in the marble flooring when Adrian tries to resume their path. "Actually, can you take a photo of us? I want to send it to my mom and Marine."

"To your mom?" Adrian whispers while Thea pushes her shoulders back, laying a hand on his chest. "Your mom knows about me?"

"Doesn't your mom know about me?"

Thea tips her head to look at him, puckering her lips ever so slightly as he leans down toward her. "Of course she does. But you're the grumpy and heartless one between us. I drunk texted my mom the night I met you."

"Really?"

He nods. Both ignore Aria as they stare into each other's eyes, failing to notice she has Thea's phone pointed at them, filming the interaction. Eternalizing how they both smile with a short-lived giggle.

"What did you say?"

"That I met the woman I was going to marry."

"Did you really?"

"Cross my heart and hope to die. She then texted me, '*Addie, go back to sleep. If you think she's the woman you'll marry in the morning, then call me,*' and I called her. There wasn't much to say other than you were a grumpy brat who offered to sing me a lullaby. What did you tell your mom about me?"

"Oh, nothing much," Thea lies instead of sharing how she asked her mom how she knew her dad was the man she loved, the man she wanted to marry and have children with.

Oddly her mother had laughed before saying she asked Thea's grandma the same question, wanting someone else to tell her what she already knew to be true.

"That's disappointing."

"Find me an editor, and I promise to take you home to meet my parents, deal?"

"Deal."

"Can I take the photo, or are you not done flirting yet?" Aria jests with a grin on her lips.

"Sorry," They apologize in synchrony. A sheepish smile adorns their lips as they glance at each other when a flash startles them.

Posing for several photos, Thea and Adrian try keeping their attention on Aria while stealing glances and failing to bite down a smile until the petite girl gets tired, handing Thea her phone and clutch before she disappears down one of the many hallways in the apartment.

"We look quite good together," Adrian chimes in, peeking over her shoulder as she scrolls past the recent photos, quickly putting her phone in her bag when a nude photo comes on by accident. "That looks better."

"Shut up."

"Make me."

"Good try, trust fund baby, but I'm not smudging my lipstick. You should probably put on some shoes before we leave, no?"

Leg slung over his knee, Adrian scrolls through the photos on Thea's phone, selecting the ones he likes the most to send to himself despite knowing no part of him has the willpower to change his phone background from the photo he'd taken of her when she'd fallen asleep in his couch a few nights ago.

"If I knew you'd like the ceiling of this car so much, I would've taken you to the garage instead of my apartment," Adrian says as she keeps her gaze on the black ceiling dotted with tiny points of light—reminding Thea of Ether's reimagined night sky with shooting stars.

Thea rests her head on Adrian's shoulder, dropping a hand on his thigh, her fingers moving back and forth as she gasps at a shooting star, making Adrian chuckle against the slope of her neck.

"It's just so pretty."

"You are prettier," Adrian says nonchalantly.

"And cheaper to maintain."

"Well, I'd much rather do your maintenance."

Thea laughs as she shifts to look at him, preening at the way Adrian leans toward her to plant the faintest of kisses on her lips.

"Do you truly think I'm prettier? My brother would disagree with you. If he wasn't single, I'm pretty sure he'd trade off his girlfriend for a Phantom."

"Thank you for giving me the key to your brother's approval," Adrian teases, stealing another kiss. "Where does he live again? I'll buy him one."

"Seattle. And you aren't buying my brother a car."

"Can I give him this one and buy a new one for me?"

"Adrian," Thea whispers, leaning closer to him with a shiver running down her spine as Adrian brushes the back of his fingers on her jawline. "I have plans for this car on our way home. Would you want to be gifted a car your sister had sex in?"

His brows raise in surprise as a smirk slowly unravels on the corner of his lips. Gray eyes flit across her face in search of any sign that shows Thea is joking, but all he finds is solemn truthfulness.

"I'm so glad I called for a driver."

Thea laughs, plotting back on the black leather seat as she cuddles against Adrian, turning her attention back to the ceiling.

Searching for another falling star for her to repeat the wishes she'd been making since they got in the car—praying she can attend next year's gala with him.

"When, I mean, if we get engaged. I'll plan dinner with your family and mine, and the party gift will be cars."

"Get fucked."

Thea pulls his hand closer to her chest, fidgeting with the silver rings adorning the long pianist's fingers as she wonders how the gala will be. If people will be awfully arrogant, or if there will be judgment in their eyes as they behold her.

"Can I send myself your nudes?"

"Yeah," Thea mutters, kissing the back of his hand. "Do you truly think it's a good idea for me to be your date tonight?"

"If you don't want to attend, we'll go to a McDona—"

"No, it's not that. I'm nobody, and you are you. I don't want people judging you because they are judging me. I could pretend to be a foreigner and just nod to whatever people say?"

"Ah, but I love how rude you can be to people. It would be criminal for you to deprive me of your little feral self."

Thea bites into his hand, stealing a hearty laugh from Adrian, who pulls her closer, peppering kisses on her shoulder, soothing Thea's anxiety over the idea of making a fool out of herself, of making Adrian seem foolish for choosing her out of everyone else.

Leaning into Adrian, Thea watches the ceiling while he watches her, smiling at how her eyes widen slightly at the shooting stars flying by the lights every thirty seconds.

It doesn't take long for them to park in front of a red carpet with a few photographers waiting with their cameras ready to capture every guest.

Adrian untangles himself from Thea, leaving the car as someone opens the bulletproof doors. She watches from inside as he straightens his suit before walking around the black sedan.

Thea's heart beats faster in her chest, loud enough for her thoughts to be smothered by the blood rushing in her ears, yet she waits. Seconds stretch as Thea wonders if perhaps she should leave through the same door as Adrian or wait for someone to open the door on her side.

"Are you nervous, Thea Tea?" Adrian asks, pulling her door open before offering his hand and a crooked smile.

"Very."

Gliding out of the car, Thea stands straighter as his hand drops to the curve of her ass. "Does it help that no matter what people talk about, I'll be thinking about how beautiful you look tonight?"

"If you think I'll wear makeup every day, you are out of your mind. I can't do half of what Aria did to my face. It was exhausting trying to understand how she was changing my face with just powders and creams."

"Lucky me, I like when you are barefaced, dolled up, lying down, standing up, upside down, downside up. However, barefaced Thea lets me kiss her more often," Adrian says, effortlessly posing for the photographers. "This is just a different side of you, and all sides of you are beautiful."

Fighting against the urge to push the man back into the car that has already driven off, standing between the disorienting flashes of cameras and the steps clad in a red carpet, Thea clings to Adrian with a silent prayer on her lips, thanking whatever stroke of fate made her choose a dress without a long train as they walk up those steps without an anchor pulling her down. But Thea knows if she'd chosen a dress with an obnoxious train, Adrian would carry the skirt up the stairs.

The flashes suddenly fade to nothing, unraveling a familiar building where pale flooring and walls greet them with piano music reverberating throughout the entrance hall.

The Stephen A. Schwarzman Building of the New York Public Library, Thea muses, remembering how that'd been one of her first destinations when she had just moved to New York.

A few guests venture deeper into the building, seeking the room holding a plethora of tomes, but Adrian takes Thea to the stairs flanking both sides of the room, leading her into a darker room with murals on the walls.

"Wow," Thea gasps, leaning into Adrian's chest as he positions himself behind her in hopes of catching a glimpse of the world through her eyes, following her gaze as she tips her head to take in the murals from top to bottom, mesmerized by the art depicting the history of the written word, something that pulls on the deepest strings of her soul. It gives Thea a certainty that if past lives are real, then she'd been a writer in all of hers.

"It's funny, isn't it?" Adrian asks, running a hand over her arm while she holds onto their woven fingers. "Humans, since the very first of us, had this shared need to record life as they knew it, to find ways for future generations to understand them. Somewhere along the line, this urge evolved into mythology, into made-up stories that are somehow still rooted in their lives."

"Meaning?"

Thea whirls in his embrace, holding the lapel of his blazer as Adrian allows his hands to rake over her spine, relishing in the soft touch of Thea's gown and how she arches toward him.

"Think of writing as a painting. If you hate red with every ounce of your being, you won't use it. Except with writing, you can use the things you hate in the antagonist. What someone writes is entirely about who they are. Even if they are writing sci-fi that is out of this world, it will in one way, or another, be a snapshot of life now but woven with the things you want future generations to know, things you hope they'll learn. From the first piece of writing to the very last, that will always be the goal."

"And if it's not?"

"Then they have no business writing anything more than a grocery list. There is a reason I'm so careful with the books and writers I choose to work with. Fiction is a safe space in which writers explore reality. If in three out of three books someone is fucking a character with wings, then I wouldn't trust them with a pigeon."

"I never expected a trust fund baby to enjoy reading. Truthfully, I barely expect them to know how to read," Thea pokes fun at him, tugging his black tie until Adrian's lips are on hers. "Astonishing."

"Remind me to send a letter to my first-grade teacher. If she hadn't taught me how to read, then I wouldn't have fallen for you as quickly as I have."

Thea's smile falters.

Heart tightening with grief for Adrian, hating the uncertainty with which he is entangling himself by falling for her.

"Don't scold me," He whispers, raising a hand to cup her cheeks. "I have control over a lot of things, but my hands are tied when it comes to you."

"I don't want my life to end yours."

"Have a little faith in me, Thea Tea. I know the best of the best in this industry, and you deserve someone who is phenomenal. I'll even begin editing romances if that's what it comes down to."

Thea can see the longing in his eyes, desperately wanting to hear she is falling or has fallen in love, but she refuses to love someone if she has to leave them.

Instead of telling him the truth she has buried deep within herself, Thea kisses him without caring if her lipstick gets smudged or if Adrian's face will be red the whole night.

A hand on his tie and the other in his hair that's been brushed back with pomade, Thea sinks into the kiss, controlling everything except how Adrian presses her against the mural, his hand dipping between her legs, raising a shiver from her as the cold metal of his rings kisses her warm thighs.

Adrian's grunt at the lack of underwear makes Thea smile into the kiss. A smile that turns into a gasp as Adrian slips his fingers inside her.

"Fuck," She whispers, glancing over his shoulder to find the room blissfully empty, yet they are practically in a hallway, a passage between the staircase and the rest of the second floor. "We can't do–ah, fuck."

"Let me have you, Thea," he whispers, thumb caressing her clit as he licks his lips. "Please let me have you."

Nodding, Thea wraps her arms around his neck, letting Adrian's kisses silence her as Thea has never been very good at staying quiet when Adrian touches her.

Not when he's learned too quickly what she likes. Mastering the outline of her pleasure, in the few times, they'd been alone in the elevator carrying them to his apartment, pleasuring her before allowing Thea to see a single piece of feedback he had to give.

"I love seeing you like this," Adrian speaks against her mouth, arm snaking around her waist, holding Thea against his chest as her legs begin to tremble. "I love it, love how you want to scream my name. You might not say it, Thea, but I can see it in your eyes. You fell for me as quickly as I fell for you. You love me, don't you?"

Thea bites into his neck, jerking her hips toward his fingers, sinking him deeper without caring about where they are, certain the Pope could be in the room, and she would still want Adrian inside of her.

"I can't," She moans, sucking on his neck.

"But you already do, Thea Tea."

"I don't want to."

"I'll just have to love you for the both of us." Adrian kisses her, tasting the despair on her tongue. "Now, come for me."

Thea buries her face in his chest, practically roaring with relief as she didn't realize she'd been waiting for permission, didn't realize she'd want Adrian to dictate when she'd climax.

Unaware of the world around her, Thea only feels the kisses Adrian peppers over her face as he pulls his fingers from inside her before licking them clean.

"Dripping wet," He whispers under the sound of footsteps, thumb caressing her spine as Thea slowly descends from cloud nine, jerking as his fingers brush against her entrance once more. "Sorry, but I'm not letting that elixir go to waste."

"You can have whatever you want, Adrian Friedman. Tonight, I'm yours."

17

Through the years of working at Ether, Thea has seen a lot of drunk fools smiling ear to ear because she'd given them a free serving of french fries and some water.

Yet, she's never seen someone smile as widely and for as long as Adrian has been, sustaining a toothy grin for an hour and counting.

"You're scaring people," Thea mutters against the flute of champagne in her hand.

"Tonight you're mine," Adrian carols giddily, stealing a kiss from her before he turns to a waitress walking by with a tray full of champagne flutes.

Champagne and water are apparently the only things rich people will drink when dwelling in their wealth.

"Doesn't mean we are together."

"I know, I can go home with anyone in this library if I want, and you can go fuck your boss. Yet, you're choosing me for the night."

"Are you truly that happy over something I said because of orgasmic bliss?"

"Orgasmic bliss is something that unshackles the truth, and the truth is that you have chosen me."

"Yes, you've mentioned."

"Mentioned what?" A woman clad in a green dress asks, her blue-greenish eyes raking over Adrian's body, not failing to notice how Thea weaves her fingers through Adrian's before returning the favor.

Eyes move from the woman's blonde hair down to the silk grown that is too vibrant for a place so muted in colors —where white marble caves into a red tile border that matches the stone walls.

"Madison, please meet Thea Scriven."

"Ah, so you are Thea," The woman says with a hint of recognition in her voice. "Everyone in the office has heard a lot about you."

Her lips turn into a smirk as she assesses Thea, skipping past the choker on her neck but lingering on their hands—the way Adrian's thumb caresses her knuckles.

"From how highly Adrian has spoken of you, I expected more than an underwhelming book. Trying to fuck your way into publishing is very crass, don't you think?"

"I assure you that publishing fucked me long before Adrian ever did," Thea says, glancing at Adrian, who sustains his silly smile. "I presume you are an editor? Perhaps one responsible for all the best sellers out there?"

"Not quite," Adrian chimes in.

"That title belongs to him, at least in fantasy." There is a slight blush on her cheeks and longing in her eyes. "You should've written a fantasy or just picked someone else to —"

"Thank you for your input, Madison. When I want to hear your opinion, I'll ask for it. Until then, you can refrain from being rude to Thea."

Both women look at Adrian with their brows raised and mouths agape, except Madison blushes while Thea leans closer, resting her chin on his shoulder.

With a huff, the woman disappears through the throng of incredibly wealthy people and editors, who, except for Adrian, aren't the wealthiest of people.

"So," Thea preambles. "When was the last time you two slept together?"

"What makes you think I slept—fine, three weeks ago. Yes, I knew you already."

"Did you lead her on?"

"No. I'm always honest when I'm only interested in casual sex. As fun as it is, casual sex is nothing like being with someone you care about."

"Don't puppy love your way out of this," Thea chides as Adrian gives her the most innocent glances. "You told her you didn't want anything serious, then proceeded to blab about me? A terrible move, Friedman. Very bad. Don't you even dare blame Madison for her enmity toward me. You planted that seed."

"I see the flaws in my ways, in my defense, my work best friend kept prying information from me. She was relentless. Don't worry, she's a raging lesbian. I'm fairly certain she slept with Olivie a few months ago."

"Delightful information," Thea taunts, taking a sip of champagne. "Don't hold Madison's behavior against her. I've acted that way before, realizing that antagonizing another girl who liked the same boy as I did wouldn't make someone like me. Love isn't a battle, is it?"

"I'd fight for you."

Thea smiles, smoothing down Adrian's tie as he leans closer to steal a kiss—making Thea thankful for how long-lasting her red lipstick is when the man's been stealing kisses all night.

“Stop talking about me when you are at work and don’t be cruel to someone who likes you.”

“But it’s hard not to talk about you," Adrian pouts against her lips. "You are all I think about. It's sickening."

"Poor baby," Thea pats his cheeks, not daring to mention how hard she finds it to talk about Adrian when words fail to do him justice, leaving her in a maze of words. "I think people want me to leave you alone so they can talk to you."

"You've noticed their glances?"

"Go be your charming self while I stand here looking pretty."

"You always look pretty, and you are the charming one." Adrian deepens his pouts, resting his forehead against Thea's. "Besides, I'm shy."

"You are not shy, but how about instead of counting down to ten, you have to talk to ten people before you can find me? Tag, you're it!"

Laughter chases after Thea as she saunters away, fighting the urge to run as she used to do when playing Tag with Jules and their cousins when they would venture into the woods, using small branches as swords while pretending to be fearless warriors in some fantasy world until someone would get hurt and cry.

Cradling the flute of champagne in her hand, she roams the empty space where long oak tables usually fill the library. Thea's gaze flits over the countless books adorning the dark shelves as she seeks comfort in tomes otherwise unknown to her, many of which she’s likely to not be smart enough to fully grasp their meaning.

It's not their story that Thea finds comforting, nor is that why libraries and bookstores have such a special place in her heart, but rather the dreams they carry within their walls.

The dreams of countless authors, some of whom are far more talented than Thea will ever be, with stories crafted to perfection, while others write as if they suffer from chronic stupidity, writing pieces of literature often offensive not only by their quality but what they include in the text.

From racism and ableism to misogyny and xenophobia, the disregard for the struggles and mere existence of so many people is weaponizing books as another form of oppression. Yet great and terrible writers have managed to achieve the dream that slips between her fingers.

If the spawn of the devil could achieve their dreams, then maybe so can I, Thea muses as she sinks into the reminder libraries and bookstores carry, whispering to her that her impossible dream isn't as impossible as she believes them to be.

Thea tries to imagine the excitement of the authors whose work has taken residence within the library have felt upon learning of their success, learning their words would be printed for the world to see.

"Finally, someone who appreciates the books within the library."

Thea spins to find a woman with short hair, clad in a vibrant red gown accentuating the lean curves of her body and her arms that are muscular in a delicate way.

"Did I startle you?" The woman offers Thea a smile. "Shouldn't you be networking, miss?"

"Thea Scriven."

Thea knows she should take the opportunity to network and pitch her book to the editors in attendance, but she prefers to seek solitude over making a fool out of herself when she doesn't know who's who in a room with a CEO, editor, and personal assistant.

"You're Adrian Friedman's date, right?"

"Is that a problem? People have been glancing at me all night. At first I thought they weren't fond of me, but I'm beginning to wonder if Adrian has some dark secret I should know about."

The woman laughs, head tipping back before looping her arm through Thea's, pulling her down the hall. Her brown eyes are focused on the leather-bound books, quickly reading their titles while Thea assesses the stranger.

"No dark secret. People are just surprised, that's all. I've known Adrian my whole life, and I've only seen him date one girl. Even then, he wouldn't take her to events."

"And you are?"

"Our grandfathers were best friends who founded the company our dads inherited and built an empire together. I'm fairly certain they wanted a Ferragni child to marry a Friedman, but when you grow up together, it's hard not to see the Friedmans as siblings."

"I'm glad."

"As am I," The woman says, still not offering Thea her name. "May I have your number, Thea? The idiot forgot to send it to me."

Brows furrowed together, Thea takes the phone the woman offers with a kind smile, one that lingers as Thea creates a new contact.

"Great. Don't be surprised if I text you invitations to join family dinners. We are very loud, so take painkillers before you attend any," The woman says, slipping her phone into her clutch bag. "Can I get you another flute of champagne?"

"I'm fine."

"Please, I insist. When I'm back, I want to hear more about you."

Thea watches as the woman walks back to the center of the gala, where people are gathered to network as their boisterous laughs echo against the stone-clad walls, ignoring the most fundamental rule of a library.

Fingers brushing against the dark shelves encompassing the main hall, Thea tips her head to the ceiling with a recessed mural framed by a richly adorned crown molding in shades of gold and copper.

A world of utter beauty that is a guardian of countless other worlds, of the past and future, dreamt by writers long gone.

Thea lingers in the same spot as the soft crescendo of a violin echoes toward her, but her attention is on the mural where its details get lost in the distance.

"Mademoiselle, may I have this dance?"

A smile tugs on the edge of her lips as Adrian snakes an arm around her waist, tugging Thea toward his chest while being careful not to drop the clutch bag he'd been carrying all night for Thea—keeping the crystal etched bag under his arm.

"Claro que sí."

"You know that's Spanish, right?"

"I know. I took Spanish in High School. It's a civic duty for me to use the knowledge I gained thanks to taxpayers," Thea conspiratorially whispers as she whirls in Adrian's arms. "I don't think you had time to talk to ten people?"

"You didn't stipulate your rules, so I joined conversation in a group of ten."

"Sneaky."

"Or am I just smart?"

"I do think you are deceivingly smart."

"Are you calling me stupid?"

Thea gasps, sprawling her hands on his chest as Adrian mirrors her gasp, leaning down until his forehead is against hers. "I'd never call you stupid. You like me. That's something only smart people do."

"In that case, I'm a genius."

"The smartest."

"My dance?"

"I don't know how to dance. At least not in a pompous way, and this gala is very pompous."

Weaving their fingers together, Adrian leads Thea further down toward the main reading room. Leaving behind the throng of people clad in luxurious clothes and expensive jewelry.

The orchestra playing becomes a soft echo, the melody barely gracing their ears as Adrian pushes the petit clutch bag into his pocket before dropping into a curtsy with a kiss on the back of Thea's hand.

Cradling her hand in his, Adrian lays Thea's free hand on his shoulder before he pulls her closer, thumb caressing the slope of her back as gray eyes explore the planes of her face.

"Just follow me," Adrian whispers as he steps forward with his left foot. "Dancing is a lot like sex."

Thea snorts a laugh while keeping her eyes on their feet, watching his right foot slide sideways to the right. Her brows knit in concentration, anticipating Adrian's next move.

She mirrors his movement, moving her feet to the left as his left foot glides toward his right before stepping back with the right foot.

"How so?"

"Well," Adrian preambles, stepping back with his left foot to give Thea time to catch on to the gist, "sex is only as good as your partner's ability to move with you, as good as they trust you."

Thea tips her head back, focusing on Adrian's eyes as if she desperately needs to prove they are compatible, that they can move in tandem with each other.

"But, Thea Tea, sex is also meant to be fun. So if you misstep, I won't be turned off from dancing with you again. Step on my toes if you want, and I'll slow down so you can catch up."

"I didn't step on your toes."

"That's because I'm a really, really good dancer," He susurrus against the shell of her ear. "I know when you're about to take the wrong step. Whatever we are doing isn't a waltz, but I'll always follow your lead."

"This is very much a waltz," Thea argues, jerking her chin down to their feet. "See, I'm waltzing."

"Oh my, oh my, you are waltzing."

Thea's scowl melts into a smile when Adrian plants a petite kiss on the edge of her lips. Bringing their dance to a halt, Thea wraps her arms around his neck as Adrian peppers kisses all over her face while they sway in place, rotating ever so slowly.

"Are we still waltzing?" He quips, moving a hand down on Thea's back as he dips her toward the floor, kissing her lips to silence the yelp that rises in her throat.

"Is this what you do on a boring Thursday night? You hit a waltzing club?"

"A waltzing club?"

"Yes, instead of tight dresses, the wealthy will wear expensive clothes and pretend they are in some British noble countryside manor."

"If that's how you want our boring Thursday nights to be, then I'll set up a waltzing club. There is nothing I wouldn't do for you, Thea Tea. You are quite bewitching."

"Even murder?"

"Okay, maybe there are a few things I wouldn't do for you," Adrian says as she rests her head against his chest. "I promise to visit you in jail. I'd be very punctual for our conjugal visits."

"Wouldn't we need to get married for those?"

"You make it sound like that's supposed to be a problem when I'd marry you in a heartbeat."

"Shut up, Friedman."

"I wouldn't even get a prenup."

Thea laughs at that. Finding it incredibly annoying how often the trust fund baby makes her laugh when he's far from being funny but pries on how giddy she feels around him to make her laugh.

"Let's go find a courthouse. I could use half your money."

"All I have to my name is my salary. The black card in my dad's name."

"I guess I'll settle for your terrible jokes and boring galas."

Gasping loudly, Adrian buries his face against the crook of her neck with a fake sob. "Can we go home, Thea Tea?" Adrian asks, making Thea pull back to look at him.

"Don't you have to stay and rub elbows with more people?"

"I do, but I can't be pleasant to people when I see you wandering the library. It makes me want to scream and grab your attention, and we really shouldn't be screaming in a library."

"Let's go home then."

"I like the sound of that."

"Of what? There were four words there," Thea teases despite knowing he's clinging to the idea of her seeing his place as home—of seeing anywhere with just the two of them as home.

In long strides, Adrian practically runs across the main reading room, ignoring the few people who call his name as they wave at him, bypassing the waiters and waitresses with silver plates brimming with champagne.

Heat raises over Thea's cheeks as they walk by the woman she'd met not long ago—arching a brow at Thea before she chugs the content of one of the two flutes of champagne in her hand.

The orchestra and the soft prattle fade to nothing as Adrian takes her down to the entrance of the library, guiding Thea toward the area where a valet boy nods in recognition, not needing to walk up to them for him to find their car and driver.

Adrian lets go of her hands, smiling when her digits find their way to his waist while he slips his blazer off, tugging at his black tie.

"You are blushing."

"Well, we practically ran a marathon."

"They are fairly busy. It might take a moment," Adrian says, jerking his chin toward the valets as many luxurious cars park in front of the library.

Thea grins as he drops his blazer around her shoulders before pulling her close, cocooning Thea against the chilly breeze of night.

"We were running. I'm not cold."

"Thea Tea, please understand that you are always hot."

"Aren't you a trickster."

"Aren't you a beauty," He says, hand moving to the nape of her neck, caressing the skin that raises a shiver down her spine. "Should we go to that courthouse?"

"Is that even where people get married? Isn't that where they get divorced?"

"Frankly, if you said people only get married on Mars, I would make a few phone calls to arrange that."

Thea grimaces.

Biting at the air in front of her as a blind dog would do when someone beeps their wet snout.

"Don't be that kind of rich boy."

"What kind of rich boy? Also, I'm more of a billionaire boy. You'd be marrying into wealth."

"The kind that is like *'Mars is my amusement park,'* or the kind that would harass their secretary until the poor girl is in love because they said all the right things."

"But I do say all the right things."

"You don't. You are charming because of how bad you are at being charming."

"Ouch? Or should I thank you? I'm somewhat confused."

"Just don't act like, because you have money, you are better than people. That's a turn-off, and I'm too horny to be turned off."

"Okay, no marrying on Mars. Then where do we go?"

"How about we think about the honeymoon first?"

Adrian smiles at that.

Slithering around Thea to press his chest against her back, Adrian leans down, planting kisses from the arch of her jaw, down the slope of her shoulder, before moving back up.

"First, we'd leave from wherever we are getting married on a private jet," Adrian whispers, pressing his hips against her ass. "The crew is discreet, so they wouldn't bother us unless we wanted them to, and I'd want my wife all to myself."

"I don't know. I think I would be quite tired after a ceremony, reception, dancing."

"Shush, this is my fantasy."

"Did you really shush me?"

"I did. Now, because my beautiful wife is tired, I would naturally do all the work. I'm used to it by now—ouch," Adrian moans as Thea elbows his ribs. "I'm used to, but not tired of it. I quite enjoy pleasuring my beautiful wife. If I died between your legs, then I would greet God with a smile."

Adrian unravels his arms from around Thea, helping her down the red carpet-clad steps as his car comes up in the line.

He leaves his driver to offer the valet a bountiful tip as he opens the door for Thea before slipping inside after her. Marveling at her gasp when he presses a button and the divider glass between them and the driver turns black.

"Oh, that's fun," Thea muses, reaching for the button with an amused huff as the glass becomes transparent before returning to the privacy setting.

"It's soundproof too," Adrian chimes in, dropping a hand to her thighs. "Where were we? Ah, that's right, you'd be in my father's jet, pulling your beautiful dress down your even more beautiful body."

"I am quite beautiful. I'll give you that."

Thea slouches against the seat, spreading her legs a little bit for Adrian before she pulls away, teasing him until he's sitting in the middle of the seat, his hand firmly on her thighs.

"I'd finger you first, making you even wetter as you'd been wet the entire day. Waiting for the nuptial night but unable to touch yourself. My beautiful wife would be starving for my touch, but I would take it easy, have your legs quivering from nothing but my teasing touch."

"Then you'd eat me?"

"Then I'd eat you. Making you cum so many times you'd be painfully sensitive to my touch. So many times that if I said *'cum for me'* at any point of the night, you would climax."

"You aren't hiding that this is a fantasy, but it sounds fun."

"I could train you to do that. I read an article about this a while back. Regardless, stop messing with my fantasy," Adrian chides with faux annoyance. "Where were we?"

"How about I tell you my fantasy?" Adrian gestures for Thea to continue as his fingers caress her inner thighs. "We are leaving a gala, on a boring Thursday. Your hand is on my thigh until I move to ask you to pull down the zipper of my dress so I can breathe."

Thea swivels in her seat, waiting a few seconds as Adrian trails kisses down her spine before unzipping her dress a little, savoring the soft sigh that precedes a deep breath for the first time in hours.

"I hear him unbuckling his belt before turning back to face him," Thea says, biting her lips as Adrian obeys her fantasy. She works on the zipper of his pants before palming his bulge. "He's impressively hard, and my mouth is watering, but I also enjoy teasing him."

Thea pulls on the skirt of her dress before she kneels in her seat, stroking him through the thin layer of cloth.

"He moves to kiss me, bringing his hand between my legs," Thea whispers with a malicious smile as Adrian moves as if she'd been controlling the strings of a marionette. "He slips three fingers inside at once, just how I've told him I like, savoring the way it makes me feel so dirty."

"You aren't dirty."

"No, I'm positively slutty," Thea says, pulling his shaft from his briefs. "You know, I never had sex somewhere so expensive."

"Just wait until we get home, and I'll make sure you can never say that to anyone else."

Thea smiles against his mouth, biting down on Adrian's bottom lip before she parts her lips for his tongue, moaning as he kisses her gently while his fingers move faster inside her.

Nearly making her forget the way she'd been teasing him, stealing her focus for a moment too long.

"You'll fuck me tonight, Adrian Friedman?"

"No, I'll worship you tonight, Thea Scriven."

"I know you will," Thea whispers, rolling her hips against his fingers as she strokes him harder. "There is a reason I play with myself to the idea of you, fantasizing about telling you to fuck me because I'm yours."

"Are you really?"

Thea pulls away, bending down to his cock. She licks the crown of it, smiling at how Adrian grunts as his fingers move to bury themselves in her hair.

"You didn't answer me, Thea."

With a Cheshire smile on her lips, Thea takes him in her mouth, body trembling in doing what she'd fantasized about for so long.

Both hands around his shaft, Thea rotates her wrist as she focuses on the head. Sucking as her tongue moves around it, making sure no part of him goes untended.

"Fuck," He curses, slapping her ass. "You take me so well."

Thea grazes her teeth against his shaft as she pulls back with spit running down her chin. Her hands never stop working him, thumb teasing the head that leaks pre-cum.

"Where do you want to cum?"

Adrian brushes her hair back, thumb caressing her jaw as he pulls her into a kiss. "Your pick," He breathes between kisses. "I'll let you know when I'm close."

In a second, Thea is sucking him off again, taking him deeper as she sticks her tongue out, moving all the way to the hilt, holding him in the back of her throat until she needs air.

Adrian shifts in his seat, grabbing her ass and the headrest to keep himself from wrapping his hand around her head. Wanting her to use him however she desires, even when he wants to fuck her mouth and throat.

"Finger me," Thea orders, moaning as Adrian slides four fingers inside her, making stars appear before her eyes. "Too much. Fuck, Adrian."

"I'm sorry," He mutters as she rests her head against his chest. "I'm sorry."

"That felt good, way too good."

"I'll go slow."

"I won't," She whispers, tightening her grip around him.

The tip of Thea's tongue brushes the bit of skin on the back of his cock, a sensitive part often neglected.

Her strokes match his; the faster Adrian thrusts his fingers inside her, the faster Thea moves her tongue. Sucking him off for minutes at a time before teasing her, feeling his cock grows taunt, twitching a few times before cum paints her cheeks and chin.

Moaning, Thea strokes him, taking Adrian in her mouth as she tastes every drop of his cum. Humming at how he tastes—something salty but oddly pleasant.

In a hazy bliss, Adrian wraps his hand around her neck once more, pulling Thea toward him as she sticks her tongue out for him to see his cum dripping from her tongue.

"Swallow," he demands in a plea.

"What's the magic word?" Thea asks as she slips out of her dress, letting the beautiful gown join his blazer before she straddles him.

"Because I said so."

"Bossy."

But she does as he requested, opening her mouth when Adrian pulls her closer, licking the cum on her face before kissing her, savoring the taste of himself and Thea.

His hands rake over Thea's naked body, slowly creeping toward the diamond choker around her neck. Lips assault her feverish skin, making Thea roll her hips against his groin.

"You are phenomenal," Adrian grunts, bucking his hips as Thea positions his shaft between her slit.

"Good. I want you to be impressed after all the times you ate me out."

"The pleasure is all mine, Thea Tea."

Adrian bites down on his lip as she moves against him, teasing and pleasuring herself at the same time, head lolling back as Adrian kisses her throat to the rim of her ear.

"I want to be inside of you," Adrian moans, wondering if it's the champagne or maybe it's Thea herself that makes him brave.

"Here?"

"Right now. I need you like I never needed anyone."

Thea raises her hips, letting Adrian guide himself toward her entrance as she kisses him, pressing herself into him before she sinks onto him with a moan that reverberates through the car.

"Fuck," She curses, trembling as he stretches her. "Too girthy."

"Sorry?"

"Don't be."

Adrian moves his mouth to her breast, sucking on one while pulling on her nipple until Thea moans, but she still doesn't move.

"We can wait until we are home where we have lube?"

"No, no, I need you," Thea moans, moving up with her brows knit together. "You feel too good inside of me. I fucking need you, Adrian. I need you."

"You need me," He mutters, blowing hot air against her nipple. "Then fuck me like you belong to me."

Nodding against the crook of his neck, Thea cries out as she sinks back down, thrusting hard against him, body contorted toward his touch, wanting her skin pressed against him.

"You feel so good," He moans, a hand on her ass pushing her against him. "My beautiful, beautiful Thea. You feel so fucking good."

Thea yanks the loose tie from around his neck, lips assaulting his as she pulls his shirt open. Buttons fall onto the seat, some gliding to the floor as she rides him.

"Oh God," Thea moans, head lolling back once more as she moves faster and harder, clenching around him as he lifts his hips against her, getting deeper than he'd been before. "Oh, fuck—fuck."

"Let me see your face as you come for me."

Looking into her brown eyes that gleam with lust and something else, Adrian holds Thea, cupping her cheek as she bites down on her lips, nails sinking into his chest. Thea clings to him as Adrian unravels her, scattering her across the ether as if life as she knew ended, erasing the past and future, leaving Thea with nothing but Adrian.

"Beautiful, so beautiful," He groans, cumming inside her when he sees in her eyes what she refuses to say. "I love you too, Thea."

With Adrian still inside her, Thea cuddles against his chest, hips lazily rolling as she kisses his neck. Unbothered by the cum dripping down from her pussy, and onto the leather seats.

Unbothered by everything when she feels safe in his arms.

18

There are worse walks of shame than walking from a garage with cars that probably cost more than Thea's entire building with nothing but a blazer covering her naked body, but there is no hiding the cum dripping down her thighs.

"Are you blushing?" Adrian asks against the shell of her ear, draping an arm around her shoulder before slipping a hand under the blazer to squeeze her breast. "There is no one but us and my driver."

"And cameras."

"I'll have the footage deleted as soon as we are home."

"Still embarrassing."

Adrian chuckles as they walk into his private elevator, holding Thea, who buries her face against his chest—taking comfort in how Adrian is also disheveled with his shirt hanging open, belt abandoned in the car, and trousers unbuttoned.

"You are a cutie."

"Get fucked, Friedman."

Fingers move to the nape of her neck, coaxing Thea to raise her gaze to his. A grin blossoms on her lips as he kisses the tip of her nose.

"I thought you liked to be slutty?"

"Only when no one can see it," She argues, rolling into the tips of her toes. "I like being your slut, having you relish in the sight of my body, how you'll get hard for me, nearly losing control while still letting me have my way. I don't like being the object of someone else's fantasy, surely not a stranger."

"I love you too much. It's disproportionate for how long we've known each other."

"It's scary, isn't it?"

"The greatest things in life often are. That's why you are terrifying."

"I'm sorry," She mutters, burying her face against his chest.

Thea knows she doesn't need to say why she's sorry. Nor does she need to feel sorry about not being able to say she loves him when everything in her life is up in the air. When she doesn't want to say she loves Adrian just because he could be the spark that ignites her dreams.

"Did you know my mother is Brazilian?" Adrian blabs suddenly, breaking the silence that'd fallen over the elevator.

"Really? Does she speak Portuguese?"

"It would be odd if she didn't. Don't you think? Growing up, whenever someone was pissing her off, she'd use her favorite phrase under her breathe, *'Vai se foder seu filho de uma puta do caralho,'*[2] and people would look at her as if she was summoning Lord Lucifer himself."

"That sounds so pretty. What does it mean?" Thea weaves her fingers through his, brows knitting in confusion when Adrian's chuckle tells her he won't translate the sentence to her. "Do you have a favorite phrase?"

"Me fode."

---

2 Translation: "Go fuck yourself you fucking son of a bitch."

"What does that mean?" Thea asks just as the elevator reaches Adrian's penthouse.

The man drops his hand on her lower back, guiding her into his apartment when the elevator doors disembogue in his foyer.

Adrian watches her. Waiting for the gleam of wonder to adorn her eyes as Thea seems unable to grow tired of the view he has from the living room despite having been there many times already, spending hours working on edits while sitting in front of the large window framing the whole of Central Park.

"I love that view," Thea mutters, beelining toward that window, basking in how the city lights paint her a different kind of starry sky. "It's beautiful, isn't it?"

"It is. I have the perfect view."

Adrian meanders toward Thea, snaking an arm around her so he can see the world through her eyes—a privilege, although not quite as beautiful as seeing Thea react to the world.

"Do you think your mom would like me?"

He chuckles against the slope of her neck. "Remember that girlfriend I told you about? My mom adored her, but when she broke my heart, Mommy Friedman nearly hired a hitman. She says she loves anyone who makes me and my sisters happy, pampering them more than we would, but the opposite is also true. If there is someone we don't like, then she's unforgiving."

"Color me terrified."

"She's dying to meet you. If you think me wanting to buy your brother a car is bad, don't be surprised when she buys your parents an estate near my parents."

Thea whirls around in his arms, skin glowing faintly in a post-orgasmic gleam, tinting her cheeks pink while her lips remain slightly swollen, either from making out or sleeping against his chest.

"So your mom is like you, but on steroids?"

"No, my sisters are like me on steroids. My mom is something else. You'll love her."

"Tell me what that phrase meant," Thea points out, drawing idle patterns on Adrian's chest.

"Oh. It means *'fuck me,'* preferably now. An order and a plea woven in two short words."

A wolfish smile spreads across her lips before she slips away, stealing her clutch from Adrian's hands as she allows his blazer to fall from her shoulders.

"You are out of luck. I'm a bit sore from fucking in a car."

"Liar. You are sore because I'm *girthy*."

"Maybe I am."

"Go take a bath, Thea Tea. It should be filled by now," Adrian says, arching a brow as Thea raises hers. "What? Did you forget I'm a trust fund baby? There is an app for everything in this house. Now, go take a bath. I'll bring snacks soon."

"And water," Thea carols as she wanders down hallways that are less of a maze when it comes to knowing the path to Adrian's bedroom.

Everything else is still fairly confusing, but she blames it on how every room has the same aesthetic with pale flooring and walls to compliment the art and vases—all things that would leave Thea rich if she stole even a single relic or art piece from Adrian.

Hopefully, Adrian is the only one with access to those apps, Thea muses, waving at the cameras that capture her naked body as she prances down the mazy apartment to his bedroom.

There is a moment of surprise when she slips into his room to find the clothing rack gone and the room tidied to perfection as if there'd never been a single person inside the room since they left.

As inviting as the fluffy comforter appears, the sound of water coerces Thea toward the bathroom, where the gargantuan bathtub is filled with water with the jets keeping it warm.

Thea quickly works in adding the jasmine, mandarin orange, and Ceylon bubble bath—something Adrian had bought for her when she pointed out how most of his bath products were unscented.

Meandering toward the sink, Thea smiles at the post-it stuck on the mirror, with arrows pointing down to a whole range of skincare.

Remove your makeup!!! Follow the order from left to right!!! P.S. The first one is a cleansing oil, add water after the makeup has melted from your eyes, and you can figure out the rest.

Enjoy your sexy night, Aria.

Thea chuckles at the note, yet she absentmindedly obeys, following through the routine with little interest but trusting the girls who'd gotten her ready for the gala to get her ready to bed.

Once her skin is glistening, with all the luscious moisturizers, Thea sinks into the tub, blowing the bubbles as she sighs under the jets of water massaging her sore body.

Her lids grow heavy as the warmth envelops Thea in a cocoon of safety, working the tight muscles from wearing heels for hours on end.

In that hazy bliss, Thea doesn't think of how long it's been since she's given herself an entire day without writing, where she'd allowed herself to sleep for a few more hours in Adrian's arms before she made breakfast for them since the man couldn't use his appliances for more than boiling water.

A day when she'd eat her food slowly, stealing lazy kisses and caresses before they'd take a shower together. Somehow they later ended up on the couch, watching reality shows about people Adrian had met in real life.

"I come baring gifts," Adrian's voice startles Thea. "Did you fall asleep?"

"No?"

"So, whose snore did I hear?"

"I don't snore. You should seek medical help."

Adrian laughs, settling a change of clothes from his closet on the countertop before moving toward Thea with a bowl filled with fruit salad.

"Scoot over."

"What? Why?" Thea asks, taking the bowl from his hands, eyes focused on Adrian, who undresses in front of her with a faint blush blooming on his cheeks. "This bath is mine, Friedman."

"I know, but I would rather it not be your last one, Thea Tea. If I'm in the bath with you then you can fall asleep without drowning in bubbles."

Thea pouts with a spoon in her mouth.

Shivering as his fingers brush against the nape of her neck to unclasp the choker she'd forgotten to take off. Adrian tosses the diamonds on the floor as he joins Thea in the bath.

Wrapping an arm around her waist as he whispers, "I do love the birthday suit, Thea Tea."

"Really? I love the bubbles."

"Odd, I hate them." Adrian kisses her neck, hands cradling the edge of the tug as Thea rests her head against his shoulder. "They ruin my beautiful view."

"Have your parents ever told you to see with your eyes, not your hands? Do the opposite, Friedman."

A low chuckle reverberates against her body, making her skin tingle, and a smile blossoms as Adrian's hands glide over her body in a soft caress, causing Thea to arch against him as she eats her snack, content to end the day with Adrian.

Thea's attention shifts from the jets, focusing on the soft hand exploring her body the way one would mold clay into a sculpture, a touch both soft and firm, gentle yet precise, with every stroke.

She feels Adrian's smiling against her neck, the way his heart thrums faster with each beat against his chest, echoing through her body as if they were meant to share a heart.

"Adrian?"

"Yes, Thea Tea?"

"Can I ask you something?"

"Yes."

"Where does your fantasy end?"

"With you fully sated?"

"No," Thea chuckles, smacking his arm around her waist. "After the sex, after the countless amounts sex, where does your happily-ever-after end?"

Adrian remains silent, nibbling on her neck as he thinks about it, almost as if he'd never pondered it before meeting Thea.

"First, we are getting the fuck out of the city. Maybe the country? I want kids, not too many, but I don't want them to grow up here. I'd love to raise them in Brazil, but with business, we'd have to settle for Europe, probably England."

"When?"

"Honestly, when I was younger I thought I'd have them by now."

"You are too hot to be a dad just yet," Thea jests, craning her neck to gaze at him.

"That I am. But I want my kids to grow up somewhere with fresh air, where at night they can see the stars while rolling their eyes when I tell them about how I met their mother in a bar in Brooklyn."

"I bet she's a fantastic writer."

"The best."

Adrian heaves Thea into his arms, water spilling over the dark flooring as he carries her bridal-style toward the shower to rinse the bubbles from their skin and wash the hairspray from her hair.

Head tipped back, Thea watches as Adrian shampoos her strands, massaging her scalp while being careful not to let the water run down her face.

"And you, Thea? Does your happy ending involve children?"

"Would you hate me if it didn't?"

"I could never hate you, but I wouldn't force you to have them, nor would you force me to live without them. Sometimes your soulmate isn't the person you are meant to be with, sometimes the love of your life is just the person who teaches you what unconditional love means, not the one you build a life with."

"Three," Thea says with a shiver as the man rinses her hair, turning off the water and leaving her cold.

Dark brows knit with confusion as Adrian walks toward the change of clothes he'd brought her, taking a long fluffy towel he then wraps Thea in.

"Three what?"

"Three children. That's how many I'd like to have. That way each uncle and aunt can be someone's favorite, and we'd have thrice the babysitters."

"Wicked genius," Adrian says conspiratorially.

They walk to the vanity, where Adrian sits Thea on top of the marble countertop while he searches the cabinets for lotion—knowing Aria would scold him for not pampering her skin.

"What are you doing?"

"Just brush your teeth," Adrian mutters, triumphantly raising a bottle of lotion for Thea to see.

"I can put lotion on my own."

"Oh, I know, but you'd decide to do it in bed, and once you're in bed, you'll be knocked out."

Not bothering to argue, she raises a leg, planting her feet on his chest as Adrian spreads the pearly lotion over her wet skin.

His touch is firm, massaging her muscles while Thea tries not to moan with toothpaste in her mouth, amusing Adrian with the sight of her sitting with a towel draped over her head as she clings to it with one hand while brushing her teeth with the other.

"Do you also want to raise our three beautiful children outside of New York?"

Nodding, Thea spits the white foam, dropping one leg before raising the other to his chest. "I wouldn't even be in New York if I had been published five years ago. I love the quiet, and I hate having cockroaches as roommates."

Adrian chuckles as he quickly works the lotion on her body, pulling Thea off the vanity, and his lips find hers. Savoring the way her tongue tastes of mint while he tastes of champagne, savoring the slow and lazy kisses as he spreads the lotion across her stomach, back, and breasts.

Arms wrapped around his neck, Thea pulls Adrian down toward her while ignoring how ridiculous their reflection looks with her skin whitened by lotion and Adrian's butt naked between her legs.

"No sex tonight?" Adrian moans against her mouth.

"Just cuddles."

"Naked cuddles?"

Thea bites down on his bottom lip, pulling on it with a laugh. She doesn't answer him as she slips away from his captivity, sauntering toward the change of clothes he'd brought her with a bounce to her step, knowing gray eyes are focused on her reflection.

Venturing into his bedroom, Thea pulls on the hoodie Adrian had set aside that night as she slips under the thick blanket, trying to wait for him as her lids grow heavy with sleep.

19

Head buried in the crook of his neck, Thea drones as fingers glide lazily over her leg as Adrian tugs her closer until her body is mostly on top of him, protected from the sun streaming through the floor-to-ceiling windows.

"I could get used to this." Adrian's voice is husky with sleep. Goosebumps spread over Thea's skin as if he'd glided a cube of ice down her spine. "Is this the next step?"

"To what?"

"For you to conquer every aspect of my life? I'm already addicted to the poison of your lips. Will you make me think of you whenever I'm forced to wake up alone in bed?"

Lips peppering kisses on his neck, Thea rolls her hips against Adrian, gasping lightly as his fingers dig into her thigh with a low grunt in the back of his throat.

"Will you speak more Portuguese to me?" Thea asks as if he hadn't said anything. "I like how you sound. It's cute."

"My relatives would disagree with you," Adrian whispers as Thea sits up, pulling the blankets around her shoulders. "They tease me for my gringo accent."

"My poor Brazilian trust fund baby."

"I'm not Brazilian nor Latino. Those are titles that only apply to my mom. She nagged me endlessly about how I didn't grow up with enough aspects of Brazilian culture to consider myself Brazilian or Latino. I'm very much a white American trust fund baby."

"Thank you for the geography class. Now, the cute gringo accent?"

"*Bom dia, amorzinho da minha vida.*[3]"

Thea squeals a little, planting a kiss on his nose as she asks, "What does that mean?"

"Look it up, Thea Tea," Adrian's hands glide from her thighs to underneath the hoodie she wore to bed. "*Você já fodeu seus dedos pensando em mim? Já sentiu a sua bucetinha molhada enquanto gemia o meu nome? Emplorou por mim em um quarto vazio?*[4]"

Even though Thea doesn't understand the words, she bites her lips as she grinds against Adrian when there is no mistaking what he's thinking.

"Are you talking dirty to me in Portuguese?"

"Maybe I'm asking you a question."

"Let me answer them for you then," Thea says, pulling the hoodie over her head. Throwing the item away as Adrian's hand from her stomach to her breast. "Your voice gets deeper, more guttural when you start talking with your cock."

"Then you always know when I want you?"

"You always want me."

"Touché," Adrian says nonchalantly, sitting up as Thea lays down, allowing him to loom over her, allowing the sunlight to catch on his dark hair and light eyes. "You are addictive, Thea. I crave the taste of your lips, the sound of your laugh, and the way your eyes twinkle when you look up to find me staring. I crave the freaking echo of your

---

3 Translation: "Good morning, love of my life."

4 Translation: "Have you ever fucked your fingers when thinking about me? Ever felt your wet pussy as you moaned my name? Begged for me in an empty room?"

steps when I'm home alone, the way your skin smells, and how your hair feels on the tips of my fingers."

"Oh no, I broke you," Thea jests, wrapping her legs around Adrian's waist.

"You did, and I don't ever want to be whole again."

Adrian kisses a path from Thea's stomach to her navel. Hands move along the slope of her waist as he looms over her before Thea opens her mouth to him, welcoming him without a moment of hesitation as if she wants him as much as he wants her.

Her smaller hands find their way to his dark hair, tugging his head back as Thea moves to kiss his neck, rolling her hips against the bulge in his sweatpants.

"Break me," Thea pleas.

"I think I already did, but I'll give you time to cling to the fissures. I know you won't admit to anything until your books are on the shelf. You are afraid that your heart beats faster when you see me isn't about me but rather what I've given you so far. But all I've done is give you a chance, Thea."

Thea dips her hand between them, stroking Adrian as he shimmies out of his pants, crashing down on her as he struggles to kick them away. Adrian rolls from on top of Thea, opening a drawer on the bedside table in search of lube. Settling between Thea's legs, she watches as he pours some lube into his hand, coating himself before Thea guides him to her entrance.

"Thank you," Thea mutters in a moan as Adrian nudges at her entrance. His thumb caresses her clit as his eyes flit over her body, assessing every freckle and mole on her pale skin as if she's a puzzle he's so close to putting together. "God, you really are girthy."

"It's a blessing and a curse. I've been with girls who couldn't take me at all, girls whose pussy were deeper, and I didn't do much for them. One time, I was with a girl who didn't feel anything. Later, she told me she liked to use a dildo thicker than a soda can."

"Odd choice of dirty talk," Thea jests with a moan as Adrian thrusts into her, slow and gentle as if to not break her. "But you have the whole package. Girthy cock and length, not giant where it hurts, but big enough that we'd need to take it slow."

"All I hear is that I have the perfect cock for you."

"Circumcised too. I don't like foreskin. The first penis I ever saw was uncut, and I was far too young to see that. I was searching for different wood types for a school project, and I still don't know why there were dicks in there."

"And I'm the one with the odd choice of dirty talk?" Adrian jests as he pulls out. "Turn around, Thea. I want to fuck you from behind."

The sheets ruffle as Thea rolls in bed, arching her ass toward Adrian. A moan rises from her throat when a slap echoes against the bedroom walls. Adrian's fingers close around her waist, holding her down to the mattress as he slips inside her, groaning when Thea clenches around him with a moan. Her fingers dig into the blanket, holding on with each slow thrust.

"I love your ass," Adrian grunts with another resounding slap. *"Gostosa pra caralho.[5]"*

Thea glances at him over her shoulder, pushing herself to her elbows as Adrian pulls back inch by inch. His hand

[5] Translation: "So fucking hot."

slithers under her stomach, hoisting her toward his chest, thumb caressing her collarbone as he thrusts into her.

"Go harder. I want every step of mine to be a reminder of you."

"I love you," He groans against her lips, a hand spreading her legs wider. Fingers playing with hers as he moves faster and harder, each stroke eliciting a moan from Thea, making her squirm and pull away before sinking back onto him.

Their body contorts to each other with the sound of skin on skin, sweat beading on the nape of Thea's neck, dribbling down her spine before Adrian pushes Thea down into the mattress.

He licks her spine, grunting at the taste of her, at how she writhes beneath him, burying her face against the blankets, nails digging into his skin in a plea.

Harder.

Faster.

Deeper.

There, *right there*, her body seems to say as she clenches around Adrian.

"Fuck! You feel good, Thea," He grunts, grabbing her ass as she cries out. "God, your pussy feels amazing."

Thea can feel him twitching inside of her as he cums when his strokes halt for a few moments—seconds that drive her into near insanity before he thrusts once more, fingers moving on her clit, pushing her to climax not long after.

Her body quivers, shuddering with a wave of pleasure threatening to drown her as Adrian plants lazy kisses down her back, arching her ass up as he licks the cum dripping from inside her.

"Fuck, no," She moans, pulling away from Adrian and rolling in bed. "I worked hard for this cum."

"What?"

Adrian crawls toward Thea, pinning her hands above her head as he moves down toward her breast. She arches toward him, breath catching in her throat as her legs wrap around him once more.

"God, you are evil."

"Why?"

"I'm still trembling, and you want to fuck me again."

"In my defense, I didn't get to see your little orgasm face. You bite down your lips, furrow your brows, then open your mouth in a gasp. It's cute."

"You make an excellent case," Thea concedes. "Just be quick. I want to write today, and I can't do it if you take forever to make me cum."

With a wolfish smile on his lips, Adrian licks a path down her stomach, lifting her hips as he rests his head against her thigh. Running a finger down her slit, Adrian smiles, nibbling on her skin.

"Pink and swollen," He says with a growl. "Glistening and throbbing, I truly must have died, and this is paradise."

Before Thea can say anything, his tongue is on her, and all that escapes from her lips is a loud moan.

Feet propped on Adrian's lap, Thea reads through the chapter she'd finished editing, searching for any typos or mistakes that seem to proliferate within the pages of her book.

"Adrian?"

"Yes, Thea Tea?" He says without raising his gaze from the manuscript he reads while lazily massaging the soles of her feet.

"Will you proofread this when you are done with your chapter?"

That'd been part of their new arrangement, Thea to letting Adrian help her edit without getting in the way of his workload, not wanting him to abandon his obligations while preparing the book he sent to editors—although she doesn't know if Adrian only offered a summary or if he sent editors the earlier chapters they already worked on.

Thea reaches for her phone, finding a few email notifications about sales she doesn't care about before she finds a text from Marine.

"Aw, Jolly is having a blast in Marine's apartment," Thea mutters, raising her phone for Adrian to see a picture of the cream-furred cat pouncing for a red laser dot on Marine's apartment walls.

"You know, you can bring Jolly here when you are spending the night."

"Stop trying to steal my cat. She adores you as it is. If Jolly knew she could live a life without chasing rats and roaches, she would abandon me."

Adrian chuckles, lifting his eyes to Thea. Holding her gaze, he says in a near whisper, "I already own one pussy. Why not get the other?"

"Get fucked, Friedman."

"You need a cute nickname for me," He pouts as Thea averts her gaze back to her phone.

"Is Thea Tea supposed to be a cute nickname?"

"It is cute because you are cute."

"How is calling me tea a cute thing?"

With a sigh, Adrian tosses his tablet on the opposite side of the couch before reaching for the computer he'd given Thea, claiming it wasn't a real gift since she only used it in his apartment.

Thea spreads her legs as Adrian crawls to her, settling the computer on the floor before resting his head on her chest.

"What is tea?"

"A hot beverage? Are you having a stroke?" She jests, resting her cheek against his head as Adrian rakes a hand over her thighs.

"Shut up. Tea is hot, often too hot for one's own good, but people drink it because it's comforting, no?"

"Yes?"

"So, you are hot like tea, and I've often been graced with your taste. So, you are my own tea."

Thea laughs as she runs her fingers through his hair, relishing the way Adrian contently groans as if he's a giant lazy cat.

"You really are awful at being charming. It often makes me wonder why I like you when you are so dorky."

"It's because I'm extremely sexy. My wealth is equivalent to my sex appeal. I'm the male equivalent of a femme fatale."

"You know, a fatal man isn't nearly as appealing. Men already tend to be fatal to a lot of women," Thea mutters, a hand moving down his back. "You are sexy, but you are dorky and cute. You are a gentleman, not because you think I'm too incompetent to even wash my hair, but because you like being close to me. You'll open doors for me because you don't want my hand to leave yours. There isn't a word to describe how pure you are."

"You are good with words. Have you ever considered being a writer?"

"Maybe I should write wedding vows?"

Adrian tips his head, brushing his nose against Thea's neck as he moves to bury his face against the slope of her shoulder.

"What would you write for our vows?"

"Propose to me first, and read the chapter I wrote since you've discarded your work to cuddle me?"

"You are exploiting my sexy brain," He moans, sitting up to reach for the computer before swiveling until his back is to her chest. "At least be the big spoon for once."

Laughing, Thea sprawls her hands on his chest, planting kisses across his cheek as Adrian scrolls back to the beginning of the chapter.

Taking her hand in his, Adrian kisses the back of it while reading through her book, nibbling on it to keep himself from laughing at the love interest's lack of interest in playing the role of enemies.

"You know, St.Clair is very charming. I don't know how Cecilia managed to dislike him for so long. I'm also so glad you didn't name her something like Lizzie. I never met an author who named their character Lizzie who wasn't white and racist. Sophie too, there are plenty of names like that," He mutters before falling silent once more while reading another page. "Oh, I remember this elevator sex scene. Is that a kink of yours?"

"No comment."

"Duly noted."

"You make some odd observations, you know."

"Have you ever met a person of color whose nickname was Lizzie? Or a person of color with a friend whose nickname is Lizzie? Names tell you a lot about someone, and in books, they tell you even more about the writer. People write what they know. Someone won't write racism or misogyny into a book unless they are those things."

"It's so hot when you talk books to me," Thea's voice is a low groan, akin to the ripple in a still lake. "It's even hotter when I agree with you."

Adrian doesn't say anything as he reads more of the elevator scene with Thea biting on his ears that grow red, clearing his throat to hide the little startled yelps as the main characters have sex in the small space.

“Tell me, Ethan St.Clair, do you want me to fuck you?” Adrian reads out loud.

“Isn’t it the other way around?” Thea asks, quoting the scene she just edited to be a little dirtier.

“No, not with me. I always get what I want. Your pleasure is secondary to mine," Adrian squeals lightly, biting down on the back of Thea's hand.

"Be gentle," She whispers as she imagines what St.Clair would do. "It’s the first time a woman fucks me.”

Adrian tilts his head to look at Thea, baring the blush on his cheeks to her. "If you ever said anything like that to me, I could be half away across the world from you, and I would bust a nut so fast."

"Finish reading so we can order some Indian takeout."

"You know I could fly us to India, right?"

"Shut up, Superman."

"Not my favorite hero, but I'll take it."

Adrian pulls Thea's hand to his beating heart, grinning as she's unable to stop herself from playing with his hair and pampering him with kisses.

Yet, the man doesn't progress past the elevator scene, shifting between her legs as he rereads the scene over and over again until his phone rings.

"That's my mom's ringtone," He declares, settling the computer in front of him before reaching for his phone on the marble coffee table. "*Oi, mãezinha...*[6]"

Thea sighs as Adrian ambles down the hallway, lingering on the threshold as he glances over his shoulder, arching a brow before slapping his butt.

"His mom has her own ringtone," Thea mutters while reaching for her computer to work on the next chapter, giving Adrian double the work for when he's back. "God, I love him."

The magnitude of what she said doesn't crash down on her for a few minutes, but when it does, Thea's heart hammers against her chest. Bringing a wave of terror, a fear she's only felt when convinced the Brooklyn Bridge would be the last thing she'd see before death.

Thea leaps off the couch, petrified, as she wonders if she should leave before Adrian comes back or pretend she didn't slip up and say something she hasn't even allowed herself to confess in the deepest recess of her mind.

---

[6] Translation: "Hi, Mom..."

"Oh, this is bad," she whispers, rubbing her shaky hands over the hoodie she'd stolen from Adrian. "Oh, this is really bad."

Thea reaches for her phone, video calling the one person she always ran to in a crisis—who would calm her down when she was a little girl and had nightmares.

"Pick up, please pick up—"

"Where are you?" Jules asks, his face tinted pink by the sky in Seattle.

"A friend's house."

"Should I call the cops? Why do you look so frightened? Should I send Aaron over?"

"God no, I just missed you."

Although Thea did miss her brother, Jules sees through her lies but decides not to press for answers. His hazel eyes focus on the background surrounding Thea, his brows arching slightly.

"Is that Central Park?"

"Aaron told me you're in love. Why didn't you tell me about her?"

Heat spreads over Jules' sharp cheekbones, something many of Thea's school friends would fawn over. Lusting after her brother and his sharp jawline, *a man built on raw edges,* they used to say when Jules was anything but raw.

"She's a client, so no, I'm not in love."

"Do you blush for all your clients?"

"I do for the infuriating ones…you'd like her."

"You are in love!" Thea jests, walking toward the large window she has grown to find comfort in. "How is she? What's her name?"

Jules rolls his eyes, pushing his chair back as he walks out of his office in his apartment. "Hana Sakamoto, and she's the most beautiful woman I've ever seen, but strictly a client."

"Prettier than Taylor?"

The high school sweetheart Jules had been engaged to for a couple weeks before they both left for different colleges across the country with the promise of maintaining their relationship long distance for four years before getting married.

Within a month, the girl mistakenly sent Jules a video of her being fucked by four guys at a sorority party, claiming she was finally getting good sex after her vanilla boyfriend.

"Don't," Jules hisses, hating that part of him still loved the blonde girl, hating how, from time to time, they'd meet up and Jules would prove he'd grown in many aspects. "Taylor isn't important here."

"I like this Hana of yours. Taylor has never not been important to you. Can I meet her?"

"Don't you have work? I can buy you a plane ticket if you want to visit, but she's a client, so no, you can't meet her."

Thea pouts, allowing her brother to distract her from Adrian, from how her heart still beats too fast for a man she didn't know all that long.

"Jules?"

"Yes, little one?"

"Do you think fast love can be a long-lasting love?"

"Have you met someone?"

“Not like that.” Another lie Jules sees through but allows Thea the comfort of it. “It’s for a book.”

“I think love is kinda like a plant? Some will grow super fast, others will take longer, but whether they thrive or die is entirely dependent on how well you take care of them.”

“God, you really show you were mom’s helper in the garden. A plant nerd.”

"Did you call just to bully me? I don't appreciate my kid sister bullying me. Stop bullying me."

Thea laughs as she sits on the floor, facing Central Park, but her eyes remain on her brother as she rests her cheek against her knee.

"You seem happier than I've seen you in a long time. Work has been doing you wonders."

"Let me show you something."

Jules rolls his eyes at her, but the corner of his mouth curls into a faint sketch of a smile as they fall silent while he ambles around his apartment, tapping the screen of his phone to change the camera direction.

"Is that a dog?" Thea asks, bringing her phone closer to her face. "When did you adopt a dog?"

"I was coerced to adopt a lost Samoyed pup."

"By who?"

"A client."

Thea laughs, noticing the blush spreading over her brother's cheeks. "What their name?"

"Sana Banana."

"Like the first and last syllable of Sakamoto Hana, if we are following the Confucian family values, the same values you studied extensively for a project in high school?"

"No," Julien denies too quickly, forgetting all the training he has as a lawyer. "Sana as in Nasa backward, like the syllables flipped over?"

"Jules, you hate the cosmos. The mere idea of Black Holes sends you into anxiety overdrive."

"Why can't you believe I'm an improved man? Who is that?"

Hair whips across her face as Thea looks over her shoulder to find Adrian frozen on the threshold of his living room; a skittish smile blossoms on his face as dread tarnishes his silvery eyes.

Caught between wanting to be introduced to her brother, to gain a little more access to her life, but dreading, she doesn't want him any further into her privacy.

"That's Adrian," Thea speaks in a near whisper. "He's someone I'm scared of."

"Send me the address. I'll ask Aaron to pick you—"

"Jules, I'm fine. I'll introduce you two eventually, but right now, I want to order some Indian takeout," Thea says over her brother, hanging up on him before he can argue.

Adrian doesn't move as his gray eyes track Thea, watching as she stands up, throwing her phone on the couch before taking a step forward. She halts, tilting her head to the side as she mirrors his attentive gaze.

"Adrian?"

"Yes, Thea Tea?"

"Remember a while back when you said you could marry me because I scare you? What did you mean by that?" She asks, curious as to why he fears her when she knows why she's scared of him.

Scared of how quickly her heart beats when he walks into the same room as her, how her eyes drift toward him only to find him stealing glances at her, scared of how she shouldn't care for him as much as she does when there is so much she doesn't know about him, but that only makes her all the more curious.

Thea is scared of how quickly she's falling.

Plummeting into a new unknown when she's already lost in a desert of impossible possibilities, lost for so long that she fears Adrian is nothing but a mirage.

"I'm scared of not being a man worthy of you, and not in a *'you make me a better man'* kind of way, but rather you believe in a narrative you created, one that will never fit who I am. This is something I've seen happening far too often, and I'm afraid you only lo—like the idea of me, preferring fantasy over the real me."

Thea's lips part as if she's about to say something, but no words come out as Adrian ambles toward her, slipping his phone into the pocket of his sweatpants.

"You are the best thing that has ever happened to me, Thea. There isn't a day I'm not in awe of how spectacular you are, and I see the real you, the things you wish I didn't, and I love you more than I could love any fantasy. So I'm afraid because if there is one thing you're certain of, it's your worth. That's why you gave yourself five years instead of giving up."

"Better than a $333 million penthouse?" Thea jests as her feet drag against the floor, carrying her to him, but Adrian meets her halfway as he'd always done.

Tucking a strand of hair behind her ear, Adrian chuckles lightly, a sound that fails to convey just how profoundly happy Thea makes him.

"You mean the $333 million penthouse where my mom saw a naked girl walking down its hallways and called me angry because she didn't know if it was the same girl I've been babbling about?"

"Oh no, she didn't? She saw me naked?"

"She said you have a beautiful body, although your hips could be wider for childbirth."

"Oh no," Thea echoes, wrapping her arms around Adrian's neck.

"She wants to meet you," Adrian heaves Thea, wrapping her legs around his waist. "She demanded I take you home this weekend, but don't worry I said the family can meet you when you are ready to meet them. Oh, and I asked her to log out from the security system."

"Does the bedroom have cameras?"

"Just the hallways. That's where the valuable items are all located. Everything else is something easy to replace."

"Like that fifty thousand dollar couch?"

"Rich people are a different kind of varmint," Adrian spins as if they'd been dancing to no melody. "Now, what do you want to order?"

"Samosas, Chicken Tikka Masala, biryani, and pork Vindaloo. Oh, and naan, make sure there is naan."

Adrian throws Thea on the couch, smiling as her laugh grows louder when he lays on top of her, hands prodding her ticklish waist while he grazes his unshaven face against the slope of her shoulder.

"I love a hungry lady."

"Shut up, Friedman. You haven't fed me since we woke up because you don't know how to turn on your stovetop."

Adrian sits up between her legs, hands raking over her thighs as he looms over Thea—the tips of their noses touching each other.

"You didn't know how to turn it on either."

"It's not my appliance to know how to use. Besides, I'm not touching a single thing that kitchen of yours. It's more expensive than my childhood home."

"You seem to keep forgetting you're dating a billionaire. There is no such thing as *mine.* You don't even need to make me your wifey for my money to be yours," Adrian argues, fishing his phone from his pocket before handing it to Thea, who raises a brow. "Text the concierge what you want. He'll handle it while I read your masterpiece."

"You know we aren't dating, right?"

"Then what are we doing? I've made you cum three times just today. I washed your hair and—"

"We are in an editor and writer relationship."

Adrian chuckles as he settles against Thea, pulling her hand to his chest as he picks up her computer, finally scrolling past the elevator scene.

"I don't remember fucking and taking any writer of mine to a gala," Adrian mutters, peppering kisses on the back of her hand.

"I'm keeping up with our bargain. The day my book is released, you'll take me on a date. Until then, we are not in a relationship."

"So, I can fuck Maddie if I want to?"

"That's usually what being a free man entitles. You can stick your meat in whatever hole that will accept you with enthusiastic consent."

"Every hole accepts me with enthusiastic consent. It's a glorious meat, but can we stop calling my dick meat?"

"What should we call it? Mozzarella sticks because those are also made from milk?" Thea jests, nibbling on his ear. "Banana split because there are two balls of ice? Breakfast because you get sausage and eggs? Birdie because you have a nice peacock?"

"You are dreadful, but sword of thunder has a nice ring to it, and I make you quiver beneath me."

Thea's laugh rises and billows in the openness of the room, resounding against all the marble surrounding them, stealing a smile from Adrian as he pretends to be oblivious to what's so funny.

"You could've said it's because you bring the thunderclap?"

"Please, we are discussing my penis, not my balls clapping for you."

"Adrian!" Thea yelps in a fit of laughter. "You are disgusting, Friedman."

"Can we settle on gigantic? No gargantuan penis?"

"No, I'll stick to Alexander the Great because you've conquered my body," Thea whispers against his ear, hand trailing down his chest, creeping dangerously near the band of his sweatpants. "I think I'm due for a history lesson, don't you think?"

20

The heat of Ether's kitchen shifts into the cool kiss of the night as Thea slips past in the direction of the back door, where the rats scurry away to the sound of her boots thumbing against the concrete ground.

Her hands wander to the pockets of her apron, reaching for her phone with a smile on her face as she reads the notification on her screen—where the Brooklyn Bridge crumbles into a photo of her and Adrian cuddled in his bed.

Adrian Friedman sent you $1000.

"I miss you :(Are you sure you can't come home tonight? I can pick up Jolly from Marine and we could go to your place together?"

You sent Adrian Friedman $1

"No can do, trust fund baby. I miss sleeping in my own bed."

A lie, but one she intended on telling until she had to work at Ether upon Isa's request for her to cover the shift of a coworker who'd gotten sick. Only when Thea had walked into Ether and Aaron hadn't deigned to look at her that she remembers the night she spent eating Indian takeout with Adrian was also the night she was supposed to meet Aaron for dinner so he could update her on the renovations.

Except she'd forgotten. Leaving Aaron to wait for her in the restaurant before he went to her apartment, knocking on her door only for him to have no answer, for his texts and phone calls to fall to voicemail as Thea ignored her phone to favor running her hands through Adrian's hair.

Adrian Friedman sent you $1000.

"Cruel woman! My bed is infinitely comfier than yours, and you have me to wash your body. Zero effort on your end. I can even send you my driver."

You sent Adrian Friedman $1

"You have plenty of photos of me, you won't miss me too much, and I left you a T-shirt so you can still smell me."

Thea perches herself against the crates loitering the alley, peeling her gaze away from her phone to look down the alley where the bright headlines cast a yellowy light against the red brick wall, echoing the voices of people meandering home from work—maybe going over to visit a friend or a lover.

Raising a little inkling of envy in the pit of her stomach, wishing she could be cruising on Brooklyn Bridge to meet Adrian when being in his arms makes it so easy for Thea to ignore the time ticking and cling to hope for what the stars have written for a future that, for the first time in years, isn't daunting.

But hope is a funny thing. It will blossom and wither from nothing, capable of surviving under cruel conditions, yet at times it will crumble and slip from her grasp when everything seems to be well.

With a sigh, Thea turns her gaze toward the night sky. Pretending the airplane or helicopter flying above the city's skyline is a shooting star as she hopes for more days with Adrian, even when a part of her will always keep hope at arm's length.

Not allowing herself to daydream past the slim possibility of being published when Grim the Reaper is counting down the days before knocking at her door, demanding what she promised.

It seems cruel that she might have only five months with Adrian when she had four years with Aaron, something that borders on sacrilegious.

Thea mulls over how to let Aaron go gently. How she can part ways with a man she loves but has never been in love with, never felt the same peace with Aaron as she feels with Adrian.

"Maybe I don't love Adrian either," Thea murmurs under her breath, feeling the weight of that lie as she knows that Adrian being a beacon of hope isn't the reason she loves his company, why she feels so blissfully content to have someone so interested in everything about her.

Adrian feels like a breath of air for someone who'd been drowning in sorrow for too long.

Phone vibrating in her hand, Thea glances down with a sigh on her lips that quickly melts into a smile as she reads the notification.

Adrian Friedman sent you $1000.

"Break is over, Thea Tea. Time to take your glorious booty back to work. P.S. I still miss you and I have news to share. You might want to see me tonight."

Not bothering to text back, Thea drags her feet over the concrete, slipping back into the heat of Ether, where the kitchen staff bellows as if they'd been cooking with the Great Wall of China separating them.

It always amazed Thea how hearing loss after spending years in noisy kitchens isn't more common amongst retired restaurant staff.

"Thea, table fourteen."

She falls into the routine of piling plates on a tray, amazed by how the dishes served in the restaurant weigh less, yet Thea has no urge to steal anything on the plates despite knowing it'd be an orgasmic experience—she'd much rather steal french fries than Beluga caviar.

There is just something comforting about the simplicity of deep-fried food and how melted cheese becomes stringy in a bite of pizza.

Perhaps that's why there are more patrons found laughing loudly in a bar with deep-fried delicacies than from patrons relishing in fine dining.

Thea ambles down the elegant parlor of the restaurant, sustaining a meek smile that goes unnoticed by patrons whose arrogance is exponential to the number of zeros in their bank account, acting as if their wealth somehow elevates them closer to the God they worship. Something they must have learned from the Catholic Church, one of the wealthiest institutions whose alleged purpose is to spread righteousness, justice, and peace, yet the scandals involving priests seem to be swept under the rug with the same quickness as one will buy art for a better tax return.

Thea places the plates in front of the patrons decked with expensive watches and suits that would probably be laughably cheap in Adrian's world but impossibly unattainable for Thea.

"We'll take your finest wine," A bald man with a slightly crooked nose says.

Thea lingers for a moment, waiting for any of the four men sitting around the table to say either *please* or *thank you*, lingering there until it becomes clear she's more likely to be struck by lightning and win the lotto than for any of the patrons to offer common courtesy.

Boots dragging against floors polished to perfection, Thea ambles toward the restaurant's bar—which is smaller, but it holds bottles of wine that cost a few hundred.

"Table fourteen wants the best wine someone with a twelve dollar watch can buy," Thea tells the barkeep, whom she didn't know the name of—she'd never been good at remembering the restaurant staff.

"Not a very good wine."

"It surely can't be better than five dollar wine," Thea bemoans, resting her chin under the lip of the silver tray. "What?"

"Nothing. I don't expect you to respect the craft of vinification after the shit you pulled with Mr. Mariani."

"And what shit would that be?"

Thea arches a brow, standing straighter as she holds the man's gaze. A corrosive smirk forms on the edge of his lips, his blue eyes glimmering with poison, yet he remains silent.

"That wasn't a rhetorical question. I'm waiting for an answer."

"You fucked him for years, getting him wrapped around your fingers, in a literal sense too, while claiming you want to keep your relationship a secret despite it being obvious. Then when you have enough of sneaking around, enough of leading him on, you decide it's time to share the news with the staff, and not even a week later you ditch him? That's the—"

"That's enough," Aaron's voice raises over them, sending a chill down Thea's spine as it's the first time he's spoken to her in a long time. "Noah, your job here is to be a sommelier, not tend to my personal life. Go do your job and fetch table fourteen's wine."

Thea slowly turns to face Aaron, sucking in a breath as she'd nearly forgotten how beautiful the man is, how electrifying his gaze is.

Making her skin tingle as green eyes rake down her body, igniting a fire deep within her belly with the way Aaron tilts his head as if appraising a prey he knows he'll chase after and conquer.

"I missed you," Thea whispers.

"Did you?"

"Yes."

"It didn't seem like it when I waited for you outside a restaurant like a damn fool or when I went to your apartment believing something bad happened to you. I had your landlord come over to open your door only to find your apartment empty. Not even Jolly was there. Did you miss me when I called you? When I texted you worried? Fuck Thea, I only learned where you were from Marine, and then it all made sense."

"I'm sorry."

"We'll talk later. I've asked Isa to take over for the night. Your place or mine?"

"Yours." Thea takes a step closer, wanting to weave her fingers through his but knowing she'd only hurt him further. "I'm so sorry. I didn't mean to hurt you."

"Yet, you did."

Aaron leads Thea toward the back of Ether, waiting for her to place her tray amongst the pile left unused for the night. He lingers in the busy kitchen as Thea ventures into the locker room with her heart thundering in her chest, conflicted between the way Aaron has always made her feel, the life she once envisioned with him, and the one she craves now.

Apron hung on her locker and phone in the bottom of her bag, Thea takes languid steps back toward Aaron, following him to Ether's backdoor as her fingers itch for his hand, but the man trudges ahead.

Thea watches his back, letting Aaron maintain whatever distance he wants from her as she can see the muscles in his back growing taut with every piece of emotional armor he clads himself with to guard the heart he knows Thea will break.

The world seems to hold its breath as the usually busy streets surrounding Ether are vacant, the cars being far between. Even the trash usually littering the sidewalk is gone, allowing more room for the few people walking with their eyes focused on their phones.

For the first time in a long time, Thea pays attention to the people around her, the way their gazes are glassy as if functioning on autopilot, and how the smiles of people sitting near the windows of bars and restaurants don't reach their eyes.

The curl on their lips is fleeting like a dandelion in blustering winds—a smile that isn't the pinnacle of joy but a facade of contempt.

Something Thea had seen on her face for many years, yet she couldn't remember the last time a factitious smile graced the curve of her lips, and Thea knows the reason for it is the same person she wished was waiting for her in the lobby of Aaron's apartment.

The palms of Thea's hands grow sweaty as his building comes into view. The cool LED light in the lobby drizzles over the sidewalks, illuminating the specks of sand in the concrete slabs.

Lingering a few steps behind Aaron, Thea watches as his lustrous shoes tap rhythmically against the flooring as Aaron holds his head high, rolling his shoulders and curling his fingers into a fist that bleaches his knuckles, yet all it truly achieves is transpiring his pain for anyone who cares to see it.

Thea hears the slight shift in the air, the faint metallic sound of the elevator motor that announces itself a few moments before the door slides open. Aaron plants his hand on the small of her back, coaxing her to step into the elevator before him.

Her eyes fixate on the numbers growing from zero to fifteen. They move undisrupted, zooming floor after floor without a single person to dampen their progress, to give Thea a moment to organize thoughts pelting down.

"Aaron?" Thea calls for him as the elevator reaches the penthouse, doors sliding open.

The man marches to his front door, typing a new password on his digital lock. Aaron doesn't hold the door open for Thea as he slips inside his apartment, dropping his blazer on the back of a leather armchair.

"Yes," His voice is curt, not carrying the inflection of a question but sounding more like a demand.

Thea watches as Aaron trudges to the kitchen, opening a cabinet door in search of glass before reaching for a bottle of bourbon.

He pours the amber liquid without looking at her, without arching a brow as she approaches him while keeping the island between them, almost as if Aaron is a caged animal—one she needs to keep her distance from, but perhaps she's the danger, not him.

"Aaron, you know, don't you?" Her voice is nothing but a whisper.

"That we won't ever be together? I suspected as such."

"You know that I love you, don't you?"

"But you aren't in love with me."

"I'm not in love with anyone."

Aaron's laugh is bitter, evoking a burn in her throat as if she'd been the one drinking the bourbon as if she was the one whose heart was breaking.

"Don't fucking lie to me, Thea. I saw you falling for him. You'd lay your head on my chest, playing with my fingers as you thought about him. I've wrestled for your attention since the first time he sent you a text. I'd know he was texting you because you'd smile in a way I've never made you smile. You fell in love with a man you've known for weeks while I lived in the shadows of your affection for years," His voice raises at that, not quite a shout, but enough to bring tears to her eyes. "I carved a space in your heart, and he earned the love I fought so hard to gain."

"I do love you."

"Spare me of the fucking bullshit, Thea. All I ever was to you was someone to fuck, and pity sex is the last thing I wanted from you."

"That's not true," She argues, reaching out for him, but Aaron pulls his hand away when the tips of her fingers touch him. "I've loved you for a long time, and I thought I'd been in love with you for equally as long."

"Great, at least I'm not the only one you fooled, nor do I think I'll be the last. From rich boy to billionaire, what's next, Thea? Who else will you fuck before breaking another man's heart?"

"What?" Thea hisses, hand slipping into her bag, brushing against her hand sanitizer, keys, and the packet of polaroid pictures Adrian gave her of them at the gala before her fingers reach her phone.

Aaron watches as she proffers the phone to him. "What am I supposed to do with your phone?"

"Take it. If you think I've fucked you for your money, take your goddamn phone back."

"That's not what—"

"If you think I'm a fucking whore, then you are not the man I thought you were," Thea speaks over him as her body trembles with anger and hurt. "I know, I'm breaking your heart, and I am sorry. I'm so incredibly sorry Aaron, but being heartbroken doesn't give you the right to act like a fucking asshole."

"Getting on your knees a lot doesn't make you a fucking saint, Thea."

Staggering back as if he'd hit her, Thea watches as regret cloaks Aaron's anger, smothering the man as a pained sound bubbles past his lips.

"Congratulations, Aaron Mariani. You just proved why Jules never wanted me to be near you. Next time a woman is on her knees for you, remember that you're no God. You don't get to make judgments on others."

"Thea, I didn't mean to say that."

Raising a shaky hand between them, Thea walks away from the kitchen island, her phone left behind as her steps echo against the tall ceiling.

The street light pouring through the giant windows becomes hazy as tears line her eyes, and her heart tightens as she feels like she's disappointing everyone.

From Aaron and Jules, down to herself as if she should've known better than to love Aaron, better than to fall for Adrian when she could've stuck with Aaron.

"Thea, please, please don't go?"

"I don't care how much I love you, because I do love you, but I'll never allow a single person to talk to me that way," Her voice is carefully stripped of emotions, making it hard for her to breathe through the sorrow lodged in her throat. "No matter who, I'll always choose myself, and maybe that makes me evil, but it's better to be the devil than be walked over. Good night, Aaron."

Thea doesn't let the tears fall as she walks out of his apartment, letting the door close behind her as she bites on her tongue while pressing the elevator button several times, tasting copper long before the elevator skids open.

Every fiber in her body is clamoring for her to run out of the building, to disappear into the night before allowing herself to shed the tears lining her eyes.

Thea jolts against the telltale sound of glass shattering against the wall, and a pained cry echoes down the darkened hallway.

She listens to the havoc in his apartment while waiting for the elevator, knowing Aaron would never chase something he knew he couldn't have, that was the first lesson his father ingrained in him, but perhaps Aaron also knew Thea would never speak a word to change his mind about her actions.

Nor would Thea ever listen to someone shame her for her freedom.

21

"Thea Tea," Adrian's voice is cheery as he ambles down the hallway to greet her in the elevator, but his joy melts into worry as he sees the redness in her eyes. "What happened? Why are you crying?"

"I need a new phone."

Adrian's brows knit in confusion as he pulls Thea into his arms; a hand moves to the nape of her neck while the other lies on the small of her back, holding her close as sobs wreck through her body.

"Please don't cry, Thea Tea. It breaks my heart," He mutters, planting a kiss on her temple. "I'll have Josh go buy you a new one."

"Who is Josh?"

"The concierge?"

"Your concierge is named Josh? That's such a young-sounding name," Thea speaks between sobs, quivering in Adrian's arms. "And I don't want you to buy me a phone."

Adrian sweeps Thea into his arms, carrying her from the elevator down the hallway that leads to the staircase descending into the living room Thea enjoyed the most—feeling more comfortable laying there than on Italian leather.

"Josh is a young guy. Were you expecting his name to be something like Alfred?" Adrian murmurs against her temple as he sits on the shearling couch. "I'll buy you a new one. They are really cheap, and you said you need one."

Thea pulls back with a sniff as her hands move toward the neckline of his nondescript T-shirt that looks like something she could pick up from a mall. In reality, every clothing piece in Adrian's closet is custom-made by an Italian tailor—each piece costs more than a new phone.

"I don't want you to think I'm a whore." Thea's lips quiver with each word she speaks as tears dampen her skin. "I'm not a whore. Well, I am if you think a whore is someone who enjoys sex, but I don't want to get paid for it. I couldn't handle selling something else I love, whoring my books is already painful enough."

"I'm so entirely confused right now, but I could probably get away with murder if you'd like me to. You'd be surprised how good of a lawyer money can buy."

Adrian runs his thumb over her cheeks, wiping the tears that still fall as she tries not to grin through her pouty lips.

"You have snot running down your nose, and I'm still in awe of how beautiful you are. If there is a whore in this strictly professional relationship, I'm truly the biggest whore for you."

"Shut up."

"Make me."

"As you said, I have snot running down my nose," Thea protests as her loud sniff morphs into a shriek when Adrian wipes her nose before cleaning his hands in his sweatpants. "Gross."

"I can throw them in the washer." He shrugs, puckering his lips in a silent demand—one Thea is happy to comply as she leans closer to give him a small, quick kiss. "Tell me what happened, so I know why I'm going to jail. Who was the imbecile who made you cry?"

"The list is quite long, but it's only one name tonight."

"Aaron?"

Thea nods as tears well in her eyes once more. She leans into the hand, cupping her cheek, shivering as Adrian brushes a strand of hair behind her ear.

"Did he touch you?"

"No, he would never. Quite the opposite. He wouldn't even let me touch him."

"But he called you a whore?"

Nodding once more, Thea buries her face against the crook of his neck, trembling against his chest as she tries not to cry.

"Was it because of me?" Adrian asks, but Thea doesn't say or do anything, allowing the silence to prolong as he runs his fingers down her spine. "Do you want me to distract you?"

"Please."

"Well, today at work we received a survey about the reading comprehension level in the US. Apparently, fifty-four percent of adults from ages sixteen to seventy-four lack proficiency in literacy, having worse reading comprehension than a sixth grader. Even if those numbers were only for people with learning disabilities, it would still be ridiculous that they aren't receiving the right tools to achieve the same outcome when they are more than capable. Which several geniuses prove that to be true."

Thea pulls back, looking at Adrian with her brows furrowed and the corner of her lips twisted in a snarl. "Are you serious? People can't have worse reading skills than a twelve-year-old."

"Give or take, about 104.67 million people do."

There is a slight inflection to Adrian's voice, making his words sound like a question, an estimation when he ran the numbers of the US population in those age brackets compared to the sale records of bestsellers.

"That's why we have bestselling books with lines about being prepared to be cremated for playing with fire and about concrete being stiffer than usual. Thea, it's concrete, that's the opposite of pliable; it doesn't change forms. The definition is in the word itself. It can't be stiffer; it has one state of being. If someone fucks up using the word concrete, I'm forced to ponder if they ever had a single thought in their head."

"What are you hinting at, trust fund baby?"

"I'm saying that besides the never-ending misogyny, racism, xenophobia, and oddly zoophilia, present in books, this industry is, for the most part, publishing books fit for a person whose reading comprehension is worse than that of a pre-teen, and those books become bestsellers when they should have never been acquired in the first place. This industry and its readers are not how one should judge talent because more likely than not, you're writing books an eleven-year-old couldn't begin to grasp. So, you either dumb down your writing or pray the education system gets better."

"Harsh criticism you have of an industry you are the heir for," Thea reminds him of the obvious—something Adrian often tries to forget.

"There is a reason I went on to become an editor for a competitor instead of taking a role in my father's company. Editors are, in a philosophical way, the guardians of quality, yet we are also the people allowing authors like the strikethrough author to be published, picking the incredibly bad stories and terribly written books among fantastic novels."

Thea cuddles against Adrian, moving her legs from wrapped around him, laying her head on his chest with her knees brought to her chest while Adrian keeps a hand on her butt and the other on her thighs.

She listens to him, clinging to his words as much as she savors the steady beat of his heart, each of them reminding Thea she's safe.

"A lot of people are leaving publishing because there isn't much prospect of advancing in their careers, but by allowing these sixth grade level books to exist in the world, and readers to buy them, it tells the higher-ups there is no value to what editors do, no reason to invest in an editor's talent when any half-assed book published six years ago can still sell 768,700 copies. It's a vicious cycle of mediocrity, and the bestseller list is often a reflection of how bad writing has become and how little publishing cares because there is still a profit in those books that an eleven-year-old could've written."

"I'm so confused by this conversation."

"I'll take confusion over sadness," Adrian says, stealing a kiss as he holds her closer. "It's frustrating to see literature diminish to this. In the fifty books I've read this year, I couldn't find anything other than a level of entertainment I can get from scrolling through social media, and I don't even like social media. Books should make us think, make us reevaluate our life based on what we read. Instead, you'll see people claiming they write empowered female characters when they are truly writing sex dolls with a heartbeat, perpetuating the idea that a woman should live in the shadows of men."

"Like you and I?"

"You don't live in my shadows."

"You're a billionaire, Adrian. That's a *'pretty big'* shadow to overcome." Adrian lays his hand under her chin, tipping it back so her eyes meet his. "What? You can't say I'm wrong."

"But you are. Everyone in that gala was curious about you. Not a single question they asked me were about me or work. Besides, when you become a worldwide bestseller, which will be happening soon, people will search your name, curious about your age, where you were born, and your spouse."

"I'm married now?"

"Not right now, but you'll marry me eventually. You are falling for me, Thea Scriven," Adrian speaks in a near whisper, planting a kiss on the tip of her nose with a broken heart over how red her eyes still are. "Regardless, when they see my name there, they won't go 'oh, the billionaire boy,' they'll be flabbergasted about how mundane I am compared to you."

"They'll surely say I'm too pretty for you."

"It would be criminal if they didn't. You are utterly beautiful, far smarter than me, and infinitely more passionate than anyone I've ever met. It breaks my heart that literature means so little to so many when it means so much to us."

"Yet, none of that has been enough so far."

"You chose an industry where nepotism runs wild, Thea Tea. If you don't have a friend who knows an agent, it makes life that much harder. I've asked many agents I know about how much time they'll spend on a query. At best, they'll deploy ten minutes for something you've dedicated months or years to, ten minutes to read the blurb, bio, and the first three chapters of a book. So many hit rejection based on the bio alone, on a name sounding too foreign, but will deny and claim they want diversity in their client list of fifty shades of white."

"So you hate agents?"

"No, they make my job easier, and they fight for writers' rights, but that doesn't mean they are always fighting for the right people. Everyone wants authors to be paid fairly. Personally, I don't want to work with a racist or someone whose work belittles women, whose work romanticizes abuse, not only physical but emotional abuse. That's why I like your work and why I love you."

"You don't love me. You barely know me."

"I do love you. The only thing you could do to change that is if you participated in an anthology to raise money for a cause when in reality it's just a publicity stunt, a way to get those other authors' readers to read your work. That's a very lowly thing to do, don't you think? That might be the only thing that would make me ask for a divorce."

"You are so opinionated, Adrian Friedman."

"That's how you know you are damn good, Thea Tea. You survived all of my layers of criticism. The only critic I have is over your—never mind."

"My ex-boss-friend?"

Adrian throws Thea on the empty side of the couch before he stands up while she pouts with her brows furrowed—cushions dipping beneath her knees and the palm of her hands as she moves toward him.

"God, you are cute," Adrian lays his fingers underneath her chin, thumb caressing her jawline as his eyes sparkle with pride. "You'll be proud of me."

"Why?"

"I had Dev teach me how to use every appliance in my kitchen."

Thea smiles at him, certain every kiss and caress since Josh, the concierge, called to inform Adrian she was going up to the penthouse to ease the sadness lingering in her heart.

"Show me. I won't believe you until I see you fry an egg." Thea stands up on his couch, gesturing for Adrian to turn around before she wraps her arms and legs around him. "Piggyback me to the kitchen."

Adjusting how she sits on his back, Adrian does a little jump, and Thea squeals loudly, tightening her hold around his neck as she buries her face in the crook of it.

Keeping his hands on her thighs, Adrian does another little jump, laughing as she squeals once more before slapping his chest.

"I'm not going to drop you, Thea Tea. I'm never letting you down," Adrian says, doing a third jump that steals yet another yelp from her. "See? You aren't going anywhere."

"Adrian?"

"Yes?"

"Stop stalling. I want to see you start a grease fire in your million-dollar kitchen."

"Blasphemy," Adrian declares as he trudges ahead, taking thunderous steps that steal giggles from Thea.

In retaliation to his antics, Thea blows air against his ear. Making Adrian curl away from her with a shriek that melds into the sound of her laugh as he lets go of her legs, swaying his body as she clings to him, legs dangling in the air as Thea chokes Adrian.

"Come here, you little devil," He wheezes, catching her legs and holding them close to his chest as her breathy laugh makes him smile like a fool.

"No! Oh god, I'm going to fall!"

Her voice echoes against the empty hallway, reverberating on the stone flooring and the walls clad in paintings.

"Adrian, please."

Without a moment of hesitation, he lets go of Thea's legs, crouching a little before spinning around when her arms unravel from around his neck.

Gray eyes track the ruddy glow in her cheeks, the way her lips curl into a smile rather than a sad pout, but the glimmer in her eyes steals the breath right out of his lungs.

"What?" She asks, arms moving around his waist as Thea tips her head back, lids fluttering as Adrian runs his fingers through her hair.

"Just thinking of how I wish a slow and terrible death to each and every person who's ever made you feel sad, to anyone who has ever deprived the world of your smile."

"Like drowning versus burned alive kind of death?" Thea muses at his cruelty.

"The kind of death where their flesh melts from their body, where their organs begin to decompose while they are still alive. I don't care who and how, but anyone who ever made you feel anything short of happy deserve undiluted anguish."

"How cruel of you, Adrian Friedman."

"You deserve a lifetime of happiness, Thea. Anyone who gets in the way of that should quite simply die."

Thea scrunches her nose as Adrian leans down, resting his forehead on hers while gazing into her eyes with a slight smile on the lips she knows the taste of far too well.

"Adrian?"

"Uhm?"

"There is small possibility I'm in love with you."

"Finally."

22

Waking up has never been something Thea enjoyed, as she enjoyed sleeping a bit too much, savoring dreams where her writing meant something more to people than herself.

The beauty of dreams is that, unlike life, she could control them, yet she doesn't have many complaints waking up to Adrian spooning her.

Waking up to their fingers woven together, holding his hands close to her heart, or maybe he'd been the one to move his hand over her heart as if needing to feel the soft echo to soothe him.

“I have a question,” Thea preambles, rolling to face Adrian as he’d been cuddling her, hiding his face from the sunlight pouring through his windows as they always forget to draw the curtains down before stumbling into bed. "If we had a child together, what's a name you'd never give them?"

A faint blush creeps onto his cheeks before Adrian says, “Other than the obvious? Because I should've known better than to date a Lauren. Especially when my mom would always tell me names have an imprint.”

"How so?"

"Have you ever met a Jake or Lucas that wasn't a class clown and douchebag? Or a Lauren that isn't more poisonous as the plant they are named after? Names tell a story. It's up to us to read through them."

"What story does my name tell?"

"That you love my silvery eyes?" Adrian asks, batting his lashes at Thea to steal a laugh from her. "It tells that you're kind, that when you love something, you do it with every part of yourself, and living that life isn't easy. Not when you don't want to do anything else, but you consider it to be as much of a blessing as it is a curse."

Thea falls silent, eyes flitting over the curves of his face, noticing how the faint layer of facial hair from the night before is a little more prominent now. Making Adrian seem older than his usual boyish mien, seem wiser, like someone Thea could grow old with, practically seeing the days that might be robbed from them. Because Adrian is right when it comes to Thea wanting to be a writer to a point it became a curse, leaving her with no desire to do or be anything else.

"Are you thinking about how beautiful my eyes are?"

"No, I was thinking our child's middle name could be the place they were conceived at, at least if it sounds good."

"*Adrian Taboão da Serra*[7] *Friedman*, doesn't sound very good to me."

"Where is that? Brazil?"

Adrian nods, burying his face against the crook of her neck, eliciting a chill as his stubble scratches her skin, leaving it red as she shrieks away with a laugh.

"Mine would be Thea Grand Canyon Scriven. Promise we'll take better vacations than our parents?"

"Sex vacations?"

"Don't twist my words, Friedman."

---

[7] Taboão da Serra is a municipality in the state of São Paulo in Brazil.

Adrian gasps as he rolls into his back with a hand over his heart—an exaggerated sob bubbles past his lips as he pulls Thea toward him.

"I'm gorgeous. The best-looking amongst the Friedman's children, going on a sexcation with me is a dream of many."

"Didn't you say you were the ugly duck as a child?"

"In the eyes of high society, yes, I was." Adrian rolls, pinning Thea beneath him as he assaults her neck with scratchy kisses—pulling back only when her laugh becomes breathless. "My mom let me indulge in all the Brigadeiro I wanted while other moms were enforcing a strict diet, I had pimples while other kids went to spas more often than a child should, and I had a tooth gap. So I was a normal boy, but in the high society, I was considered a demonic entity. Nothing braces, some basic skincare, and a growth spurt didn't manage to make me beautiful."

"Just that and a homme fatale surged?"

Adrian lays down on top of Thea, nearly purring as she wraps her arms and legs around him, holding him close enough for their hearts to beat in synchrony.

"It still took me a few years to grow into myself, and getting cheated on by my girlfriend and best friend didn't help. Eventually, I became a major slut. If it had a pulse, I'd be fucking it."

"Oh, really? Did that phase end?" Thea asks, biting on his shoulder.

"It ended the moment I got chlamydia, gonorrhea, and syphilis. That was not a fun doctor visit. My parents were very disappointed, but I'd already made up my mind on putting the well-being of my dick before the urges of my dick."

Laughs echoing against Adrian's bedroom walls, Thea slithers away from him—or rather, tries as he wraps his arms around her waist.

"Let me go, Adrian Chlamydman," She teases him, prodding at his biceps. "I want to take a shower before I go buy myself a new phone."

"Oh, I like the sound of that."

Thea slouches against Adrian, letting him curl up against her as she glances over her shoulder. "That wasn't an invitation. I don't want your triple STD dick near me."

"But I'm cured?"

"Really? I thought you were stuck in medieval times," Thea flicks the tip of Adrian's nose as he pouts in his best efforts to lure Thea with puppy eyes, lids fluttering close when she runs her fingers through his mussed dark strands. "Come on, Chlamy. Don't you have to go to work?"

Adrian sighs, letting Thea go as he slithers out of bed, slipping on his fuzzy slippers before catching up to Thea and throwing her over his shoulder, eliciting a laugh from her as Adrian drums his fingers on the back of Thea's thighs.

The dark marble in his bathroom is bleached into a sad gray by the sunlight enveloping the apartment, leaving the air slightly balmy.

Thea slides down Adrian's chest, her arms lingering around his neck even when her bare feet touch the floor. "Thank you," she says as Adrian tugs on the zipper of the sweatshirt she slept in.

"For carrying you from bed to here?"

"For replacing sadness with joy."

"You still won't let me buy you a new phone, will you?" Adrian asks, fighting against a smile at curls on the edge of his lips—something that'd become natural instinct when seeing Thea smile.

"Nope."

She turns away, letting the only clothing item she'd been wearing pool around her feet before she steps into the large shower—crooking her head to the left while trying to remember the function of the four faucet knobs.

"First one is temperature, second is the left side faucet, third is the right faucet, and the last one is the rainforest faucet."

"Why do rich people need that many shower heads?" Thea probes, glancing over her shoulder to find Adrian stripping down.

Adrian cocks a brow as Thea's eyes linger on the thumbs he has hooked around the band of his black brief. When he doesn't slip them down, Adrian watches as her gaze moves up his naked torso before meeting his eyes.

"Enjoying the view?"

"Chlamydia never looked so good."

Laughing, Adrian sways his hips as he carols, "Tananan-nan-nan-tananan-nan."

"Oh! A striptease. I've never had a striptease start so late in the game." Thea whistles as she leans against the glass shower box, pressing her body against the cold panes as Adrian spins around slowly, pushing his brief down a little bit before gliding a hand toward his butt and the other to his neck. Adrian caresses his own body while biting his lips, giving his best impression of a homme fatale as he arches his back to make his butt look bigger.

"Now you're being a little tease," Thea jokes as he pushes the thin layer down his body, practically taking a downward dog position that is less than flattering. "Oh god, I'm just so wet."

Briefs pooling around his feet, Adrian turns around to face Thea. "Fuck," His voice deepens as gray eyes rake over her naked body pressed against the glass.

It takes a second before Adrian prowls toward Thea, who pushes her butt out to imitate him. She gasps when Adrian slaps her ass, snaking an arm around her waist, pulling Thea flush against his chest as he turns on the rainforest faucet.

Thea presses into his body as the water hits her skin, hand moving to the nape of his neck, coaxing him closer, needing him to kiss her until the warm water runs cold.

"You wicked little thing," Adrian says, pulling back as Thea tries to kiss him. Their lips hover close to each other, the air of their lungs shared but not by a kiss. "Say it."

"No, not until I'm sure of it."

"Then lie, Thea, make a fool out of me. Fill my veins with the poison of your lips until I fall on my knees for you."

Thea doesn't say anything as she angles her head slightly, allowing her to peer into his eyes as she pulls his hand down her chest.

Gliding down her stomach until a moan escapes her lips when his fingers search, press, and glide against her.

"Say it. Lie to me."

"I love you," Thea whispers as if sharing a secret, something she didn't even tell herself. "I love you more than I've loved anyone else, and it terrifies me. It terrifies me that this love might be an illusion because I don't want to love you."

Adrian cups her cheeks as he asks, "Why?"

"Because if I love you, that means I could lose you, and I'd rather not have you at all than to ever lose you."

"You have all of me for as long as there is a beat in my heart. So, have me, Thea."

This time Adrian doesn't pull back when Thea tries to kiss him, nor is their kiss a wildfire that burns down to nothing—leaving nothing but destruction in its path.

No, their kiss is slow.

It's like a drizzle in its softness, something that ignites sparks as their lips move in tandem. Caressing and savoring the way Adrian runs the tip of his fingers over her stomach while Thea scratches the nape of his neck.

"I love you," Adrian mutters against the kiss, smiling. "God, I love you so much. How can I love you this much, Thea?"

"Because I'm incredibly hot and an even better writer?"

"Must be why." His finger moves around her jaw, pulling Thea into another kiss. Stealing a moan from her as their tongues brush in tandem to her bum grinding against his groin. "Not to mention, you are wicked good."

Thea bites down on his lip, pulling back as she reaches around her—silencing the groan in his throat as she curls her fingers around his semi-hard cock.

"How disappointing. I thought you'd want to fuck me."

"Thea, I was thinking about my grandma so I wouldn't get hard." Adrian takes a step forward, pressing Thea against the wall as he relishes in the whimper as her nipples touch the cold surface. "Body or hair first?"

"Really, Chlamy?"

"Hair first then."

Thea feels as Adrian stretches himself toward the cutout in the wall where bottles of shampoo and rinse are lined up beside the shower oil cleanser.

"I think there are more pressing matters than washing my hair. Don't you think?" Thea asks, tipping her head as Adrian lathers the shampoo against her scalp—stealing a moan with the pressure he applies as if he'd been a hairdresser in a different life.

"I'm not stopping you, Thea," he mutters. "My cock is still in your hand."

In the blink of an eye, Thea faces him as she trails kisses down his body. Her nails elicit shivers as they dig into his pale skin while one hand works diligently to work his length.

Her knees pop as she kneels before Adrian with water pelting down her face. Planting kisses down his length, a smile tugs on the edge of Thea's lips.

"Don't be a tease," Adrian muttered, running his hands through her hair.

"Make me."

"Hands up."

Thea does as he asks.

Moaning as he wraps his fingers around her wrists, pushing her against the wall, Thea relishes in the shiver evoking goosebumps down her body, but Adrian watches as her nipples grow hard.

"How do you want me?"

Thea doesn't say anything as she opens her mouth, tongue sticking out in an invitation—moaning as he pinches her nipple before thrusting into her mouth, pushing himself down her throat as her cheeks hollow to suck on him. Thea's teeth graze lightly against his shaft as Adrian pulls back with drool slipping down her mouth.

Thea moves her mouth to the side of his cock, tongue teasing him as she sustains his gaze, humming as her lips move up and down his shaft.

"I've never seen someone look so pretty with a cock down their throat."

"I don't currently have a cock down my throat. What a tragedy," She says in mocking sorrow before taking Adrian in her mouth once more.

Adrian thrusts into her mouth, moving in tandem to the tongue caressing underneath his cock, to the way Thea bobs her head back and forth with droll being washed away by the streaming water.

She pulls one hand out of his hold, touching herself as she takes him down her throat, moaning as he thrusts into her, each stroke coming faster than the one before as Adrian's groans grow louder.

"Fuck, Thea. I wanna cum inside of you," Adrian pleas.

But her hand moves to his hips, holding him against her, urging him to cum in her mouth, pleading for him to let her taste him.

Thea smiles as she feels him twitching against her tongue. Pulling her head back, she sucks on the tip of his cock. A hand curled around him, stroking the man that climaxes with a loud groan that nearly makes her come.

"Fuck," He curses, thrusting into her mouth, pushing every last drop of cum down her throat. "Fuck, Thea."

Adrian's body quivers every so slightly as she stands up—hands gliding from his shaved legs up to his waist as she rolls onto the tips of her toes, kissing him with his cum still in her mouth.

"Fuck," He groans against her mouth, savoring the way he tastes against her tongue. "I think it will take me months to cum again after that."

"A pity, I quite like making you cum. You whimper a little."

"No, I don't. I'm a manly man. I groan."

"No, you whimper between groans. It's hot. I like it. You sound like a pornstar."

"I thought that was a bad thing?" Adrian asks, pulling Thea onto her feet before resting his forehead against hers, neither particularly caring about the water bill.

"It is bad to fuck like a pornstar. I wanted to see if you remembered that."

"The only thing I'll forget you ever said is that I whimper. Because I don't."

"Whatever you say, Adrian Chlamydman."

Adrian rolls his gray eyes, hands gliding down her body until they rest against her ass. "Should I repay the favor, Thea Tea?"

"When I climax, I want you cumming inside of me, and as you said, that might take you months. Now, wash my body so I can wash yours."

"Bossy."

"That's because I never got an STD. Who would say poor little me always had money to buy condoms, and the billionaire didn't."

"Funny, because we've never used a condom before."

"You're the first man I've fucked without a condom. It took me months to fuck Aaron without one, and I've had an IUD since I turned eighteen. If you gave me anything, I'd sue your ass, Chlamy."

Adrian gasps loudly, dropping his head to the crook of her neck as he mutters, "You are after my STD money?"

"I'm after your girthy cock."

"Because you love me?"

"Shut up, Chlamy."

Thea stares at the phones on display, wondering if she should buy the least expensive one in case she doesn't use the item for more than a few months or if she should be hopeful for the first time in five years.

"A middle ground, maybe?" She mutters to herself, glancing over her shoulder in search of Adrian, only to find the billionaire standing beside a store clerk.

Intently listening to the man wearing a blue polo go on about the different features in the brand's wireless headphones compared to their competitors—at least that's what Thea thinks when, in reality, Adrian is making sure whatever purchase they make is paid for on his black card.

"Chlamy?" Thea calls out to Adrian, who raises his head as a golden retriever would when called on.

Thea smiles as he walks toward her with a non-existing tail wagging behind him until his arms wrap around her waist.

"Don't use your sexy nickname for me in public," He scolds her in a jest, planting a kiss on the tip of her nose as his fingers run over her damp hair. "What do you require my wisdom for?"

"Which phone should I get?"

"Color-wise?"

"Quality wise."

"Get the best one. You deserve the very best, Thea Tea," Adrian mutters, resting his chin on the crown of her head. "I think I should call the CEO and have him develop a better phone for you."

"Don't brag about your billionaire best friends. Only fools like billionaires."

"Yet you love one."

"Your dad is rich, not you," Thea argues, pushing Adrian away as she turns to face the clerk, who is busy with another customer. "And I don't love you. I just might love you, but I'm not sure."

Adrian prowls toward Thea.

The tips of his fingers brush against the nape of her neck as he pulls her closer, thumb caressing her jaw as he kisses her face.

From her forehead to the bridge of her nose, down her jaw before he circles back, planting a kiss on each corner of her mouth before giving her a quick kiss, and another, and another, until her arms wrap around his waist.

"You should wear glasses more often," Thea mutters against his mouth. "It's cute and sexy."

"I'll throw all my contacts out when we get home."

"Don't be wasteful, but you should wear your glasses when we are home."

"There is one time I don't want to wear glasses."

"When I'm sitting on your face, and you make me cum so good I nearly squirt on you?"

"Jesus Thea, there are kids around," Adrian chides, glancing around before leaning down to whisper against her ear. "But yes, I need my contacts for that. I truly can't fathom the idea of you orgasming and me not seeing your face during it."

"Jesus Friedman, there are kids around."

Adrian chuckles as he turns around to call out for the clerk, "Hey Garrett, she'll take the top-notch phone in..."

"Green," Thea compliments. "Thank you very much, Garrett."

"And I'll take the headphones in green too. Thank you."

Garrett and the client he'd been talking to turn to face Thea and Adrian, both furrowing their brows, but the clerk only nods along, muttering something for the client before he walks away.

"That's a terrible name, huh," Thea mutters, resting her head against Adrian's chest, feeling as he chuckles while running his fingers down her spine.

"You think so? I think it fits him."

Thea doesn't argue as she listens to Adrian's heartbeat —a sound she's often fallen asleep to, perhaps one she's grown more used to than Jolly's purring.

A pang of guilt hits Thea as she thinks of how much time Jolly spent with Marine since Adrian waltzed into her life, conquering Thea's undivided attention as if there'd been a silver thread connecting them, coaxing them to seek each other since the knot fell in place.

But even worse, Adrian would easily steal Jolly's heart. Making the kitty adore him far more than she'd ever adored Thea.

It doesn't take long for Garrett to return with a sealed box. Thea watches as he peels the plastic around it, allowing gravity to pull on the bottom of the box before proffering the phone to Thea.

She doesn't waste time, turning it on and typing in all of her info again while hogging the store's WIFI to download her apps.

Too preoccupied with logging into her email, Thea doesn't notice as Adrian pays for everything, doesn't notice as he weaves their fingers together, leading her toward the large glass doors leading to the streets of Manhattan as she scrolls past newsletters she had to make time to unsubscribe as she truly couldn't care less about their sales.

Making time to delete the emails with updates from authors she'd like before resenting them a little bit for achieving the success she hasn't —and one they wouldn't have achieved without the right friends.

Thea sinks the heels of her boots into the concrete ground as she reads an email that makes her heart beat faster. Adrian glances over his shoulder, noticing her face is caught between hope and dread.

Dear Thea Scriven.

My name is Rue Hayes. I am an editor at Harpy Editorial. I received your manuscript through a colleague of mine, and he informed me that you live in the city, so I'm interested in meeting you to discuss your book. I'm free this afternoon. If that doesn't work for you, we can arrange another day.

"Thea?"

"Can you meet me on the Brooklyn Bridge after work?"

Adrian nods as he asks, "What for, Thea Tea?"

"I'll have either really good or terrible news. Either way, I want to share them with you."

"I'll bring cake," He mutters, pulling Thea into a quick kiss before she practically runs across the street, where tourists hog the sidewalk to take terrible pictures of the Pulitzer Fountain as if the fountain was unlike any other they'd seen in a mall—or as if their photos would be better than anything they could find online.

Thea prances down W 59th Street, stealing glances at her phone as if to make sure the email wasn't a figment of her imagination, to make sure she isn't dreaming about the first glimmer of hope she's ever truly had.

"Oh fuck, I need better clothes," Thea realizes as the street light turns red. "Fuck."

23

A chill runs down Thea's spine as she walks into the imposing yet incredibly mundane lobby of Harpy Publishing, or rather, the building the publishing house runs its business.

"Hi, I have a meeting scheduled with Rue Hayes from Harpy Publishing," Thea says to the woman chewing gum behind a large desk in the center of the lobby.

"I'll need your name, some form of ID, and a moment, please."

With shaky hands, Thea slides over her driver's license that might as well have moss growing attached to it since it's been utterly useless since she moved to New York.

Her nails, painted in a light shade of pink, tap against the marble countertop, matching the clicking sound of the keyboard as the woman, whose blonde hair is pulled back into an elegant bun, types away, checking something Thea can't see despite trying to peer down on the screen in front of the woman.

The wheels on the woman's chair graze against the polished floor as she swishes across the desk, picking up the most distant phone and speaking in a near whisper.

Thea bites her lips, tasting the cherry-flavored gloss she reapplied before walking into the building, wanting to appear somewhat put together when she didn't have Aria to work her magic.

"Ma'am, you may proceed. Miss Hayes is expecting you on the eighth floor."

Thea squeals under the woman's watchful blue eyes, following Thea as she walks to the access control gate, where a security guard swipes a card through a machine to allow Thea passage.

Seconds seem to stretch into hours as she lingers in front of the elevator, watching the numbers go down with a few stops until the metal doors slide open and a group of workers walks out.

Chatting amongst themselves, they split around Thea as if she was an invisible force pushing through them until the new pair of high heels she bought that morning touch the elevator floor.

Pressing the button for the eighth floor, Thea pulls her phone from her pocket when she sees a new notification.

Adrian Friedman sent you $1000.
"Good luck with whatever you are doing. Unless it's a pregnancy test, I don't think we are ready for a kid yet. You aren't pregnant, are you?"

Thea laughs as the knot in her stomach comes undone while searching for a picture of a positive pregnancy test before sending it to Adrian with a single text saying, "PP?"

Slipping her phone into her small bag, Thea whirls to face the back mirror of the elevator—inspecting her makeup to ensure the curl of her lashes and the thin eyeliner weren't disrupted by something on her way here.

Thea takes a step back to take a measure of her outfit, unlike her usual dark wash jeans, combat boots, and T-shirt. Instead, she is wearing rather well-fitted khaki dress pants with pleats in the front of them, accentuating her waist.

She pulls on the green knit top that cinches in the white dress shirt, worn the same way as styled on the mannequin, minus the neon pink bag that seemed like the wrong fit even to someone without much knowledge of fashion.

So, she picked a little black bag that doesn't hold much beyond her phone, hand sanitizer, wallet, and keys.

"Too late to change now," She mutters.

Fidgeting with the collar of her dress shirt, she whirls back to the elevator door as the vehicle slows down, opening its doors to the eighth floor, where the Harpy Publishing House slogan displays on the glass wall separating the office from reception.

"Thea Scriven?" A woman with blonde hair and rounded cheeks says as a greeting, smiling when Thea nods—too nervous to utter a single word. "Thank you for making time for a meeting so last minute."

"Thank you for reaching out."

High heels click against the laminated flooring as Thea gingerly approaches the woman, following Rue with her eyes peering through the glass wall where half is covered in a matte film, yet the way the publishing house smells leaves Thea in awe.

Wondering how they managed to make a corporate building have the same smell as a library, of a cozy room where a thousand stories reside.

They walk further down the long hallway in silence, allowing the sound of phones ringing and conversations to billow past the layer of glass separating Thea from the office, yet her feet linger when she hears a laugh she recognizes.

Her eyes flit over the office, glossing over the people seated around in the cubicles for Adrian as she would never mistake his giddy laugh, not when that sound makes her heart swell.

"There he is," Thea mutters to herself as the man walks out from a meeting room with his head tipped back as he laughs, yet the sound is a little bit scornful.

Thea watches as Adrian pushes his glasses higher onto the bridge of his nose before turning to face a younger man and woman—young enough for them to be interns.

The bright look on their faces showing Thea they respect Adrian's opinions, valuing whatever wisdom he shares with a stoic look on his handsome face.

Lecturing the future of publishing about the value of books and how one should strive to publish books that enrich society, as entertainment and quality don't need to be paradoxical—at least they shouldn't be.

Fiction is a safe space in which writers explore reality, Adrian told her a while back, putting into words something Thea believed down to her core. A principle that should give a voice to the voiceless, should bring to the limelight the stories that have been ostracized by society.

Yet, Thea only thinks of how captivating Adrian is at work. His mere presence demands the attention of his colleagues, who either glance or stare at him as if to make sure Adrian is real, something Thea is also guilty of doing far too often.

"Miss Scriven?"

"Sorry, I got distracted."

Rue chuckles as she gestures for Thea to follow her, this time without the interruption of Adrian's presence—although the man continues to linger in her mind.

The echo of their high heels fills the silence as Thea is led into a small meeting room surrounded by windows that flow from the floor up to the ceiling, allowing for a view of the monstrous buildings piercing New York's polluted skyline like deformed mountains.

Settling in a seat, Thea watches as the woman walks around the table before sitting behind the leather journal and a short stack of paper.

"You know," Rue preambles, writing something on a new page of her journal. "When Adrian asked me to read a romance manuscript he'd come across, I almost said no."

"That's surprising. I didn't expect people to deny a Friedman of anything."

"I thought so too until the little heir told me the reason he chose to work here is that he wanted people to tell him no. Adrian knows if he had worked under his dad's empire, there wouldn't be a single person who would've denied him."

Thea fidgets in her seat, annoyed how a surname could grant someone so much power, irked by how unfair it is that knowing the right person takes precedence over being the right author.

Annoyed how that can grant someone a publishing deal in a corrupt system that allows a rapport to speak louder than talent and art.

"Adrian could've pitched a book from the point of view of toilet paper, and people at F&F would see it as a genius book, but here at Harpy, it took him a good few years before being allowed to pitch. He would need a phenomenal book and arguments to be allowed to acquire a book. There had even been times when he was our senior's scapegoat for why a book didn't sell as much as expected."

Nodding along, Thea bites on her tongue to keep herself from commenting on the irony of how Adrian didn't work for his father's company for a fair chance, and Harpy didn't offer him that. Forcing Adrian to prove himself more than his colleagues had to, even when he's more passionate about books than anyone Thea has ever met.

"May I ask how you met him? Adrian is a bit of a workaholic. He isn't one to meet a lot of new people, surely not unknown writers."

"I don't see how it would be appropriate for me to talk about something Adrian hasn't told you himself."

"Good answer," Rue mutters with a smile tugging her lips as if Thea passed a test she unknowingly subjected to. "I really enjoyed reading your book. It was...refreshing."

"You don't sound happy about it."

"I am, but it's unlike other books we've published and unlike any book I have personally acquired."

"Meaning?"

"Meaning, I'd like to know why you wrote your book the way you did, why you touch on the things you touched on, such as Cecilia saying the only reason she isn't seen in the same light as other girls are because they weren't given the same respect as Cecilia was, a respect she didn't feel as if she earned but rather inherited because of her father."

The edge of Thea's lips curl at the memory of that conversation shared between her characters when Cecilia pointed out the obvious to the people who choose to remain oblivious to facts—preferring the ignorance of saying they abhor misogyny while upholding those principles.

Yet, that's not the answer to what Rue asked.

"When I was fifteen, I was known as the Jane Austen wannabe. That name brought me relatively close to one of my classmates as she was always seen reading a romance book. The darker and smuttiest, the better. At least that's what she used to say, and I used to agree."

Thea turns her gaze to the buildings surrounding them, catching a glimpse of people sitting at their desks or chatting amongst themselves, leaving Thea to wonder if they, too, feel as if they carry blood on their hands.

"At the time, I didn't see the problem with what we would read. Trading recommendations was a way for us to bond while swooning over lines like 'You're mine. No other man shall ever touch you'. The relationships in those books were all we wanted in a relationship, craving a man to love us so much he'd be overbearing and possessive."

"You thought those things meant love?"

Thea nods, her gaze still distant as she sinks into her memories, remembering the peach-colored frames of her friend's glasses, the freckles that coated her pale skin, and the nails she'd always paint in a color that matched the art of the book cover she'd been reading.

"You are mine," Thea speaks in a whisper. "That's what her older boyfriend would say. That's what he said while stabbing her frail body seventy-nine times. '*Without you, I'm lost,*' '*You're the only reason I have to live,*' these were the things we were told to think of as love, as things we should not only settle for but strive for. We are lied to,

convinced these were the terms and conditions, made to believe love was a twisted game when the love portrayed in those books had always been a hateful lie. Those stories aren't about love, but they are sodden with the blood of women murdered by their boyfriends, husbands, fathers, even strangers who'd been told a woman's body was their birthright."

"I'm sorry for your loss."

Thea's smile doesn't quite reach her eyes, lingering closer to being a snarl than a smile, lacking any warmth as Thea would always push emotions down to the pit of her stomach when relaying that story.

"Did you know fifty-eight percent of registered murders against women are committed at the hands of an intimate partner or a family member? Every eleven minutes, a woman, as young as fifteen, is murdered in their home, like my friend who died in a rug that'd been a family heirloom because her boyfriend couldn't stand the idea of her having a male best friend because he didn't like that she had an older brother. He even complained about the way her father would look at her because she was his. So how dare she be anything to any other man? Fiction and reality collided when that boy wrecked his life by ending hers, taking her family to the grave as they could never recover from her death, while he sought to be redeemed."

Rue's cheeks drain of color as she listens to every word Thea speaks. Her knuckles bleaching around the fountain pen she's been scrawling within her journal until Thea began to explain the thought process behind her book—behind every book she's written and will ever write.

"Since the day she died, I started to wonder if she would've run away from her boyfriend if she didn't read books romanticizing behavior that leads to women being brutalized. I wonder if she would be alive if we hadn't fallen prey to the narrative written by older women who aren't wise despite their age, whose hands are covered in innocent blood, as they are the ones establishing the fine print of what women should desire in a relationship. By selling the ideal man as one who is possessive, they feed the cruel fire of misogyny, sending girls to the gallows before they are even old enough for their first drink."

"We publish what sells," Rue mutters, her eyes reddened with sorrow—or perhaps it's guilt as Thea can see how the story impacted Rue, making her wonder the same things Thea had dwelled on for years. "We just hope the book is good."

"It's a vicious cycle as readers buy into the narrative that killed my friend. Believing they are capable of distinguishing fiction from reality, but we've all been gullible enough to believe the same thing. After all, media literacy isn't something we are taught in school. It's her death that hovers in my mind when I'm writing a new book, going back to that day in early November when my hands became tainted with her blood too."

Thea closes her eyes against the memory that appears before her eyes, the red and blue lights zooming past her house after the boyfriend called the police, claiming he found his girlfriend in a pool of blood.

A part of her would never forget the howl of pain that reverberated against the forestry surrounding her childhood home as her friend's mother got home to find a stretcher carrying a black body bag.

"I cling to hope, not a single one of my readers will ever fall prey to the things Mr. Douglas committed, and any writer who cares, any writer who isn't misogynistic, would write with a similar mindset. Instead, they use the blood of victims to write their next novel. They spit on rotting corpses by romanticizing behavior that traps women six feet under. Women who were once full of life, who had dreams and ambitions, who had so much love before falling into traps laid out by screenwriters, producers, and authors, because while their work may be fiction, the abuse against women is very much real, 736 million women globally kind of real."

"I've never thought of things the way you do. Perhaps I should reevaluate the moral compass I abide," Rue says, standing up as she plasters a smile on her face. "I'll go fetch us some coffee. Would you like anything else? Harpy has a fully stocked snack bar."

"I'm fine. Thank you."

Thea hides her trembling hands between her legs as Rue walks around the table before leaving her alone in the meeting room. She waits a few moments before fishing her phone out of her bag.

Adrian Friedman sent you $1000.
"Do you really think I wouldn't be able to recognize your fingers? That's not you. So, no trip to PP and Reginald Friedman-Scriven has to wait until he's actually conceived."

You sent Adrian Friedman $5
"The day you name our child Reginald is the last day I'll ever say the L word."

Adrian Friedman sent you $1000.
"Odd, not once have you looked into my eyes, and said, 'I lesbian you,' which for your information is something Olivie said to her first crush when she was 12 and thought there was only one girl she could crush on."

With the edge of her lips tugged into a smile, Thea puts her phone back in her bag. Ignoring Adrian as she waits for Rue to return, Thea stares at the gray wall as seconds bleed into each other, growing into minutes that move all too slowly as the only sound in the room comes from Thea's heart thundering inside of her chest, blood soaring in her ears as if she couldn't feel her anxiety through the shakiness in her hand or the sweat in her armpits.

Marring the polished surface with her fingerprints, Thea raps her nails against the glass surface of the table as she fights the urge to stand up and search for Rue, resisting the urge to text Adrian to inform him she's down the hall. Craving his support in this situation when she could really use someone reminding her of the worth of her stories, on why she matters as a writer.

Thea sighs in relief when she hears the air shift as the door swings open, and the click of high heels precedes Rue's voice as she says, "Sorry to keep you waiting. My supervisor needed help with some tech thing a simple search would've solved."

"Ah, I've seen people talking about building their own list while still being expected to fulfill tasks fit for assistant editors. Quite an industry we've gotten ourselves into, huh?"

"That's when we don't keep the title and are still expected to acquire our own list," Rue mutters, settling a little tray of danish butter cookies and a mug of caffè americano on the table. "Can I be honest with you?"

"I think that's the least you owe me after everything I shared."

Rue smiles through the rim of her glass holding black coffee—which seems to be without a single cube of sugar by how the woman frowns at the first taste.

"I really want to work with you."

Thea practically slouches against the stiff chair as relief washes over her, yet her throat tightens with tears as she doesn't allow herself to cry.

Not until her dream is no longer a figment of her imagination but rather dried ink.

"I don't know what your agent has told you," Rue speaks, gaze focused on papers scattered in front of her, missing how Thea furrows her brows in confusion. "But before editors make an offer on a manuscript, it will be discussed by many people. From the acquiring team to marketing, all of it is to ensure we are publishing books that can actually sell."

"Yes, I'm aware. Though, I suppose those guidelines don't apply to every author. Does it? Some people don't need to hit the 5K threshold to enter a bestseller list, right?"

"You are awfully aware of the industry's dirty secrets, but yes, networking will do wonders for your career. More than talent and quality ever could."

Thea doesn't allow her discontentment to trespass her face. Not when this has been a common discussion for her and Adrian when they work together.

Even though he hates it as much as Thea does, Adrian has grown callous about the discongruity in the industry. Able to shrug and remind her talent and skill aren't primordial requirements across the board in the publishing industry.

But unfairness is something Thea never accepts with a smile on her face, preferring to dismantle the issue like a Trojan Horse, pointing out the flaws in a system that smothered the life out of her.

"I just have one question. Nowhere in your manuscript have I been able to find your agent's information. Maybe it was overlooked on your part, but—"

"No," Thea says, curling her fingers into a fist. "It's not a mistake. I don't have an agent."

"May I ask why?"

"You would need to ask the people who rejected me. They never deigned to give me a reason for their rejection."

Rue nods as she raises her cup of coffee back to her lips, savoring the beverage, prolonging the moment as she avoids Thea's gaze, fidgeting with the edge of her journal.

"For us to move forward, you'd need to find an agent. It's quicker and easier to negotiate with one. It ensures, a few years from now, you won't say you got a bad deal because you signed a contract you didn't under—"

"No," Thea repeats as she feels the prick of tears, feels the lodge in her throat depriving her of air. "I won't sign with one now when they've had countless opportunities to represent me before."

"Then this is as far as you'll come, Thea. I urge you to reconsider. When you do, you have my email and my phone number. I look forward to hearing from you again."

"You will." Thea's chair screeches against the sleek flooring. "One way or another, you'll hear from me again, but don't think it will be because I've signed with an agent.

If I've made it this far without an agent, I'll get to the end without one."

Rue smiles at that, watching as Thea marches toward the meeting room's door before raising her voice, "Thea?"

She nods, unable to speak a word as tears line her eyes.

"I won't forget what you've told me today. You have given me a lot to think about, a lot to reconsider about the things I've held as true, or at least the things I'd been reluctant to take a closer look at. Thank you."

"That's what writers are meant to do, whether it is within the margins of their books or if their words bleed into the real world. If a writer doesn't make you think a little deeper, then they aren't a very good writer or the receiver isn't very bright. You should reconsider who the writers you give your time to are."

24

The murky water beneath the Brooklyn Bridge flows toward the ocean as all rivers do, disemboguing into something far greater than it had been—a fate Thea believed to be the way of life.

Believed some people were rivulets meant to become a steady stream, a small river bleeding into one bigger, more powerful, but very few people would bleed into a part of the ocean.

Perhaps there were also people meant to be a part of the Dead Sea, where no life could blossom. A place for dreams to wither.

Thea can feel the low thrum of vehicles driving on the bridge and the steps of pedestrians trudging by as they relish in the view between Brooklyn and Manhattan or look down at the screens of their phones.

With tears running down her face, Thea wonders if those strangers have ever been so absorbed in their pain that they wished to go against every single programming the brain set in place to protect life, a simple command etched into every person, making it so every fiber of the human body clamors for life even when one just wants to rest.

Thea smells the scent of his cologne before feeling Adrian's arms wrap around her, allowing her to seek refuge in the warmth of his embrace, but she doesn't move, keeping her eyes on the murky water, her fingers curling around the cold railing.

"I'm sorry," Adrian mutters without knowing what he's sorry for.

Planting a kiss against her temple, Adrian keeps his arms around her, giving Thea time to wallow, for the lump in her throat to wane enough for her to speak when just breathing is all too laborious.

Slowly, like a withering tulip, Thea rests her head against Adrian's chest, raising a hand from the cold railing to wrap her fingers around his wrist, needing the steady ebb and flow of his pulse to soothe her, giving Thea something to anchor herself in.

"Death is all but a fleeting moment, just a second, in which the ether of life evades flesh and seeks something else, don't you think?" Thea asks as a blustering wind suddenly sweeps over Brooklyn Bridge, flogging her face with the long strands of her brown hair. "One moment your heart is beating, the next your brain is fighting to keep you alive. The blood in our veins yearns to live, our lungs crave air, then the curtains fall, and there is a moment of silence. *Finis*."

Adrain slithers around her, holding Thea against his chest as he feels the languid beat of her heart. A false mirror to the sorrow ravaging deep within her being as he buries his face against the crook of her neck, breathing Thea in as he waits for her to continue.

"The final act of life comes and goes without an epilogue, without a cliffhanger for the next act, but life and death aren't about the body, are they? Our bodies are a vessel made of bones and muscles to protect something, or maybe it's the manacles that trap us in purgatory? Why is it more tempting to find out what happens after death than to keep trying?"

"I'm the wrong person to ask, Thea Tea. I care about you too much not to selfishly hope you'll keep trying, give your dreams just another chance. Just try one more time."

"It's so tiring to be a constant failure. I'm so tired."

"You aren't a failure."

"I'm not a prodigy either."

"By whose definition?" Adrian spins Thea around, his large hands cupping her cheeks until there is a pout on her lips. "Because if you ask me, nothing about you is short of elysian."

Thea arches her brows as her hands flutter toward his waist, tugging Adrian closer as the wind raises a shiver down her spine.

"I feel like I'm stuck in limbo. Like I'm caught between an ellipsis."

"How so, Thea Tea?"

"An ellipsis indicates what wasn't said. So if I die, I'm robbed of my voice as suicide is nothing if not an intentional omission of life, a life neither joy nor sorrow were given the chance to blossom, like pouring salt over roots before hope could grow into happiness."

"And if you live? If you keep trying?" Adrian asks, gray eyes seeming brighter against the redness as Adrian tries not to cry, to remain strong for Thea—needing her to be none the wiser about how much sorrow the mere idea of life without her evokes in him.

"Then my voice is just another echo in an endless chamber of how inconsequential my work is, and I don't want my work to be inconsequential, for my words to be a ripple in treacherous waters, a bluster in a hurricane. I want my work to matter to others, but no one cares."

"I care. Thea, I despise the romance genre, and I've reread your books four times, three of which weren't related to editing. I like your voice, I like how you write, and I love you. Your books are a mirror of who you are, and you are phenomenal. Not many people can stare into the sun without being blinded."

"So I'm the sun?"

"God no, I hate quotes comparing someone to the sun. It's a nuclear ball of plasma. It will obliterate anything that comes near it, there is nothing romantic about it."

The sketch of a sad smile casts a shadow on Thea's lips as she watches how quickly Adrian gets sidetracked when his mind leads him down a detour.

"You, Thea Katherine Scriven, are heaven on earth. You're the laughter someone feels deep in their belly, depriving them of air as they laugh without an end in sight. You're an afternoon nap on a rainy day. The first snow of the year, and the last summer night. You're everything good, everything powerful, and everything beautiful life has to offer."

"Where did you get Katherine? That's not my middle name," Thea murmurs through her pouty lips.

"I don't know. It seemed like a good guess."

Adrian's fingers caress the nape of her neck, stealing a kiss from her while keeping her close, kissing her all too slowly as he can feel the lingering weight of sorrow in how taut her body is, feeling somehow heavy against his chest.

"Well then, Chlamythea, may I whisk you away for the weekend? And before you ask, I've gone to Marine and successfully collected Jolly after being interrogated. I didn't realize I'd been interrogated until I left her apartment. I wonder if she's had CIA training?"

"Close enough. Her dad was a CIA agent."

"That's so much cooler than being a billionaire's son." Adrian weaves their fingers together, tugging Thea toward the Manhattan end of the bridge.

Trailing behind Adrian, Thea tries not to think of the four people that have survived jumping into the river's murky waters. Wondering if they dove into the water with their feet pointing down, their arms up, and dropping straight down as they'd break the surface of the water.

But, if she fell at an angle instead of sinking, the impact would be the same as falling onto concrete. Fracturing her bones and lacerating her organs in ways only her soul had broken before.

"Thea?" Adrian calls, pulling her from her reverie only for Thea to see a hazy version of the man she was growing to love.

Her body trembles as sobs wreck through her in a deluge of tears, yet Thea can see Adrian's heart breaking before he pulls her closer.

A hand on the nape of her neck as Thea weeps, clinging to him as she would until her dying breath.

Jolly's tail smacks Thea's face as the cream-colored cat climbs Adrian's chest to lick his face, completely smitten with the man who's hidden a little portion of catnip in his jacket pocket.

"She loves you," Thea points out as she fidgets in the seat of Adrian's car, laying her head in his lap without bothering to watch the view as they've been stuck in traffic for the last fifteen minutes.

Adrian runs the fingers of one hand through her hair, the other scratching Jolly's back, stealing a purr from the cat and a sigh from Thea.

"A trend amongst the Scriven girls."

"Don't think my mom will love you. She's a Mariani girl before a Scriven girl. My brother won't like you much for a while, but my dad will love you. Give him a nice watch, and he'd consider marrying you instead."

"I won't even need to ask them the thirty-six questions that lead to love?"

Thea rolls until she's facing him, although she doesn't dare to put her feet into the seat of his car. She can read the smugness in his face as Adrian's thumb traces the arch of her brow, gliding down toward her jaw as if to coax Thea into satisfying his conversation topic.

"What thirty-six questions?"

"In 1997, a psychologist, Dr. Arthur Aron, came up with thirty-six questions in a study aimed to speed up the development of intimacy between two strangers. Those questions are divided into three sections that increasingly become more intimate and personal."

"Ask me one."

"Before making a telephone call, do you ever rehearse what you are going to say? If so, why?"

Thea slightly blushes as she nods, and Adrian offers her a little smirk when she turns to bury her face against Adrian's abdomen. "I'm anxious! I worry I'll forget the reason I'm calling someone. I don't like talking on the phone, even with my family. Now you answer one."

"If you could wake up tomorrow having gained any one quality or ability, what would it be?" Adrian says, peeling his gaze from Thea's face toward the window, watching as they move a little bit. "I'd like to be your personal genie in a bottle with infinite wishes to offer you. Oh, you want your grandma's cookies? Here you go. Now you want to visit the Eiffel Tower? Open your eyes, and look down on Paris. I wish I could fulfill each and every desire of yours in a mere second."

Thea pulls Adrian's hand to her lips, peppering kisses from the tips of his fingers down to the inside of his wrist, making Adrian squirm lightly with a shiver running down his spine.

"You are too good to me, Chlamy."

"What do you value most in a friendship?"

"A nice cock." Thea laughs as Adrian flicks the tip of her nose with a roll of his eyes. "Honesty. I don't think any relationship is capable of thriving without honesty between both parts, yet it's incredibly rare to find."

Jolly meows discontentedly as Adrian peels her away from his shoulder before scooting into his seat to give Thea more room for her legs.

She kicks away her high heels before curling against Adrian with Jolly in her lap, squeezed between them.

"How close and warm is your family? Do you feel your childhood was happier than most others?" Adrian voices another of the thirty-six questions. "What do you think?"

"You surely struggled a lot as a child. How dare your father not give you a private jet at the ripe age of five years old?"

"Actually, he has a private jet for each family member." Adrian watches as Thea's jaw drops, eyes widening before she catches onto his deceit, smacking his chest. "Two jets have been enough for everyone to use without overlaps, but we're close like a knit sweater and warm like a cinnamon bun. So yes, I'd say we are happier than other families around us. My mother never allowed money to be a defining part of our character."

Thea runs her fingers through Jolly's fur, smiling as the cat rolls around in a sleepy request for belly rubs.

"I like hearing you talk about your family. It brings light to your eyes. It's unlike the way you become subtly happy about other things you care for."

"In that case, I'll share this one story about when Ollie had been a brat to one of the many people who worked in our estate. She believed our parents would take her word over the staff, but my saint of a mother trusted each and every person there as she'd handpicked every employee, taking care of them with the same gentleness she wanted them to care for us. Needless to say, she was utterly disappointed in Ollie's behavior, even more so because she lied. Mommy Friedman explained why my devilish sister was wrong and demanded an apology."

For a moment, Adrian doesn't speak.

Gray eyes catch every little speck of sorrow in Thea's eyes, catching the way she pets Jolly with one hand while running her fingers over the inside of his wrist.

Adrian runs his thumb over Thea's lips, wiping away the lingering residue of gloss now smudged on the front of his shirt from hugging her tightly as she'd wept in his arms.

"Ollie refused to apologize as the dutiful brat she was. So my mother told her until she apologized to each and every member of our staff, they were to not aid her in any capacity. The next day, she had to serve herself some cereal as not even a glass of water was brought to her, then she had to use a hair straightener on her wrinkled uniform since no one had ironed or washed it for her the night before. That's when she heard our driver turning on the car to take me to school, but even taking her to school was a task she wasn't given access to. Every single thing someone would've done for her, she had to learn to do herself. Many of which she was too young to figure out."

"I feel bad for her," Thea mutters, the corner of her lips turned down, brows knit close together.

"My mom didn't let her starve, but she'd eat what my mom made instead of what our private chef prepared. That went on for a full month until Ollie broke into my parent's bedroom with tears running down her face at four in the morning, apologizing for her behavior. She wanted to apologize to all fifty members of our staff at that very moment, but mom said she'd have to wait until the morning came, and she couldn't wake them up that early. To this day, I have yet to see a more heartfelt apology than the one she gave to every employee."

"Have you ever been a brat?"

"I don't think that's in the thirty-six questions to falling in love. Which the next question is, tell your partner what you like about them, but not something you would say to someone you've just met."

Mischief glimmers in Thea's eyes as Adrian moves his hand down, the back of his fingers caressing her chin on his way down her throat.

Thea nearly waits for him to close his fingers around her neck, but all Adrian does is crook a brow. Waiting for her answer as his thumb glides down toward her protruding collarbone.

"I like that you grant me a voice. When we first met, you could've interrupted when that guy was talking to me, but you waited to see if I'd been someone raised to silence their own voice, and if I had, I know you would've cut your meeting short. Even with Madison, she's your colleague, and you didn't speak over me, didn't cut in to say something that would appease us both."

"Anything else?" Adrian asks, bending down to plant a kiss on her forehead, making Jolly hiss as the cat leaps toward the arch formed by Thea's legs.

"I like that you are always kind to those around you, and you'll refuse to let me wash my hair because you like how close it makes you feel to me. I like that you are always touching me, never manhandling me, but I can always feel the heat of your hands near my body. I like that you'll bury your face against the crook of my neck, holding me close as we fall asleep."

"Sounds like you like me."

"That's because I do. Now tell me your favorite color?"

"Teal," Adrian says with a quick raise of his brow as if saying you can guess the reason why. "Oddly enough, it sounds like Thea, don't you think?"

Do you think they make teal caskets? The words form on the tip of her tongue as Adrian scoops Jolly to his chest, oblivious to the new wave of sorrow that hits Thea.

Plummeting her into an abyss of sorrow, where currents thrash her from one failure to another, reminding Thea of all rejections she'd received over many different books, of how no agent saw her as worthy of anything more than empty words of kindness.

Only the men enamored with her had bothered to read Thea's work, who'd seen a glint of whom she could become, and Thea couldn't help but wonder if it was their lust speaking louder than their wit.

Maybe all they did was echo back to her the things she'd been shouting when trapped in a maze of mirrors, where she'd run into the reflection of the woman she hoped to be, only for the glass to break and cut her skin.

"Thea, don't slip away," Adrian mutters, pulling her into his lap, a hand on the back of her head as he holds her close, allowing her tears to sodden the collar of his jacket. "Don't believe the lies in your mind."

"I just want to matter. Promise you won't give up on them? Promise even when I'm gone, you'll fight for my stories to live on? Maybe that's the paradise I'm meant to go to, maybe that's—"

"None of your books will be posthumous. You are worth putting up a fight for, so I'll fight for you until you can fight for your books yourself. Give editors the time they need to get permission to make an offer. Just a little longer, Thea Tea. You just need to wait a little longer. You didn't tell me your favorite color?"

For several moments, Thea doesn't say anything, clinging to Adrian and Jolly as if they are a lifeline, the only things keeping her from deepening into her sorrow.

Her attention drifts to the sway of the car, the city becoming blurry as traffic slowly dissipates like morning dew when the sun comes out.

Fingers running back and forth on the collar of Adrian's shirt, Thea's eyes flit over the windows to the ceilings with little LED lights, to the trims on a car worth more than any advancement she could ever hope to receive for her books.

"Yellow," Thea speaks in a choked-up whisper with tears still rolling down her cheeks, lingering on her chin before they drip down on Adrian's shoulder. "My mom wears this perfume that smells like the color yellow. Yellow is like the sun rays enveloping me in a golden blanket of safety while lounging in a meadow."

"What color is your brother?"

"Phthalo green. He uses strong cologne, wears expensive watches and suits, drives a nice car, and lives in a fancy condo. For everyone who sees him, they'll think he's as lifeless as the color black, but when you take a deeper look, he's joyous like spring, giddy. Julien is playing a role, but he's the best man I've ever met."

"And me?" Adrian runs his fingers over Thea's thighs, coaxing her into taking a deeper breath, into expurgating the tension in her muscles.

"Yellow."

"I love you too, Thea. Now, what is too serious to be joked about?"

Skyscrapers become miniatures before bleeding into trees as they escape the city. Each taking turns to ask and answer questions well beyond the initial thirty-six.

Conquering little pieces of knowledge about each other's childhood, learning the stories behind the few scars on their bodies—from when Thea threw a glass during frat party because one of the guys had been harassing a girl, but the shards ricocheted against her to when Adrian needed surgery on his shin after a skiing accident in Gstaad.

They talk until Thea follows Jolly's cue and falls asleep curled on Adrian's lap while he murmurs all the things he likes about her.

Things he'd only ever share with years of being married to anyone else, but he was happy to share it with a sleepy Thea, etching the crescent love he feels for her in

Thea's subconscious mind, hoping hypnopedia works to ensure she'll never doubt her worth as that's been something Adrian never doubted, knowing Thea was worth more than the finest things life could offer.

"People don't deserve your tears, Thea," Adrian whispers with a sad smile as her cold nose brushes against his warm neck. "Your blood is something no one is worthy of, but please don't leave me. Not because of this, I can't stand the idea of losing you when you just came into my life, when I know you could leave such a beautiful mark in the world."

25

"Where are we?" Thea asks as she climbs down from the car, tipping her head back to take in the sheer size of the house, located in the center of a woodsy area.

Adrian spins around, stretching his arms with a cocky smile that doesn't quite fit his usual mien, as Thea wraps an arm around his waist while holding Jolly in her other hand.

"Hudson Valley, more precisely, the estate my parents own. Don't worry. They are home with Cove."

"Why are we here? And how many estates do your parents own?"

"I wanted you to get a taste of life in a palacete[8] outside of the city," Adrian steals Jolly from Thea's embrace, cradling the cat close to his heart before he trudges forward. "And there are far too many properties under the Friedman name. I wouldn't know the answer to that."

Barefooted, Thea runs after Adrian, taking only a small moment to appreciate the fluffy grass between her toes—not even in Central Park had the grass been squishy enough for her to think about sleeping there.

Thea jumps on Adrian's back, nearly sending him to the ground, but he manages not to fall. His hand reaches for her thighs as Thea wraps her arms around his neck.

---

[8] Palacete is a Portuguese word for a small palace, bigger than a mansion but not quite as large as a palace.

"I'm never living in a pala...whatever you called this place. I'm not the governor's wife, Friedman."

"You'd be my wife. That's far more beneficial than marrying a politician. They are incredibly corrupt despite being nice, yet they'll take vacations in countries where the legal age is closer to a preteen than an adult for no good reason. Spend a day amongst powerful people, and you soon realize how rare it is for people to be good. Instead they abide by the law and think of it as being the same thing."

"I hate nice people," Thea murmurs as Adrian carries her up a few marble steps. "My mom always said that niceness is a demeanor, that some of the most backstabbing, racist, misogynistic motherfuckers tend to be the nicest people. Goodness is a core value, and those people tend to be hellbent on abiding by their morals."

The front door swings open without Adrian raising a finger to it, making Thea turn her head toward the frame as if to search for some piece of technology available only to the ultra-rich, but all she finds is a little old lady standing with her hands crossed over her belly.

Smacking his hand from her thigh, Thea slides down Adrian's back. She can feel his gray eyes on her, can sense the curl on his lips.

"It's been far too long, huh?"

"The wish I made upon that wishbone seems to have come true," The woman says, voice soothing Thea's nerves as Adrian steps toward her, nearly bowing to hug the lady. "Is she the reason you've been too busy to visit?"

With heat spreading over her cheeks, Thea stands there with her brows raised and a smile plastered on her face as she wonders if maybe Adrian was wrong and his parents are indeed home.

A mask meant to hide a discomfort Adrian sees past, but he quite enjoys the sight of her ruddy cheeks, of how Thea will fidget with the hem of her sleeves to keep herself from shifting her weight from one foot to the other.

Prolonging her misery, Adrian rests his chin on the woman's head, who watches Thea with too relaxed of a smile.

"Thea, please meet Monica." Adrian's voice echoes faintly in the vast foyer. "Monica, meet Thea, the woman I'd marry in a heartbeat if she allowed me to."

Dipping in an awkward curtsy, Thea mumbles, "Pleasure to meet you."

"Monica was my parents' governess until three years ago when she retired, and they said she could pick one of their houses to enjoy her retirement. In a way, I suppose she's still the governess as the staff here obey her."

Thea gasps in a near sigh of relief, evoking a meow from Jolly.

The woman's brown eyes flit over Thea, taking a measure of Thea's body. When her gaze falls on Thea, wiggling her toes in discomfort, a fleeting smile tugs on her lips with faint wrinkles surrounding them.

"I don't know why your mother said the girl doesn't have good hips for birthing."

"Probably because Adrian is quite taller than me," The words slip past her lips before she can bite them down, much to Adrian and Monica's delight. "He'd give me chunky babies."

"Not chunky," Adrian protests, prowling toward Thea.

He leans down, scrunching his whole face as his fingers glide to the nape of her neck, tugging Thea closer despite Jolly's jealous meows.

"Then what?"

"Supermodel height baby with all your beauty and wit," He explains, immediately forgetting Monica is watching them. "Can you imagine a little baby Thea? She'd be so grumpy and adorable."

"Hopefully none of those babies are conceived under my roof. As luxurious as this house is, the walls are awfully thin."

Thea prods his waist as Adrian smirks at her, daring her to challenge just how thin those walls truly are—eliciting a deeper shade of red as Thea gingerly hides her face against his chest.

"Come girl, the princeling called earlier, and the staff bought you some clothes for a few days. Night will fall soon, come and change into a pajama set."

Adrian pulls away, stepping back when Thea reaches for Jolly. Clinging to the kitten, Adrian disappears down a hallway with an arched ceiling and a rich work of plaster that gives the house a false sensation of belonging to a king of a long-gone era.

A warm hand brushes against Thea's back, coaxing her toward the double staircase carved on solid wood—from the wrought railing to the steps covered in a nondescript rug, every part of the staircase has been polished to pristine condition.

A marvelous gasp bubbles past Thea's lips as the soles of her feet touch the rug that is somehow fluffier than the grass surrounding the palacete, as Adrian called it.

Thea only peels her gaze from the floor when she reaches the top of the stairs that disembogues into the floor-to-ceiling windows, granting her a view of a large aquamarine pool with water cascading from a hot tub, the polar opposite of the plastic hot tub she grew up with.

Long before the property is enveloped by the woods, Thea sees a darkened outline of a tennis square beside a basketball court.

"You'll have time to explore some of the facilities before going back to the city." Monica loops her arm through Thea's, pulling her toward the east wing of the house.

The ceilings there are also arched, giving a sensation that the house is closing in on them, embracing them in a way that's comforting rather than oppressive.

Perhaps it's the dark colors on the wall, Thea muses without noticing Monica leading her to french double doors that open to a room that reminds Thea of Adrian's bedroom in the city.

Except here, the bedding is teal, matching the long curtains drowning over what Thea supposes are equally enormous windows that would grant her a view of another set of facilities.

"The bathroom is behind that door," Monica says, pulling Thea from her reverie before she can wander around the room. "I'll bring you a change of clothes."

Thea lingers there, head tipped to the side as she studies Monica the same way the woman had done to her, noticing the few lines around Monica's eyes that are less prominent than the ones around her lips.

Noticing the few strands of white in a head of hair so dark, it nearly appears to be black, matching well to the natural tan of her skin. A shade reminding Thea of an owl's feathers, and the way Monica looks at her tells Thea she shares the animal's wisdom too.

"What?" Monica asks.

"You seem like a difficult woman to please."

"I am, especially when it comes to Adrian and his sisters. Those kids are the closest things I have to children. They have taught me how to feel love beyond words and wrath beyond human."

"Break his heart, and I'm dead?" Thea carols as she walks to the bathroom. "Luckily, you won't need help for that."

A shiver travels down Thea's spine as her feet touch the slabs of white onyx, a creamy shade that matches the light green taking up the wall designated for the shower and elegant bathtub.

Thea tiptoes to the tub, its edges nearly overflowing with bubbles giving the space a floral scent that makes her nose itch as it reminds her of her grandma's perfume.

Leaving a trail of clothes behind her, Thea sinks into the warm water, resting her head against the polished edge as her mind struggles between enmity and amity.

Thea blows the bubbles she cradles in her hands as she thinks about those three words that send her stomach into a flurry, making the palm of her hands sweaty as her heart beats faster.

You are mine.

The words echo endlessly in her mind, stealing the breath from her lungs as she imagines the pain of that sharp knife cutting through her skin.

You are mine.

Her hands tremble with a scream lodged in her throat, the urge to scream as her classmate couldn't when blood poured from her mouth.

You are mine.

Thea knows if her stomach hadn't been empty, she'd retch in her bath, unable to stomach the guilt she's carried in the deepest recess of her mind, where she could say she didn't know better.

You are mine.

For years she tried to convince herself that her hands hadn't been tainted with blood as she hadn't been the author who romanticized abuse—would never write a book where the female characters were meant solely as a glory hole and to advance the fictional life of men.

You are mine.

A sentiment Thea buried deep within herself but came out whenever she thought of her friend who never got to live the life she dreamt of.

You are mine.

There is so much blood on Thea's hands, the only gift she'd gotten from the many authors Thea used to support as a teenager, and she knows she didn't make those books bestsellers on her own.

Her hands aren't the only ones sodden with blood, but Thea would recommend those books to all of her friends, to anyone who'd be willing to listen and trust her judgment—many of which ended in unhealthy relationships, with scars covering their bodies.

You are—the voices in her head become silent when Thea hears dragged-out footsteps.

"Why are you crying girl?" Monica's voice makes Thea raise her head, finding the woman to be hazy through the tears lining her eyes. "If my boy has done anything—"

"No, it's not him. It could never be him, Adrian is perfect. Far better than anything I'd ever be worthy of."

Monica walks toward the green onyx countertop settled beneath large windows, allowing one view of the woodsy area as they brush their teeth instead of staring at their reflection.

"What is it then, girl?"

"Why do you keep calling me 'girl'? I don't know if Adrian didn't bother to tell you, but my name is Thea."

"He did. Earlier today, he called to say he would be stopping by for the weekend, but before he shared that little bit of information. He told me about you. I held Adrian when he was born, he's my little boy, and if you are someone he loves, then you are my girl to care for. So tell me, *girl,* why are you crying?"

Thea doesn't speak as she watches Monica's hand move against the onyx counter, inspecting for dust when the house seems pristine. Thea wonders if even dust motes think of themselves as unworthy of such splendor, or perhaps magic exists solely within the Friedman clan.

Surely there must be an explanation as to why the Central Park penthouse is always immaculate in the mornings, even when Thea and Adrian have left the living room in disarray with pillows on the floor.

"I won't ask again, but I can't be of aid if you don't share what is weighing on your mind."

"Why is life so unfair?"

"How so?"

"Why is it a fifteen-year-old girl, someone who dreamt of being a doctor because she wanted to help people, is the one whose body is now nothing but bones left in the hollow husk of a casket, while the man who murdered her lives a comfortable life in prison?"

"Life in prison is a lot better than a life not lived, isn't it?" Monica asks despite seeing the truth reflected in Thea's eyes. "Life is everything but fair. The least deserving people are often the ones who face little suffering, being handed the riches they desire but passionate people, ah, those are the ones who feel as if they have so much to prove, the ones who'll go step by step without going anywhere."

Monica has a melancholic look in her kind eyes and a sad smile on her lips as she looks at Thea, seeing all the things Thea has tried to hide away—the way Thea has bent to her limit.

"Many give up before they can see the stars. Before they can raise the bar that sunk so low, choking their potential as they wonder if they are good enough when they'd always been too good. It's exhausting, isn't it? Trying to do good when the masses acclaim the bad?"

"It is so frustrating."

Monica saunters toward Thea, softly grunting as she kneels beside the bathtub, running a wrinkly hand through Thea's hair.

"Was she a friend?"

Nodding, Thea says, "I feel so guilty. I doubt the people responsible for her death feel any remorse."

"Then why are you feeling guilty?"

With quivering lips, Thea tells Monica the same story she told Rue, how that death impacted the way Thea writes, how she sees books, and how disgusted she becomes when seeing what is essentially a misogyny manifesto gaining traction until the title becomes a bestseller—writing countless more names in patriarchy's death note.

Thea shares the number of times she'd cry and retch when one of those manifesto books was independently published, scrubbing her skin until she bled as she knew those books would now reach new victims.

"Can I give you a word of advice, Thea?" Monica asks, wiping away a single tear that rolls down her cheeks. "Don't blame yourself for a problem you are trying to solve. You aren't the one doing those things. That blood isn't on your hands, and the blood that had been on your hands before your classmate died, that was washed away when you opened your eyes to see the harm these women bring to other women."

"But is it enough?"

"No. Bigotry is a metastasized cancer. One that affects the brain and brings out the utmost stupidity in people, spreading from one person to another. And guess what? Stupid people think of themselves as being smart, those writers think they are writing stories about strong women, but the cancer of their hatred has spread beyond repair. Be thankful for your health when very few people are."

"And the readers too?"

"What do *you* think?" Knees cracking, Monica stands up, ambling toward a heated towel rack. "Get up, girl. If you stay any longer in that water, you'll be as wrinkly as I am."

Thea chuckles, standing up with bubbles lingering on her wet skin until Monica wraps her in a warm towel, patting her skin as Thea had seen her cousins do with their children when they'd get out of a lake.

"You know, girl, just make sure you have a community. I've been around enough authors to know they need one."

"I don't care to have community with people whose bonanza reeks of misogyny, racism, and other forms of crimes against humanity. I'd rather be isolated and lose opportunities than bid farewell to my morals."

"I can see why my Adrian is smitten over you. I've never seen him like this."

"He's a man of taste," Thea mutters, stepping out of the tub as Monica pulls back, ambling out of the room to give her privacy.

Thea sighs as being alone brings back the exhaustion woven deep within her being, something she's carried long before the five years she promised herself. At that point, she'd already been broken.

If only the Universe, God, or fate showed her an act of kindness, taking the choice from her hands. It's far better to be the one who died in their sleep than the one who drowned in murky waters.

Pulling silky pajama pants over her damp legs, Thea trudges forward while ignoring the annoying urge to cry when there are no tears left.

Working on the buttons of her blouse, Thea ambles without paying attention to where she's going. Not minding the hallways or trying to remember the direction Adrian went as she trusts fate to bring her to him.

That's the one thing fate hasn't failed, although she did find it cruel to bring him as a witness to the end of her life.

Footsteps echo against the windows flanking the beautiful staircase, yet all Thea can do is cling to all of her broken pieces, to the million little fragments of her being as she searches for Adrian through the fog of sorrow.

"There you are," Adrian's voice follows the muffled sound of him patting the cushion beside him. "Come here, Thea Tea."

So she does, blindly following the sound of his voice until his warm hand brushes against her fingers, pulling her down onto him.

"Still sad?"

"I'm fine."

"Don't lie to me. I can read you like a book."

"What kind of book am I?" Thea runs her fingers through his hair as she straddles Adrian, her legs wrapping around him.

Adrian offers a sad smile as he lays a finger under her chin, tipping her head back when Thea hadn't noticed how low it'd been.

"That's better. Defeat doesn't look good on you. You know how every writer makes their protagonists suffer through the seven layers of hell before reaching paradise?"

She nods, head falling a few inches before Adrian tips it back up, mirroring her as if to remind Thea she's not one to let herself be defeated.

"You, Thea, you're the best kind of book, made from the same stuff that makes Shakespeare loved to this day. A dude who died in 1616, and people still care about his work. I dare say you are made from the same stuff as those stone slabs with passages of the bible."

"Stop flattering me and be honest, Friedman."

"I am. Don't tell my grandma, but I'm not overly religious, yet I'd get on my knees every day to pray for you, pray to you. I'd give up everything I have to see you achieve everything you want."

"Why?" Thea asks, chin trembling as she refuses to let those tears fall.

"Because if you were a book, then I'd be your happy ending."

Thea laughs, leaning down to steal a kiss from Adrian, sighing on his lips as he wraps his arms around her, squeezing Thea against his chest as if to prove a point.

"You are so cheesy, Adrian Friedman."

"And you bring out the romance love interest in me. It's quite annoying how I just think of the most disgustingly sweet things when you cross my mind."

"Such as?"

"Well, I often wish the book of our life was an erotica. Just fucking until my dick has a rash."

"In this erotica, can you have two dicks? That seems fun."

"Please, Thea, I think I can afford to buy us a dildo, a vibrator too. A flogger, a paddle, whatever toy you want."

"You are enough for me. I'll take a vibrator for when you are gone."

"Understand one thing, Thea Scriven-Friedman," Adrian says, smiling at the brow she arches. "What? I gotta practice so I can get used to saying it but understand one thing, Thea Scriven, I'll never be gone. You are stuck with me until you tell me to go."

"Then we are stuck together, Adrian Scriven. What? Why hyphenate when you can take my name instead?"

"My grandpa will hate that, but anything for you. Remember, Thea Tea, say the word, and the world is yours."

Thea knows the hidden meaning there.

She knows with a mere please, she'd get her book published because of Adrian, a book deal far too generous and above anything any writer would ever get.

"What are we eating, and what is the plan for this weekend, Chlamy?"

"No plans, and I ordered some tacos. It should be getting here soon. You just gotta lay down and relax."

26

Sprawled over a lounger, Thea's caught between being awake and asleep as she listens to the sound of Adrian swimming laps in the impossibly large pool while the sun relaxes her body.

No plans, Adrian had said the night before, but Thea hadn't believed him, expecting him to have some grand surprise of sorts when all he wanted was to give them a break from life.

Tipping closer to sleep, Thea doesn't hear as water drips against the concrete slabs surrounding the pool nor the little grunt Adrian lets out as he stretches himself, gray eyes lingering on the towel covering Thea's butt as she'd been uncomfortable with how petite the bikinis offered to her are.

Adrian perches himself on the edge of the lounger, sweeping her long hair to one side. The tip of his finger like a feathery touch against her naked skin, evoking goosebumps and a sleepy moan.

"Minha bebê dorminhoca, é tão bonitinha dormindo que nem parece ser endiabrada.[9]"

Thea practically purrs as Adrian's fingers glide down the divot of her spine, brushing past the string of her bikini top, tracing all the way to the dimples in the small of her back before he goes back up.

---

[9] Translation: "My sleepy baby, she's so cute sleeping that she doesn't even seem to be devilish."

"Stop harassing me. I'm trying to sleep," Thea mutters, shifting to take his hand from her back.

Pouty lips and all, Thea holds his hand as a toddler would fall asleep clinging to a teddy bear they have owned since birth. The edge of her lips curls up as Adrian leans down to plant a kiss on her temple.

"Are you hungry, Thea Tea?"

"A little."

"Should we have hot, wild, and rough sex before I make you something to eat?"

Laughing, Thea shifts to lay her head on his lap, smiling as she raises a hand to run her fingers through Adrian's wet hair, preening at how the man melts with that naive touch.

"Out in the open? Where all the members of your staff can see us?"

"I sent them all home for the weekend. Only Monica is here, but she told me she was going downtown to buy groceries."

"And since when do we have hot, wild, and rough sex?" Thea asks, appreciating the faint shade of pink spreading across Adrian's cheeks.

"You almost broke my nose. I'd say that's hot, wild, and rough sex, don't you think?"

A vulpine smile blossoms on Thea's lips as she taps her lips, and Adrian leans down, moving his hand to the back of her head, giving her a quick kiss as his free hand falls on hers.

Weaving their fingers, Thea shifts once more, allowing Adrian to settle between her legs as she opens her mouth and Adrian slips in his tongue, stealing a moan from both of them as the kiss deepens, teeth nibbling on each other's lips while Adrian runs his thumb over her knuckles.

"Hot, wild, and rough kiss," Adrian mutters against Thea's lips, smiling when she hits his chest.

"Shut up, Chlamy."

"Make me."

So she does, kissing him once more as she wraps her legs around Adrian, savoring the little whimper he lets out with his hands exploring her body, rediscovering the curves already etched into his memory.

Rolling her hips against Adrian, Thea kisses a path down his neck, biting on his flesh as her tongue darts over the wet skin.

"Consider me silenced." Adrian tips his head back, hands squeezing Thea's but just so he can feel her smile against his skin. "God, I love you."

"There is no God here, Adrian Friedman. Just two sinners."

"I like sinning, I'm great at sinning. I'm a sinful boy."

"Shut up. Stop being so cute," Thea says, leading his hands to the string of her bikini top.

Shivering as the knot comes undone, Thea buries her fingers in his hair, relishing in the silkiness of it, while Adrian tosses her bikini aside. Thea arches toward Adrian, shivering as his lips trail down her body, hands roaming freely, moving all too slowly for how her blood clamors for him, needing him to touch her all over.

"I'd go to hell and back for you, Thea Tea."

"Take me to paradise first." The words morph into a moan as Adrian takes her breast in his mouth, tongue flickering against her nipple.

Her nails leave vermillion streaks on his pale back, urging him to ravage her, but Adrian doesn't bother to do as he's told.

Not as his lips move further down, peppering kisses on Thea's stomach while he pulls on the strings of her bikini bottom before moving back up, kissing her sternum, then her jaw, before laying kisses on the tip of her nose and her closed lids.

"I want you, Adrian."

"Out in the open?" He jests against her mouth. "Where all the members of my staff can see us?"

"Let them see who I belong with."

"No, Thea Tea. You don't belong to anyone. You are the wildest of flowers. You are not meant to be tamed."

"I said I belong with you, not to you. I'll never belong to anyone other than myself, but I want you, Adrian. I want you more than I ever knew possible. I'd choose you over and over."

"Say that again, Thea."

"I want you? Or that I choose you? Maybe you want me to say that I love you because I do. Which is it?"

Adrian dips his fingers down between them, hissing as Thea spreads her legs for him, feeling how wet she is from nothing but mere kisses.

"Fuck."

Thea smiles as he brings glistening fingers to her lips, smiles as her tongue laps around his fingers, and Adrian's eyes become wide.

"I taste so good," Thea drawls, taking his hand in hers. "You make me so wet."

"Do I?"

Adrian positions himself between her legs, caressing one leg while kissing the other as Thea licks her lips. Her breath becomes labored in anticipation, fingers grabbing onto the cushioned lounger instead of grabbing his hair.

Kisses growing nearer to where she needs him the most, Adrian coils his arms around her waist, pressing her down into the lounger with a hand on her stomach.

"Eyes on me," He demands before lowering his mouth to her with a groan of satisfaction.

Adrian watches as her lips part for a silent moan when he kisses her with gentle despair. Needing to taste her but knows he has all the time in the world for it.

Gray eyes remain focused on Thea's face as his tongue runs in and around her folds, pausing to graze her clit with the lightest of strokes before dipping down at her entrance. He watches as Thea bites down on her lips when he pushes his tongue further into her sex, as he hums with her taste and scent.

Adrian has always enjoyed eating a girl out, enjoyed the taste of pussy, but there was something exquisite about Thea—perhaps it's just the fact of how sated he can be with merely watching her climax, with the lingering taste of her in his mouth, but Adrian doesn't think he'd ever grow tired of being between her legs.

He watches as Thea's body flexes, tightening with his lazy caress. Adrian moves up, making Thea grab onto his hair when he envelops her clit, flicking his tongue over it as a hand moves over her naked torso.

"Fuck," She curses, laying a hand over his as he kneads her breast, thumb running circles around her nipple. "Thank God for whatever girl taught you how to eat pussy."

Pulling back and relishing in the sight of her distress, Adrian mutters, planting petite kisses on her thighs, "I thought there was no God here?"

"Adrian Friedman Scriven, if you don't fucking go back to—" her words fall into a loud moan as Adrian gives her pussy a light slap with the hand over her stomach.

His entire body stiffens as Thea's legs quiver against his shoulder while he kisses her thigh, fingers raking back and forth until she can breathe again.

"I didn't know you liked that.

"I didn't know I liked that. I'm confused."

"It was delightful to see," Adrian murmurs with a mischievous smile as his lips creep further down. "Look at you, breath caught in your throat with just kisses."

"Don't get cocky."

Adrian blows her a kiss before licking her from the base up to her clit, driving Thea to whimper as her legs wrap around his head, holding Adrian there as he explores her.

Savoring the way she tastes and the sounds of her moans. The way Thea purrs as he slides a finger inside her, how her hips move in tandem with his tongue.

Flicking his tongue, Adrian slides another finger inside Thea, relishing how her body tightens around his digits that curl as he sucks on her.

"I need you," Thea moans, tugging his wet hair. "I need you, Adrian, please?"

"Not ye—"

His words die on his lips as Thea pulls away from him before forcing him down on the lounger. Straddling him,

Thea kisses him, tasting herself on his tongue as she pulls down his swimsuit with trembling fingers.

"Feet on the ground, or you'll fall," Adrian mutters, hands running down her spine. "I'd hate for you to get hurt."

Thea doesn't answer as she spits in her hand before stroking him, watching as Adrian closes his eyes for a moment, enjoying how her thumb moves over the tip.

"Why do you make me feel like this?"

"Like what, Thea?"

"Like I'll disintegrate without your touch? Like I'm a fire that aches to burn down to ashes? Like I lose sight of everything when you kiss me with that little smirk telling me you want much more than innocent cuddling?"

This time it's Adrian who doesn't answer as he pulls her down toward his cock. It's him who relishes in the way her body shudders, nails sinking into his chest while her head lolls back.

"Beautiful." Adrian lifts his hands toward her waist despite knowing one should never touch a masterpiece. "You are impossibly beautiful, Thea Scriven."

Laying her hands on his thighs, Thea raises herself to the tip before sinking back down with a roll of her hips, stealing a groan from Adrian as his cheeks grow flustered.

She moves back and forth, riding Adrian as his hands tighten around her waist, trying so hard not to thrust into her, not to roll around to fuck her how he wants.

Thea's head tilts back with a moan as Adrian drops a hand to her clit, drawing circles as she bounces on him with beads of sweat gliding down her spine.

"Fuck," Adrian groans before softly whimpering as he thrusts into her while cupping her breast.

Chasing his release, Adrian doesn't notice Thea moves her hands to his chest, moaning against the shell of his ear, doesn't notice as she kisses his neck before biting down on the slope of his shoulder to muffle the startled yelp as his large hand comes down on her ass before she can feel him cumming inside of her.

Adrian slouches against the lounger, feeling his cum dribble from Thea's thighs down his leg. Slapping her ass once more, Adrian relishes in the moan of half-pain and half-lust—a moan that makes his soft cock twitch with need.

"Listen very carefully, Thea Tea, " Adrian drawls. "I'm taking you back to our bedroom. I'm going to throw you on the bed and fuck you until you are so sensitive the mere brush of my finger will make you cum."

"You wouldn't dare."

"Is that a challenge?"

"It's only a challenge if you can catch me."

Thea smacks her lips against his before running away with a laugh fluttering in the air between herself and Adrian as she runs up the marble staircase leading back to the petite mansion.

She leaps two steps at a time, squealing loudly as she can hear Adrian's footsteps creeping closer. Thea runs past the large doors that'd been left open, blurring the division between interior and exterior.

"Stop running. My feet are still wet," Adrian bemoans, voice echoing against the vaulted ceiling as his fingers brush against Thea's waist, stealing a yelp from her as she pivots around the couch, throwing pillows at Adrian and on the floor, littering his path toward her.

"Where is the finish line?" Thea asks between gasps of breath.

"The kitchen?"

"I don't know where that is."

"Exactly."

Karate chopping a pillow back at Thea, Adrian pounces forward, missing Thea by an inch as he slips and falls on the couch.

Thea runs away once more, laughing as she used to when playing with her brother, much to her parent's dismay, as they'd bring havoc to their home.

When more than a few mass-produced vases would be collateral damage to them, bumping against side tables and the pillows they threw at each other.

Afraid of breaking something she'd need to work four lifetimes to be able to pay back, Thea holds her arms close to her body, but her laugh echoes against the walls, resounding over the arched hallway ceiling as she goes from the living room to a TV room.

The rooms blur into each other, the warm wood flooring caving to cold marble when Adrian manages to wrap his fingers around her wrist, tugging her to himself as she squeals, hitting his chest while trying to free herself from his embrace.

"I caught you," He says, leaning down to rest his forehead on hers when gray eyes flit over her shoulder. "Mom?"

Thea whirls around, finding a woman with beautiful blonde hair and gray eyes staring at them. A smile curls on her lips as Adrian pulls Thea to his chest, dropping a hand to Adrian's forearm that covers her breast.

"Mom?" Thea mutters, sinking her nails into Adrian's wrist as his free hand drops over her unclothed mound. "You said your parents weren't here? Why is your mom here?"

"I didn't know she would be here. She told me she was in London visiting Olivie."

"Yes, indeed, but when Momo said you'd come over for the weekend with your girlfriend...well, I couldn't miss the opportunity to meet her."

"Mãe, eu te falei que é cedo demais pra apresentar a Thea pro resto da familia,[10]" Adrian mutters in Portuguese, grunting when Thea steps on his toes in a silent demand for him to not speak in a language she can understand—at least not when he name drops her.

"Adrian Friedman, não ouse falar assim comigo. Você é meu filho, eu tenho não apenas o direito mas como o dever de conhecer a sua namorada.[11]*"*

Cheeks painted in the deepest shade of red, Thea sustains a smile, annoyed at not understanding a single word while too embarrassed to make any demands.

"She's not my girlfriend."

"I'm really not."

"So you both share a habit of running naked around friends?" His mother asks in a thick yet adorable accent. "It

---

[10] Translation: "Mom, I told you it's too soon to introduce Thea to the rest of the family."

[11] Translation: "Adrian Friedman, don't you dare speak to me like that. You're my son, I have not only the right, but the duty to meet your girlfriend."

is lovely to meet you, Thea. I've heard many great things about you."

"The pleasure is all mine, miss, I mean- ma'am, or is it, missus? Maybe mistress?"

"Gabriela is fine."

"Gabriela Friedman?"

"Yes, dear. Last time I checked, my husband and I haven't divorced," Gabriela speaks with a motherly smile. "Now, I'll go meet Monica for lunch. That should give you one or two hours to get dressed. Later I'd like to talk to you, Thea. In private and hopefully fully dressed."

"Of course," Thea mutters, still clinging to Adrian's arm draped over her naked body. "I'll never be naked again."

Gabriela laughs as she picks up a crocodile leather bag from the kitchen island before walking away with high heels peeling against the marble flooring.

Slouching against Adrian's arm, Thea lets him sweep her off the floor, carrying her back through the hallway they'd run through.

"Please kill me," She mutters against the crook of his neck. "I've never in my entire life been so embarrassed."

"Don't worry, Thea Tea. My mother was a model before she became a photographer, which is when she met my dad. She's quite used to seeing naked girls."

"Naked girls that don't have her son's cum running down their legs, Adrian!"

Adrian laughs, thumb caressing her thigh as he climbs the beautiful staircase, peering down the large windows to find Thea's bikini still discarded near the pool.

"Not the first time my mom has seen a girl with her son's cum. See, Thea Tea, my mom has a terrible habit of not knocking while being incredibly light on her feet. One time I thought I was home alone with my then girlfriend when my mom walked into my room as ropes of cum flew onto my ex's face, which I then proceeded to use her face to cover myself. Luckily, her mouth was already open."

"I hate that." Thea hits his chest a little harder than she'd been hitting him before—which Adrian pretends it's jealousy over a story with another girl. "I want your mom to like me, and now she'll despise me."

"Because she saw your ass and tits for maybe three seconds?"

"Because I've been running around naked in a house far more valuable than me."

"Nothing is more valuable than you, and if my mom were to hate you for whatever reason, then she wouldn't be my mom. If anything, Olivie's next girlfriend will have to be *phenomenal* for my mom to like her better."

Thea groans, kicking the air in frustration as she wraps her arms around his neck. "Adrian, I don't have enough money to pay for a single candle in this place if I were to break it by accident."

"And it would be just a candle. They are bad for your lungs anyway. You'd be doing us a favor."

Adrian stands on the edge of their bed, holding Thea close to him as she hides her face against the crook of his neck. Oblivious to the foolish grin adorning Adrian's lips as she savors the way her body melds into his.

How his arms never seem to tire of holding her, but mostly, he enjoys the proximity and how Thea's body relaxes against him.

"Thea?"

"Yes?"

"We have a few hours to kill—"

"Get fucked, Adrian Friedman."

"That's what I'm trying to do."

Adrian throws Thea against the bed, smiling at the sight of blushed cheeks, the way her nose scrunches as if she's trying to disappear into herself.

Pulling the blankets toward her body, Thea crawls to the edge of the bed, wrapping her arms around his waist as she whimpers with mocking tears.

"I'm so embarrassed."

"You know, in Spanish, that would be embarazada."

"*Embarazada* means pregnant, not embarrassed."

"We could work on that," Adrian jokes, poking her forehead. "A few practice runs would help."

"Adrian, your mother saw me naked. Why are you so nonchalant about it?"

"Because you'd be even more embarrassed if I were to freak out? My heart got lodged in my throat when I saw her, but not because of our...precarious situation. I don't want you to feel uncomfortable with my family."

Thea plops down on the bed, feeling Adrian moving to lay beside her, weaving their fingers together before bringing her hand to his lips.

"Even if they've seen me naked?"

"You are two down, three to go before my family can say we've all seen you naked...at least if we only consider my immediate family, if we include uncles, aunts, cousins, grandparents, then it's a higher number. I'm sure they'd all love to see you naked. You're beautiful, a work of art. Vermeer wishes he could've painted the perfection of your existence."

"How very romantic of you," Thea says, rolling on top of Adrian, resting her forehead on his as his hands wander down her spine.

"I'm nothing if not a gentleman."

"You don't fuck like one."

"At least I don't fuck like a pornstar either. Which, how do you know how a pornstar fucks like?"

"What do you think?"

Adrian arches a brow, rolling as he pins Thea's hands over her head. "You've fucked a pornstar?"

She nods, wrapping her legs around his waist.

"From zero to ten?"

"Ten with tongue, four with cock," Thea explains. "He'd fuck me good, making me scream before he'd stop pull out and genuinely flex while looking at a mirror? He had a mirror in front of his bed, and his closet had mirror doors, so plenty of surfaces for him to check himself on."

"What am I?"

"Last I checked, you are a trust fund baby."

Adrian groans, burying his face in the crook of her neck. Thea squirms as he bites on the sensitive skin, rolling his hips against her.

"You know what the best sex one can have is?" Thea probes. "A musician or a dancer. They know tempo, and know how to keep up with it."

"Did you know I can play the piano? I know you know I can dance."

"I don't know if I consider waltzing as dancing."

"What are you trying to say, cruel woman?"

The corner of Thea's mouth turns downward as her brow quirk up. "I did tell you fuck me good, didn't I?"

"Good as in a seven out of ten or as a ten out of ten?"

"Wouldn't you like to know, Chlamy."

"I would, actually."

Thea sits up, biting on her lips as her gaze rakes down Adrian's chest, fingers trailing with a few inches of delay, eliciting a husky groan from the man.

"I'd need a reminder to say for sure," Thea drawls, chest raising faster as memories flow, reminding her of how Adrian makes her feel.

"I can do that."

"Uhm, but I think getting caught by your mother made my pussy rival the Sahara Desert. A pity."

"Okay," Adrian says, gingerly pushing Thea away as he scoots closer to the center of the bed while she remains perched on its edge.

With a pout on her lips, Thea walks to the bathroom, feet dragging over the flooring as she puts more bounce to her languid steps.

The golden doorknob is cold beneath her digits when Thea hears the telltale sound of wet clothing slamming against the floor—the sound of a low moan.

Head pushed against the cushioned headboard, Adrian strokes himself with one hand while pulling his phone from the nightstand with the other.

A sense of betrayal flutters in her stomach as she whirls to watch him, annoyed he'd use his phone for visuals when she's naked in the same room.

"Are you fucking kiddin—" Thea hisses until her moan echoes faintly from his phone.

Her voice sounds mechanical as she pleas for Adrian in one of the many videos she's sent him when he was at work, and she was left to write alone, often writing sex scenes that would have Adrian taking the role of the love interest but it only left her aching for release.

Scenes that left her needy for Adrian, wanting him there to recreate them with her, but all she had was herself, so she'd send him photos of her wet fingers in her mouth in nothing but her birthday suit.

I need you in me, she says in the video. Adrian now watches while his thumb caresses the tip of his cock. *Need you to pull my hair as you fuck me. I'm so wet for your cock.*

"Fuck Thea," Adrian moans, snapping Thea from her trance to find gray eyes on her—on the hand that wandered to her mound. "Are you wet for me?"

Thea watches as he reaches for something on the nightstand. She doesn't see what as her eyes move back toward the firm grasp he keeps on himself.

"On the foot of the bed," Adrian orders, pulling the cap of lube open with his teeth. "Let me see how you touch yourself for me."

"But—"

"Now, Thea Tea," he hisses, and Thea trembles with a moan. "On the foot of the bed, and spread your legs for me."

Thea does what he asks—or orders, but she's not too sure which one it is, but at that moment, she doesn't care all that much.

Smoothing the thick blanket so there isn't a single crease in the fabric obstructing Adrian's view, Thea lays a hand on the mattress, propping herself up as she waits for Adrian to say something else.

"Lube?"

"Yes," She moans despite not touching herself.

Goosebumps cover her skin as the cold gel touches her. With a single hand, Thea spreads the oily gel over her breast, fingers gliding down her stomach, but she doesn't touch her pussy.

Adrian watches as she kneads her breast, biting her lips to keep herself from moaning as if they were in a bubble where the faintest disruption would shatter the moment.

"You are so beautiful," Adrian mutters, savoring the slight smile on her lips that grows wider as he continues. "Wicked smart. I'm terrified of you, of the power you have over me."

Head lolling back, Thea dips her fingers a few inches down before running her nails against the inside of her thighs, shuddering with the shiver that makes her jolt in bed.

"You are so wet for me, aren't you?"

"Yes."

"Touch yourself," Adrian orders, and her hand darts toward her lips, grazing her clit slightly but enough for him to groan. "Fuck Thea. Do you want me?"

"Yes."

"Rub yourself, Thea Tea."

Thea slips her middle and ring finger against her clit without bothering to hide the moan bubbling past her lips as she moves them back and forth, alternating between circles.

Her brown eyes move back to Adrian's cock, mesmerized as he pumps himself in slow strokes despite how his finger glides over his thick shaft.

"I want you in my mouth," Thea pleas while licking her lips, hips rolling in tandem with her fingers.

"I want to see you play with yourself."

"You have the—"

"No, Thea Tea, I want to relish in every curve of your body as you ache for me, needing my touch without being able to receive it. I want to see how badly you want me."

"I always want you."

"Then show me," he says, and Thea slides those same two fingers inside her as she plops down on the bed.

Pulling on her hard nipples, Thea curls her fingers, pumping them in and out of herself as she presses down with the palm of her hand against her clit.

Thea matches her fingers to Adrian's strokes, rubbing herself to his overly slow movements, but the pressure against her clit makes her whimper.

"I need you inside of me," Thea moans, wanting to crawl to Adrian, but something in the way he looks at her, his eyes consumed by his pupil, keeps Thea from moving.

"How?"

"I need your cock deep inside of me, stretching me so good that I have to bite down a scream." Adrian grunts as her legs quiver. "I want you to fuck me fast, to pull on my hair as you kiss down my—"

The words trail down to nothing as Thea loses herself in the fantasy, imagining Adrian rolling her body, lifting her ass before thrusting into her without caring if she'd been ready or not, imagining how he'd pound into her with a hand on her hip and another around her throat, holding Thea against his chest as he'd kiss her, tongue moving all too gently for how he'd fuck her.

Thea moves her hand faster, feeling that pressure in her stomach as her body tightens, legs quivering before an orgasm crashes down on her, and the only thing she can say is Adrian's name, inflating his ego with how Thea writhes with pleasure, whimpering and humping her hand. Oblivious to how ropes of cum land on his chest as Adrian watches the beauty of her bliss.

"Still want me?" Adrian's voice is husky.

Thea pushes herself up with trembling arms, crawling toward him, hands moving up his legs as she plants kisses from his ankle to thigh, licking the cum in his chest with a satisfied moan.

"You are so annoying, Adrian Friedman," Thea mutters, running her wet fingers over his chest, scooping the cum before taking her hand toward his mouth. "You fuck me so good even when you aren't fucking me."

Sucking on her fingers, Adrian brings a hand to her cunt, making her whole body quiver with a single slap against her clit.

"You have no idea how many times I had to excuse myself from a meeting because of your little torturous videos, how many times I lingered behind after a meeting about some YA book and had to handle the problem you created when all I would think about was lavishing in your pussy, and having your legs wrapped around me."

"Two hours," Thea reminds him, hands stroking his cock that'd never quite become soft after his orgasm. "I'd argue it will take me one hour to recompose myself."

Adrian pounces on her.

Tongue on her neck and hands all over her body as he lets her guide him to her entrance before Thea wraps her beautiful long legs around his waist.

"How?" He grunts against her throat.

"Fuck my brains out."

Undulating his hips, Adrian drives into her with a single hard thrust that makes Thea sink her nails into his back with a moan bordering on a scream.

Adrian doesn't wait long before pulling back before sinking into Thea, whose body bounces as she captures his lips. Fulfilling her fantasies with the gentle kiss when his cock is far from gentle, stretching her as she can feel him growing harder while inside of her.

"I fucking love you," Adrian groans against her mouth. "You feel so fucking good."

Drawing blood from his back, Thea pulls him closer. Needing him deeper, needing every single inch of Adrian against her, needing to feel his teeth in her neck and his tongue on her breast.

Her legs tighten around his waist, pulling him down, sinking him deeper as his thrust doesn't slow down but grows more frantic until he pulls out.

Thea moans in frustration as he throws her around. Hand searching for him, Thea whimpers with the weight of his body on top of her.

"I'm right here," Adrian whispers as he guides himself back to her entrance. "Scream into the mattress."

"Why—fuck."

Thea screams when he pulls on her hair, not hard enough to hurt her but just enough to fulfill the fantasies she shared with him a while back, fucking her from behind to reach a little deeper.

Making her see stars with each long stroke as he pulls out before sinking back into her. Striking a balance between rough and gentle with how Adrian kisses her shoulder as Thea grabs the blankets beneath her sweaty body.

"Fuck, fuck, fuck," The words are muffled as Thea moans with the white blanket between her teeth. "Fuck!"

"Come for me."

"Fuck, I can't."

Snaking a hand under her body, Adrian reaches her clit, feeling Thea shudder with the touch as she clings to the edge of bliss, toes curled as she squirms under Adrian, trying to escape the overwhelming surge of bliss.

"Come for me, Thea Tea."

"Fuck, I can't! It's too much, I—fuck, Adrian."

"But I'm so close," He groans. "I want to cum with you."

"I can't—fuck."

Thea's body is strung like a hunter's bow, and she knows the release of that tension would be unlike anything else—Adrian has already been unlike anything else in far too many aspects. She doesn't know if she can fall any deeper.

"Please come for me."

But Thea denies herself that pleasure for as long as she can, yet all it takes is for him to bite on her neck as he reaches his climax for Thea to follow him to cloud nine with a bellow.

"I got you," Adrian mutters, kissing her spine as he slowly thrusts into her, giving Thea every last bit of himself before he pulls out.

Toppling beside her while pulling Thea against his body as she still quivers, moaning against his shoulder for several moments.

"I got you."

"Fuck Adrian," Thea whimpers, sinking her nails against his sweaty chest. "I'm broken for anyone else."

"Ten out of ten?"

Thea doesn't say anything as she cuddles against Adrian with shivers that push her close to another orgasm as his fingers leisurely rake over her spine.

"I love you."

"I think love you too. Now shut up before I come again."

"Is that a challenge?" He drawls, yet his caress remains light. "Did I hurt you, Thea Tea?"

She shakes her head, biting down on Adrian's shoulder, purring with the fingers rising toward the nape of her neck, with the way he kisses her temple.

"The only hurt I feel is in knowing you could've been fucking me like that all along."

"I prefer taking my time with you, prefer being gentle, but you looked too good for me not to give you everything you asked for. Always remember, I can read you like a book."

Thea tips her head back, finding a smile adorning his handsome face. Adrian bites on her finger as she raises a hand to trace the shape of his lips, making Thea laugh as he lifts a hand toward hers, weaving their fingers together.

A shiver and giggle billow inside her with the kisses Adrian plants on the inside of her wrist, being impossibly gentle after being so rough with her.

"I do love you," Thea confesses in a whisper, feeling his smile against her skin. "You have bewitched me."

"Did I? I'll go draw you a bath—"

"No," She moans, holding him close.

"You should at least pee, Thea Tea."

"I will in a little bit. I just want to say here with you, catch my breath, then I want you to do it again."

"Gentler this time?"

"Only in your wildest dreams, Chlamy."

27

Thea tries to pay attention to what Gabriela, Monica, and Adrian prattle about, trying not to think of how the wetness in her panty is entirely Adrian's fault, how their marathon of hot, wild, and rough sex left her nerves raw to the point of orgasming when Adrian kissed her neck.

Thinking about how it felt as if she was overflowing and drained at the same time, begging for mercy while plunging toward a summit—all because Adrian dares to exist in a perpetual state of perfection.

"Are you alright, dear?"

Startled, Thea jolts in her seat. Lifting her gaze to find Gabriela's gray eyes clouded with worry, oblivious to how Thea doesn't trust herself not to open her mouth to beg Adrian to fuck her.

"Sorry?"

"Are you not hungry?" Gabriela asks as her son drops a hand to Thea's leg, pinky finger inching closer to the apex of her thighs. "Should we ask the chef to prepare you something different?"

"I think I know what she wants." There's an edge of danger to Adrian's voice and how his eyes drop to her lips as if knowing Thea had been licking her lips for lingering tastes of him. "Thea loves eating salmon prepared in a bed of tomatoes and onion. She likes how...moist it gets."

Thea reaches for her glass of wine with slightly shaky hands. Managing to not grimace despite still thinking the finest of wine tastes too much like vinegar.

"I'll pretend you didn't flirt by using a freaking fish as a decoy." Gabriela shoots a smoldering look at Adrian, who raises his shoulder in faux innocence. "My son told me you are a writer?"

Gabriela settles her cutlery on her plate as she brings her elbows to the table, weaving her fingers together before resting her chin on them. Thea mirrors Gabriela's smoldering glance at Adrian, watching as he shrinks into himself with a slight blush surging his cheeks.

"I am, but I haven't gotten anywhere with it. I'm not entirely sure if I qualify as a writer."

Gabriela laughs at that.

Her laugh is the type that, at the very least, will steal a smile from those around her. But it makes Thea want to join Gabriela's laughter to bask in her joy.

"Nathaniel, my husband, is always complaining about the market for that very reason. Writers who publish retellings of stories they didn't read or mimic parts they enjoyed the most from their favorite novels, some of which have been forgotten from the collective mind. Not everyone is meant to be a writer, yet the bestseller lists are filled with people like that. So tell me, darling Thea, which one are you?"

"A failed writer?"

"Nuh-uh," Adrian quips, his blush melting into annoyance. "Mãe[12], she's incredible, you know I don't like romance but Thea's book is the first I've not only devoured but reread."

"Have you made an offer?"

"Mãe, I'm a fantasy editor."

---

[12] Translation: "Mom."

"And?"

"I don't acquire things outside of my genre, nor would I want to work with Thea in that capacity. Business and relationships always get messy. I'd rather miss out on having another bestseller under my belt than miss out on having Thea in my life."

"Meu deus, você realmente tá apaixonado,[13]" Gabriela says, confusing both Thea and Monica.

Hoping that being a little bit drunk will make the jumble of words make sense to her ears, Thea reaches for her glass of wine.

"A gente pode, por favor, não falar em português? É rude conversar em um idioma que as pessoas em volta não entendem,[14]" Adrian says, reaching for Thea as he steals the glass of wine from her hand. "You'll get drunk if you keep drinking like that."

"I kinda want to get drunk."

"No, you don't. My mom will get anything she wants from you with you sober. If you are drunk, she'll get more than she wants."

"Shut up, Friedman," Thea mutters before heat rushing to her cheeks when Gabriela raises a brow. "Oh, not you, Gabriela. I'd never talk to you like that."

"Thea is only rude to the people she's sleeping with."

"Shut. Up. Friedman." Thea sibilates each word, raising her knife at Adrian, who smacks his lips against hers before raising his hands in defeat.

"Oh, to be young and in love."

---

[13] Translation: "My goodness, you truly are in love."

[14] Translation: "Can we please not speak in Portuguese? It's rude to speak in a language those around us don't understand."

Monica chuckles at that, chiming in, "You and Nathan are as in love as the day you met."

"Because he's as handsome today as he was back then."

Thea clings to the shy smile all too fleeting on Gabriela's lips, the way her gaze lowers as she bites her lips with some memory that elicits a blush.

The kind of love Thea had written and read about countless times, but one that's so rarely seen in real life as life would often make love hazy, buried beneath one's daily responsibilities and routine.

Perhaps it's a privilege reserved for those who do not need to worry about money, or maybe it's a choice a couple makes to never allow their love to become mundane.

Thea glances at Adrian, finding him looking at his mom with the same curiosity Thea harbors before gray eyes flit over to her, and he offers her that same shy smile.

A smile that makes her stomach flutter with excitement, not the nervous knots her stomach would be in before a date with a boy that turned out to be terrible, but rather a giddy joy in knowing Adrian loves her.

"God, they really do love each other," Gabriela murmurs to herself. "Come on, Thea darling. I'd like to speak with you alone."

"But dinner?" Adrian chimes.

"You two are more likely to eat each other's face off than finish the pasta."

"But it's shrimp pasta. Shrimp is kinda expensive." Thea spins her fork around the pasta, taking a mouthful as if to prove a point.

Gabriela's chair glides against the dining room floor without evoking a sound, carrying her glass of wine as she says, "Then take your plate with you. Monica and Addie, you stay here."

Planting a kiss on the crown of her son's head, Gabriela taps on Thea's shoulder, awakening her from her trance as she cradles her plate against her chest before following Gabriela down the hallway of the palacete, ambling down the dark halls illuminated by faint lights woven into the walls. Thea muses about how she'd have the house painted in a beautiful beige shade bordering on white, bringing light to a house that is overly dark for her taste, wishing there'd be a contrast between the dark flooring and walls.

A frown slowly creeps between Thea's brows as she thinks of ways she'd redecorate. Taking some of the art out of the living room that caves into a view of the illuminated pool, making the curtains thinner to allow more light into the room without fearing it would damage the art.

Crossing the threshold between the living room and exterior, Thea breathes in the air, laced with the smell of rain, of grass that seems all too aware of the weather change when lightning strikes far away.

"Take a seat, darling Thea," Gabriela says as she plops down on a sofa carved from nautical wood.

Thea does as Gabriela orders, resting the plate against her knees while gingerly eating her mostly untouched pasta. Peeking through her lashes, Thea studies Gabriela as she nourishes a glass of wine, tipping her head to look at the moon. Gabriela's gray eyes become nearly silver as her gaze flits over the stars, leaving Thea to wonder if they speak to Gabriela in a way they never did to her.

"I met my husband when he was a rich man, and I was a supermodel turned photographer," Gabriela speaks with a sigh as her lids flutter close, almost as if feeling the moon tug on her. "A bit of a cliche, I know, but at the time, not many people took me seriously, and many still don't. Not Nathan. He always saw my value before seeing my beauty."

"He sounds like a good man."

"He is, but I'll be honest with you, Thea. I don't know if my younger self would've chosen Nathaniel had I known how difficult it is to be married to someone so important. There is a reason I raised my children to be as mundane as possible, yet they are still the child of a billionaire."

"Meaning?" Thea muffles with the creamy sauce smudged on her lips as she chews on the shrimp.

"It's an isolating life to marry into. Your family will see you as a well of money, and they'd be right as marrying my son grants you the means to many problems. You'll gladly help them, but with time you'll feel used, noticing how they only approach you to ask for money, or they'll expect and demand you to be the one paying for everything. It makes you feel used in a way that you'll wonder if they ever truly cared about you."

Thea smiles to hide how familiar that all sounds, although for a different reason as money had never been something she'd have in abundance, yet, worrying if people cared for her is a thought often depriving her of sleep.

"Adrian hasn't told you about my promise, has he?"

"What promise?"

Thea shakes her head as she turns her gaze to the night sky, trying to read her fate written in those bright silvery dots. "I'm not sure if the future is something to worry about," Thea mutters without explaining why. "Have you ever felt as if you are running out of time?"

"My mother used to tell me all things are like the sand on a beach. If you try to cling to it, they'll evade through the gaps of your fingers until there is nothing left, but if you allow the sand to rest against the palms of your hands, it will stay there, trickling much slower."

"I don't know if I have enough sand left."

"Perhaps there is some in your pocket," Gabriela says as she stands up, strutting toward Thea. "I like you. Just please don't hurt my son. Love wasn't always kind to him, and he loves you more than he loved others. He's terrible at hiding it."

"He really is."

"Will you do me a favor, Thea?"

A breeze runs its fingers through Gabriela's blonde hair, making the woman close her lids for a mere moment as if relishing in a lover's caress.

Thea has no doubt she'd only grow more beautiful with age, allowing the years to show on her face as the thin wrinkles around her eyes and lips tell Thea the story of her life—one replete with laughter and smiles that reached her eyes.

"Yes, of course."

"I'm quite curious about your book. Will you send it to me? I have a long flight back to London tonight, and I'm afraid I'm too excited to catch any sleep."

"You're leaving already?"

"Tomorrow is the opening night of my daughter's play. Not even death would make me miss that. Cove and Nathan are joining us too. Perhaps one day you'll join us?"

"One can hope."

Tears line her eyes as Thea watches Gabriela walk away, leaving her outside with silver veins cleaving the pure darkness of night a few moments before the thunderclap echoes in the distance.

Settling her plate on the empty seat beside her, Thea curls against the soft cushion, bringing her knees to her chest as her gaze falls on the horizon.

Thea often enjoyed watching thunderstorms, mesmerized by how quickly they darkened the world, bringing havoc with their lightning, burning trees down to nothing before the storm blew them away.

With luck, the storm would leave behind a beautiful rainbow. Thea often hoped her life would have the same fate as those thunderstorms, but she often felt like the trees burning down.

"One can hope," Thea repeats to herself with a sigh before walking back inside.

"I don't like when you are quiet," Adrian declares, reaching for the remote to pause the movie they'd been watching in bed. "Why are you quiet?"

"Because we are watching a movie?"

"Not good enough. You always murmur commentary. I miss your commentary, it's cute."

Chuckling, Thea tips her head back, finding Adrian's brows knitted together in worry as he pulls Thea's hand toward his lip.

"Not my fault you choose a movie about deep sea oil extraction."

"It's an interesting topic," Adrian protests, tightening his arm around Thea and pulling her into his chest. "Can I share a secret?"

"Always, Chlamy."

"My dad has been pestering me to watch this movie. He claimed it was *intellectual pornography,* so I figured we could watch together, but it's insufferable, isn't it?"

"Intellectual pornography?" Thea asks with a brow arched in confusion. "What does that entail?"

"He calls any topic worth discussion. Abortion, gun control, or the many wars our country wedges its way into, intellectual pornography."

"That oddly makes sense. Do philosophical debates fit into intellectual pornography?"

Adrian nods, lips moving down to Thea's wrist. "Philosophical debates are my dad's favorite kind of intellectual pornography. We could watch something else? Perhaps the non-intellectual kind of porn?"

"What do you propose?" Thea leads him on, shivering as Adrian nibbles on her skin, his lips moving along the slope of her shoulder.

"I was fifteen when my uncle gave me a DVD with this movie, *As Brasileirinhas,* it was life-changing in a very depressing way, learning I didn't have the world's largest cock. I did, however, have the best cock in the locker room and received the biggest tongue-lashing my mom had ever given me. Traumatizing in many ways."

Thea's laugh reverberates against the tall ceiling as Adrian smiles against the crook of her neck, planting a kiss over her quickening pulse.

"Was that your first contact with porn? My mom imbued in my brother and me that porn was terrible, claiming it would fuck us up and it was disgusting to support an industry that exploits young women."

"She's not wrong, but don't forget that at fifteen, I was still an awkward teen. The only pussy I'd seen at the time was through a screen, at least until I was seventeen, and then the same uncle took me to a brothel. That was the last time the Friedman's saw him. My mom didn't appreciate him sexualizing her son."

"Thank God, I'd never let my children near your uncle."

"Your children?" Adrian asks as Thea slowly slides her legs over Adrian, running her finger through his hair as she straddles him. "I think you mean *our* children."

"I'm sure you would just hire a nanny to act as—"

Her phone vibrating against the nightstand interrupts Thea, who ignores Adrian's groans of protest as she stretches toward the device.

"Where the fuck have you been?" Jules's voice raises as she picks up his video call, pulling away from Adrian not to show him

"In New York."

"Don't lie to me, Theodore."

"Don't call me Theodore!" Thea protests as she knows Jules only uses the name their parents had picked out in hopes of having two boys when he's mad at her for some reason. "It's not my fault I wasn't born a boy. Besides, Thea is a full name."

"If you won't tell me where you are, I'll call the cops on you."

"And tell them what? That you are being a jerk to your little sister? I'm little. You shouldn't be a jerk to me."

"I'll tell them Aaron, mom, and I have been trying to reach you since Thursday, and this is the first time you deign to pick up."

Adrian arches a brow at Jules' near shout. The muscle in his jaw tightens as his fingers sink into Thea's thigh, tugging her closer with a need to protect her.

"Did Aaron bother to tell you anything else?"

"What do you mean?"

"Oh, so Aaron didn't tell you how he said that getting on my knees a lot doesn't make me a saint? Did he also fail to mention how he called me a whore and a gold digger?"

"He said *what*?"

"Get fucked, Jules. When did Aaron ever call you to ask about me? Did you really have nothing to ask him before blindly believing I just up and left? Do you truly trust Aaron more than you trust me?"

"That's not what I—" Thea hangs up on her brother, turning her phone off before turning to face Adrian as he cups her cheeks. "What?"

"You never told me exactly what Aaron said nor what happened between you two."

Thea sighs.

Lips quivering, she rests her head against Adrian's chest, stealing the remote from his hand to search for a new movie.

"It's not exactly fun to talk about being called a whore, and I didn't want you to think I'm with you for your money. I'm not."

"Thea, you don't let me pay for the one cookie you order when we are out for lunch. The idea of you being with me for my wealth has never crossed my mind. I find it more concerning how uninterested you are in my money. It's one of my best qualities."

"Your cuddles are your best quality," Thea mutters as Adrian rests his cheek against the crown of her head, feeling her heart beating steadily against his. "I wish I could stay here forever, trapped between the folds of time with you."

Hand slipping under her sweatshirt, the ghost of Adrian's touch elicits a shiver down Thea's back. Making her arch toward him, tightening her arms around him as her eyes linger on the crackling fireplace under the large TV—she remembers reading somewhere that looking at a source of light keeps one from crying.

"Worst case scenario," Adrian murmurs, thumb caressing the slope of her waist. "No one makes you an offer—"

"I got an offer from Harpy Publishing House."

"You did?"

Thea can feel Adrian's heart beating faster as his fingers dig into her waist, squeezing her against his body.

"Rue Hayes said she'd love to acquire my book, but first, I'd need an agent. She said it's quicker and easier to negotiate with one, protecting Harpy from me ever saying I got a bad deal."

"That's not a Harpy policy."

"It doesn't change shit, Chlamy. Do you know how many agents I've sent that fucking book to? How many rejections I've received because no one was interested? And now I'm supposed to do it all over again, all while I dangle a book deal in front of an agent who did nothing to earn their fifteen percent cut from it? I'm just supposed to give them fifteen percent of my advancement and my royalties when they had their chance to represent me?"

"If I were to change jobs, you still wouldn't sign up with a sexy agent?"

"No, I wouldn't. As I told Rue, I've come this far without an agent. They will have nothing but my blood in their hands."

"Then they'll have nothing at all."

"I hope you are right."

"I'm rarely wrong. Perks of being me."

"Indeed," Thea concedes as she settles on watching the first Captain America movie, mainly for eye candy. "You are quite an exquisite gentleman. It's a wonder you haven't made it as the eighth wonder of the world."

"My application is under review, but they are considering making all seven world wonders about me. Lucky you."

Thea's laughter wakes Jolly up from where the cat had been curled on the foot of the bed, basking in the sliver of moonlight as if it was the sun.

Jolly pounces, sinking her sharp teeth into the edge of the blanket covering them. The cream-colored cat rolls around, twisting its neck as if to kill prey that doesn't exist.

"You little rascal," Thea murmurs, startling Jolly by poking the cat's pink belly. "Tell me, Chlamy, how shall you replace the seven wonders of the world?"

"First, we have my height. I'm the tallest of the three living creatures in this room, Jolly is second, and you are the smallest," He jests, not bothered by how Thea changes the subject away from herself. "Tiny legs."

"I'm not short! You're just taller than me, but let me guess, next is your face? An architectural masterpiece at risk of being destroyed by the heat between one's legs?"

"A danger I'm always willing to face for your entertainment," Adrian speaks gallantly, smacking a kiss on Thea's forehead as she blushes faintly. "Third is how I linger in people's minds as a mysterious man. You did think of me as mysterious when we first met, didn't you?"

Thea pretends not to hear Adrian as she rubs Jolly chin, stealing a low purr from the kitty while Adrian gasps in betrayal, rolling in bed and taking Thea with her.

"Betrayer!"

Laughter reverberates against the walls of the vast room as Adrian vindictively tickles Thea's waist—annoying Jolly enough for her to leap down from bed, curling in front of the fireplace.

"I yield," Thea wheezes between fits of giggles. "You were very mysterious. For fourth place we can say it's your intellect?"

"Pornographic intellect or scholarly intellect? Don't answer that. I'll take whichever makes you happier, Thea Tea. Next?"

"Phallus the Redeemer? That is a very redeeming quality of yours, truly a wonder."

"Thea 'Theodore' Scriven," Adrian chides, raising a hand to his chest in mocking horror. "There is a baby in the room."

"She's my baby. You're her stepdad at best."

"Jolly likes me better. Don't you?" Jolly meows at Adrian without opening her eyes from the kitty's dreamland. "See? That's why she's living with me when we go back home. No more chasing rats and roaches."

"They are crunchy. She likes the—"

Thea glances at the phone discarded between the folds of the blankets at the first ring buzzing softly, but her screen remains black.

"It's mine," Adrian murmurs, patting the empty space on the kingsize bed until he finds his phone. "Hello?"

Thea strains to hear the voice on the other side of the line, but the words are muffled, spoken too quickly for her to understand anything beyond her own name.

"No, I'm not in the city...yes, she is," Adrian mutters, planting a kiss on Thea's cheek. "Why? No, tell me wh...because I'm not leaving to back to the city without a good reason."

Adrian's hand wanders from Thea's waist to her back as she turns to look at him, trying to decipher why his brows are drawn together, why his lips, which usually have a perpetual curl, are tight in a near scowl.

"Can you send it over?" He asks, and Thea prods his waist, curiosity billowing in her stomach. "Did you not hear when I said I'm not going back to the city without a good reason."

"We can go back to the city if you need to work," Thea whispers, leaning closer to hear the conversation.

Planting a kiss on Thea's forehead, Adrian slips out of bed, ambling toward the hallway as Thea slouches against the mountain of pillows, trying to on the movie but instead, she listens to Adrian's pacing, hearing his voice slip beneath the gap in the door separating them.

"I'm curious. Aren't you curious, Jolly?"

Purring is the only answer Thea gets from the pink-pawed cat, leaving Thea envious of how quickly she'll fall asleep even if she'd heard her name in a conversation.

Captain America is about to receive what Marine once called the *hotifying* serum when Adrian walks back into the room.

"Are you up to going back to New York tonight?"

"Why?" Thea doesn't lift her gaze from the TV.

"Remember the gala?"

"Uhum."

"Did you meet a woman with short hair?"

"Uhum."

"Did she mention she's practically related to me?"

"Uhum."

"Well, she tried calling you before, but she called me when you didn't pick up."

"And?" Thea feels the bed dipping under Adrian's weight.

A purr bubbles in her throat as he runs his fingers through her hair, hand gliding toward her jaw as he makes Thea tip her head toward him.

"She works in the UK side of the company, so she passed your manuscript to a few of the editors at F&F." Adrian smiles as Thea sits up, fingers curled around the edge of the luxurious duvet with a gleam in her eyes that is half-threat and half-hope. "It took her a while to do that since she doesn't want to work with writers like the strikethrough one, but she liked your book enough to pass it forward."

"Meaning? Adrian, please don't play with me. Please don't tease me with something that isn't real."

"Amy, an editor at F&F, wants to acquire your book. She knows you don't have an agent, which Ayla claims that's why she's interested in your book."

"That's the contract you asked to see?" Adrian nods, and Thea reaches for her phone, the screen lighting up as she holds his gaze, needing to anchor herself in him.

Needing Adrian for her to know this isn't another of her many cruel dreams—as if he can read the fear in her eyes, Adrian leans closer, resting his forehead on hers as tears line his eyes.

"Can you send me the contract? I want Jules to read it over."

"Already sent it to you, and I'll read it over too."

"Adrian, is this real?"

"It will be real as soon as ink dries on that sheet of paper," He mutters as a single tear rolls down his cheek. "I told you to trust me, Thea Tea."

FOUR MONTHS

THREE MONTHS

TWO MONTHS

ONE MONTHS

THE DAY

28

Hope had never been Thea's strongest suit.

Her mother used to call her overly pessimistic, while her dad would defend Thea by saying she was merely realistic. The truth is, Thea had never felt worthy of hope, never believed herself as good enough to be enough.

Something proved true with her average grades in school and college, by the rare tips she'd get from patrons in Ether as she'd rarely measure her words when dealing with customers who'd been rude to her.

But publishing had never failed to make Thea feel worthless.

It'd been the one place she desperately craved to be good enough, the one hope she'd desperately clung to while spending countless nights staring at her computer screen as stories grew from nothing.

"Are you sure?" Adrian asks, voice disrupted by the soaring winds and the cars driving on Brooklyn Bridge as his fingers rake over her spine.

Thea nods.

Gaze lingering on the distant ripples under the bridge, watching as the murky water flows toward the ocean. Thea supposed it only made sense to end things where they started, where five years ago she'd given herself time to prove, or rather, to find if there was any worth to her life.

Perhaps the Universe or God had been punishing Thea for her hope that readers' life would become a mirror of the things they read, believing that only then they would be more mindful of what they consume—an ideal that fueled Thea to write books that wouldn't add blood to her stained hands.

"I don't think I can do this," Thea confesses with a sigh. Tears run down her face, descending toward the same waters that would proclaim her body. "I'm terrified."

Five years have come to an end. 1,826 days of begging God, the Universe, or whoever was listening for a chance to make her dream become a reality, and now she no longer needs to be a juggler, no longer needs to hide her cries clamoring for help.

Thea can finally let go of those dreams that have become a thing of the past. She's allowed to relinquish the threads she'd knit to keep everything from crumbling into failure as she yearned for the day her body would hit the water beneath the Brooklyn Bridge.

"Thea Tea?"

The wind blows against her hair, softly moaning as if remembering a night so long ago when Thea had been hopeless, stolen the privilege of dreaming because of wintry rejections.

Five years have come to an end, but Thea is no longer adrift.

Thea remembers how cold the railing had been when she decided to give herself time to live. Giving herself the grace to keep trying, and she often regretted that decision, wishing she'd anchor her life into the bottom of the East River.

Adrian snakes an arm around her waist, letting Thea plummet into his embrace as her lids flutter close with fear of something new, dreading what's ahead of her as it is all uncharted territory.

"There is nothing to fear," He whispers against her ear, wishing they could stay together like that forever. "We spent four months working on this. Amy said your book is this year's most anticipated release."

"Being the not-yet-girlfriend of a trust fund baby has its perks." Thea's gaze doesn't move from the drafted email that holds the difference between life and death. "I truly can't believe you contacted all your billionaire best friends to promote a debut."

"There is nothing I wouldn't do for you, Chlamythea."

Thea smiles, resting her head against Adrian's chest as her lids flutter close. The winds of New York run through her hair, which had grown far too long as she'd barely left Adrian's penthouse during the months it'd taken her to work through the final rounds of editing.

Thea and Jolly officially moved in with Adrian three weeks ago, a brush of fate as her landlord raised her rent, and Thea had grown too used to sleeping in the same bed as Adrian—twisting and turning sleepless in the few nights they'd spend apart.

"At 7:77?" Adrian asks, and she hums in agreement. "We'll be late for our first date."

"It's not our first date. Today isn't the release day of my book."

"I can't wait that long. I just want to call you my girlfriend. I mean, you already are my girlfriend. You met my parents, and I'm meeting yours next month. And next year, I'm trading companies so we can be under the same publishing house much how we live under the same roof."

Thea loved that, loved knowing she'd wake up beside Adrian, that at six p.m she could run down the hallway of the penthouse to find him stepping out of the elevator when he gets home from work, giving her a few more hours of his day to help edit her book.

Thea opens her eyes, watching the minutes pass as she sends the email with the final draft of her book to Amy, leaving it in her editor's hands to forward the email to the other departments.

There is a long way to go until Thea can call herself a published author, but she still cries at the sound of the email being sent out into the Internet's ether.

"Next month," Thea whispers, body trembling as she tries not to weep in Brooklyn Bridge once more. "It's been so long since I enjoyed the sound of that."

"Next month, next year, next decade. We got it all, Thea Tea. You made it. I'm so proud of you."

EPILOGUE

There is something despicable about LA.

A place abundant in false advocacy. Where unpalatable people clamor for the betterment of society, posing as great examples to follow when LA is known for its corruption—at least it should be known for its bottomless misogyny masked as radical liberation, for its racism disguised as 'we see no color' when the only color they see is white.

Thea never liked the artificiality in LA, nor did she enjoy the idea of walking on faulty lines. The weird perpetual summer and nonchalance LA operates under certainly doesn't help the city's case.

But it'd been the idea of sitting through a meeting where men known for sexual misconduct and pedophilia dissect the script written around her book. Highlighting changes made so her story would appeal to the masses.

Earning the studio a few hundred million, and in exchange, Thea would become Hollywood's newest sugar baby at the small price of tarnishing her work to make it fit into a film.

Writers had long been made to believe a book-to-movie adaptation is the peak of their careers, that it's some grand compliment when it's just whoring themselves out to the highest bidder.

"As I've said countless times before," Thea preambles, managing to hide the anger she feels at how the studio insisted on an in-person meeting even after Thea voiced her lack of interest. "If I desired my stories to be made into movies, I would've become a screenwriter."

Thea stands up before any of the men can argue. She marches toward the glass doors, high heels peeling against the concrete flooring as Thea holds her head high, reaching for her phone in the bottom of her bag.

"This way, ma'am," A secretary murmurs, leading Thea down a maze of hallways that recoil around themselves.

Adrian Friedman sent you $1000.
"How did the meeting go, Thea Tea?"

Thea smiles at the notification, allowing her mind to drift away from the past two hours of her life that were somehow more infuriating than the five years she spent suffering.

You sent Adrian Friedman $10
"If my driver were to get into a crash when taking me back to my hotel, well I don't think I'd be terribly annoyed to lose my short-term memory in the accident. There should be a nicer way not to sell them the rights of my book than telling them to shove it up their asses."

Adrian Friedman sent you $1000.
"Does that mean you're coming home earlier? Jolly misses you. She's meowing like a kitty with a broken heart, but I still miss you more."

The secretary walks with a bounce to her steps, almost content in walking Thea to the black SUV car that picked her up from the airport before bringing her to the studio.

"I hope I'm not overstepping," the blonde girl preambles as Thea remains silent, paying attention to her mien as they linger in front of the building, waiting for Thea's driver to come up. "I'm glad you didn't take their offer. You're my favorite author, and I've been dreading today since the meeting came up on my calendar."

"Why is that?"

"There is this phenomenon of a writer's name getting printed bigger than the book's title on the cover? Of how that's when their books go from great to more of the same? Well, that shift often happens when there is a movie deal on the table, and I selfishly didn't want to lose my favorite writer."

Thea nods, containing her smile, as the black SUV slowly emerges from the garage. "I like to think that what sets me apart from my peers is how my beliefs are unbendable. No amount of money can deter me from doing what I believe is right, and as much as I believe in sustainability, recycling is one of the many things I avoid when it comes to my writing."

The girl smiles widely, taking a step ahead of Thea when she moves to open the door of her car. "Have a good day, Miss Scriven. Is there anything else you need? Perhaps you could share a bit of your next book?"

"I'm fine, unlike Hofmann, who may or may not get entangled in a fake dating situation to hide his sexuality in a sport that is less than accepting."

Thea hears the girl's squeal of delight through the echo of the door slamming shut. Her gaze moves toward the little white bag sitting exactly where Thea left it.

Stealing glances at Adrian's notification, Thea thinks about the surprise she planned with Josh, the concierge, for when she flew back to New York, where the elevator leading to the Friedman's penthouse would be filled with pink and blue balloons, hiding her from view until they trickled out into the hallway.

Caving into what Thea had betted $1000 with Josh that Adrian would be confused by; however, the concierge was adamant that Adrian would begin to cry at the sight of the first balloon.

Either way, Thea and Josh agreed Adrian would ask the meaning of it all whether he knew or not. He'd want to hear it from her, but all Thea would do is put that white bag toward his face.

Thea's reverie is cut short when her phone vibrates in her hand with an incoming call.

"Did I beat him to it?"

"You haven't been able to beat Adrian in the two years we've been together," Thea says, smiling as she always does when talking to Aaron, content that they are slowly mending their friendship and learning how to be friends without the expectation of sex. "Did you boys end up meeting for lunch? Where did he take you to eat?"

"Ether, and Adrian made me pay for it. He told me he's learning how to be stingy from you."

"Maybe Adrian will forever be mad that you and I have history."

"Probably that too," Aaron concedes before he pulls the phone away as he speaks to Ether's staff, allowing Thea to hear the familiar clank of plates and cutlery. "So? Are we getting a movie?"

"It's not like I need the money. My debut did great. My sophomore book coming out at the end of the month is a bestseller with pre-orders alone."

"And you have a billionaire boyfriend."

"Who I don't take money from, at least not unless he breaks up with me, then Adrian would have to pay child support. But no, there won't be a movie."

"That makes sense—wait, wait, wait, wait, what did you say?"

Thea smiles as she glances down at her flat stomach, which won't remain flat much longer. It couldn't have been six months since she and Adrian decided she would take her IUD out, allowing fate to decide when and if they were to have children.

"Child support? Or are you scandalized I'm pregnant out of wedlock?"

"You are pregnant?"

"The stick I peed on said I am, and my doctor sent me the results of my blood test, so yeah. I think Italian air made me more fertile."

"Does Adrian know?" Aaron whispers as if Adrian could somehow be eavesdropping on their conversation.

"Not yet. Only my mom, Marine, and now you know."

"I beat Jules to it? Please lie to him about this. He'd kill me for learning he'll be an uncle before he did."

Laughing, Thea lifts her gaze to find the driver pulling up to her hotel. She picks up her bags, waiting for the car to park before unbuckling her belt.

"Oh, you mean like how you got to meet Hana before I did? Jules is a tad too in love with her to care about anything else in the world. It's quite disturbing."

"Meeting her was an accident," Aaron defends himself, not mentioning how that happened because he'd booked a flight to Seattle on a drunk night. "I never intended on seeing her naked. Well, not in real life. In theory, I saw her naked long before your brother ever did, but still."

A few months after Aaron and Thea had their falling out, while Thea focused on editing her debut novel, Aaron's efforts were on vanquishing his extensive liquor collection.

"I'm proud of you, T."

Slipping out of the car, Thea mouths a *thank you* to the same valet she'd given a thousand-dollar tip when she got to the hotel the night before—she quite enjoyed redistributing Adrian's wealth as he still refused to text her instead of wiring her money, claiming it seemed wrong to contact her in any other way. In truth, Adrian enjoyed the mental image he had whenever wiring her money, as if seeing how Thea rolls her eyes and sighs before smiling foolishly.

"There hasn't been a single day when I didn't believe you would achieve all of your dreams."

"I might make you the Godfather."

"You really do want Jules to kill me."

"No, you were my first fan. I just think it would be fair. Jules hasn't even read my book yet."

The fresh and fragrant flowers in the lobby greet Thea as her high heels peel against the marble flooring made of different types of stones to craft a simple yet elegant circular design that extends itself across the entire lobby.

"At least you won't have to sit through Cove and Olivie fighting for Godmother," Thea says, bag swinging back and forth as her steps have a giddy bounce to them. "They'll be impossibly excited to become aunts. It's tiring to think about it."

"Are you back at the hotel?"

"Yeah, why?"

"Oh, nothing. I'm just curious. You're carrying precious cargo now," Aaron speaks too nonchalantly for how his voice quivers ever so slightly, something that only happens when Aaron is lying about something.

"Aaron Mariani, tell me."

"I just have a surprise waiting for you. Most of it will be useless now, but enjoy, maybe take a nap too."

"I plan on it," Thea concedes between a yawn, pressing the bottom to call for the elevator. "I don't know if it was the flight, the meeting, or being pregnant, but I'm tired."

"Enjoy your surprise, T. I gotta go. Love you."

"Yeah yeah, love you too."

Thea lets her phone fall back to the bottom of her purse as the elevator doors slide open. The metal handrail is cold beneath the palms of her hand as Thea sinks against the glass back of the elevator, watching the numbers climb to the presidential suite.

A courtesy of getting Adrian to book her stay in LA.

"One night away, and I miss him," Thea mutters, wishing the elevator could move faster so she can take a nap with the shirt she stole from Adrian before leaving for the airport. "I shouldn't love him this much after almost three years."

Watching the penthouse floor creep closer, Thea slips out of her high heels, holding them by the tip of her middle and index finger as she steps toward the elevator door, waiting for that telltale sound before the gilded doors slide open.

Surrounded by boring gray walls, Thea fishes out her room card as she ambles toward the large double doors that swing open with a loud beep and a push of her hips.

Thea rolls onto the tip of her toes when the warm carpet in the hallway shifts into the foyer's marble flooring, displaying a trail of rose petals for her to follow.

Letting herself be guided by an invisible force, Thea drops her bags on the raisin-colored velvet couch as the marble melds into wood flooring. Her jacket falls on the white armchair before Thea follows the petals down a hallway leading to the main suite.

She finds the floors of her suite covered in petals; not a single inch allows for the rug there to peek through. In the sitting area adjacent to the bedroom, there's a bucket filled with ice and a bottle of champagne over the glass coffee table.

"Cute," Thea murmurs, prancing toward the balcony that grants her a view of the city until she pulls the curtains over it. "Fuck LA."

"I kinda need that curtain open."

Thea wails as she spins around, reaching for a lamp nestled against the nook between the wall and the boring couch.

"Did I scare you, Thea Tea?"

"What the fuck are you doing here?" Thea asks, settling the floor lamp back at its rightful place as her brows knit into a scowl.

"Open the curtain, and you'll find out."

Scowl contorting the planes of her face, Thea does as Adrian asks. Staring down at Beverly Hills, with the hills painted in that beige color of vegetation that is on the brink of death while the trees growing around it are mysteriously still green.

Peering out of the window, Thea only listens as Adrian creeps up behind her, wrapping his arms around her waist. Smiling against the slope of her shoulder, Thea lays a hand over his with a smile of her own.

They linger there, waiting for something to happen, but the minutes bleed into each other, stretching into the brim of boredom.

"What am I waiting for, Chlamy?"

"It should have happened already. Fuck, I think we'd been timezoned."

"For what?"

"Well, you know those planes that leave smoke behind?" Adrian murmurs between kisses on her sensitive skin. "That people use to write little messages on the sky?"

"Yeah, I always found those things to be tacky, it's second only to flashmobs. When those were trendy I used to have nightmares about being proposed with a gaudy flashmob."

"It's such a good thing I didn't plan for either of those things." Adrian pulls the curtains close before stepping away from Thea. "If time zone didn't fuck up my surprise, that's certainly not what you would've seen."

"Right, I'll pretend I believe you, but you know I didn't plan on selling my book's rights to the studio. What were you planning to have the plane write? *Fuck Hollywood, Thea wins, Hollywood loses*?"

Chuckling, Adrian lets Thea prowl toward him as he slowly backs into the bedroom, sitting on the edge of the bed when she wraps her arms around his neck with her brows hiked up.

"Lovely suggestions, I'll take note of those, but my original idea was more along the lines of *'Marry me,'* and you'd turn around with that same curious look you have on your face right now."

"I'm glad we were timezoned," Thea murmurs, fingers digging into Adrian's shoulder—partially hoping he's joking.

"As am I, but I'll tell you, if you checked the side table in the main area of the suite, you'd find a little sage green —"

Thea slips away, turning back only to weave her fingers through his before hauling Adrian with her back down the hallway leading to the main area.

A nervous giggle bubbles past her lips as she finds the sage green box while clinging to Adrian's hand without daring to take a step toward it.

"Pick up the box, Thea Tea."

"You do it. I'm nervous."

Planting a kiss on her temple, Adrian moves around Thea, picking up the box before he leans down to rest his forehead on hers.

"Back to my plan, I'd open the box slowly, teasing you since you like that in the bedroom," He jests, laughing as she smacks his chest, but her gaze remains on his gray eyes. "If you were to look down, Thea Tea, you'd find a 3.4 Carat oval green diamond because you look beautiful in green. The band is surrounded by smaller diamonds, in a ring version of the necklace you wore for that first gala and our first non-official date, wearing it only for our anniversaries and extra special dates."

"What are you trying to say, Friedman?"

"I'm trying to say that I had my family jeweler—"

"You have a family jeweler? You are disgustingly wealthy, Adrian Friedman," Thea chides, finally taking a peek at the ring resting perfectly against the small box. "Is there a question at the end of this?"

"Indeed, Thea Tea. I couldn't buy a common ring for you when there is nothing common about you. It would be sacrilegious to ask you to marry me with something that wasn't made exclusively for you."

Tears line her eyes, nails sinking into his wrist as Adrian smiles like a fool, watching her every expression and how the pulse in her neck quickens.

"I'm still terrified of you, Thea Scriven," Adrian says. "Every day, I grow a little more scared and a lot more in love with you. Every day, I fall asleep daydreaming about our future together, of becoming a husband and a father beside you. I want to experience life with you. So, if you were kind enough to please marry me, I would be a very happy man."

"I mean, since you are pleading for it."

"So you'll marry me, Thea Tea?"

Thea raises her shoulder in an all too feline movement as the edge of her lips tugs downward. She lifts a hand toward his cheek, making Adrian lean toward her.

Practically melting until she says, "One condition."

"I pay for it?"

"I mean that too. I've made enough to retire, not afford a wedding with a billionaire groom."

"Technically, you have more money to your name than I have to mine. My credit card is still attached to my dad's bank account," Adrian points out, seeming to forget his dad passed the penthouse to his name.

Believing a man should own a house if they are to live in it with a woman—and a cat. Although, Jolly has yet to conquer her grandfather's heart.

Thea jerks her chin toward the bag discarded on the couch. Adrian arches his brow, sweeping Thea off the floor as he walks to the couch.

"Will you please say yes? Or no, any answer is better than this suspense," Adrian says, heaving Thea as he ambles toward the couch, plopping down on it with a hand on Thea's waist as he pulls the white paper bag.

Thea shakes her head, biting down on her tongue to keep herself from blurting the surprise she wanted to take place at home, but she supposes there is no better time for it.

"What? No teasing?"

"Open the bag, Friedman."

Smacking his lips against hers, Adrian sighs as he pulls out the wrinkly paper stuffing in the bag before he reaches for a small white box.

Adrian arches a brow, letting a smile creep over his lips as he pulls the lid over, enjoying the suspense he gives himself by torturing Thea in the process.

"For fuck's sake, Adrian, open the goddamn thing," Thea complains, stealing the box from his hand as she pulls perhaps the tinniest onesie she'd ever seen.

Blinking slowly, Adrian's mouth drops as he stares at the green onesie with ruffles around the collar with petite white buttons running from the front down to the feet.

"Well?"

"You are pregnant?" He asks in a whisper as if they are sharing the biggest secret ever. "You are pregnant with Reginald Friedman-Scriven?"

Thea laughs, throwing the onesie in his face. "We are not naming our child Reginald."

"True, it could be a girl, which then she'd be Reginaldina Friedman-Scriven," Adrian jests, laying a hand on Thea's stomach. "Are you really pregnant, Thea Tea? You aren't just being a little shit-head?"

"You sound like Aaron, but yes, I am pregnant. Want me to pee on a stick for you?"

"Do you know how I planned on fucking you for hours after you inevitably said yes to my emotional proposal?"

"Your proposal wasn't emotional, and you can still do that?" She points out with a pout, gingerly working on the buttons of her blouse.

"It was emotional, and I don't want to hurt my babies."

"It's twins now? Reginald and Reginaldina will be fine, Adrian Friedman-Scriven"

"Meu Amor," Adrian preambles, gray eyes focusing on the curve of Thea's collarbone as she lets the blouse slip down her shoulder while undoing the last few buttons. "I'm a dad now. I can't put my kid's in harm way."

"So we'll go nine months without sex?"

Thea stands up as her top pools around her feet. She arches a brow at Adrian, demanding an answer from the man that leans forward to plant a kiss on her stomach.

"Those pants look tight around the waist," He mutters, tugging on the only button of it. "I'll unzip it for you, and yes, I could go nine months without sex. I could go a lifetime without sex if you didn't ever want me to touch you again, it would be hard, but that's nothing compared to the torment of life without you. Or the guilt of hurting my babies."

Thea shimmies out of her pants, kicking away the black dress pants with pleats in the front of them. Goosebumps spread over her skin as Adrian's fingers rake over her thighs, his lips moving across her stomach.

"Adrian?"

"Yes, Thea Tea?"

"You terrify me."

"Is that a yes for my emotional proposal?"

Thea doesn't say anything as she ambles to the side table where the sage green box was left. Thea sucks in a breath at the green diamond, a ring far too beautiful for her.

"I don't even need a paperclip ring to say yes," Thea mutters, slipping the ring over the fourth finger on her left hand. "You could take me to a courthouse to get married as a surprise date, and I'd still sign the papers without a moment of hesitation."

"We could do that right now."

Thea glances over her shoulder, finding Adrian resting his chin on the back of the couch. Gray eyes sparkling with unspilled tears of joy. "We could, but I'm really horny right now. You can come and watch."

Not waiting for Adrian, Thea unhooks her bra before walking down the hallway, letting her black lacy panty fall on the threshold between the bedroom.

"You wicked woman," Adrian's voice echoes toward her, disrupted by the sound of the duvet molding to Thea's body and Adrian throwing his clothes against the floor as he runs to the room. "I really don't want to hurt my babies."

"Then fuck me slowly."

Adrian watches as Thea spreads her legs open over the foot of the bed. Hand trailing down her stomach, Thea holds Adrian's gaze as he gingerly approaches the bed, wearing nothing but white briefs.

"How dare you be so beautiful?" Adrian asks, fingers curling around her ankles, tugging Thea to the edge of the bed as he kneels before her.

A shiver runs down Thea's spine with the kisses Adrian plants on her ankle as a hand rakes over her other leg, coaxing a moan past her lips with his gentle caress.

Thea dips her fingers further down, arching at the wetness she finds at her entrance. "How dare you make me so wet when you don't even want to fuck me?"

"Oh, I do want to fuck you."

"Didn't sound like it."

"I said I didn't want to hurt my babies, which included you, not twins. Not once have I said I didn't want to fuck you. All you have to do is give me that little gaze you have on right now, and I'm gone for."

"What little gaze?" Thea naively asks as she bites on her lips, thrusting her fingers inside of herself with Adrian's name rolling off her tongue.

Adrian stands up in a leap, trailing a path of kisses on her stomach as he looms over Thea. Lips exploring the swell of her breast, hands roaming her hips and waist without daring to leave an inch of skin untouched.

"I want you."

"You got me, Thea. You have me, and you'll always have me. I'm yours to do as you command."

"Mine for the taking?" Her nails leave red streaks over Adrian's pale chest, inching down until Thea brushes against the band of his briefs.

Teeth sink into her neck as Thea dips her hand under his briefs, using her toes to maneuver the single piece of clothing between them out of the way.

"Ouchie," She moans. "My feet are cramping."

Laughing against her skin, Adrian slides his underwear down his legs, allowing Thea to stroke his already hard cock. Allowing her to guide him into her entrance.

"Maybe I should be on top? You love when I'm on top," Thea moans softly, knowing how to make Adrian melt into her. "You always fuck me harder when I'm on top."

"Fuck Thea, should we be doing this?"

"Adrian, yesterday you fucked me against a wall, then you fucked me in the elevator, keeping your fingers inside of me until we were inside of the car, where you fucked me again. I was already pregnant when you slapped my ass so hard I could barely sit still in the meeting today."

"That was before."

"Just fucking fuck me."

Far too slowly, Adrian pushes himself inside Thea, watching her lids flutter as her mouth parts in a silent moan, oblivious to how Adrian searches for a sign of pain rather than basking in her growing pleasure with each second he's deeper inside of her.

"Fuck," She whimpers, rolling her hips toward Adrian, who pulls out.

A hand cupping her cheek, he leans down, resting his forehead on hers, "I'm sorry, I didn't want to hur—"

"No, no you feel so good. Please don't do this to me."

"Do what?"

Thea runs a hand over Adrian's back, voice slightly trembling, as she whispers, "Don't reject me. Don't see me differently because I'm pregnant."

"No, that's not—Thea, I know it doesn't make any sense, but I'm terrified I'll fuck up, that I'll somehow hurt you, our baby, or both. I've wanted this for so long. I don't want to ruin this little dream of ours."

Heart swelling with love and cheeks ruddy with anger, Thea pushes herself onto her elbow as she lays a finger under Adrian's chin, making him look into her eyes.

"If you can't fuck me because I'm pregnant, then I want you to fuck me as if you want to get me pregnant."

"I can do that."

"Then do that."

"Okay, but you tell me—fuck" He curses as Thea rolls over, lifting herself over his cock before sinking down on it. "Fuck Thea."

Scooting higher on the bed, Adrian's hand moves to her waist, holding her until she smacks it away. "Don't touch me. I'm mad at you."

Adrian pulls his hands away with a slight pout on his lips as she plants her hand on his chest before moving against him, hips undulating slowly, adjusting herself until Thea finds the right spot and her head lolls back. A groan slips past her lips as she uses Adrian to satisfy herself, hips moving faster against him, kneading her breast and stroking her clit as Adrian watches her, fingers curling into fists to keep himself from touching Thea when all he wants is to feel the warmth of her skin, to feel how she grows feverish with lust, how sweat will bead on her flesh the longer she rides him.

"My beautiful, beautiful Thea."

"Shut up, Friedman." Hissing, Thea leans down as she moans against Adrian's mouth, wanting him to kiss her, but the man is dutiful not to touch her. "I'm so mad at you, but you feel so good."

"Do I?"

Adrian groans, opening his mouth for Thea, who kisses him as his hand brushes against her thigh, creeping toward the curve of her ass when Thea slaps him.

"Ouch? That's new."

"Sorry, I'm so sorry, but I'm so mad at you," Thea moans, peppering kisses on his face as the sound of skin on skin fills the room in tandem with the scent of sex. "Fuck Adrian, why won't you fuck me?"

"I kinda of am."

"You aren't."

Thea pulls back, crawling back to the foot of the bed as she settles herself between his legs. Eyes on his, Thea takes Adrian down her throat, moaning at her own taste. Her tongue swirls over his shaft as her head bobs down on it, coaxing Adrian to thrust into her, to take control how Thea wants him to. But all Adrian does is brush her hair away from her face as his lids flutter close. "Fuck Thea, that feels so good."

A string of saliva stretches between her lips and his cock as she pulls back, stroking him as she kisses down his shaft, licking him from the base up to the tip with her gaze on his.

Her fingers glide over his shaft in a firm grasp as she pumps him slowly. Thea kisses his thigh and hips as her long nails elicit a shiver down his spine that drives Adrian to thrust into her hand.

"Will you fuck me?"

"I quite enjoy when you fuck me instead."

Thea whimpers, crawling back up with a hand on his cheek and the other guiding him back inside her. For a few seconds, Thea doesn't move, savoring the way Adrian stretches her, relishing in how Adrian fills her up so well, stealing the air from her lungs with how he fits her perfectly. But it's not enough. She needs him to want her.

"Please?" Thea pleas against his lips, moaning with the slap on her ass that resounds against the suite walls. "Smack my ass again."

"Thea—"

"Please?" She moves against his shaft, dragging out her movement until Adrian sinks his fingers into her hips with enough strength to mar her skin.

"I'm not smacking your ass."

"Please? I want you. I want all of you, fast or slow. I just want you to want me."

Adrian rolls over, kissing Thea's chest as he pulls back before slamming into her, making Thea moan loudly. "Promise you'll tell me if it feels wrong?"

"Just fuck me, please, please fuck me?"

"Thea, promise me?"

She wraps her legs around him, fingers sinking into his dark hair as she nods, rolling her hips with a moan.

"I need to hear you say it."

"Yes, Adrian, I promise. I'll tell you if anything feels wrong, but please fuck me."

Adrian practically growls, taking her breast in his mouth as he pounds into her, eliciting moans that grow louder with each flick of his tongue over her nipple, resounding against both of them with each thrust.

His strokes are teasing, going too fast before he practically comes to a halt. Undulating his hips sensually as he edges Thea, he takes her all the way toward an orgasm before stealing the pleasure from her.

"You are so wet, so perfect." Adrian sucks on her neck, gliding down her chest where he leaves red marks on her skin, pleasuring her without needing the world to see that Thea is taken care of, without him needing to brand her as if Thea is his property. "How could you ever think I don't want you?"

"I love you so much, but I'm so scared."

"Of wha—fuck, I'm close."

The coppery smell of blood swivels between them as Thea sinks her nails on his back, pulling Adrian flush against her body, needing him to cover every inch of her as Adrian's thrusts grow frantic when he seeks his pleasure, taking Thea with him as her body trembles, eyes rolling to the back of her head with an orgasm.

"I love you," Adrian groans as he cums inside her, pulling out to kiss her through her orgasm, painting her stomach with ropes of cum that reach her breasts. "I love you, Thea."

Adrian rolls from on top of Thea, pulling her with him as her body tightens. The waves of pleasure crashing down on her as Adrian runs his fingers over her back, from the nape of her neck down to her pussy.

"Fuck," She moans, biting on his shoulder without hearing anything through the blood soaring in her ears. "That was good."

"I know. I'm a phenomenal lover."

Thea laughs as she peppers kisses on his neck, squirming as his fingers brush against her tender entrance, spreading his cum over her as she moans.

"Uhm, I like that."

Adrian kisses her temple as he slides two fingers inside Thea, holding her flush against his body when she jerks away from his digits, her body all too sensitive, yet she still wants him.

"Keep doing that, and I'll need all of your cock."

"How greedy of you, Thea Tea."

"I always want all of you, Adrian Friedman," She speaks with devout certainty, yet her voice is sleepy. "I'm truly terrified of how much I love you, even more so of how our life is about to change. I'm scared you won't want me and that you'll grow to see me only as the mother of our children."

"Nonsense, I only fear causing you pain," Adrian explains, pulling half of the duvet over them as he can feel her heartbeat slowing down.

Thea hums, nestling herself in his arms, burying her face against the crook of his neck as the soft brush of her fingers over his arms comes to a halt.

"The best things in life tend to be the scariest, don't they? That's why I've always been terrified of you, Thea Tea," he confesses with a smile on his face. "Sleep well. I'll be here when you wake up."

BONUS SCENE: BIRTHDAY

"My baby is coming, cha-cha-cha," Adrian singsongs, fingers tapping against the carbon fiber steering wheel as he shimmies in a gleeful dance. "Cha-cha, I'm going to be a daddy, cha-cha-cha."

Thea watches through slanted eyes as the planes of Adrian's face are accentuated by the red traffic light as they wait for the light to turn green when Thea sucks a deep breath, lids fluttering close, partially from the pain and partially from the annoyance of seeing Adrian so excited when she's stuck with the discomfort and pain; fearing something bad will happen with their baby or will happen to her, and she won't get to see their child grow.

"We are almost there, Thea Tea," Adrian reassures Thea as she begins to regret not accepting Adrian's suggestion to spend the last month of her pregnancy living in a hotel neighboring the hospital.

What seemed like an unnecessary indulgence while they have a perfectly fine apartment, now feels like a big mistake when all Thea wants is the comforting presence of her doctors.

"You installed the baby's car seat, didn't you?" Thea's knuckles bleach around the armrest of the car door, wishing she also hadn't turned down Adrian's offer to turn one of their guest bedrooms into a mini hospital room and have the staff taking shifts there for the last week.

A waste of money, Thea claimed as she ran her hands over her belly, amused by how Adrian's zealous nature had grown into bordering excessive.

"There is one in all of our cars. All inspected by professionals." Adrian's face is painted green a moment before the wagon's engine roars, propelling them forward. "My dad put one in his car, and I should probably remind Jules to do the same for his rental."

Humming through a contraction, Thea doesn't pay attention to how Adrian dials Jules while driving at a snail's pace through mostly empty roads.

Taking the exact path, Adrian insisted they practice driving through at different times of the day as he wanted to know the quickest way to the hospital while avoiding the streets that reminded Adrian of the moon crevices.

If she'd gone into labor during the day, Adrian was ready to call a helicopter as it would take them up to an hour to get to the hospital, but at two a.m, it should only take twenty minutes from their apartment garage to the hospital.

"Good morning, mate," Adrian speaks in a faux Australian accent when Jules picks up his call. "My beautiful, precious, and perfect baby is making its way into the world as we speak."

"What?" Jules grunts as Thea swivels in her seat, trying to find a position that is a little more comfortable. "Are you at the hospital?"

"On the beautiful day of October 16th, I am on route to the hospital with my beautiful, strong, utterly perfect, and lovable wife, who is glaring at me—"

"Please stop talking," Jules speaks over him, somehow knowing Thea just wants five minutes to breathe in silence. "Should Hana and I leave now or in a few hours?"

"I don't think she's that far off," Adrian confesses gleefully, not bothering to hide that he just wants someone other than himself and Thea—and Josh, the concierge—to know their daughter will be born within a few hours. "Up to you, mate."

"Thea?"

"We'll call after she's born and when I feel like interacting with people," Thea says, and Jules hangs up on them. "No more calling people, Chlamy."

"Not even my parents?"

"No."

Thea picks up her phone to send her parents a text as they were the only ones in the family who didn't join Adrian's plan for everyone to fly out to New York two days before Thea's due date and spend the month there to meet the baby and help them.

She tries not to think of how her parents would've carved out the time if it'd been Jules's firstborn or even his fifth, but even with Adrian's jet left at their disposal, Thea's parents will take a day or two before flying to New York.

Adrian hums, reaching for Thea's fingers to keep himself from tapping the wheel as she leans into him, resting her head against his shoulder, enjoying the few minutes without pain and rambling, allowing Adrian to let his giddiness crumble into the worry he carried in secret for nine months.

Flickering between pure excitement about becoming a dad, of seeing Thea fulfill dreams she had about how her own life would play out, but mostly Adrian was excited about seeing the world through a baby's eyes.

Adrian knows he loves their child, but every ounce of excitement is laced with fear that he won't feel the same visceral connection Thea has with their baby girl.

Terrified he won't ever feel the urge to sing the lullabies, the ones Thea has been caroling since the first kick she felt, and that when their daughter falls or has a fever, he'll be clueless as to how to comfort her.

Adrian is afraid the only connection he'll have with his daughter will be through blood and not love, and he knows that's something that would break Thea's heart.

Something that would make Thea see him differently, and Adrian really didn't want Thea to love him less, really didn't want her to ask for a divorce when the ink on their wedding certificate barely had any time to dry.

A ridiculous fear, Thea would say, if Adrian had the courage to voice his concerns, but Adrian prefers to push his fear aside in lieu of basking in those few moments of bliss where he allows himself to feel nothing but joy.

Thea bemoans in pain, digging her fingers into Adrian's biceps as the red and blue lights of ambulances come into view, painting their dark green car in its hues, dribbling into the dark interior as Adrian drives towards the parking lot attached to the hospital.

"Here we are, Thea Tea," Adrian says, his voice coated in excitement. "Should I go to the reception while you wait here, or do you want to go together?"

"Together."

Planting a kiss on the crown of her head, Adrian opens the trunk before slipping out of the car. The soles of his feet hit the ground with a soft thud, matching his determined steps that don't quite match the fear billowing in his veins.

What if I don't love my baby?

What if something bad happens to my baby?

What if something bad happens to Thea?

What if I feel nothing at all?

What if, what if, what if.

The questions soar in his mind as he pulls Thea's luggage and their baby's maternity bag that's been carefully packed with the help of a pediatrician, stocked with the daintiest baby clothing Adrian could find.

"My baby is coming, cha-cha."

For something considered a miracle, there is something incredibly grotesque about childbirth.

Adrian could list all the things he didn't like, starting with the fluorescent lights that are unflattering to everyone in the room and the sterile smell of clean hallways, but it's mostly the amount of needles stabbing Thea and the blood involved that makes him queasy, draining his face of color.

It is something that, despite reading all of the baby books available—even medical books—hadn't prepared Adrian for the brutality of birth.

"I can't do this again," Thea bemoans, lifting her gaze from the doctor between her legs to face Adrian, who runs his fingers through her hair, sodden with sweat. "I can't do this."

"One push, Thea Tea."

"I can't!"

The doctor glances up at Adrian, arching a brow before glancing at a nurse who runs toward him as he leans closer to Thea, resting his forehead on the crown of her head.

"One push, and we'll have our baby."

"I'm tired," Thea wails through gritted teeth, head lolling back in exhaustion. "Why would you do this to me?"

"I'm sorry, Thea Tea. We don't need to have another child, I promise, but we do need to get this one out."

Tightening her grip on his hand, Thea sucks in a breath before pushing when the doctor nods. Adrian grunts in tandem with her as a bone come out of its righteous place, shattering a bone as her grunt becomes a battle cry.

"You're doing great," Adrian whispers when she stops pushing at the count of ten. "Just one last push. I'm fairly certain you broke my hand. You can do this for me, no?"

"What?"

"One push, and we are even."

Tears run down her cheeks as Thea glares at Adrian, taking a deep breath before he begins to count down again, patiently waiting for his personal torture to end.

Time seems to slow down for a moment, the fluorescent lights blurring Adrian's vision. Everything snaps back into focus when a nurse holds their baby in her arms, doing a routine of quick examinations.

"Why is she not crying?" Thea asks, fists sinking into the mattress as she pushes herself up, trying to see her baby.

"Not all babies will cry at birth. Some of them are quite content with it," The nurse explains before lying their baby on Thea's chest. "She's quite healthy."

Thea doesn't notice how Adrian's attention remains focused on the doctor, waiting for the all-clear that the birth went well and Adrian doesn't need to worry about losing his wife.

She no longer pays attention as the world comes down to the goopy gremlin lying on her chest with its umbilical cord still attached. She doesn't notice anything but how tiny fingers wrap around Thea's index finger as gray eyes wander around the room, mouth opening as the lights grow dim.

"Oi, bebê[15]," Thea whispers in Portuguese—she began learning the language shortly after finding out she was pregnant, hating the idea of not being able to understand her child.

Thea doesn't notice when a nurse takes Adrian away, muttering something about checking his hand before he gets to hold their daughter.

A part of her wishes she could walk around the room, cooing Alara into falling asleep but rocking her baby will have to wait until she can walk or until Adrian is back.

"Hi, Alara, yes that's you, bebê. My little Alara Florence Friedman-Scriven."

Running her thumb through Alara's blonde hair, Thea smiles as gray eyes find hers, gazing intensely at Thea while the staff slowly trickles out of the room, giving Thea between thirty to sixty minutes before they pester her about delivering the placenta.

"Hi," Thea says again as Alara babbles, startled by the own sound she produces."I'm your mommy, and you're

---

[15] Translation: "Hi, baby."

the best thing that's ever happened to me. I'm so happy to be here, Alara."

Seeking the details of Alara's face, Thea clings to her baby, running the back of her finger down Alara's little nose and pouty lips, a carbon copy of Thea's. While the shape of her face and the color of her eyes and hair are a gift from the Friedmans, leaving Thea to wonder if they'll darken with time or if Alara will remain looking like a mini version of Cove.

The minutes pass too quickly as Thea fills her mind with questions about whom Alara will grow to be, curious if maybe her baby will take after her aunt and be a fashionista or if Alara will love books as much as her parents do—perhaps she'll find a field no one in the family loves.

Regardless of whom Alara becomes, Thea knows she'll always be filled with more love than she ever thought one could feel for another person, bringing to the surface a devotion and selflessness no person should be able to feel.

A knock on the door brings their moment of solitude to an end as a nurse comes to teach Thea how to feed Alara, demanding the little energy Thea had left before a different nurse comes to bathe Alara where Thea could see.

Wishing she trusted her legs enough to be the one holding her baby in Alara's first-ever bath. "You should get some rest," The nurse chides as she wraps Alara in a swaddle, settling the baby in a small acrylic crib close to Thea's hospital bed, close enough for Thea to keep a hand on Alara's chest but not enough for her to be able to raise her baby comfortably.

"It's funny how tired I am, but at the same time, I feel like I could spend eternity watching her."

"Just close your eyes for a minute. Let your mind catch up."

Thea does as the nurse asks, falling asleep long before the older woman leaves the room. Shrouded in a mantle of sleep, Thea doesn't hear when Adrian knocks on the door with his hand covered in a cast.

Only the sound of the monitors still attached to Thea fills the silence in the room as Adrian gingerly saunters toward Alara, who's been staring at the ceiling as if she's all too intent on memorizing the exact shade of the beige walls and how the fluorescent light stripes fill the room with a warm glow.

It's as if the hospital room is a work of art, Adrian muses, building up the courage to pick his daughter up. Maybe anything is a work of art to a newborn.

Alara opens her mouth, sticking her tongue out as Adrian just stands there, hands on the edge of her crib as his heart thrums loudly, filling his ears with the sound of blood rushing through his body as anxiety threatens to overflow.

"You clean up nice," Adrian tells Alara as if sharing a secret or maybe just trying not to offend her. "The blood and white goo didn't look good with your complexion."

Alara sticks her tongue out once more, squirming in her swaddles as Adrian smiles at her, falling in love with how Alara's face is familiar to him—almost as if Adrian had seen her in a million dreams before.

She stares at him with the same odd fascination Adrian has caught Thea looking at him many times before; sometimes, it's a glance filled with love, and other times, it's out of pure annoyance.

First, Adrian decides to unravel her swaddle despite having yet to learn how to wrap babies into little burritos, but for some reason, he wants to hold her with as few layers between them as possible.

Arms springing up in a stretch, Alara babbles as Adrian struggles to pick her up with only one hand, but he quickly settles her tiny body against the cast enveloping his wrist and forearm.

"Hello," Adrian whispers, bouncing back and forth with his back to Thea. "I'm your dad, Adrian Friedman, and that's your mother and my beautiful wife, but she probably introduced herself already, didn't she?"

Alara's sigh becomes a yawn as she glances around, seeming more interested in the popcorn ceiling than in her own father, moving in his arm enough for Adrian to bring her closer to his chest.

"I'm your dad, you know, you could pretend to care. Dad. That's a funny word, isn't it?" Alara kicks her legs, and Adrian takes that as a yes. "I'm terrified I won't be a good dad. I had a great dad, so if I fuck this up, it will be all on me. It's not like there are any excuses for shitty dads, but you and your mom deserve better than a shitty dad, wouldn't you agree?"

Adrian places his hand over Alara's chest, smiling when she looks down at him. Hand blindly seeking his before constantly babbling when she finds it, trying to wrap her fingers around his, but Adrian's hand is just a bit too large for her.

"Sorry, you'll grow up and be able to hold my hand," Adrian explains, feeling tears welling in his eyes as something shifts in his heart and mind. "Oh God, you are my baby, and I'm your dad. I'm your dad, and I've been worried for so long."

Alara's faint blonde brows knit closer as she looks at Adrian when he pokes her cheek, yawning and tugging on his finger as she opens her arms.

"My baby Lala."

Tears fall down onto her onesie before Adrian plants a kiss on her head, feeling like the world's biggest fool for ever doubting he'd love her, yet Adrian finds himself unable to breathe when everything comes down on him.

Depriving him of air as if he's drowning in a deluge of love, leaving him to gasp for air when the love Thea had nine months to grow into, slowly adjusting to fit that love inside of her heart, all of it crashing down in one second.

"Are you crying?" Adrian whirls around at the sound of Thea's husky voice. "You love her, don't you?"

"So much. It feels like she ripped my heart from my chest."

Thea pats her bed, and Adrian cruises toward her, letting Thea wrap her arms around him as Alara's gray eyes flit between the two.

"How's your hand?"

"You could break all of my bones if it meant getting her here."

"I'll keep that in mind for our next baby, but I think I'll want you here for the first hour of their life."

"Thank you, Thea Tea."

"For what?" She asks, running a finger across Alara's cheek.

"Everything? For trusting me with your art, for being my wife, for giving us our daughter, and for giving me more happiness than anyone should ever experience. I don't know what exactly I'm thankful for. I can't even think."

"You can thank me by being the one to wake up for night feeding and do all of her diaper changes home."

"Deal."

ACKNOWLEDGMENTS

I've always been an avid believer in starting things from the start, and Ellipsis began with my experiences and frustration, with my hopelessness and fear that if my stories wouldn't matter to others, then neither did I, but I've made it—at least I hope I did, so yay me.

I'm acknowledging my own importance at this moment because, for almost four years, I've worked relentlessly to achieve this dream of mine. Trying to conquer a little space in the publishing world, and while it didn't happen the way I hoped it would, there is nothing wrong with trying a new path.

But this new path has made me cry and brought me to the edge of my personal Brooklyn Bridge more times than I could ever bring myself to admit, and certainly more times than anyone around me would ever know.

Thea's story is a deep dive into my turmoil of emotions, anger, and envy, of the solitude that comes with the certainty that I've been alone on this treacherous road. While I've been alone on this journey, it doesn't mean there weren't people supporting me from the sidelines, so cue to the gratitude parade:

Melissa Üstünsöz was the first person I reached out to read the first book I've ever written, giving me the very first glimpse of hope when it came to my work having value.

Cassie Mannes is a literary agent that has always made me believe in the rare goodness within this industry, and while she's not my agent, she has always shown how deeply she cares for writers, been a beacon of light for me, and a reminder that some few, rare people care deeply about the people behind the keyboards, hoping each writer finds the best route for their work.

While I never intended Ellipsis to be a blank statement encompassing all agents as thoughtless and uncaring—because they aren't all thoughtless and uncaring—it would be a lie for me to say there haven't been many agents other than Cassie whom I see answering writers questions on Twitter, always willing to support others.

Cassie was the first person who made me consider self-publishing as an option for me, the first agent I'd seen talk about the matter without an ounce of judgment behind it, without making it seem like self-publishing is settling for less, but instead something full of opportunities.

I'll always be thankful for this kind human, for how she cares deeply about books—even the ones she can't monetize and earn royalties from.

Next, I'd like to thank Adah B, I already thanked her for her kindness and sweet words a long time ago, but she's the second person to give me another first glimpse of hope when offering me her professional opinion while being so lovely about it. Adah, your kindness is something I'll never forget. It's something that brings me to tears even now. It has been something I think about often as I often feel like giving up on writing and myself. Saying 'thank you' doesn't seem like enough.

Sara Cerutti, what a delight it is to call you a friend, you're an actual angel in my life, and I couldn't be more thankful for you, even when I feel nauseated with fear whenever I send you an excerpt from Ellipsis or something else I'm writing at that moment.

You're one of a kind, Sara. Truly one of the smartest and kindest people I know. Your patience is unmatched. I'll forever be thankful for your patience when explaining the different kinds of licensing and listening to me rant about the same things so often. I'll also always be grateful for your phenomenal music taste.

Perhaps kindness and intelligence are something common amongst the name as Sarah has been someone I can rant to, someone I can be flabbergasted about so many things, who'll always be someone I can have the utmost interesting conversations with as our opinions and world views are so similar.

Both Sara and Sarah have made me feel less lonely and a lot less angry after chatting about how fucked up this industry is. (Truly, what a f-king mess.)

Asma A. Lovelette, thank you for being such a thoughtful and kind person. Your feedback about Ellipsis has been immensely helpful, and I say 'has' because your commentary inspired me to write a novella about Theadrian. Thank you for leading me on this journey.

There aren't words to describe how thankful I am for you, nor to express how much I wish you the best of luck in your career as a writer. I pray you have a successful career, as the world needs stories with your moral compass at its core.

I'd like to thank my parents for supporting me all of my life in everything I've wanted to do and believing I could achieve anything I set my mind to. Thank you for believing me even when I didn't. Thank you for loving me to the moon and back, allowing me to grow from a grumpy child to a significantly *less* grumpy adult (I still don't like being told what to do, though).

There are many people I am grateful for: Asmaa (a different one, I promise), Valentina, Kammy, bb Sarina, Ainsley, Genshin Impact for being such a good procrastination companion.

Then there is you. Yes, you reading this. I'd like to thank you, whoever you are, and wherever you are. Thank you for reading my book and being here to give it meaning. It is truly more than I could ever ask for.

Thank you for joining me in this. Thank you for making my life a little less lonely and allowing me to (hopefully) entertain you, allowing the stories I've made to touch you in any capacity—even if all I achieved was making you horny. I'm still ethereally grateful you took the time to read it.

I hope to see you in the acknowledgment of Theadrian's novella (It's the next book I'll release) and see your review (good or bad, I'm curious). I hope you'll keep up with my next books and the extra content I plan on posting over social media (You can follow me @EllieOwenAuthor on Instagram, Twitter, and TikTok).

Hopefully, you'll follow my journey, and I'll follow yours. Thank you for being here, and if you're wondering, "Ellie, this is a romance book. Where is the playlist?" And to that, I must say there is a playlist (check my site ellieowen.com for it. It's a good one, if I may say so myself), but it's also with great joy to inform you that I have successfully aged past my pubescent years.

While you can expect a playlist for every book of mine, never expect me to include the playlist in the actual book—I truly love music and coming up with a playlist that fits the stories I write, but come on, guys, I am not a toddler.

Lastly, there is one person who is pivotal for Ellipsis's existence, and that is my friend, editor, and multitasker, Alyssa Joy.

Alyssa, you've been the greatest support I could've had through this dream—or nightmare—of mine. I know this position is one you would likely prefer to not have taken, but please know I'm forever thankful for everything you've done for me, rather it be editing this beloved book of mine, hearing me rant and vent about all the insecurities publishing has a way of bringing to the surface.

You've supported me long before I even thought about writing Ellipsis, but you have also inspired many aspects of it—our miscommunication inspiring Thea and Marine's dynamic, Aaron being the only one who believed in Thea for a long time, and aspects I don't think it's necessary to mention here as you know what the are, but thank you for never trying to censor me in any way.

Thank you for understanding my vision for Ellipsis even when it came at the expense of a few of your favorite things and people; thank you for trying to see this story through my eyes even if the view was a bit too hazy for you to understand what you were seeing.

I love you, Jolly Joy. Thank you for being my friend, and for being such a great editor. I know our friendship isn't perfect, but you've given me something no one else will ever be able to give me, through your support you've allowed me to fulfill my dream to publish a book, I don't know where Ellipsis will take me, but you've made the greatest difference in my life, you've given me the opportunity to add meaning to my work and there is nothing I can ever do to repay you for that, but I'll always pray for you to achieve your dreams.

There is greatness ahead of you, Alyssa Joy, so go chase it.

(If this part was a mess that's because you didn't want to check my grammar, and I'm kinda busy crying.)

P.S. I'd like to thank every teacher of mine who never deserved to be in a classroom. Some of you said I'd never be anyone important, maybe you're right, but I do hope you aren't still cheating on your wife. If you are, then hopefully, she's not pregnant this time around. I hope erectile dysfunction becomes as trusting of a companion in your life as your bald spot is.

And to the ones whom this may concern, even if I never become anyone important, at least I'll always know sleeping with students is a crime, especially when they are minors. Please stop teaching. Schools would be safer without you in them.

Made in the USA
Las Vegas, NV
21 May 2023